THE FIFTH SEASON

THE FIFTH SEASON

Mons Kallentoft

Translated from the Swedish by Neil Smith

HODDER &
STOUGHTON

First published in Great Britain in 2014 by Hodder & Stoughton
An Hachette UK company

Originally published in Swedish in 2011 as *Den femte årstiden* by Natur och Kultur

1

A CIP catalogue record for this title is available from the British Library

Trade Paperback ISBN 978 1 444 77630 0

Typeset in Plantin Light by
Palimpsest Book Production Limited, Falkirk, Stirlingshire

Printed and bound by Clays Ltd, St Ives plc

Hodder & Stoughton policy is to use papers that are natural, renewable and recyclable products and made from wood grown in sustainable forests. The logging and manufacturing processes are expected to conform to the environmental regulations of the country of origin.

Hodder & Stoughton Ltd
338 Euston Road
London NW1 3BH

www.hodder.co.uk

Prologue

Early December, 2010

I don't understand why . . .

My body is fire.

All the seasons.

I have a hundred wounds that someone has scratched, torn and cut into me, and I am stumbling through the forest. Burning cold and icy pain.

It is me.

I have become pain.

What is there after pain?

The trees are hydras, whose thousand blazing heads are lunging at me, their teeth wanting to rip me to shreds, their poisonous blood seeking a way into me, and a millipede is crawling up one of my thighs, up inside me, where it unfurls its devilish fangs.

I scream.

Is this the end? Blood is running down my forehead but I stumble on, feeling the roots of the trees free themselves from the cold ground and wrap around my ankles, calves and thighs, trying to drag me to the ground, opening me up to the hydras' barbed-wire tongues.

How did I end up here?

Who am I?

Why am I going to die now?

I am alone.

I don't even have myself any more.

And something is hunting me.

What else is in that predator's arsenal?

Every root, every branch, every cold wind wants to tear me to pieces and lap up my blood, eat my guts, my kidneys, my liver and my heart.

Mum.

There you are.

I can see you standing in the kitchen and I call out to you.

'Mum, Mum!'

The branches are digging into me now, the cold and heat are me, and it's raining and snowing and hailing and they're howling now, the hydras, and where have all the flies come from? They want to lay their eggs in my wounds, so they can be born as maggots in what was once me.

Who will remember me?

Male faces carved into the trunks of the trees.

I can no longer breathe. The branches and twigs and thorns are cutting my feet to ribbons.

I want them to catch me, so that something else, a whiteness, a different sort of warmth can begin.

I move forward.

Burning. No skin on my lower legs.

I don't want to feel any more, I don't ever want to have another branch stuck inside me.

Hear the panting.

Hear the darkness.

Hear the loneliness.

Hear someone being suffocated by their own fear.

Hear someone who refuses to give up, refuses to die.

That someone is me.

★   ★   ★

I am howling now.

It is my last scream, the last air I manage to force out of my lungs.

I am lying on my back on scalding roots, watching the trees' branches lower themselves towards me, their faces spitting and hissing corrosive acid onto my cheeks, into my eyes, making me blind.

But the pain isn't blind.

It's all that's left now.

And the masks carved into the trees.

Something cold in my side.

Snow is falling.

White stars are falling on my naked body and the steel cuts at my insides, slicing my genitals, piercing something new, and there is nothing there but my scream.

I can't even scream any more.

The forest is deaf.

Doesn't want to see.

Mum.

I never want you to find out what happened to me.

I want you to believe that I died without fear, without pain, surrounded by good people.

I want to believe that myself.

But I know it wasn't like that, and something cuts into me again, a polished tree-trunk, a millipede with a thousand knives for legs, I shudder and I'm dying, Mum, giving my body to the flies.

I leave myself, see my naked, mangled body lying in a glade in an abandoned patch of forest in Östergötland, and I become someone else, *someone who drifts in a space separate from that of the living, and I'm free, Mum, I am, aren't I?*

I see myself being left there.

The ferns sniff at my sides; the trees want to eat the flesh that was me.

Someone walks away.
Wiping the knife on rotting leaves.
I am dead, Mum, burned, cut to pieces, raped and murdered.
I am not alone in that fate.
And it has to end.
The hydra must be killed, even if it has eternal life.

Maria.

That's me.

Maria Murvall.

I am mute and the world does not exist, but I know where I am, even if I still lack a foothold in my own world, or that beyond.

There is no logic where I am.

It's pointless looking for any.

I'm sitting on the bed, tucked into the corner of a room in Vadstena Hospital.

A madhouse.

This is where people like me end up.

People in white coats.

They all doubt whether I'm actually in their world, if I can hear what they're saying, what they want with me, and if I understand what happened to me, if I remember anything about it, how the forest raped me.

I remember everything.

But I'm done with their life, I've left it behind and now there's no way back, I no longer have the language of tongues.

I do not exist.

Not to the doctors or carers, not to my brothers, or Malin Fors, who comes here sometimes and tries to get me to talk, tries to get me to answer questions she doesn't even know if I can understand.

I don't want to exist.

And if I don't exist, then the evil can't exist, and then nothing evil has happened, and if nothing evil has happened, evil doesn't exist.

It's summer, or maybe spring, outside my window. Or is it late winter?

An in-between season that has no name. The world is out of joint, they say, and I know it's been that way for a long time.

I no longer dream. I live in sleep and wakefulness and I still want the hydra, all its heads, to disappear.

But it can't be killed. Not the hydra.

The first time it came was in the forest, then again and again, and then some time just before Christmas.

I screamed then.

Inside myself. It never stops moving, seeking out new flesh to debase, devour, destroy.

It never stops.

And now a cloud is drifting in front of the sun, a big, black, swollen, sulphurous cloud of evil.

Evil can't reach in here.

Because I don't exist.

My heart is beating but I'm not alive.

Definitely not.

If someone were to connect electrodes to my head they would see activity. But not as you know it. Not the flickering traces of the soul, when synapse after synapse is activated by curiosity about the world.

I embody all that is mute.

A different pattern.

But now it's happening again, and I want to scream and I am screaming but my screaming can't be heard, because I don't exist.

But the hydra exists.

Those teeth.

The jaws that drag women into the very darkest depths, depths where there is nothing but fear, pain and loneliness.

It starts with women. Women come before children. And that's why it has to start with women this time.

Women like me.

It's moving now, the evil that exists in the depths.

It's moving.

And I, Maria Murvall, curl up in my corner and scream my soundless scream, which the woman by the car a long way from here can't hear.

A car door opens on the gravel drive in front of a large, gothic villa surrounded by trees, where the wind is dancing through dense foliage.

The woman being carried to the car has been drugged. Someone has stuck a needle in her arm and injected her with a sedative.

Her wrists bear the marks of the chains that have held her shackled to a wall.

A black case full of used notes changes hands.

The car door closes.

The car drives down a paved road and disappears into an unfamiliar landscape where a patch of water is constantly changing its appearance in the light. Then the car carries on into an unfamiliar season.

A room is waiting for the young woman in this season.

The room is merciless.

A room created of hidden darkness and cruel light.

A room without feelings.

A room in which life and death have no dividing line.

The room where a person can forget that they are human.

PART I

The First-Mentioned Love

I

Skåne, Saturday, 14, Sunday, 15 May, 2011

Can clouds close their eyes? Malin wonders. Choose not to see what happens beneath them?

Can clouds forget?

She pulls Peter closer to her as she looks out across the Skåne fields that his father owns.

She leans her cheek against his shoulder as they walk towards a low, green ridge a kilometre or so away.

Is everything OK now?

At long last?

Have I finally got peace in my life, come to terms with what has been and what can yet be?

Doesn't the fact that I'm here in Skåne with Peter's family, to help celebrate his father's seventy-second birthday, prove that?

Before, a walk like this, without any real goal or purpose except the walk itself, would have made her restless, and left her wondering where the nearest bar was, so she could drink herself into a pit.

But now she is walking here.

Beside Peter.

Putting one foot in front of the other and not really wanting to be anywhere else.

It's OK, just walking here.

Like this.

It's OK doing this, right now.

Peter's green corduroy jacket.

The fabric soft against her cheek.

His voice soft as well as he talks about the intrigues in the neurosurgery department rather than all the things he sometimes wants to talk about, and which she definitely doesn't want to discuss.

Or do I?

The ridge is getting closer.

Closer.

And then Malin Fors and Peter Hamse are standing at the foot of the ridge, and they look at each other and nod, and then they begin their ascent.

She's faster than him.

She starts to run, and feels herself sweating under her top. She hears him panting behind her.

I'm going to win.

And love is a competition here on this unknown ridge in the south of Sweden, and run, Malin, run, because there's always something to run from, isn't there?

If nothing else, then the very feeling that things are OK?

Boring.

At the top now.

She's got there something like fifty metres ahead of him.

She sits down on a rock.

Looks out across the world.

Looks at Peter as he comes towards her, panting and smiling and happy, as if she were a present waiting for him at the top of the tallest mountain in the world.

He sits down beside her.

Wraps his arms around her and gives her a sloppy kiss on the cheek.

'You'll be the death of me,' he says. 'You know that?'

'I won!' she says.

'I didn't even know it was a race.'

They look out across the landscape in silence. The fields where the earth is coming to life again, Lund to the north, and off to the west the chimneys and grey-black buildings of Copenhagen on the other side of the Sound.

Behind them is Martofta, Peter's father's estate, and Malin turns to look at the big house, glistening like a white fairy-tale castle in the distance.

The windows of the house are glinting in the sunlight.

The windows are eyes, Malin thinks.

They want something from me.

There's a reason why I'm here.

I felt it before, but now I know. Something's going to happen.

And Peter pulls her to him.

Starts saying how beautiful it is here, and she knows what he's leading up to, she can hear it in the tone of his voice.

She hushes him.

'Can't we just enjoy the view?' she says. 'It's beautiful here. That's enough.'

'Is anything ever enough for you?'

Warmth in Peter's voice.

No accusation. Or is there?

'How do you mean?'

'I mean that you're the most obsessive person I've ever had the honour of meeting.'

Malin is dazzled by the warm, playful light of the candles in the sconces on the walls.

She looks around Martofta's dining room, letting her eyes move from face to face around the enormous walnut-wood dining table.

What am I doing here?

On an unfamiliar estate a short distance north of Malmö,

in the middle of a vast, windswept prairie in Skåne. What am I doing in this oversized house with all these strangers?

It's been a wonderful day, like something out of a lifestyle magazine.

But this?

The watch on Rudolph Hamse's arm. The little jewels sparkling in the light. A painting by Zorn on the wall behind him, a farmhand and a kitchen maid surrounded by hens on a sloping meadow.

'Skåne's car-tyre king. That's my dad,' Peter said the first time he talked about his family. 'He sold the business five years ago.'

Rudolph.

Named after the silent movie star Rudolph Valentino.

Must have been just as much of a charmer in his youth, the features of his face still sharp even though he's over seventy.

Thirty people around the table.

Malin only knows a few of the guests at the 'modest' seventy-second birthday party. Most of their faces are flushed with Martini, champagne and wine, and the venison from the estate's own deer, and to Malin's ears their conversation sounds like a raging spring torrent. She can make out individual words as separate drops, but the context is lost in their shared drunken excitement.

Only water in the glass in front of her.

The nails of her forefingers are deep in the balls of her thumbs as the smell of alcohol threatens to get the better of her. The new, expensive and uncomfortable black dress from Hugo Boss that Peter bought her is chafing, the silky fabric is itchy and her shoes feel too small, their heels too high.

But I look lovely, Malin thinks. Just like the other guests.

Most of them are older than her. The sort of people who

tell lies because it's fun, who judge others according to the size of their bank accounts.

Peter.

He's sitting opposite her, and she looks at him, his sharp nose and short blond hair, and his eyes are twinkling, aren't they?

And she feels embarrassed.

Just from looking at him.

Warm.

Her cheeks blushing, just like everyone else's.

'I'm not like them,' he said.

But that's not true. He fits in perfectly here, with his quick-thinking doctor's mind.

Dipping into conversations at exactly the right moment, with exactly the right comment, sitting back and waiting, going on the attack, making jokes, and he has just given a brilliant speech in his father's honour.

The car-tyre king.

Smoking a cigar now, and he gets up, taps his glass and calls for quiet, clears his throat, snaps his head back and pulls his stomach in under the crocodile-skin belt and white dress-shirt, and it's as if a lifetime of hard graft and deserved gravity suck the guests' words out of the dining room in just a few seconds.

And then he begins to speak, Peter's father.

He turns towards her, towards me, Malin thinks, and she wants to get up, but her backside feels as if it's stuck to the green leather of her chair and she wants to throw herself at the half-empty wine glasses within reach.

Peter.

Help me.

But he's just grinning at her with an amused, slightly sadistic look in his eyes. 'Malin,' the car-tyre king says.

Rudolph.

'Malin Fors. Never did I think I'd be welcoming a tough, beautiful female cop into the Hamse family.'

The speech of the silent Valentino.

'I never thought Peter would meet anyone who could hold his interest for more than five minutes. From the little I know and have heard about you, Malin, I like you a lot. Keep hold of each other.' Then Rudolph's gaze moves on to his wife, Peter's mother, Siv, the face-lifted blonde in a clearly very expensive red dress, who must surely have hoped for better for her son than an alcoholic, albeit reformed, single mother from fucking Linköping, of all the wretched places in the country.

Give me something aristocratic, she's probably thinking behind her cheery smile. A bit of tradition. And lots of money.

He's swaying slightly, Rudolph, at his place at the top of the table.

But he's done his homework, and talks briefly about the murders she has solved.

Admiring oohs from the other guests: lock all criminals up. Flay them alive.

Names of murderers. Threats to society. Rendered harmless, thanks to her.

Now we have nothing to fear from them.

'Thanks to you, Malin Fors.'

'Welcome to the Hamse family and Martofta. A toast!'

'Cheers!'

Thirty strangers raising their glasses to her.

What do I do now?

Drink a toast with water, a toast to longing. For what? My daughter Tove, perhaps, or maybe just to feel Peter's body next to mine.

★ ★ ★

She's making conversation with a car-dealer from Simrishamn.

A bone-dry local in his sixties who has made a fortune from 'the artistry of German engineering'.

Then the car-dealer goes to the toilet.

And Malin gets a chance to look at Peter.

At his face.

An archetypal shape for her. The lines that the first person etched in the sand of the first beach.

I'm lost, she thinks as she looks at him.

Surrounded by his family, and I'm the person who just happens to be his.

We're both lost, aren't we?

There's no way back. No matter what your mother might want.

You started talking about it six months ago.

The child you'd like to have.

The child you'd like us to have together.

'It would be a good thing, Malin. And it's the right time for me, otherwise it will never happen.'

That's what you said to me one evening when you found me at home in the living room bent over the contents of my file on Maria Murvall. The thirty-two-year-old social worker who was found brutally raped and abused on a forest road south of Hultsjön, a lake north of Stjärnorp, one autumn morning seven years ago.

The papers had been spread out over the floor. Like a sort of creation myth trying to make sense of itself.

Love.

Evil.

Like night and day.

Cold and heat.

Maria Murvall. Mute and distant in a room in Vadstena Hospital. A shell.

My brother.

Stefan.

Abandoned by his mother. Incapable of ever learning who I am. But you can feel that I'm here, can't you, Stefan? Somehow I've found a way into you.

His thin arms on the covers, he sleeps on his back with his mouth open and the Hälsingland night keeps watch outside the care home where he lives.

My bloody father, pretending that my brother didn't exist. Keeping him secret from me for almost thirty-five years. Bastard.

Dad's back in Tenerife. Haven't spoken to him since he went back. He's called, but I haven't called back.

Forgive? Move on?

Never. Never ever. Not everything can be forgiven. And Mum. Dead and buried now. I'll never be able to understand her betrayal. I know that now. And what does that sort of betrayal lead to?

Stefan's cold, limp hand in mine, a tepid fallen leaf with soft bones and protruding, warm veins.

You can feel that I'm with you, can't you?

You feel me, don't you?

The world is a tormented scream.

A child. In this world?

Sure, Peter. Sure.

'Coffee and liqueurs will be served in the drawing room.'

Siv's voice reedy but full of contented warmth as she announced the next stage of the evening.

Peter took Malin's hand as they made their way out of the dining room and sat down on a large blue Howard sofa facing an open fire with a gaping bearskin on the floor in front of it.

He fetched coffee for them both, and a cognac for himself.

Sat down beside her and whispered in her ear.

'They might think you're pregnant because you're not drinking.'

That had occurred to her as well.

She decided she didn't give a damn what they thought. I'm thirty-seven now.

'I don't care what they think. You know that.'

'I know,' he replied. 'And that's why Dad likes you. He's only ever respected stubborn people.'

'So you think I'm stubborn?'

'That's just the start of it, and you know it.'

Then he held her tightly and kissed her on the forehead.

'They're OK, aren't they?'

She nodded.

'It was nice, what he said about me.'

And then she closed her eyes. Thinking about Tove, and how she was probably at a party up in Lundsberg, how she seemed to be happy at boarding school, and how the gaps between their telephone conversations had got longer during the past year. At first they had spoken every day, then every other day, and now perhaps once a week, and then it was almost always Malin who called, with the anger of rejection bubbling inside.

But she had Peter now.

They had each other, and they practically lived together, even if they both still had their own flats. His dad hadn't been wrong, she could very well imagine becoming part of this family, and maybe, just maybe, she already was.

Two weeks' holiday.

It had been a quiet winter in the police station. No spectacular murders had shaken Linköping. Two alcoholics had managed to kill each other in a flat out in Berga in February, but that was pretty much it.

Malin had been longing for a difficult case. And had felt

guilty about that. But solving difficult murders is what she does, and she knows she's good at it. To fill up the time she's been working on the Maria Murvall case.

It was as if she'd been raped by nature itself, and she is still in hospital, silent and shut off.

But Malin hadn't got anywhere with the case. She'd exhausted every angle, examined every nook and cranny.

'Take a couple of weeks off now, Malin,' her boss, Police Superintendent Sven Sjöman, had said. 'Go and visit Tove, do something nice.'

'You think I look worn out?'

'No, quite the contrary. But this quiet patch won't last forever.'

She hadn't gone to visit Tove, the timing was all wrong, but she was going to try to drive up for the end of the school year in a few weeks.

Instead, Peter had taken some time owing, and nagged at her to go down to Skåne with him for his father's seventy-second birthday party. He had bribed her with a few days at the Hotel Angleterre in Copenhagen, assuring her that she'd love it.

She had to meet them again some time. The first time had been in Stockholm, before Christmas, at a Christmas meal in Operakällaren.

Rudolph and Siv.

The car-tyre king and his wife.

Peter's sister Theresa, a researcher for Gambro, a pharmaceutical company in Lund.

And now I'm sitting here, Malin thinks, and what am I feeling?

I don't know.

I've got no idea. Beyond the fact that I want to be with Peter.

And that something has to happen.

2

Alcohol makes a promise to an alcoholic: I will give you peace and quiet and a few hours free from pain.

I will make something happen.

Then I'll destroy you.

But isn't it wonderful, being destroyed?

Malin digs the nails of her index fingers deep into her thumbs and thinks: How can anyone handle a party like this without drinking?

You steel yourself.

Think about how disgusting strong spirits taste.

How terrible it is to be hung-over.

That you get invisible medals for strength of character and good behaviour if you abstain.

You think about other things.

Fascinated by those who are drunk, how they permit themselves to become temporarily crazy.

You simply deceive yourself, Malin thinks.

Because you know how insanely wonderful it is to get drunk. Drinking your way into the mire, soft as cotton wool.

And that feeling, that longing never ends, Malin thinks. I'll carry it with me as long as I live.

Malin is sitting alone on the sofa. None of the drunken guests appears to have the time or desire to talk to her, the cop. Even the men don't seem to want to come over and chat about police work, which is what usually happens.

The fire in front of her.

Small sparks are jumping out of the hearth, but lack the strength to set fire to the well-polished parquet floor.

Someone puts some music on in a distant room. Dance music. Where's Peter? Everyone must be dancing now, because the drawing room, so full of people a short while ago, is now almost deserted, apart from a fat old man in tails who's fallen asleep in one of the armchairs.

She closes her eyes.

Thinks about Janne. They don't speak to each other very often any more. Just about practical matters concerning Tove. And there aren't many of those these days, seeing as she takes care of herself up at Lundsberg. But they celebrated Christmas together. She and Peter, Janne and his new blond bimbo, and Tove.

In Janne's house.

Where Malin used to live.

Janne had cooked the ham himself, and made Christmas toffee. And to her surprise, she hadn't felt like tearing the bimbo's eyes out.

Then, suddenly, someone close to Malin.

Who?

She looks up and sees Sara, Peter's sister's girlfriend. Her surname was Markelberg, wasn't it?

They'd spoken briefly when she and Theresa arrived at the party in time for afternoon cocktails, taken on the veranda in the dying light of the weak spring sun.

'Do you mind if I sit down?'

In her black cocktail dress, with her medium-length, loose dark hair and full lips painted bright red, Sara Markelberg looks like a modern version of a forty-year-old Ava Gardner.

What does she want? Malin thinks. She pulls her Hugo Boss dress down towards her knees.

'Of course.'

'It's so noisy through there,' Sara says as she sinks into an armchair. 'I need a bit of peace and quiet. I've never liked dancing.'

'That makes two of us. The dancing, I mean,' Malin says.

Sara puts her cognac glass on the table. Crosses her legs, revealing a black nylon-covered thigh.

What does she want?

'You're not drinking?'

Malin shakes her head.

'There's no new little person on the way?'

Malin shakes her head again, and something about Sara's bluntness makes her feel like being honest.

'I'm a sober alcoholic,' Malin says, and the confession passes through her body like a shock, leaving her feeling drained and full of a strange sense of relief, and Sara nods and says: 'Bloody hell, this must be a nightmare then.'

'It's OK,' Malin says. 'I've been through worse.'

'I'm sure.'

'But you know, when you're among people who are drinking and getting drunk, it's like you're in a different world to everyone else.'

'I know that feeling well enough,' Sara says.

'Sometimes I feel incredibly thirsty,' Malin says.

Sara nods, takes a gulp of her cognac and closes her eyes, appearing to enjoy the warmth of the fire, the cave-like feel of the moment.

And Malin has the feeling that something is getting closer, that the air in the room is contracting.

Then the feeling vanishes.

Almost as quickly as it appeared.

'I'm a doctor,' Sara says. 'I think our jobs are fairly similar, you know?'

'How do you mean?'

'We help people. Make them believe that bad things don't

exist. That everything can be fixed. We create the security that every society needs if people aren't going to end up tearing each other to pieces.'

Malin laughs.

'Extreme, but true. Unfortunately.'

'Have you ever shot anyone?'

Usually this question would make Malin angry, but from Sara it seems entirely natural.

'Yes, I have. But it was unavoidable.'

'No angst afterwards?'

'Yes, but not much. How about you? Is there anything following you around?'

Sara looks as if she'd rather not answer, seems to have something to say, but holds back.

'I work in mental health, so it's usually my patients who are tormented by demons. I try to keep a distance.'

'It doesn't always work, does it?'

Sara shakes her head.

'It works all too rarely.'

She can't see me, Peter thinks.

He's standing in the gloom in a red-painted servants' corridor, studying Malin as she talks to Sara Markelberg.

Go-getting Sara. Fearless Sara. She's been improbably good for Theresa, who has always been antisocial. Opening her up to a world outside her laboratories.

Malin.

They had met by chance at the hospital after a bomb went off in the main square in Linköping.

Peter sees her lean forward now. They're almost touching, she and Sara.

What are they talking about? It seems to be something important, and he can see a hint of obsession in Malin's eyes, her desire, greater than herself, to forge ahead when she picks up the scent of something important, something that it's usually impossible for even her to put into words.

She's a riddle wrapped in a mystery inside an enigma, Peter thinks.

Just when I think I understand her, or at least part of her, she slips away, changing before my eyes, turning off in a different, unexpected direction.

Do you want to live with Malin Fors? Best fasten your seatbelt.

Do you want her as a mother to your child?

Give her something to anchor her to this world?

Peter takes a sip of his freshly mixed Martini. Cold and sharp and pure.

He sees the loneliness and fear in Malin's eyes. That feeling she carries, of something broken and irreparable, of having somehow been deceived by the world.

He walks out into the large drawing room.

Sees his father dancing with an elderly woman whose name he can't remember. Sees the smile on his face, the look of an irrepressible ladies' man.

He has been notoriously unfaithful for forty-five years. Often with several women at the same time. Mum must know, she does know, but chooses to focus on other things. On her money, her comfortable life. Putting blinkers on to shield herself from anything resembling an unwelcome emotion.

His dad is one of those men who take and take, and then take a bit more of what they want. Everything must be available to those sorts of men. And they charm the world with their smiles, their shamelessness and their money, leaving human wreckage in their wake.

Mum.

Completely disconnected from herself. One big mask of convention and ideas about how things ought to be.

Peter knows that his family has influenced him. In

relationships he has always ended up in a no-man's-land, hesitating until it's too late, until love has deflated in the face of his indecision.

That's not going to happen with Malin.

Leaning forward on the sofa over there, its blue fabric like an unfamiliar ocean around her body.

I've made my choice now. I'm going to hold on.

I'm where I should be with Malin. Wherever it is we're heading together.

Sara Markelberg got up and left shortly after Peter came over to them.

Now he's sitting next to Malin and she feels his body against hers, and wishes they were up in their room, away from the party.

'What were you talking about?'

'All sorts of things.'

'Such as?'

'We were talking about your sister, among other things.'

Peter doesn't seem interested in what they said about his sister.

'You talked about more than that.'

'Yes,' Malin says. 'We talked about you.'

'And what did you say?'

'That you're a right idiot. What do you think?'

Malin kisses him on the cheek, letting her tongue wander over his rough skin, and feels that her conversation with Sara isn't over yet, that the words are still shimmering, unspoken, and that there's a reason why she, Malin Fors, is here now, some reason that's bigger than her.

Peter's body on top of Malin's, pushing deeper inside her, and now he's there, right at the top against her innermost wall, in a vain attempt to vanquish some sort of loneliness.

No child.

Not yet.

The coil is where it should be.

She scratches his back and whispers in his ear: harder, faster, don't be so fucking gentle with me, don't be so tame, and he pulls out of her, turns her over, puts her on all fours facing the hundred-year-old oak bedstead and starts pumping, pumping, pumping, and she wants to cry out, groan, but holds back, just lets her head hit the old wood, in this absurdly oversized house, among all these people with their oversized egos, and now she yells: is that the best you can do? Huh? Harder, and the unknown beast has to be drawn out, has to be driven out, and then killed, killed, killed, so it can never come back again.

Afterwards.

Beside each other.

Wet with sweat.

'You frightened me,' Peter says.

'Frightened you?'

'Yes.'

'I don't know what got into me.'

'What are you scared of, Malin?'

'I don't know.'

His hand on her back, warm, gentle, present.

'I'm here,' he whispers. 'We're here together. You know that, don't you?'

The clock on the wood-panelled wall of their bedroom says it's a quarter past five.

Thirsty.

Malin creeps out of bed, pulls on a grey flannel dressing gown, then makes her way out of the room, down the cold staircase and on towards the kitchen.

The party finished at three o'clock. The last car left at half past. She had woken up when the music fell silent. Then she fell asleep again until her thirst woke her up, and now she's walking into the gloomy kitchen.

A dark shadow is looking out of the far window.

'God, you scared me!'

It's Sara Markelberg, in a similar dressing gown to her own.

'I felt thirsty,' Malin says, turning the tap on as Sara sits down at the kitchen table.

Malin drinks straight from the tap.

'You'd think there's champagne in that tap,' Sara hisses. 'I don't drink much, but I still have trouble getting to sleep.'

Malin laughs and sits down opposite her. Breathing in the lingering smell of alcohol and left-over food, even though the staff have done a good job of clearing up.

Sara looks at Malin through the gloom, holding her gaze before saying: 'I work in the secure unit of St Lars Hospital in Lund. We've got a girl there, barely over twenty, and she's completely distant, like she's in another world.'

Why are you telling me this? Malin wonders. Because I'm a police officer?

Maria Murvall, she thinks.

'I'm having trouble letting go of her case. Her psychosis is bad,' Sara goes on. 'And it seems to be permanent. No one knows who she is, or where she's from. We haven't given her a name. We just call her "you".'

Silence.

Curiosity transformed into a growing black lump in the darkness.

Malin leans forward.

'What happened to her? How did she end up there? Something must have happened to her, surely?'

Sara leans forward as well.

Takes a deep breath.

'She was found one morning, on a road beside a field east of Malmö,' she says, then goes on: 'Naked, raped. Mute. As if she'd been terrified out of her life, but without actually dying. That was more than five years ago now, and the police aren't getting anywhere with her case. They've dropped the investigation.'

What she's saying makes Malin feel wide awake. Alert, eager, even though she's only had a few hours' sleep.

Shameless.

Straight to the point:

'Could I see her?'

Sara looks at Malin, not surprised or curious, more like expectant.

'I've got a similar case that I've been trying to solve, up in Linköping,' Malin says. 'But I haven't got anywhere. So I'd really like to meet this girl, no matter what condition she's in.'

Inside she's cursing the authorities' failure to compile a shared, searchable database. Once the preliminary investigation was dropped, this woman's case would have been hard to find. You'd have to go through official channels, and Malin's investigation into Maria's case is anything but official. No archives get opened up for a freelancing police officer investigating an old case in her spare time.

How many women like Maria are there around the country?

How many similar cases?

She's wondered about that occasionally, and made limited attempts to find out, but nothing has ever shown up.

But the cases are there.

She's sure of that.

Sara leans forward a bit further and whispers: 'Tomorrow. We'll go to Lund tomorrow. You have to see her. God knows what happened to her.'

And inside her Malin feels something simultaneously break and become whole.

As if she were entering an unfamiliar season, where everything normally taken for granted is called into question.

3

Malin is up first, in spite of her nocturnal conversation with Sara Markelberg.

Jeans and a white top.

I'm the only one who isn't hung-over, she thinks, the only one not being chased by an internal devil wielding a sledgehammer. If there's one advantage to not drinking, it's this.

Hangover-free mornings, no feeling like a pig, no throbbing skull, a body that's not tormented by regret and shame. And, in their place, early morning moments like this one, silent and caressing.

The big country kitchen is bathed in a magnetic light from a vibrant blue sky. There's no holding back the spring out there, unless it's actually already summer? What season is this?

It was snowing less than three weeks ago.

Then the thaw, followed by a hailstorm the like of which no one had seen before.

Hailstones the size of tennis balls battered cars, and it was sheer good fortune that no one was killed.

Then almost summer heat. Shy little flowers trying to push up from the ground, only to be forced back by a sudden frosty night. Grass that wanted to grow but didn't dare, bright greens fading to grey, best not to appear presumptuous.

Shiny stainless-steel machines in the kitchen, two big

fridges, the sort usually found in restaurant kitchens, one of them bearing a note saying:

'Breakfast! Help yourselves!'

Coffee.

Malin makes herself a cup with the Nespresso machine, the strongest, blackest kind, and drinks it standing by the ten-metre-long worktop, listening to the house creak with the memories of centuries, and wondering if it's complaining that the nobility has been replaced by a robber baron?

Sunday today.

Peter ought to be down soon, they're supposed to be heading off to Copenhagen, and Malin sits down at the long table in the centre of the kitchen.

One end wall is covered with blue, flower-patterned tiles.

She inhales the smell that permeates the room, a strange mix of enclosure and freedom, of privilege and slowly simmering game stews, vases of dried lavender from the estate's own fields.

'You're up early.'

Malin looks around.

Sara isn't wearing any lipstick, and is dressed in the grey dressing gown. She doesn't seem hung-over either. She's standing just inside the door looking in Malin's direction, yet somehow past her, out through a window towards a sky that is so blue it seems to have no end.

'Peter and I are going to Copenhagen today,' Malin says after a while.

Sara sits down opposite her.

'I thought we were going to Lund,' she says, and Malin knows that Sara knows there's nothing she'd rather do.

Malin nods.

'But there isn't time. Peter's booked a table for lunch.'

'There's time,' Sara says. 'Isn't there, Peter?'

And Malin turns her head, and there he is, in his perfectly

faded jeans, looking at her, yet past her again, towards the sky.

'It's a hell of a day,' he says. 'Couldn't be better. What's there time for?'

Malin opens her mouth, trying to find the words that will persuade Peter that she has to go to Lund, to the secure unit of St Lars Hospital to meet a silent young woman whom the world has forced to turn away from life.

But she doesn't manage to say anything.

Sara gets in first.

'You know Maria Murvall, Malin's special case? I've got a woman in exactly the same state, in my ward at St Lars. Malin ought to see her.'

Peter shakes his head.

Malin has made an effort to conceal her interest in Maria from him when she talks about the case, but he's still noticed her obsession.

But has avoided making any comment.

'Copenhagen?' he says, holding out his arms.

Then he walks over to Malin and hugs her shoulders from behind.

'What a day,' he repeats. 'Perfect for working outside. And there's no point me saying no, is there? You'd still go. I'll cancel lunch, we can go this evening instead.'

Malin puts her hands on his and squeezes them tightly.

'That sounds good.'

She can't be bothered to play games and tenderly ask him if that's what he really wants, and just resigns herself to her own nature. On the other side of the table Sara smiles.

Tarmac and swaying yellow fields that seem to melt into the sky, a shimmering jade streak on the horizon.

Plumes of smoke to the west.

Faint through sunglasses that turn the surrounding rape
fields orange, and make an avenue of poplars to the east
look like wine bottles stuck in the ground upside down.

A smell of sulphur on the air from farmers' fires.

An open-topped yellow BMW.

Malin is sitting beside Sara Markelberg, feeling the wind
tug at her hair amid the noise of the world around them.

The car conquers metre after metre of tarmac, eating up
the distance between them and the mystery ahead.

Peter's sister Theresa hadn't appeared before they set off.
'She's always liked sleeping in,' was Peter's comment. 'The
hangover from hell,' Sara declared. 'Believe me, she won't
be out of bed before three.'

'What do you know about the police investigation?' Malin
yells over the howl of the wind.

'A hundred and fifty pages of nothing, from what I could
see. Some doctor, a gynaecologist, suggesting that her injuries could have been self-inflicted, but I have trouble
believing that, no one could do that to themselves, it's out
of the question,' Sara shouts, without taking her eyes off
the road. 'I read the case notes in an effort to understand
what happened, to find some way into her, but it was
pointless.'

Behind the words lurks a blunt scientific worldview: I
don't understand this, I've failed. No more than that.

Then Sara looks away from the road and turns to Malin,
looking into her eyes, a little too long, with an expression
that's almost a plea: Do something, help me find out something about this nameless young woman.

Smooth out the question marks.

Explain why.

Some fifteen minutes later they pull up outside the entrance
of St Lars Hospital in one of the parking spaces reserved

for doctors. The large, red-brick building is set apart, yet still in the centre of Lund, built as an imposing castle for madmen, with a heavy, tiled roof to press the madness into the ground.

Malin follows Sara Markelberg in through the automatic doors. They take a lift that smells of vomit up to the second storey, where a grimy yellow linoleum floor leads them down a windowless corridor. They turn a corner into a different corridor, lined with textured grey wallpaper.

Bars behind a locked door with reinforced glass.

A guard in a built-in booth.

The guard nods in recognition to Sara before pressing a button, and there's a click and the first door slides open automatically.

And now Malin can see that the bars are behind the next door, rather than in front of it, as she had thought.

Sara puts a key in the door.

'So they can't get out? Are they criminals?' Malin asks. 'The patients here, I mean?'

'Some of them are a danger both to themselves and the wider community. They're here because they've been sectioned under the Mental Health Act.'

'And our girl?'

'I don't think she cares,' Sara says. 'We've tried everything. Different languages even, but nothing seems to come close to breaking through her silence. There's no chance that she's faking. No one could pull that off.'

Behind the bars a corridor lined with locked doors.

At the end of the corridor more bars, in front of a window.

Behind the window the sky.

So blue now that it almost seems to be turning black.

'I'll go in alone,' Malin says, and Sara Markelberg doesn't protest. 'I know what to expect.'

The door to the nameless woman's room is at the far end of the corridor.

Not locked, and now Malin can feel Sara's hand on her shoulder, encouraging her to go on, to go in, and Malin presses the handle and opens the door.

A tree with fresh foliage outside a window.

A small desk in front of a whitewashed concrete wall, a green and lilac rug on the floor, and exactly the same sort of old-fashioned hospital bed that Maria Murvall has got, pushed into a similar corner, and at the top of the bed, wearing a white hospital gown, sits the mute young woman, staring out into space.

Like Maria.

Just like Maria.

And Malin wonders why Maria in particular ended up as a victim. The kind-hearted social worker about whom no one had anything but good to say, the woman who took on the cases of the very weakest in society and helped them, supported them, gave them a few crumbs of dignity in their lives when everyone else despised them, consciously and unconsciously.

Is friendliness dangerous? Did she have an inclination towards darkness? Did she want to expose herself to danger? Or was it her utterly uncompromising engagement on the side of good that led to her ending up where she did? Had she simply sacrificed herself for the sake of good? There was no question that evil had been victorious out there in the forest. Leading her to a dark, cold place that she both wouldn't and couldn't leave.

'We feed her,' Sara had told her. 'She won't eat by herself, but she does go to the toilet. She goes on living, in a way, but not properly.'

The door closes behind Malin.

There's a silence here unlike any other.

An all-absorbing silence that suggests there is a place between life and death where people can flee. That there is a place where none of the laws of nature applies, a place of silence, exactly the same silence that surrounds Maria.

How old is she?

Malin moves closer to the bed.

Twenty-five? No more, and she has high cheekbones framed by greasy dark-brown hair that looks as if it needs a wash and a good dose of conditioner.

The young woman blinks, brown eyes that don't seem to see anything, hidden ears that don't seem to hear anything. Malin sits down beside her on the bed.

The woman doesn't pull away, just breathes calmly, taking absolutely no notice of Malin's presence. Her legs are stretched out on the bed, and Malin finds herself wishing that she would curl up, pull away, try to hide, show any reaction at all, but she just sits there.

The loneliest of all lonely people.

As if abandoned by herself.

Like a very specific type of person who has known a terror that has nothing to do with life, with breathing.

'What's your name?' Malin asks. 'Nobody knows, but a lot of people would like to know. There must be people wondering where you are.'

Her breath smells, Malin thinks. It smells of emptiness, of a longing to get even further away.

'*She isn't suicidal. At least we don't think she is.*'

'What happened to you?' Malin asks.

'What happened to Maria, do you know?'

'Are you connected?'

Words.

Am I saying them, or just thinking them? Malin wonders.

But it doesn't matter, because you're not hearing anything anyway, are you? You don't even know that I'm here.

What happened to Maria? You know, don't you? What happened to you?

Right now your name is nothing, I'm going to give you your name back. If it's the last thing I do in my life, I'm going to give you your name back.

I'm going to give all lost women their names back.

I'm coming now, Malin thinks. I'm coming after you now, you bastards.

I want you to know that.

I'm coming after you now.

4

Before Malin leaves St Lars Hospital, she and Sara Markelberg have coffee in the hospital cafeteria.

The walls of the shabby room, covered with textured yellow wallpaper, are hung with colourful paintings of indistinct monster-like human faces that Malin guesses have been made by the hospital's patients.

At first they sit opposite one another in silence.

Unwilling to say anything, just letting the horror sink in, and Malin wonders what's going to happen now, and realises that she hasn't thought about Peter once since they left Martofta.

Eventually Malin asks Sara if she's happy with Peter's sister. Surprised at her own curiosity, and ashamed of being intrusive.

'We're good. How about you two?'

'Good.'

'Children?'

'He wants children.'

'And you?'

'To be honest, I don't know. Don't tell anyone, I'd rather we kept this between us. How about you?'

'No, neither of us.'

Sara takes a sip of coffee and Malin feels her compulsive thoughts creeping up on her, merging with the institutional smell and the taste of tannic acid, in the middle of this intimate yet oddly superficial conversation.

Does Peter like hunting? He's never mentioned it. Is he
a hunter?

Is his dad a hunter?

She's seen the gun cabinet in the house. There must be
at least ten different rifles, two of them extremely handsome
shotguns with detailed engraving of seabirds with serpents
in their beaks.

A beautiful death.

A swarm of shot spreading over the landscape, a tiny ball
of lead capturing and destroying something living mid-
flight.

She asks Sara about Peter's father, and she has nothing
but good to say of him. 'OK, he's a patriarch, but entirely
free from prejudice, and when it comes down to it he's
actually a very fair and kind man.'

Before they part Sara tells Malin the name of the police
officer who was in charge of the investigation, a Sören Lind.

They say goodbye with a hug on the steps of the hospital,
and Malin feels the unfamiliar woman's body against her
own.

Somehow they have a shared mission now.

Somehow they are going to save all women.

She walks towards where the railway station is supposed
to be.

Lund.

Just like Linköping.

Similar buildings, similar people. Just a bit smarter, a bit
more precious. Brown brick buildings from the seventies
with tiny windows, the smell of hamburger stalls and well-
kept little cafés with blue window frames and organic
sprouted grain on the ciabatta, sorry, *paninis*, in their chiller
cabinets.

Malin is keen to go and see Sören Lind straight away,

but knows she ought to go back to Martofta, where Peter is waiting for her.

But Sören Lind might well be at work in the police station in Malmö.

Working on a Sunday.

Nothing unusual about that. Detectives are often required to cover emergency calls. In Malmö there's presumably a rolling rota, there always is in the big cities, with officers required to work every third weekend.

She dials Sören Lind's number.

Thinks: Peter will have to wait. He can handle that.

Sören Lind was at work.

He agreed to dig out the files, everything he'd got on the case.

Then the train to Malmö, and during the eighteen-minute journey Malin reflects on how quickly things are moving now, and how she prefers it like that, doesn't want to be held back now that she's finally got a lead in the Maria Murvall case.

Maria.

Her name like a mantra in time with the sound of the train on the rails as she passes through small communities where the modest little houses square up against anything unfamiliar.

Maria.

A promise.

To me. To her. To Tove. To all bloody women, and all bloody, bloody men.

A door opens to one side of the reception desk in Malmö police station, its worn hinges creaking.

An elderly, almost unhealthily thin man with a face covered in leathery suntanned skin nods in her direction.

He's wearing beige trousers and a crumpled white shirt that's seen better days, hanging off shoulders that seem to have shrunk over the past decade or so as enthusiasm and curiosity were gradually replaced with exhaustion and eventually disappeared altogether.

His face cracks into a weary smile as he shakes Malin's hand, and his handshake is firm yet hesitant, and Malin follows him into his office.

'Well, you can see for yourself,' Sören Lind says, leaning back in his creaking office chair as Malin leafs through the photographs that were taken of the nameless young woman's naked body, the pictures pulled from a folder on the grey desktop.

The room is shabby.

Ingrained with smoke.

He probably smokes in his office, even though he's not allowed to. Smoking's banned in every police station in the country.

'You can see for yourself,' he repeats.

And Malin does indeed see for herself on the other side of the desk.

The skin on the woman's legs looks as if it's been torn by huge thorns, she has bruises as if the tree branches had turned into boa constrictors and tried to squeeze all life out of her, her face is beaten beyond all recognition, she has gaping wounds where her nipples once were, and around her navel someone has carved a flower into her skin, a perfectly formed little coltsfoot. Her vagina appears to have been burned and shredded with blunt instruments from another age, and between the wounds on her thighs there are blue bruises with yellow edges gradually fading to orange, as if the most vicious flames of hell had tried to rape her.

'She was penetrated with some sort of spiked object,' Sören Lind says.

. Just like Maria, Malin thinks.

And it dawns on her that she hasn't explained to her colleague in Malmö why she's there, why the case is of interest to her, and he hasn't asked.

'She was found by a motorist,' Sören Lind says. 'A woman on her way to work, out by the Hisna hills, twenty kilometres east of Lund, in an area of mixed forest and open farmland.'

'I heard there was a gynaecologist who thought she might have inflicted the wounds herself?'

'That's right,' Sören Lind says. 'But I don't agree.'

'It really doesn't look like it,' Malin says.

And Sören Lind adjusts his shirt, and takes a deep breath, with obvious difficulty.

'I'm not going to ask what you're doing here, or why you're interested in this case, but I can tell you one thing.'

Sören Lind pauses.

He gives her his weariest look, a look that says I don't care any more, I'm going to tell you everything important, no matter what the consequences.

'What?'

Sören Lind takes another deep breath.

'I'm due to retire next year. I've stopped caring.'

Malin puts the pictures back in the file, closes it, shifts on her chair and looks at Sören Lind.

More exhausted than Sven Sjöman, Malin thinks. Unless Sven is actually as tired as this? He's been getting more exhausted, her boss. And sometimes she's found herself wondering if he's starting to get old, or if it's something else, an illness of some sort? He's at the age where you almost start to expect that.

'You wanted to tell me that you're due to retire soon?'

Sören Lind grins.

'No, I want to tell you that there was something odd about this investigation five years ago. The prosecutor kept wanting to drop the case. Implied that the girl was probably a messed-up prostitute, and he got that independent gynaecologist, not the usual one from Malmö General Hospital, to examine her injuries, and sure enough he declared that her injuries could very well have been self-inflicted.'

'But you didn't believe that?'

'No, no one could inflict those sorts of wounds on themselves. I was in charge of the investigation, but when the prosecutor decided that the case should be dropped, there was nothing I could do. And it wasn't as if she was likely to appeal against the decision.'

'Who was the prosecutor?'

'Fredrik Kantsten. He works in Stockholm now.'

'I've never heard of him.'

'He's about fifty. He gets the pick of the really big jobs. He's a smart bloke. I always had the impression that he was the sort of man who got things off his hands quickly.'

Malin nods.

'I know the sort,' she says. 'Probably didn't want anything to do with a sexually motivated crime. There are other prosecutors like that. And if an investigation looks like it might be a dead end, they drop it quickly to improve the statistics.'

'Yes, because a case that's been closed is a crime that's been cleared up, according to the National Council for Crime Prevention,' Sören Lind says.

'It's completely insane,' Malin says. 'It just encourages weakness and passivity in prosecutors.'

'There are too many cowards among that lot.'

Bloody prosecutors, Malin thinks. They watch each others' backs, look after their own. Just look at the prosecutor who dropped the preliminary investigation into a rape allegation against Police Commissioner Göran Lindberg, although they had DNA, his car registration, and a mobile number. But at least he was given a long sentence in the end.

Career men.

Cowards in public service.

'Just after the woman was discovered there was a murder in Rosengård, an immigrant was found tortured to death in a garbage room, and to be honest we weren't getting anywhere with the girl in St Lars. Maybe Kantsten was right to drop the case after all.'

Malin stands up.

Holds Sören Lind's gaze.

'So you still don't have any idea who the woman is?'

'No. It was even on *Crimewatch*, but no one recognised her.'

I should have seen that, Malin thinks, but simultaneously, why? I don't watch the programme, no one I know does.

'So you have absolutely no idea who she is?'

Sören Lind shakes his head.

'No. None at all. But, like I said, there was something funny about the whole investigation, a sort of fog surrounding our work. Everything seemed to go so damn slowly.'

Malin recognises the feeling Sören Lind is describing, the way work on a police investigation can feel like stumbling over a terrifying field in milk-thick fog, all the while sensing predators snapping at your heels, and knowing you have to press on, into the unknown.

'I swear the investigation was very thorough. For instance, we checked if any cottages had been rented out in the surrounding area, but we didn't come up with anything. I can give you a copy of the file. Hang on while I sort it out for you.'

Alone in the room.

The pictures of the wounded woman burned into her retinas.

Malin thinks of Tove, Janne, and then Peter. Lets them fill the room, make it less empty. She thinks of her colleagues in the Linköping Police. Sven Sjöman, Police Chief Karim Akbar, her partner Zacharias 'Zeke' Martinsson, Johan Jakobsson, Waldemar Ekenberg and Börje Svärd.

There's space for them all in the room.

Filling it with her memories of them.

Good memories.

The taxi has stopped on the road cutting straight through a cornfield by a solitary tree, a large beech, where a female motorist found the mute, battered young woman who is now sitting in a psychiatric hospital in Lund like one of the living dead.

The woman I met a little while ago, yet somehow didn't, Malin thinks.

Copies of the pictures in the folder. The map.

This must be the place.

Just a few dozen kilometres from Peter's family's estate.

Could she have come from there?

Absurd, Malin thinks. Don't let your brain get out of control, Fors.

And Malin gets out and the taxi driver, a dark-skinned man in his fifties who isn't the talkative sort, hasn't asked why she wanted to come out to the middle of nowhere, and the sun is pressing her to the ground, unnaturally warm now, and she hurries into the shade of the beech, trying to see the scene before her, on a day like today, the woman stumbling along the road, bleeding, gone for good, and how the motorist doesn't believe her eyes at first, it can't be, yes, it is, oh no, oh dear God, oh God . . .

God.

Is he here? She?

Are you who I'm looking for? Malin wonders. Is your

soothing whisper what I want to hear? And she steps out into the sunlight, away from the silence of the tree, and she thinks she's going to burst into flames, and tries to listen to the blue, blowtorch air, listening out for an unfamiliar voice explaining what happened.

The nameless woman.

Maria Murvall.

Anyone else, any others?

She looks at her own shadow. Tries to step into the dark outline of herself, and the ground is full of dried blood, isn't it? Bone dry and thirsty beneath her feet.

But there's nothing except silence here.

And the ever-present loneliness.

And the stench of ill-will. Sulphur.

The unmistakable, rotten odour of bad intentions.

Why?

People confronted with evil, afflicted by it and its manifestations, always ask themselves that question, Malin thinks.

And sometimes there is an answer.

But not always.

Sometimes it's as if evil were a force of its own, something unquestionable that always exists, everywhere, just waiting for the right opportunity to show its teeth.

But there's always some sort of explanation for evil, somewhere.

The sadist takes pleasure in what he does. And everyone can understand pleasure.

But what if the evil that struck Maria Murvall and the nameless woman in St Lars was of a different sort?

A directionless evil, without pleasure, without any goal or purpose.

An evil without explanation.

An evil that is an echo of itself, and which therefore never disappears.

An evil that can't be eradicated.

Malin crouches down and picks up a handful of soil, then lets it slip through her fingers, back down to the ground again.

Then she hears the scream.

A lonely woman's tormented scream.

As if she had become aware for the first time of the deepest experience of human life, and wants nothing more at that moment than to die.

And Malin wants to shake off that scream, make it disappear, but it's there and she knows that this woman exists somewhere, that she's alive, and that it mustn't be too late.

It mustn't be, it simply mustn't be too late.

And Malin feels her stomach clench, feels her whole body surge with unfamiliar electricity.

And she gets the feeling that it's urgent.

That something is urging her on towards the evil.

That the woman is real.

Like her, like Tove.

Then the scream ebbs away.

And it's as if it had never been there.

But Malin knows she can't hold back. Whatever it was that was once in the vicinity of this tree has now moved into a hole so dark that the darkness itself seems to consist of shining light.

Fredrik Kantsten.

Stockholm.

Malin wants to set off at once, not be tramping down this ridiculous street in this absurdly bohemian city.

The top part of Strøget.

But it's still wonderful to be here, and their room at the Angleterre, an insanely luxurious hotel in overblown *fin de siècle* style, is magnificent, and is called a junior suite. Although she has no idea what could possibly be considered junior about such an obviously old room.

And now she's walking through Copenhagen on this strange spring evening, dressed in her usual jeans and fake Converse trainers bought at Skänninge market, with Peter's arm around her shoulders, walking past hundreds and hundreds of people sitting at the pavement cafés, strolling slowly along a street free of cars, lined with elegant red-brick buildings. The evening is wonderful, in the most banal sense of the word, and she can feel his body beside her, and doesn't wish anyone else were here, not even Tove, as they walk through this dream-like fine evening in a dream-like good life, yet she still wishes she were some-where else.

Back in the hotel room. With her head buried in the report from Malmö Police.

At the police station in Linköping. Showing Zeke and Sven Sjöman the similarities between the two cases.

In Stockholm. Hearing what that prosecutor, Kantsten, has to say about the case, and where the gynaecologist came from, the one who said the injuries could have been self-inflicted.

She wants the gynaecologist's name.

His report.

And Malin looks at the people going past.

Thinks: I can go to Stockholm if I want to.

I'm still on leave. I can do whatever I like.

But what would Peter say?

I'm here. With him now.

And she pulls him closer to her and rests her cheek against his corduroy jacket.

Women in floaty dresses, men with briefcases even though it's the weekend. A few of them are carrying oversized cases of shiny brown leather.

What have they got in those cases? Malin wonders. All the secrets of the world? Documents? Aftershave?

Or something worse. Like the Boston Strangler with his nylon stockings?

'We'd better speed up,' Peter says. 'Or we'll lose our table.'

'What table?'

'We've got a table booked at Noma. Best restaurant in the world. Do you know how impossible it is to get a booking there? The chef, René Redzepi, is a genius.'

Maria Murvall, Malin thinks, has never eaten there. That much is certain.

Peter stops.

Turns towards her.

'You're not really here, are you, Malin? Can you try to be here, this evening, just for my sake?'

'I'm here,' she says with a smile. 'Where else would I be?'

5

Monday, 16 May

Arlanda.

One of the arseholes of the world.

I'm here now, Malin thinks as she cruises between the businessmen in terminal four shortly after eleven. Stressed, they're hurrying to or from their flights beneath the black roof where forgotten wires dangle, evidence of sloppy electricians.

The metallic voice from the loudspeaker above her, as though it comes from the other side.

They had cut short their trip to Copenhagen by a day.

Noma had been a revelation. Twenty small, strange but refined dishes. Improbably beautiful creations that made her long for a fat steak with Béarnaise sauce.

Peter had noticed her mind was somewhere else during breakfast, and realised that she wasn't really going to be present during the visit to the restaurant, or the Glyptotek, or the shopping in exclusive boutiques at his expense.

Shopping.

When they'd been together a few months, it dawned on Malin that he had money. And that had simultaneously horrified and appealed to her. He didn't just have his generous doctor's salary topped up with antisocial-hours supplements, but had money in the bank as well. He could indulge in things for himself, for her, for them, and it was as if he'd held back on this so as not to seem boastful or arrogant, as if he had wanted to prove to her that she was good enough for him even though she was just a poor bloody police officer.

But in spite of the money, in spite of all the wonderful things they could buy in a city like Copenhagen, she had just wanted to get away.

Not even the sheets on the hotel bed could hold her there.

Thick, infinitely soft cotton sheets, washed precisely the right number of times to be able to caress a tired body, and somehow impregnated with a smell of apple blossom that transported Malin back to the garden of the house in Sturefors where she grew up.

She had loved that garden.

But the memory of budding apples wasn't enough to keep her in Copenhagen. Nor the memories of her mother and father in that house, the feeling that nothing was the way it should be, that nothing was the way it seemed.

Peter hadn't even made an objection.

He helped her book the ticket just a few hours later.

She would have liked him to beg her to stay in Copenhagen, in Skåne, beg her to let them spend some time together, but he hadn't.

He had waved her off in the taxi from the Angleterre, before himself setting off back to his family estate to do, as he put it, 'a bit of work in the garden'.

'Do what you have to do, Malin,' he had whispered. 'Do what you have to do.'

In bed on Sunday night, between the apple-scented sheets, he had whispered those same words, and they're like a mantra inside her now as she sits in the taxi from Arlanda on the E4, heading towards the central courthouse on Kungsholmen, where Prosecutor Fredrik Kantsten has his office.

She leafs through a copy of *Aftonbladet* as they pass the futuristic offices of Sun Microsystems.

Unable to concentrate on what she's reading.

Thinking: I'm crazy to do this.

I could be living it up in Copenhagen, but instead I've set off on a wild goose chase to Stockholm.

Leaving Peter behind.

Fredrik Kantsten probably isn't even there. Malin hadn't wanted to call, because he would doubtless have refused to see her if she had actually managed to get hold of him.

Because she's got absolutely nothing to show him, just a gut feeling.

Better to take her chances.

Better to assuage her restlessness.

She focuses on the paper, forces herself to read.

The chief executive of Save the Children, Sten Dinman, former minister for equality for the Social Democrats, has written an article encouraging people to donate money to the victims of a disastrous flood in Indonesia, in Sumatra. He suggests that we have to treat them as human beings in spite of their Muslim faith, and implies that he has discerned a lack of generosity towards the victims because of this.

The article has been endorsed by a whole series of big names, at least fifty of them. Some of them Malin recognises, others not. Then she sees Fredrik Kantsten's name.

In his capacity as district prosecutor he has signed the article, along with a number of his colleagues.

She looks at the photograph of Dinman.

Youthful, in spite of his forty-plus years, a broad, powerful face framed by short, fair hair. One of the people to watch in the Social Democrats. Handsome, engaged, potential prime ministerial material.

She closes the paper.

Tucks it into the pocket behind the driver's seat.

What am I actually doing here?

The taxi bores its way past Stockholm's glistening office blocks, where success seems to be taken for granted. They're packed in along the road from Arlanda. The façades are made of tinted, polished glass, through which financial power can look out, but no one can see in. Petrol stations, a steady stream of lorries in the other lane, and at the edge of a field is a diminutive factory with a sign announcing that they make vests.

Must be a huge demand for vests these days, Malin thinks. Modern chain mail. Everyone wants to protect themselves from something, everyone's afraid, so why not put on some chain mail and pretend that nothing bad can happen, that nothing can hurt you.

But all is not well in the country's largest city. The gaps that had existed between people while she was studying at Police Academy have grown into chasms now.

Beyond the glittering office buildings, hidden behind thin scraps of forest where no sensible person would venture after dark, lie Stockholm's most tragic suburbs, seemingly endless clusters of grey blocks that life seems to have abandoned long ago.

And in those districts hopelessness and resignation thrive. No one ever says so outright, but anyone who can move gets away from there as fast as they can. To make a better life for themselves and their children.

We have to be able to say things like that, Malin thinks. Talk about the problems that come with integration without being labelled as racists.

We have to talk, dare to see, dare to speak uncomfortable truths, because otherwise the Swedish Democrats will go on picking up more and more of the country's weaker souls, and their leader, the upstart Jimmie Åkesson, will be the one setting the tone of the debate.

And that simply can't be allowed to happen.

They've reached Norrtull now. The protected enclave of the inner city takes over.

There's no hopelessness here.

Here the cancer is arrogance.

Malin misses Zeke. She wishes he was with her. So she could lean on him, even if Maria Murvall is her own obsession. But she knows she has to do this alone. That it's her against the horror, but also her against herself.

Sometimes loneliness is unavoidable.

But I miss Zeke. His calmness, the way he never backs down.

Sven Sjöman and Karim Akbar would be annoyed if they knew I was actively working on the case while I'm on leave, Malin thinks as the taxi passes Vanadisplan. If they knew I was I acting on my own initiative and trying to see a senior prosecutor in Stockholm, disrupting his schedule. But I don't give a shit about his schedule, and anyway, how could Sven and Karim stop me?

Would they even want to stop me?

Would they suspend me, threaten me with reprisals? You're a vigilante, Malin, when you carry on working off-duty. A private detective obsessed with the truth.

But they must want to know what happened to Maria, everyone is interested in her secret, and if they knew about the new case, the woman at St Lars, they couldn't help but be curious.

Two mute women.

Two secrets.

The same secret?

But maybe this trip to Stockholm is a step too far.

To be honest, I don't care what Sven and Karim say, what anyone says, I'm going to find out what happened to Maria and the nameless woman.

The taxi stops outside the central courthouse.

One of the capital's largest buildings, an impregnable fortress that reminds her of a medieval castle: brown-rendered walls set with windows that are far too small, walls that seem pressed down by the abruptly sloping roof, with silly iron details fixed to the façade in a misguided attempt at some sort of aesthetic effect.

A prime example of the architecture of power. Suppressing the individual in stone, emphasising their smallness, their insignificance, making them malleable, easy to govern.

Malin had been inside the building many times when she was studying at the Police Academy, where she was the only single mother among all the students.

Tove had been two years old, barely old enough to go to preschool.

She pays the taxi driver.

Gets out.

Stockholm.

Millions of noises, all saying that no one here really cares about anything. That the broader flow is always bigger than any individual occurrence, any desires, wishes or longings.

All the huge new buildings by the Central Station. A different city from the one I knew.

But somehow always the same.

I have no official reason to be here, Malin thinks.

But my questions have a moral and ethical justification.

The justification of good intentions.

I've got that much, haven't I?

She stops outside the courthouse.

Then goes up the broad flight of steps to the entrance, lifting her legs unnaturally high because of the intentionally steep steps, and feeling herself shrink from the effort. Even the door is outsized. She opens it, and inside is an entrance hall flooded with light in every colour of the spectrum.

Straight ahead is a statue of Justitia, made of coloured glass, in the strong sun from the window behind her. Just like a church, Malin thinks, a bloody church of justice, as if anything were ever just.

She had checked out Fredrik Kantsten online very briefly.

He seems to be a real career man, moving to Stockholm from Malmö to become a district prosecutor, head of his own unit of fifteen prosecutors within the Stockholm division of the Public Prosecution Authority.

But, on the other hand, he seems fairly reasonable.

Interested in gender issues, and a regular speaker on the subject.

A supporter of stiffer sentencing for domestic abuse cases.

A proper little gender Jesus.

The nicotine-ravaged woman behind the grey, plastic reception desk looks up and evidently realises that Malin is a police officer, maybe she can tell a detective from the way their breath smells, their posture, or something.

'How can I help you?'

The woman's voice is neutral, uninterested in everything. Her face is as grey as the reception desk itself, her hair almost red, but only almost.

Malin digs out her ID.

'Malin Fors, detective inspector with Linköping Police. I'd like to see Prosecutor Fredrik Kantsten. Is he here?'

'Have you arranged to see him?'

'No. But I'm hoping he's here. It's urgent.'

'Fredrik's fully booked. He's in court now, but he'll be back after lunch. You can always try then. What's it concerning?'

'A previously abandoned case that I'm working on.'

The woman behind the desk doesn't ask any more questions, just looks down at her computer screen and goes back to work, ignoring Malin completely.

'I'll just sit down and wait,' she says in a voice that's too loud, then goes over to a pale blue sofa facing a worn wooden table covered with old magazines, mostly gossip rags. The woman ignores her remark.

Maybe I ought to call Conny Nygren, Malin thinks. Have

coffee with him. See if he's still up and about. Bask in his nicely relaxed manner, in the hope that some of it might rub off on me.

Another time, maybe. I'd better stay here.

Malin feels suddenly angry with the receptionist.

I'm sitting here for your sake, she thinks, for yours and mine and every other woman's. But you wouldn't understand that, would you?

You don't even care.

'Fredrik!'

Malin is roused from a light slumber by the receptionist's voice.

'Fredrik! Wait a moment, this is Malin Fors from the Linköping Police, she's been waiting to see you.'

Malin's eyes open.

The room comes back.

The clock on the wall behind the receptionist, she only notices it now, says 13.15, and Fredrik Kantsten is standing before her dressed impeccably in a grey suit, a pressed white shirt and a blood-red tie.

Why do I think it's that colour? Malin wonders.

He's smiling at me.

The confident smile of a man with power, a man who is one metre eighty-five tall, and knows he exudes unquestionable authority.

But there's something behind that. Malin spots it at once.

A disconnect, a sense of unbridled ambition, on the verge of carelessness.

His face.

The forehead like an open field below a sky of short, straight fair hair, watery blue eyes and a nose that adds definition to a face that is otherwise unremarkable. A few acne scars on both cheeks.

Malin stands up.

Shakes Prosecutor Fredrik Kantsten's outstretched hand. A firm handshake, and she matches the pressure.

'Do we have an appointment?'

His voice is dark, yet there's still something hunted at its core.

'No. I happened to be in the city on personal business, and I'd like to ask you a few questions about a case I'm working on.'

'Which case?'

'The case of the young woman who's in St Lars Hospital in Lund. She was found raped on a road outside—'

'I remember her . . .' Fredrik Kantsten interrupts. 'I remember her very well. Poor girl.'

You're a bit too quick to say that, aren't you? Malin thinks.

But his sympathy seems genuine. I'm just being suspicious.

'Has the case been opened up again?' Fredrik Kantsten asks. 'I thought it had been dropped long ago.'

'Do you have time to answer a few questions?'

'About what?'

'About the case.'

'By all means. I've got fifteen minutes free now. I remember it being a particularly gruesome case. What was done to her was absolutely terrible.'

Something you wanted people to think she could have done to herself. Isn't that right?

The prosecutor stressed now, impatient, male.

'This way,' he says, gesturing along a corridor. 'We never even managed to find out who she was.'

Coffee in brown plastic cups on a mahogany desktop, a wool rug on the floor, an oil painting that looks old and expensive on the wall. The woven back of a Bauhaus chair against her shoulders. The smell of lemon-scented cleaning fluid.

The prosecutor's surroundings are rather more splendid than those of an ordinary detective inspector.

Classless society.

Sweden?

Hardly.

Self-importance everywhere, a smile of self-satisfaction.

Malin made up her mind to lay her cards on the table, and talked about Maria Murvall, and how she found out about the Malmö case, and what Sören Lind said about the investigation, and all the circumstances that had roused her curiosity.

But she didn't mention Sören Lind's suspicions that the case had been dropped too quickly, or that he thought the external gynaecologist had been called in on flimsy grounds.

Trying to stay neutral. Wanting to hear what Fredrik Kantsten had to say. Or not say.

'You dropped the case because there was no evidence leading to any suspects?' Malin asked.

'That's right. The detectives weren't getting anywhere, and I couldn't see any other lines of inquiry. We'd looked under every stone, and our resources were needed elsewhere.'

'You prioritised other cases?'

Fredrik Kantsten nodded.

'Everyone knows how engaged I am in women's issues, in gender matters, everything to do with violence against women, and I'd never drop an investigation without doing everything in my power to solve it. One or two people in the investigating team might have thought I dropped the case too quickly, but we really weren't making any progress.'

Malin nodded.

'And I wanted to speed things up so that she could have some peace and try to heal her soul.'

'She's not healed yet, from what I understand.'

'That's dreadful. But, from what I remember, the investigating officers wanted to drop the case.'

And Fredrik Kantsten squeezes his nose between his thumb and forefinger.

Pressing, as if to scratch an itch.

'I think I'm getting a cold,' he says, glancing at his wristwatch.

'What about the medical report?' Malin says. 'Did that produce any significant forensic information?'

'We had a gynaecologist in Malmö who was pretty useless. He was often off-target, I thought he'd delivered some seriously inadequate work.'

'How did you get around that?'

'I brought in Emanuel Ärendsson, a professor of gynaecology, from the University Hospital in Linköping in fact. That is where you're based? He's an expert in this sort of injury. Basically I wanted to see if it was possible to find any more evidence from a second examination.'

'And did you?'

'He thought her injuries could have been self-inflicted.'

'What did you think?'

'I wasn't sure, but in cases like this I've learned that it's best to rely on the experts. And keep my own opinions to myself.'

Fredrik Kantsten.

One hundred and eight-five centimetres of masculine power in front of Malin.

He's got reasonable answers to my questions.

Sören Lind.

Probably just another victim of the eternal conflict between the police and the prosecutors, grabbing any chance to air his discontent. Maybe he just doesn't like Kantsten.

But you're answering my questions honestly.

Aren't you?

You are, aren't you?

You don't appear to feel threatened or think your judgement is being called into question, and your professional integrity seems beyond reproach.

And why shouldn't it be?

That same question, again: What am I doing here?

While I'm on leave.

I see a connection, dash up to Stockholm and take up a prosecutor's time. Is this case making me crazy? Something needs to happen in Linköping soon, something I can focus my energy on.

'Thanks for taking the time to talk to me about the case.'

Fredrik Kantsten says he knows how hard it is to do proper police work when people won't even answer your questions.

'Silence is the worst enemy of the truth,' he says.

And sometimes you need to use unorthodox methods to break the silence, Malin thinks, seeing her colleague Waldemar Ekenberg in her mind.

'I sympathise with you,' Fredrik Kantsten goes on. 'I think it's good that you're carrying on where the system couldn't quite succeed. We have to find out who she is, and what happened to her and the other woman you mentioned.'

Fredrik Kantsten's high forehead frowns on the other side of the mahogany desk.

He sucks in his cheeks as if to give them more definition.

'Maria.'

'What?'

'Maria Murvall. That's her name.'

'Who?'

Fredrik Kantsten looks at his watch again.

'She's the other woman I told you about.'

6

I've stopped howling.

Or am I still howling?

My violated body, my rotten body, I can see it, but I'm not it.

The pain is gone now. And it feels nice to escape all the humiliation.

So what am I? Who am I?

I am her, the woman lying in the forest, decaying, my flesh full of the hungriest grubs of spring, of flies with glowing pus-filled eyes, my stench so strong that not even the foxes want anything to do with me.

Am I alone?

No.

There are more of us.

But I am alone here.

How did I get here? Is anyone missing me?

I can drift off to my lonely mother, see her wondering in her constant intoxication: Where is she, where are you, only daughter of mine?

Shame drove us apart.

Cheers, kid.

Dad isn't here.

But I can hear him scream down in the flames.

And that's where he belongs.

Can I feel anything any more?

Have I got skin?

Not on my legs.

The hungry flies eject their corrosive vomit into my flesh and I wish someone would find me before it's too late, before I disappear into what I once was.

I remember the branches in my body, the burning tearing thorns, and how the millipedes with knives for legs cut me to shreds. How I was lost, how something caught up with me and how the forest, the roots of the trees, the dripping leaves of the ferns, consumed my body, frozen under the pale light of the winter stars.

How I was pierced through.

I drift upward.

I'm still scared.

Someone must find me, because otherwise I'll have to return to this place over and over and over again.

I want to be free.

Who can set me free?

They parked the car approximately nine kilometres from Stjärnorp Castle, on land owned by a farmer named Fridman, ten kilometres or so from both the abandoned Workers' Education Centre and Sjölunda, on a narrow forest road meant for lumber trucks. Then they walked straight out into the blossoming forest, where there was still snow under some of the fir trees, and Roger Andersson thought that nature seemed confused, as if it couldn't make up its mind what season it really was.

To the delight of the children, his son Erik, six years old, and daughter Ida, eight, there were already a few wild strawberries.

Last year he and the children had found morels here, just five hundred metres into the forest, in a patch of woodland felled a few years before.

There were bound to be morels this year as well. The

finest delicacy offered by the forest, the very best taste of the right to roam.

The children love the forest, love pushing their way through thickets and undergrowth and ferns, clambering up onto ancient moss-covered rocks and feeling like explorers in a world wide open for them to conquer.

Food in the rucksack.

Chocolate milk, sourdough sandwiches with Italian salami.

No malted bread with pink sausage, like when he was young.

It's just after three o'clock, the sun is no longer as strong, and down here under the crowns of the firs and ragged pines it's almost dark, shady, a bit scary if you were to ask the children.

Sandwiches.

And chocolate biscuits.

Roger Andersson sees his children ten metres further away from him in the forest.

The children, he thinks.

And prays that nothing bad ever happens to them.

I can see something now, feel something vibrating in my rotten flesh, even though it's no longer mine, and they're close now, and why are they getting closer, why don't they go in a different direction when they notice the smell?

Or is the wind coming from the wrong direction?

So that they can't smell my unmistakable perfume of death? Of a human body that's in the process of decay?

I sink lower.

Who are you, my saviours?

Children.

Two little children.

You shouldn't have to see this.

You shouldn't have to see me.

You're just children, just metres away from me now, and I want to scream at you to turn back, because I want to spare you from seeing me, I'm not suitable for children, I shouldn't be part of anyone's childhood.
But there's no point.
No one can hear me scream any more.
And I do want someone to find me.
That's what I want, almost more than anything.

Roger Andersson notices the stench.

It comes unexpectedly, as if the wind has suddenly changed direction to fend him away, and he sees the children stop in a glade where the ground is covered with ferns.

A dead animal.

A cadaver.

They usually stink, but not this badly, and an animal cadaver isn't something he wants the children to see, nor even to smell.

Bloody hell.

What could possibly smell this badly?

He's smelled plenty of dead, rotting animals before, but none of them had this sort of ungodly stink.

The stench cuts right through him, as if it were the most terrifying smell he can think of, and he sees the children hesitate, then move forward as if driven by some relentless force, and he starts to run after them, as if he knows what is lying in the little glade now, still hidden from the children's eyes.

He runs to protect them.

So they won't have to see.

He stumbles.

He runs on, but when he hears their screams he knows he's too late.

That the children have now, once and for all, seen what

life can do to a human being, that they now know what death can accomplish.

You see me now, children, and you scream. That's my face you can see, it's strangely untouched, isn't it? As if the world wants to put my beautiful face on display now that I've gone.

Learn from this, children, learn to celebrate life and not to be scared of death, because that sort of fear is pointless, because death will come to you sooner or later no matter what you do or say, no matter how ingenious your protests.

You've found me.

I'm sorry if I've scared you, and now you can't see anything because your dad is holding his big, warm, tobacco-scented hands over your eyes, so you can't see what he sees.

What are his eyes looking at?

My eyes are looking at evil, he thinks. He thinks that I must have lain here for a long time, and when he feels his stomach clench he's glad they haven't yet eaten the sandwiches.

Then he wonders if there's any mobile coverage here, in the middle of the very deepest of forests in Östergötland.

I have to call the police, he's thinking.

This woman has been murdered.

Violated and left to rot in a forest glade.

I have to call someone, he thinks.

Call someone who can sort this out.

7

It's four o'clock in the afternoon, and the sun is still high in the sky, but lacks the strength to illuminate the world below.

The darkness is a noose around the forest's neck, the trees catch at each other with invisible barbs, tearing and ripping each other apart in their imagination.

Zeke Martinsson, detective inspector with the crime unit of the Linköping Police, looks over at forensics expert Karin Johannison, his former lover, and sees her poking at the body he knows is lying on the ground beneath the trees.

A young woman.

Bloody hell.

And he doesn't know why, but the image of his own grandchild – she's only a few months old, the little thing – pops into his head.

It's not her lying there. But one day, when she's a teenager and life gets properly dangerous, it could be.

No one's safe.

Zeke is sure of that much.

You have to keep an eye on girls.

On Malin, even if she's seemed calmer since she met Peter Hamse, her nice if somewhat bland doctor. Up ahead Karin leans slightly to one side, and he can see her generously proportioned bust under her white coat.

Is my life a mistake?

Zeke runs a hand over his shaved head, then feels his

rough cheeks with his palm. His stubble has become increasingly grey over the past year.

What if everything just comes to an end soon, like it did for the woman over there in the glade?

What have I got to show for myself?

Children. Grandchildren. A wife that I . . . Well, what? I'm not exactly in love with her.

But I respect her.

Maybe I should have carried on with Karin. Kept hold of her. Dared to take the decisive step. See where it would have led me.

On the other side.

Maybe that's what the woman over there did.

Stepped out into the unknown.

And look how it turned out for her. Not even Sven Sjöman's warmth and expertise can save her now.

Sven Sjöman, head of the crime unit, sighs and thinks: At least it isn't hot.

The forensics team has secured the area around the glade where the Andersson family found the body.

The blue and white tape of the cordon encircles the place where death has manifested itself, arriving prematurely to complete its task.

They've questioned a badly upset Roger Andersson. Morel-picker, forest-lover, father of two, and sent him home with a number to call if they need counselling.

The father and children had been waiting for them in the forest beside their silver Volvo, at precisely the GPS location he had given them, and the children had been quiet, but didn't seem shocked.

They had gone back into the forest with them, to the body, refusing to wait by the patrol car with the uniformed officer who had gone with Sven and Zeke when they got the call.

The stench had been a portent of what they were going to find.

The body, the remains of it under the ferns.

Sven had seen similar bodies before. From the description the man gave back at the car he had already understood that the body had been there for a long time, that they didn't have to take any great precautions, because the winter would have eradicated any clues that might have been there. She had been frozen by the snow and cold however, and hadn't decomposed entirely, in fact she was remarkably well preserved, and Sven thought she was something of an open book. Karin Johannison ought to be able to tell them a reasonable amount.

This was murder.

If there was one thing that was certain, it was that the woman in the glade hadn't received those injuries by accident, but that she had ended up here because of someone else's evil actions.

Sven is standing by the body now, leaning forward slightly, feeling his back protest by sending shooting pains through his nerves.

He looks at the face, wide-open to the world, as if it were completely untouched by time, as if death had left her head unmarked.

But death had taken her eyes.

There's no life in the little round spheres adorning her symmetrical face.

Yet it still feels as if she's looking at me, Sven thinks, as he takes a few steps back.

Karin has a young male assistant with her, one Sven hasn't seen before.

She's working on the body, and the assistant is examining the surrounding ground, he looks frustrated, as if he knows there's no point, and it occurs to Sven that Karin might have looked like the woman on the ground when she was younger, perhaps Karin had been a more innocent beauty then than she is now? Today she has the appeal of ageing beauty, with little wrinkles that make her clear-cut features even more refined.

Johan Jakobsson has also arrived and is waiting over by a tall pine, and Sven thinks about how Johan is growing year by year, and how the hesitant young father has been replaced by a determined detective who is aware of both his strengths and his weaknesses. That doesn't stop his jeans hanging from his hips, or the jacket he's wearing over his dark blue polo top drooping off his shoulders. There's still a hint of insecurity in his features, as if everything in his face is slightly too small to give it any real character.

Börje Svärd and Waldemar Ekenberg are missing, they're in court giving evidence on an old case that's being tried for a second time.

Malin, Sven had thought when he got the call about the woman's body in the forest. You ought to be here now. I must call you.

The same forest in which Maria Murvall was found.

Twenty kilometres or so from here. But the same damn forest.

A broad sweep of forest in which you can get lost and never find your way out. A forest in which it looks as if absolutely anything can happen.

Malin's on leave, but given her obsession with Maria's case she'd never forgive him if he didn't call.

And she's seemed brighter recently. Perfectly OK, considering that she's Malin Fors. And she's seemed sober.

So he called.

She was sitting on the X2000 train, on her way back from Stockholm. She hadn't wanted to tell him what she'd been doing in the capital, just said it was good of him to call, and sounded excited in a reserved way.

'I'm on my way. I'm tired of being on holiday.'

A young woman dead.

Somehow violated by the forest in the same way as Maria Murvall.

The forest glade.

The frayed ferns, all the nooks and crannies where the sun's rays never reach.

Her injuries.

As if carved by alien knives.

What force lives in this forest? Sven wonders as he watches Karin pick at the corpse with a pair of tweezers.

What sort of hungry black greedy snarling evil lives here, hidden, lingering in the black spaces between the tree trunks?

I want to know.

Malin wants to know.

We all need to know.

Everyone must know. That's what the police's job is.

And now he hears noise in the forest, someone heading eagerly towards him, then Sven sees Malin's blond bob shimmering in the light between the lush green foliage of two bushes.

Malin approaches Sven.

He's sixty-three years old now. Just a few years away from retirement, and he's managing to keep his gut under control, holding any more heart attacks at bay. His arms are hanging by his sides, his hands like large, withered bunches of flowers sticking out of his white shirtsleeves.

The gentle paws of a craftsman, finely tuned, able to fit the smallest screw into the smallest hole.

He sees her coming, and smiles in the way a teacher does when he sees a favourite pupil return after a school holiday.

After an illness.

The way he smiled when she came back from rehab at the clinic for alcoholics.

But this time his eyes aren't smiling, they just look tired, the mournful eyes of someone who's seen too much.

The smell of the corpse doesn't seem to bother him. He must have got used to it, the way she herself is trying to. But it isn't possible to get used to it, only to learn to bear it.

Behind Sven, some ten metres deeper into the forest, Karin Johannison is crouching over something, she's got a mask over her mouth, and her long blond hair seems to be in the way, but Karin brushes it aside with a practised gesture.

Karin.

Almost forty. Childless and recently divorced from her husband, who discovered she'd been having an affair with Zeke and threw her out. Zeke had ended the affair shortly after that, when presented with an ultimatum by his wife Gunilla.

'You end this at once. I'll forgive you this time, but never again. You can't manage without your family, you know that.'

Karin.

The gorgeous forensics expert.

Now she's the one who's alone, not me, Malin thinks.

Yet somehow her back seems straighter, she seems freer, and Karin has told Malin that she's thinking of trying to adopt a Vietnamese girl instead of trying to find a decent man to make kids with.

Her choice of words had surprised Malin, they had seemed too unpolished for the lithe, elegant, and occasionally rather smug Karin Johannison.

But perhaps she's moved on from all her pretentions now?

Zeke is hovering five metres to Karin's right, and his shaved head is shiny with sweat. His black eyes aren't visible, but Malin knows they're glowing with an eagerness to find out what happened to their victim, and that he won't hold back in their search for the truth.

He misses Karin.

Malin can tell.

But Zeke has love. With Gunilla. And since his son Martin suffered a serious knee injury in the NHL, he's back in Sweden with his family more often now, with the two grandchildren Zeke can't get enough of.

He's forty-six now, Zeke, and a grandfather twice over, and Malin often teases him about that, calling him old man, but he's no old man.

Quite the contrary.

Best not to get in his way at the wrong moment.

Zeke waves at her, shakes his head, and she can see Johan Jakobsson in the gloom between two trees just behind Zeke.

Johan's children are getting more and more independent, and he looks more alert with each passing day. He's grown into his role as the team's computer expert, and sometimes Malin can't help wondering if there's anything he can't find out with his manic tapping on various keyboards.

A few of her colleagues are missing.

Waldemar Ekenberg, the chain-smoking loose cannon from Mjölby, easily the most violent officer in the team.

Capable of cutting someone's balls off if it would help him get information.

But we need violence sometimes.

Don't we? Sometimes the ends can justify the means. Malin isn't so naïve as to doubt that.

It doesn't mean you abandon your soul. Just that it gets a bit fuzzy sometimes.

But where's the boundary? How much force can police officers use before they themselves become the bad guys?

Börje Svärd isn't there either.

He's found a new woman since his wife died of MS a few years ago, and it's done him good. A bit of love, a bit of company apart from his Alsatians and his beloved rifles and pistols.

Malin stops.

Inhales the acrid stench of the corpse.

Shuts her eyes, letting the moment flow through her body like a distant breeze.

Within her she can see the troubled faces of her colleagues, the expectant way they were just looking at her, as if to say: be brilliant, Malin, solve this case, don't let us find another girl, another woman in these forests, don't let another woman be found staggering along a forest road out here one morning, apparently raped by the forest itself, by its barbed evil.

Maria Murvall.

Perhaps she staggered along in this very place, fleeing something, what were you fleeing, Maria? There was no way out, was there?

The nameless woman in Lund.

The gynaecologist who examined her. Emanuel Ärendsson, from Linköping of all places. Coincidence. A little trick of reality.

But Maria.

The woman in the glade.

The nameless woman in the fields of Skåne.

It's all connected, you're connected, aren't you?

I can smell it, from the stench here.

Maria Murvall.

We've got DNA from the person who was, in all likelihood, her attacker.

Malin opens her eyes again.

The little glade is an enclosed room.

Maria's sickroom.

My brother Stefan's.

The woman in Lund's. The cells in which people from cases she's solved in the past have been locked away.

And other faraway cells.

Josef Fritzl's.

Fred and Rosemary West's in Gloucester.

They tortured and murdered eleven women.

Evil's room is the room to which we always return. Sooner or later, even if we don't want to.

Rooms where anything at all can happen.

And does happen.

I'm feeling my way through those rooms, Malin thinks. Can't let what's concealed in them destroy me.

Must I destroy them, all those feelings, to get close to the person who did this?

And she thinks that in the innermost of those rooms sits a man who is nothing but a man, everything else stripped away, his whole being reduced to violence, self-justification and lust and instinct.

How many times have she and her colleagues seen women like this? Raped, beaten, tortured and ruined, and always, almost always, it's because of a form of masculinity that was out of control.

We women, Malin thinks, we're never finished with our struggle against warped masculinity, we have to fight it when we see it, otherwise we're doomed to go under.

Malin knows these forests. She's walked through them alone in her hunt for the answer to what happened to Maria Murvall. She's plotted possible routes on maps and followed them, in an effort to see what she could find.

But she found nothing, and her search expanded wider and wider.

She came across buildings, deserted cottages, an abandoned training centre, rusting car wrecks, and forest, and still more forest, and then open, mist-shrouded fields with deer sniffing at the edges of the forest.

They fled when they picked up her scent.

The scent of the enemy, of danger.

But she doesn't want to think of her searches through the forest now.

Her fear during those hikes. She brushes it aside.

Instead she goes over to Karin, crouched beside the body.

She sees the face on the ground, beneath Karin's gloved, milky-white hands.

The face.

Open, closed, dead yet oddly alive, its blond hair dirty with earth and pine needles and the remains of the previous autumn's leaves, the mouth slightly open, as if she's trying to tell me something from wherever she is now.

8

I'm whispering: You've found me now.

I'm whispering, but no one can hear me, can they?

A woman is picking at my wounds with tweezers, but I can't feel anything.

They've searched the ground around me. I could almost hear their thoughts: There's nothing here, there's nothing left.

But I'm still here, the memory of me, my story of how I ended up here, in this evil forest.

Someone else has arrived now.

Her. The woman on whom I'm pinning my hopes.

She's standing behind the one with the tweezers now, in the hesitant light of the dying day, and she's pulling a face. Does it smell? Do I smell? Or is she grimacing with fear?

Maybe she's grimacing because she can feel my fear, and recognises it as her own.

Who is she scared of finding like that?

Maybe she's got a daughter, maybe she sees herself lying here in the forest glade, waiting to be found.

I'm a mystery.

A mystery, a many-headed hydra, a head for every feeling.

Fear.

Fury.

Shame.

Arrogance.

Some other inexpressible feelings, and then lust, always always always this wretched lust.

Can evil exist without it?

Cruelty, pure and clear as distilled water.

And the desire for cruelty, the most perverse desire of the sadist, the desire to cut, to break crush destroy everything that is beautiful and hopeful.

You're standing down there, Malin Fors, you want to know what happened to me, don't you? Not for my sake, but for yours.

And that's your curse.

Malin sucks the air into her lungs, trying to suppress the cloying, filthy stench that the corpse is giving off, but it's impossible.

'Karin,' she says, and Karin Johannison, evidently completely absorbed in her work, turns around quickly, as if the murderer had crept through the forest and taken her by surprise.

'Am I OK to walk here?'

Karin pulls herself together and nods at Malin.

'No problem. We've searched the ground. Nothing in the immediate vicinity.'

'What have we got?'

Malin wants to ask for herself, in spite of what Sven Sjöman has told her. She wants to hear it from Karin, to anchor what's happened in reality.

'Woman. About twenty. White. Scandinavian appearance, possibly central European. Difficult to say exactly. Severely abused. The skin on her legs has been burned off. Possibly with acid, possibly with hot liquid. Probably raped. Possibly with a sharp, barbed instrument, maybe a knife, it's impossible to say right now. And the perpetrator cut a hole in her stomach. I have to admit, I've never seen anything like this.'

Malin looks at the young woman, laid open to her gaze, as ants run across her wounds and the twigs and pine cones and needles seem to want to force their way into her, and show her how painful death is.

Who are you? Malin wonders.

And without knowing why, she finds herself thinking of a girl she was at school with, what was her name? Malin remembers her round, freckled cheeks, similar to those of the girl on the ground, and Malin recalls her backside, prematurely curvaceous, and her swelling breasts, but she can't remember her name, and somehow it feels important to remember it, here in the woods, in the presence of this girl.

Kristina.

Kristina the Slag. That was her name.

She was too plump too early, and too well developed, she wore clothes that were always a bit too tight, as if she had an adult at home who wanted her to look like that.

Malin remembers how the boys used to lock Kristina the Slag in the boys' toilets, then make her dance with her breasts uncovered, and pull down her trousers, and then they'd toss coins at her.

Kristina wasn't stupid. But she didn't know any better. And I didn't know any better than to leave the bastards to it, Malin thinks. Or did I? And just didn't care?

Kristina the Slag got pregnant when she was fifteen.

And had an abortion.

Everyone knew, but no one knew how everyone could know.

And no one cared.

She was Kristina the Slag, and there were rumours that her dad had got her up the duff, that Kristina had enticed him with those eyes, that backside, and those big, big breasts and those clothes that were too small.

That it was her fault.

Then Kristina the Slag moved away with her family.

And no one thought about her any more.

Least of all me.

And Malin feels herself blush with shame at the memory.

At the heartless inadequacy she had demonstrated then, when she hadn't lifted a finger to help Kristina.

Malin realises that this is probably only the second time she's thought of the loneliest of all the girls she was at school with.

Is the woman lying in front of me a Kristina? Someone let down by everyone, allowed just to drift off into the darkness?

Malin hears Karin say something about 'extreme violence', and the words drag her from her thoughts.

'So she was tortured?' Malin asks, and is back in the forest, beside the girl, the dead, violated girl.

'Purgatory couldn't be worse than this,' Karin says, looking down at the body again, using the tweezers to look under the girl's, the woman's eyelids, as if looking for the last image she saw when she was alive.

'How do you think she ended up here?'

'She walked or ran through the forest,' Karin says without hesitation. 'If you look at the soles of her feet, they're cut to pieces, in an irregular pattern, just as if she's run barefoot on frozen, or almost frozen ground.'

'Are you sure?'

'Yes. In all likelihood she got her injuries somewhere else, fled, and they caught up with her. Do you see here?'

Karin points to the back of the girl's head, at an indentation in her blond hair, the result of a blow.

'The murderer smashed her skull in with something, possibly a rock.'

'Could the rock still be here?'

Karin shakes her head, and her fine blond hair brushes her cheeks.

'We haven't found it yet. We'll keep looking. But don't

get your hopes up. The shape of the wound to her head would have changed over time.'

'And the wound to her stomach? Was she conscious when that was inflicted?'

'Impossible to tell if she got it before or after death. But she could hardly have been conscious because of the pain.'

'She still looks so well preserved,' Malin says.

'Yes, her face is almost untouched, almost as if she could turn up in the papers or on television to say who she is. But the body's been here for a long time. All winter, probably, frozen, and then lying here hidden in the shadows, where the snow must have lingered. It's remarkably well preserved, in spite of the warm days we've had.'

'DNA from the perpetrator?' Malin asks, without mentioning the connection to Maria Murvall.

'I doubt it, that's extremely unlikely.'

No, that would be too good to be true.

Where are the others? Malin finds herself wondering.

Sven, Zeke, Johan? Shouldn't they be here with them, or have they already spoken to Karin, do they know all this? They must do.

And she turns around and sees her three colleagues standing in the shade of a pine some twenty metres away, to escape the smell, judging by the wind direction.

It smells of cadaver.

But also something else.

Something sulphurous.

An unfamiliar smell.

Sven waves her over to them.

Two minutes, Malin gestures, holding two fingers in the air.

'Shouldn't she have been eaten by predators?'

'The foxes, you mean? Yes, but they probably didn't want to,' Karin says.

'Didn't want to?'

'I think her nipples were burned off with hydrochloric acid. Foxes can smell that sort of thing from quite a distance. And would have stayed away. And sometimes predators don't bother with easy pickings. No one knows why.'

'Is there anything more you can tell me about her, anything else you've found?'

'No, sorry Malin, nothing.'

'Do you think,' Malin goes on, hesitating in the face of the obvious stupidity of what she's about to ask, 'there's any way she could have inflicted these injuries herself?'

Karin looks up, her eyes black, full of sudden, uncharacteristic anger.

'Malin. What kind of fucking question is that? You can see her injuries for yourself. Do you think she came out here and smashed a rock into her own head? Burned her nipples off with acid herself? And no one cuts a fucking hole in themselves.'

Karin.

She's never sounded so hard, so angry before.

'Sorry, it was stupid, I was just wondering. I don't know why I asked.'

When Malin goes over to Zeke, Sven Sjöman and Johan Jakobsson, Zeke pats her on the shoulder, amiably, as if to welcome her back from her truncated holiday, as if she needed that.

A first, informal investigative meeting in the forest.

They need to draw up a plan of how to get closer to the truth, and Malin wonders what to say about what she's found out in Skåne, about her trip to Stockholm, and the new case's evident similarities with Maria Murvall's case.

Practically the same forest.

Similar wounds.

One woman dead.

The other like one of the living dead.

But her instincts tell her to hold back, let Sven start the investigation the best way he can, without any preconceptions. The others know she's been working on Maria Murvall's case, but aren't aware of how obsessed she's become with it.

It wasn't even the Linköping Police's case, it was dealt with by Motala.

No one but Sven would probably even make any connection between them.

'Look upon this as the first meeting about the investigation into the murder of Woman X,' Sven says. 'We can regard it as murder from the outset. According to Karin, there's no doubt whatsoever about that, and I agree with her.'

Zeke shakes his head.

'No normal person would do to an animal what someone did to her.'

Sven summarises what they know, what Karin has managed to come up with.

And he says what Malin's already thought, that they haven't had any reports of a young woman missing from Linköping for the past year or more.

'We'll have to check reports for the whole of Östergötland, the whole of Sweden. The first thing we have to do is establish her identity. Any ideas about who she might be?'

Malin, Zeke and Johan stand silently in the forest as a couple of uniforms talk too loudly over towards the road, one of them laughing coarsely.

'If she was an ordinary woman she couldn't just disappear without trace, without anyone reporting it for six months, could she?' Zeke says.

'So what are you thinking?' Johan wonders.

'Maybe she was a prostitute,' Zeke says. 'A victim of

trafficking, maybe a domestic or an au pair, someone no one would notice had gone, someone no one would miss. Someone who came here illegally and has been living underground.'

'That sounds plausible,' Sven says. 'But we need to proceed without any preconceptions.'

He's about to go on when Malin interrupts him: 'Someone's missing her, somewhere, we can't doubt that. Maybe she's just a young woman who went off the rails.'

She tries to conjure up Kristina, Kristina the Slag's face, but it's gone.

'We've all seen girls like that. Haven't we? And we know what can happen to them.'

Zeke nods, and Malin finds herself thinking of Tove, even if she knows that Tove takes care of herself, but it could have been her lying here, and the forests around Lundsberg are vast, offering thousands and thousands of hiding places just like this.

'She got here through the forest,' Sven goes on. 'Even if it was a long time ago, we need to organise a search of a five-kilometre radius. Talk to anyone living nearby. The land is evidently owned by a farmer named Fridman. We need to talk to him, his farmhouse is down by Lake Roxen somewhere.'

Sven pauses briefly before continuing: 'We also need to check if there's anyone on the sex offenders' register who lives in the area, or even anyone in the whole district who's been released in the past six months.'

'I'll take care of that,' Johan says.

'Good.'

'Her face,' Malin says. 'That's our best lead, isn't it? To establish her identity?'

'You mean we should release a cleaned-up picture to the media?' Sven says.

Malin nods.

'We'll wait on that,' Sven says. 'First we need to knock on some doors. But most of all we need to see if there's a missing person report anywhere that matches, we don't want any of her relatives seeing her picture in the paper or on television before they've been informed.'

Malin shuts her eyes.

She doesn't know why, but the image of a lonely, shabby woman in a messy, shabby room comes into her mind.

A vodka bottle on a table.

The woman reaches for the bottle, but before she can grab hold of it, it transforms into a snake's head, which quickly divides into several more.

Malin blinks and the image disappears.

'We'll split the door-to-door into sections. I've called in Waldemar and Börje. They can talk to the landowner. We'll all have to join in, and it'll take us a fair way into the evening. There aren't many people living out here, so if we all pull together it ought to go fairly quickly. I've called the regiment up at Kvarn and they're organising a search of the forest for clues tomorrow.'

Sven pulls a map out of one of his trouser pockets.

'Let's get started,' he says. 'Johan, you take one of the uniforms. Malin and Zeke can go together.'

Sven's right.

It makes sense to start work straight away, while the investigation is still crying like a newborn baby.

It's strangely silent in the forest. And Malin knows what's wrong. The media haven't found their way out here yet, which they ought to have done by now.

Nice to escape the photographers' flashes, and intrusive people with even more intrusive questions.

Like Daniel Högfeldt, a journalist from the *Östgöta Correspondent*, with whom she once had an affair. She's completely lost touch with him now, but has heard that he and one of her old friends, radio presenter Helen Aneman, are living together.

Should she say anything to her colleagues about the similarities with the Maria Murvall case?

No.

Better to wait.

But shouldn't it have occurred to Sven or Zeke?

Should she tell them about Skåne, or her trip to Stockholm?

No. She can feel herself drifting about in Maria's case, like a teenage girl heading aimlessly towards some unknown danger.

She wants to stay in the glade in the forest, but from the corner of her eye she can see two paramedics pick up a stretcher bearing a yellow plastic sack, and soon, Malin thinks, this will be the loneliest place on earth.

9

An ambulance disappears off down the forest road, seemingly swallowed up by the mottled trunks of the arching birches.

Another car is coming towards them, one of the *Correspondent*'s reporters' cars.

'How was Copenhagen?' Zeke asks as he starts up his new black Saab, parked between two patrol cars and Sven's red Volvo.

'It was OK,' Malin says. 'Luxury hotel.'

'Take care not to get used to it.'

The hum of the engine fills the car, along with a faint smell of petrol. The *Correspondent*'s car is beside them now, and she sees that Daniel Högfeldt is driving.

He waves to her, and she waves back, then he makes a phone signal with his hand.

Hope you don't call, Malin thinks. What have we got to say to each other? But she knows he just wants to do some digging into the case.

'There's no danger of that,' she says. 'I feel like a right country cousin in all those smart rooms.'

Zeke grins and his deep-set green eyes twinkle.

'That's because you are a country cousin.'

Then they drive in silence to the first house. A red cottage in a wide clearing that ends in a boggy field stretching a kilometre and a half to a black wall of pine trees.

Zeke switches off the engine.

The clock on the dashboard says 17:13. It's still light, but oddly gloomy, as if some unfamiliar darkness had settled over the world.

'Hang on,' Zeke says as she's about to open the car door.

'You might be able to fool the others, but not me,' he goes on.

'What do you mean?'

'You know what I mean.'

Malin stays silent.

'Maria Murvall,' Zeke eventually says. 'You're thinking about her. That this case is just like Maria's, that the forest where Maria was found is next to this one, that there must be a connection. I know you, Malin.'

'I've been doing a bit of work on the case.'

Zeke nods.

'I know. You didn't honestly think you'd be able to hide your obsession from me? I've seen the file on the screen of your computer, the folder on your desk.'

Of course he's noticed, Malin thinks. He knows me better than I do myself.

'I worked out that it's a form of therapy for you. So I chose not to say anything.'

'Do you think I'm mad?'

'No.'

Zeke opens the car door, gets out, stretches and says: 'OK, off we go, disturbing the peace, to see if this has any connection to Maria, or if it's something completely different. We'll have to mention it to Sven when the right moment comes up, but we probably shouldn't wait too long.'

The first house was occupied by an elderly woman. She hadn't seen anything, hadn't heard anything.

And it was the same at every house they visited. A lot of the summer cottages were still shut up, and in the houses where anyone was home people just looked blank, wondering what had happened but kept in ignorance, so as 'not to prejudice the investigation'.

Malin, Malin, Zeke is thinking now.

Rubbing one hand over his scalp. Holding the wheel with the other, dodging the potholes on the forest road.

She's always been prone to tearing off on her own.

And he's felt let down on those occasions, but knows he has to give her space. Because she's still the most brilliant murder detective he's ever met.

Smart, intuitive and, most important of all, obsessive.

She's hiding something from him. He knows that. But doesn't want to ask, better to let it mature fully inside her. He knows he's got better at that over the years, listening and holding back, waiting for the truth instead of forcing it out.

But sometimes the truth has to be forced out.

Sometimes even the police have to resort to violence.

And how many times has he lain awake at night full of regret after pushing a bit too hard, or when he's heard about Waldemar Ekenberg's almost bizarre excursions into the borderland between good and evil?

But he's always chosen to look the other way.

And felt sleep come.

Aware that they are fundamentally good. He's never understood why people in the US get upset about the fact that their own troops use torture. What the hell do they expect?

Doing evil doesn't necessarily mean that you are evil. Does it?

The forest surrounding the car.

Malin's tight-lipped silence.

The trees, the pines like rigid demons on the other side of the deep ditch, their branches arms trying to catch hold of every woman, drag her to the ground and drive their grating fingers into places where they don't belong.

Over the sound of the engine he can hear the forest whispering, enticing: Come to me, I mean you no harm. But something evil lives in the forest, inside every human being.

And behind the trunks of the trees he can make out distorted human faces, gorged with desire and self-fulfilment and the need for more.

Worms. Beetles. All the unhatched rattlesnakes' eggs.

Then Zeke is pulled back to the car. Surprised at his own uncontrollable dark visions.

Not like me, he thinks. Not fucking like me at all.

How many times have I done this now? Karin Johannison thinks as she looks at the peculiarly well-preserved female body on the metal table in front of her.

The autopsy room at the National Forensics Laboratory. Hidden away in the basement, three identical metal tables lined up in a windowless room with tiled walls, lit up by merciless fluorescent strip-lights.

It's as if none of the details of death can escape that light.

The yellowing bruises. The wounds with rotting, pus-oozing edges, the torn labia, the burn marks that must have been inflicted with a soldering iron, or possibly a small heating element. And the hole that had been cut into her stomach, methodically, but with extreme violence.

The black holes where the nipples had once been.

The irregular acid burns.

The desiccated white crust of sperm, like a seal on parts of the flesh.

Maybe I can get some DNA from it? Unless it's too degraded. Looks like it.

Malin didn't mention Maria Murvall out in the forest.

Almost the same place.

I know that.

If I can get some DNA we can compare it with the sample we took from Maria. The result must be in the archive after the work we did four years ago.

It's impossible to say if the person who did this to the woman on the table was a professional, a doctor, or a butcher, for instance. Or if he has done it before. But one thing is certain: it was done out of pure malevolence.

The weather has worked in their favour for the investigation. First the cold of winter, then the spring's inability to decide if it actually wanted to be spring at all.

She once read that the Aborigines have sixteen seasons. Or was it seventeen?

Maybe we should have more seasons too, Karin thinks. In that case this strange, unnatural May could be a season in its own right, the time of year when everything seems to hesitate, and the whole world has trouble working out what it wants.

Cold. Rain. Warmth. Sun.

Rapid shifts from one to the other, as if the weather, and time itself, had got stuck in limbo.

But the alternation between cold and heat meant that the body had thawed slowly, meaning that bacteria hadn't been able to get a firm grip on the body, and she could deduce more than she actually wanted to from a simple examination.

You can't have been more than twenty, Karin thinks. Wishing that the young woman before her could be given another chance, wishing she could bring her back to life, but knowing how pointless that wish is.

No one has that sort of power.

And she thinks of what she herself was like at twenty. How self-obsessed she was. The way she thought about clothes and her looks and money, and how she had only emerged from self-obsession years later.

She had left her husband. Even if he had thrown her out.

Zeke had left her for his family.

And she'd soon be forty.

The papers from the adoption agency arrived yesterday. China still permits adoption by single people.

As does Vietnam, via Denmark.

I can't stand here poking about in death all my life, Karin thinks. That would be unbearable.

I can't give life to anything, but I can give someone love.

The other detectives have also been knocking on doors. Waldemar Ekenberg and Börje Svärd had spoken to the farmer, Fridman, a good-natured, old-fashioned fellow, but he had been unable to give them anything, and was just shocked that a young woman had been found murdered on his land.

Darkness had settled over the forest, and with the darkness came the cold, and they called it a day and went home once they'd knocked on the last door.

And now Malin is leaning back in the chair in the kitchen of her flat on Ågatan, looking out at St Lars Church and thinking about the fact that her church and the hospital in Lund are named after the same saint. She thinks about the inscription above one of the side-doors of the church: 'Blessed are the pure in heart, for they shall see God', and she thinks that her three women are innocent, and maybe they can see God.

Earlier that evening Malin had looked through the case file from the investigation in Malmö.

But didn't find anything new.

Just a sense of relative indifference to the pain suffered by a young woman.

To what she had gone through.

Peter, his face on the other side of the table, framed by

the ticking of the Ikea clock with the broken second-hand on the wall.

'What are you thinking about?' he says.

'Coincidence,' Malin says. 'Such as the fact that we'd probably never have met if it weren't for the violence in this city.'

'Violence and love go together,' Peter says. 'Sex and violence go together, they're very close. It doesn't take much for one to slip into the other.'

Malin smiles.

Knows what he means, the way she almost always 'slips' when they're making love, but she's never gone too far yet, and how would he react if she did? With his usual calm? With concern, fear?

Not Peter, he'd soak it up and give it back, play the game so that it could stay a game, albeit an absurdly dangerous, lust-filled game.

But soon. When the coil comes out. Will everything that happens in the bedroom be reduced to procreation?

She doesn't even want to think about it.

The remnants of a simple meal on the table between them. Rice, sausage, boiled cauliflower, water in their glasses. Peter had abandoned the last of his holiday as well, and drove up from Skåne after lunch.

'I couldn't handle any more of Dad,' he had said over the phone in his car. 'He kept inspecting everything I did in the garden as if I were a kid.'

Malin had thought about her own father when they ended the call.

Earlier in the day she and Zeke had been on their way into the garden of a villa on the edge of the forest.

And Dad had been there then. As if they'd been in the garden of the house in Sturefors, thirty years before. Thoughts of him had coursed through her head.

I don't give a damn what he's up to, she had thought, I

don't care if he's alive or dead, or if he's alone, he deserves all the loneliness in the world. And he used to check everything I did in exactly the same way Peter described. Unless it was Mum who did that?

'Have you had enough?' Peter asks.

Malin nods and he clears the table, and she watches his perfect athlete's body move around the kitchen.

Sometimes she's taken aback by the fact that just by breathing in her vicinity he manages to make her feel at home, at peace, how a look from him can make her relax into the moment and forget all her desires and wretched restlessness.

Is he a superhero?

Is there a superhero doing the washing-up in my kitchen? Is the dusk outside the beautiful dusk of superheroes?

Is that what love is?

The phone rings from the old plywood cabinet out in the hall.

'I'll get it,' Malin says, and picks it up to hear Tove's voice at the other end of the line. She asks her mum how she is, and Malin answers, then Tove talks about the weekend, and tells her about the party they'd had in the gymnasium, and how she and Sofia and Ebba have been practising a song they're going to perform at the end-of-year concert in a couple of weeks.

'You have to come, Mum, you and Peter have got to come.' Tove's asked her before.

Of course I'll go, Malin thinks. As long as this case doesn't drag out.

Malin had been astonished when Tove told her about the song.

She had always hated singing. And now, she and two new friends are going to sing in front of the whole school.

Have I held you back, Tove? Is that what I did?

'I'll be there. And Janne. Maybe Peter.'

'You've got to come.'

Tove's pleading like a little girl now, now all of a sudden she wants a mother again, now that it suits her, and Malin feels like putting the phone down, feels like yelling at her daughter, shouting out her anger at being sidelined, but knows that she's just being childish.

Tove has to take flight now.

Out into what will be her life.

'We'll try to come.'

'You must! You've got to hear us sing!'

Tove had liked Peter from the start, attracted by his intelligence and integrity, and the fact that he seemed to have read all her favourite books appealed to her.

Friends.

And surely there's nothing better that a seventeen-year-old can be with her mum's new boyfriend?

That sort of relationship is usually disastrous.

But Peter hadn't gone with Malin to Lundsberg in October for parents' day.

And what a fucking nightmare that had been.

All those stuck-up people behaving as if they knew each other, even though they'd never met, as if their social status alone made them the best of friends, and Malin had stuck out like a sore thumb, she'd been the black on the beach full of white people, she was the immigrant who'd strayed into the posh supermarket on Karlavägen in Stockholm.

The headmaster had spoken to her. Praising Tove's achievements, and adding in passing: 'Considering how hard it can be for students like her, she's doing well.'

Malin had asked: 'What do you mean, for students like her? Should she be less talented just because I'm not as posh as everyone else here?'

Her forthrightness had surprised even her at first, then

she realised that that's just how she is, and that the sort of
people she'd been forced to mix with at Lundsberg's parents'
day scared her, because they brought out her true self, her
anger, fear and capacity for brutal honesty.

And the capacity to deal with the consequences of that
honesty.

'That's not what I meant,' the head had said.

'Of course it was,' and Malin had left him with the others
at the cocktail reception, and had gone down to the little
lake near the main building and had sat down on a jetty
in the mild, clear autumn evening, waiting for dinner.

Tove had come down to join her.

'You hate this, don't you, Mum?'

'I don't hate it, it's just not my thing. You know that.'

'But it's my thing.'

'I know, and that's why I'm here.'

There on the jetty they had hugged, and dinner that
evening had passed without any problem, but in March, at
the next parents' day, Malin had made sure she was busy.

'We're going to sing "Summertime",' Tove says. 'The
music teacher says we sound almost like Billie Holiday.'

'I wouldn't want to miss that,' Malin says, then she talks
about Copenhagen, and Tove asks her to say hi to Peter.

'Will do,' Malin says. 'He's right here,' and she calls into
the kitchen: 'Tove says hi!'

'Say hello back!'

'I heard,' Tove says, then she goes on: 'Mum. There's one
other thing.'

'What?'

Tove's tone of voice. Malin doesn't like it.

As if a secret's about to be revealed.

'Nothing, we can deal with it later.'

'No, Tove, you have to tell me now. Now I'm curious
and—'

'No,' Tove says. 'Not now. Bye.'

Tove hangs up, and her voice is replaced by a lonely, unending note.

Mirror, mirror, on the wall, who is the fairest of them all.

I couldn't tell Mum, Tove thinks as she straightens her back in front of the mirror. I couldn't ask her, and Tove can see her student room behind her in the mirror.

The muddle of books, the green-striped bedspread from Ikea. She's the only one here with an Ikea bedspread, the others have all got throws from Ralph Lauren Home.

That's what matters.

She focuses on herself instead.

She's noticed the way her face has changed during her year up here in Värmland.

The way her nose seems to point towards the sky, sharper, and the way her cheeks have got less round, more distinct, and she's let her brownish-blond hair grow a bit longer, the way fashion dictates that all the oh-so-lovely girls from Östermalm and Djursholm and all the country estates should wear theirs.

But they seem to accept me. The way you accept a foreigner who can't be completely stupid, seeing as she's managed to get to the same place as them.

It occurs to Tove that her whole being is becoming more and more like the others. I don't really like that, she thinks, I want to be who I am, but presumably that's what's meant by social integration.

Mirror, mirror.

She's started having singing lessons.

And to her surprise she's discovered both that she likes it, and can actually sing.

She likes showing off. As a contrast to the books.

All the hard-won insights found in them.

She thinks about her mum. Feels older than her, almost more mature. But still wants her to be a mum, still wants her to become a really good mum one day.

The sort of mum who comes when you want her to. Not the sort who leaves you alone all night because she has to work.

Peter.

He's OK.

But if they were to, like, have kids or something I'd go mad.

You can't have a new brother or sister when you're seventeen.

That would just be embarrassing.

10

Is there no end to this night?

Sven Sjöman is sitting in the kitchen of his house.

He sighs into the darkness, he hasn't bothered to switch the light on, and the freshly painted green cupboard doors are glowing black along the walls.

He's found it harder and harder to sleep over the past year, and has felt a strange new restlessness in his body, and his few, inadequate hours of sleep have left him tired and listless, almost uninterested in his work.

He's been to see a doctor, a young one, who recommended tests, it might be a hormone imbalance, that sort of thing can happen 'when you get old'.

One month ago.

Still no appointment to go for tests up at the University Hospital.

Is it supposed to take this long?

But everything in this bloody country is being dismantled now that the right-wing coalition is in charge.

He could always phone and make a fuss.

But he feels fine otherwise.

Can't be bothered to call. So unbelievably tired. He's thought about applying for early retirement. Seriously thought about it.

His workshop in the basement. It's a long time since he was last there, he's lost interest in woodwork, shaping the wood into a different sort of beauty from its natural state.

Dishes.

Traditional bowls with carved wooden handles.

He's grown tired of routine, tired of his job, but he makes an effort to keep up appearances for the others in the team, tries to seem keen. But they can see right through me, he thinks, especially Malin.

Sven gently rests one cheek on the table top. Shuts his eyes, feeling the soft surface of the waxed cloth against his skin, and he listens to the sound of his breathing, deep, heavy, rattling.

Malin.

Has she finally found peace now? She's matured a bit since she met that doctor, Peter Hamse.

She never talks about him, but Sven knows that they're pretty much living together. He's noticed that she talks to him on the phone a lot.

She's thirty-seven now.

How old is Tove? Seventeen? Suddenly Sven is struck by a thought he's never had before, because it has somehow always been too unlikely: what if Malin wants another child? With this Peter Hamse? She isn't too old, and her drinking in the past couldn't have wrecked her body in that way.

Maybe that's what Malin needs to become a whole person at last? A new child. I wonder if she's thought that herself?

Banal thoughts.

As if life could be summed up in a few platitudes.

But what would we do without her?

She doesn't see it herself, but she's the driving force behind the investigative team, the one who moves everything on with a strong, invisible power.

She sets the tone.

We'd have problems if she suddenly went off on maternity leave.

Maternity leave.

Somehow that phrase doesn't fit with Malin Fors.
Not at all.

Börje Svärd is also lying awake, with his arm around Matilda,
the woman he met at a Sunday dance at the Cupola early
in November last year.

He's holding Matilda, but thinking about Anna, where
she might be, and he hopes that all the suffering she had
to endure in life is over now, and that she might be an
angel in a big, white room where no pain exists, where it
isn't even possible.

Was her body beset by evil? Was the illness evil? Can an
illness be evil, or does evil have to have a conscious intent?

Not that it matters. She suffered. And then she died. No
more to it than that. Evil doesn't need a purpose.

Nothing wrong with Matilda.

But it's not love. Do you need love at this age? Maybe
sex and friendship are enough, having fun together as long
as you don't get on each other's nerves.

Is this new case going to wear at our nerves?

It's bound to.

The dead woman in the forest is almost certain to make
Malin a bit crazy, this is precisely the sort of case that
provokes her almost obsessive devotion to her work,
making me, Waldemar, and the others look like uninterested dullards.

Matilda.

She's got a bit of weight to lose, a bit of weight to hold.
Anna was just skin and bones in her last five years, and
her paralysed body couldn't even feel his tender caresses.

Was there any point to those caresses? Was the goodness
they were meant to convey just an empty gesture?

He kneads Matilda's large, soft breasts, plays with one
of her nipples, which stiffens under his fingers.

She turns towards him.

'So you're ready to go again,' she whispers, and Börje feels, thinks: This is enough, this is more than enough.

Waldemar Ekenberg is sleeping in his bed in his house in Mjölby, a dreamless sleep, deep and indecently free from worries.

His wife isn't sleeping beside him.

She's started working nights in the care home. Wants to have her own money, even though they could manage more than well enough on his salary.

She comes home just as he's setting off in the car for Linköping.

She works four nights a week.

Hello in the morning, hello in the evening.

Together yet somehow parallel, and Waldemar is happy with the arrangement, they annoy each other less this way, it's as simple as that.

In his sleep a dream begins.

He dreams of a woman, bloody and wounded, staggering through a cold forest at night.

The ground where she walks is freezing.

The blood solidifies in her wake, turning to ice, lapped up by a greedy, invisible monster.

Then the woman stops in front of Waldemar in the dream.

Holds out her hand to him in the forest.

He holds his own hand out to her, but before he can reach her she's gone, and the empty landscape of dreamlessness spreads out once more.

Zeke Martinsson is lying awake in the bedroom that is his alone since Gunilla expelled him from the bed they shared.

For life?

Who knows.

He thought she was going to throw him out when she found out about his affair with Karin.

How did she find out?

A text on his mobile.

He'd left his phone in the pocket of a pair of trousers she was going to wash.

Classic.

And stupid.

As if he wanted to be found out, to set something in motion, as if this carousel of infidelity and betrayal and lust had to come to an end, one way or another.

And Gunilla had given him an ultimatum.

Me or her.

But the words meant the family or her, Christmas, Midsummer, grandchildren, Martin, the whole fucking family or her.

So he dumped Karin, in a confusion of confused days.

'I don't feel anything any more,' he told her, and was surprised at how easy it was to say the words as long as he convinced himself that they made things easier for Karin. 'I did for a while, but now I don't feel anything. What I felt vanished among all the lies, the betrayals.'

'You're lying,' Karin said. 'And you know you are.'

'I'm not lying.'

She didn't say anything else.

Left him alone with his words about vanished feelings.

And in a month's time it will be Midsummer. And Martin and the grandchildren will be here to celebrate it with us.

Gunilla says she's forgiven him. But she'll never forgive me entirely, nor trust me, something's broken, that much is obvious, and she's threatened to kill me if I say anything to Martin.

Our boy.

Phenomenally rich from ice hockey, but injured now,

recently operated on, so we've got them here for the summer, him, his wife, and the children.

'He doesn't need to know.'

As if the shame of my human frailty, of Gunilla's own inadequacy, is the worst thing, not the act itself, the closeness, sweat, penetration or betrayal.

Open, close, count sheep.

The grandchildren had been there the evening before. He'd brought Martin's old toys up from the basement, and spent hours playing with the little boy on the rug in the living room. Building a farm, lining up cars, making a looping train track.

Fifteen sheep.

The woman in the forest, the stench, the smell of sulphur, the rotting corpse.

Malin.

He'd felt how keen she was in the forest beside the body from the way she smelled, the way her brain started to make connections to the case of Maria Murvall.

Her relationship with Peter Hamse has had no impact on her obsessive nature, but he's been good for her. Zeke is no longer as worried that she's going to slip and start drinking again, or even have a small lapse, and she's been doing more exercise than ever down in the gym at the police station.

She's in better condition than he's ever seen her.

Not at peace, not remotely, but somehow in balance, in her own way.

As long as she doesn't lose her balance now that we've got this to deal with.

Blink.

Eyes open, closed.

Counting sheep.

Gunilla. Couldn't I just sleep in bed beside you?

* * *

Police Chief Karim Akbar thrusts deep into District Prosecutor Vivianne Södergran, she's on all fours in front of him on the bed in his villa in Lambohov, and her body takes on a warm orange glow from the lamp on the bedside table.

She's groaning.

But says nothing, never does when they make love.

He's standing on the floor at the foot of the bed, the polished parquet floor cold beneath his feet.

Back and forth, out and in, and he slaps her hard on the buttocks, knows she likes that.

He doesn't want to come, not yet, knows it takes longer for her, so he tries to think about something else.

About the lamps. Pretentious things bought from Mio. The bedside tables in red-stained oak come from there as well.

He thinks about the job with the Migration Board in Norrköping, the one he turned down.

For Vivianne's sake, even if he'd never admit that to her.

Norrköping. Within commuting distance, of course, but he likes having her close during the day, just a hundred metres or so from the police station, in the courthouse next door.

Out and in.

And the Migration Board. Too depressing, too sensitive, too wrong to be the right career move.

Faster, she's whimpering now, all the way in, like that, just like that, and he can hear her getting close, and thinks about the press conference tomorrow morning, and what he's going to say to the press about their new case.

They haven't got much.

Knocking on doors hadn't given them anything, and they would be searching the forest tomorrow and over the coming days, and they could reveal some of what Karin had given them.

No details about the wounds, but the fact that she was running from something.

And the woman's identity is still unknown.

Harder.

And he slaps her.

Wants to slap harder, but holds back. He's stronger than her. Physically. He could actually do anything he wanted to with her, she wouldn't have a chance of resisting.

But he just wants to give her love. I don't want to use my muscles, my strength to make her a tool for my pleasure, my view of the world.

But it's nice to feel the power I've got now.

It's part of the intoxication of the act, approaching the point where love becomes violence and pain, and the way it's actually possible to savour that moment.

Slapping harder.

That's wrong, Karim, and you know it.

Her skin.

Warm and gentle and soft.

Don't cross the boundary. There's no way back.

He lets go.

Calms down.

Fills Vivianne with all that he is, and he is a man, a man, a man, a tender man.

You like this, don't you? he thinks, but then she whispers, just before he explodes: 'Take it easy, Karim, take it easy, enjoy it, you've got nothing to prove.'

Unless she doesn't actually whisper anything?

Is she silent?

Saying nothing?

And he lets go, pushes even deeper into her, and they come together and everything is soft and tender, tender and soft.

Waldemar Ekenberg has woken up.

Sweating from the dream he knows he'll never be able to shake off.

He got out of bed, went into the kitchen and drank some milk straight from the carton, then put it back in the rumbling old Husqvarna fridge that they should have replaced long ago.

He had once done the same thing when he was little. And his father had seen him and beat him the way he beat Waldemar's mother.

But he beat her all the time.

And hard.

And Waldemar used to hide under his bed, covering his ears to block out her screams and wondering why no one came to their rescue, her screams must have been audible out in the street and around the other houses.

He had heard her cry, and had wanted to hit his father, smash him in the head with a frying pan, but he had never dared.

He had hated the way his father smelled. Sweat, desire, power.

Cancer took him in less than a month, when Waldemar was fourteen. Eating away at his stomach. His father had lain whimpering in a bed in Motala Hospital, and Waldemar had stood beside him, and felt like punching him right on the scar left by the pointless operation, hitting him to take revenge for all his mum's bruises, all her screams, the way all joy in life had vanished from her eyes.

And he had hit him.

Twice, with his fist clenched, and Dad had screamed.

He had screamed and screamed, but none of the hospital staff had come.

It was as if they knew the old bastard was getting what he deserved.

Waldemar Ekenberg puts the milk back in the fridge.

And reflects upon the fact that he's never told anyone about his childhood.

Not even his wife.

And thinks that he only plays the chauvinist so no one will think him weak. I've been playing the part so long that I've turned into one.

He thinks of the number of occasions he's hit people since that time at his father's deathbed, for the same reason. And thinks that he'll want to do it again, and will do so.

Malin is lying like a child, close to Peter.

One arm over his chest, the other snaking over his stomach towards his crotch.

Silent.

Wordless.

That was how they'd made love that night, calm and close, careful, as if they wanted to tell themselves that the sort of violence Malin had encountered in the forest wasn't even possible, that people didn't do that sort of thing to each other, that it went against nature.

For a few short seconds they managed to convince themselves.

That the world was good, gentle.

Then they fell asleep and, just like Waldemar Ekenberg, Malin dreams. In her dreams flies are buzzing around a rotting cadaver, and the countless shining heads of a hydra, all with their maws wide open, are pulsing, swaying and lurching back and forth over the dark scene of the dream.

Peter's body.

Beside her in bed, but in the dream his body is a cadaver. And beside him yet another cadaver.

And she paws at the cadaver's face, trying to understand, to see who it is, but someone's tied a black blindfold over her eyes, and she can hear drums, strange voices singing forth a world of goodness but they're being drowned out by darker voices, voices from long burned-out campfires where people begged the darkness for help to survive.

Bang, bang, bang.

Steady and pained, the voices cry above the flames against the black vault of the dream.

The hydra sniffs at the cadaver, its heads try to eat Malin's face, tearing the flesh from her cheeks, boring a hole through her body, and the woman in the forest, her wide-open, empty face is there with her now, and she whispers into Malin's bleeding ear.

Help me, she whispers.

Help me.

Silence is our worst enemy.

Just because you pretend something doesn't exist, doesn't mean it stops existing.

You have to help me.

Us.

Maria, me, and the other nameless woman in the other room. All the others.

Who are we?

Why doesn't anyone miss us? Why don't we exist? Who thinks we're worth so little that we don't even need names?

And the violence, Malin, what sort of evil is capable of hurting us the way we were hurt?

Only you can give us clarity, only you, no one else.

We're waiting for you.

We're waiting for you to bring light to our dark world.

And in the dream Malin wants to answer the woman who has come to her, but her lips are sewn together and the many words she wants to say become a shapeless noise shut inside a dark hole, and she swallows hard, leaves the evil dream and goes into another where a little boy is sleeping in a white bed surrounded by small, shining black baubles.

11

Tuesday, 17 May

Persistent rain, unassuming grey pearls falling from low, dark cloud.

Like an autumn morning.

But that season is far away, time somehow indeterminate now, warped, rotating around its own axis.

It's a quarter past seven when Johan Jakobsson walks through the automatic doors of the police station and heads across the grey stone floor, past the curved, glossy reception desk and on into the open-plan office. There are no journalists outside yet, they're probably waiting for the press conference, even though the murdered woman in the forest must have whetted the hyenas' appetites.

He woke early, long before the rest of the family this morning, sat down at his home computer and logged onto the police server.

He carried on with the previous day's work, searching through the register of sex offenders, checking to see if anyone had been released and had settled in their area during the past year.

And he got a result.

An Arto Antinen. Forty-six years old, from Kisa.

Found guilty of raping his partner.

He denied the charge but was sentenced to two years in

Österåker, having previously been convicted for exposing himself at a playground in Tranås.

Plenty of sexual frustration in that body, Johan thinks.

And, according to the register, Arto Antinen lives just outside Stjärnorp, in a cottage just a dozen kilometres or so from where the body was found, only just outside the radius of their door-knocking.

Vile.

Johan thinks of his own children as he switches on the computer on his desk at work. His daughter has just started school. He knows what he'd do if a flasher showed up at her playground.

He'd cut the bastard's balls off, that's what he'd do.

Cut all the sexual frustration out of that sick body.

Hatred.

Nothing can summon up hatred like my fate.

Except possibly my father, my dad, for what he did to me.

He's burning.

That's some comfort to me.

Malin. I can see you down there.

Huddled beneath taut black fabric, as if to protect yourself from the evil creeping up behind you.

Don't be overconfident, Malin.

Don't think you can protect yourself.

No one.

No one can protect themselves.

Malin is walking quickly towards the police station, hunched up under her large black umbrella. The weather is so changeable that she never knows if she's going to need her umbrella, or sunglasses, a thin top, or a padded jacket.

She doesn't want to be late for the morning meeting. Her car is parked outside the station.

No charge there.

She cuts across the Horticultural Society Park, noting that some of the trees are blossoming and that the lawns and paths are as well maintained as usual. She walks up towards Drottninggatan, where an orange ethanol-fuelled bus named after an ice-hockey player is rumbling up towards the hospital.

The blocks of flats look tired in the rain. And so much smaller than the buildings in Stockholm, shrunken but without actually being so. The grey façades have white lines painted around the windows, as if to provide life with a frame. There are lights on inside the flats, but there aren't many people about at this early hour.

Linköping.

One hundred and forty-five thousand dream cocoons.

The poor living just a stone's throw from the rich. Smugness living next door to hopelessness. Lives turning around the same axis, but with radically different circumstances.

People still look each other in the eye in Linköping. But people have started to lower their gaze more and more. In line with the increase in misanthropy, pain, jealousy, and anger at crushed dreams.

Dreams.

Fulfilled and unfulfilled next to each other, always close, and blindness, the desire not to see anything.

In this city, Malin thinks, rich and poor alike are united by their blindness.

Blindness is a way of living side by side.

On the surface, Linköping is a safe, secure city. But violence and evil are here, Malin thinks. Everywhere, always.

And more than anything the inhabitants would like to turn their backs on all that sort of thing. They want to prevent their rosy dreams being turned into nightmares.

Linköping.

The city as a pressure cooker for human lives. The plain

and forests and lakes like a curling fat snake around the buildings and cathedral and factories and hospitals.

Violence has a piquant history here, the bloodbath and beheadings in 1600, the Battle of Stångebro two years before, when the water of the Stångån River was stained red with the blood of mercenaries.

Blood, still flowing red in the city's inhabitants.

And sometimes it flows on the streets, to this day.

A young boy stabbed to death in an open street one morning. A woman as well. Not far from where Malin is walking now, barely five hundred metres from the police station.

A young mother beaten to death on a cycle path in the centre of the quiet residential district of Lambohov.

Respectable members of society turn out to be paedophiles who rape their own children.

Violence is in our midst, Malin thinks. But if we choose blindness, it doesn't exist at all.

No one wants to see.

That's just how it is, Malin thinks as she shakes off her umbrella and speeds up.

Sven Sjöman is holding a blue marker pen in one hand as he rubs his eyes with the other.

He opens his mouth, and says in his most authoritative voice: 'This is officially the first preliminary meeting in the investigation into the murder of the woman who was found yesterday, murdered in the forest north of Stjärnorp.'

On the whiteboard behind him he's already written:

Woman X

Then, immediately below that, a large question mark.

And the question mark seems to summarise the atmosphere in the room, the feeling shared by all the members of the

Violent Crime Unit of Linköping Police at that moment, at the start of this first formal meeting in the investigation into a woman's brutal murder. The feeling that all the questions raised by the woman's murder must be answered, otherwise fear and insecurity will take over the city, the whole region, and instil a grain of fear in people, making them suspicious of their fellows, without them ever realising it. That suspicion means that social interaction will be tainted, and soon the whole city will be affected, becoming an inhospitable place where no one considers anyone's needs but their own.

Every unsolved murder contributes to that atmosphere.

Every solved murder helps drive the city forward in the right direction.

And their shared sense of responsibility is the best tool they have for turning Sven's question mark into an exclamation mark.

Malin looks at her colleagues.

Johan Jakobsson, on the other side of the table, in jeans and a short-sleeved white shirt, looking tired, he's probably spent half the night at his computer. Börje Svärd, in a black tennis shirt, looks as if he's had sex, and is almost cheerful, and it suits him, makes him seem more genial.

Waldemar Ekenberg, in his customary beige nylon shirt, seems to have slept well. His face isn't as sunken as it usually is, and seems less nicotine-grey, and his greasy brown hair and grey-green eyes seem somehow more lively than normal.

Perhaps, Malin thinks, Waldemar can detect an opportunity to show his dark side?

Zeke, in a tight white T-shirt, has the same expression he's worn a lot recently, the abandoned man's look of surprise: What happened? The look of someone who doesn't understand his own feelings, and has to live with the consequences of that.

Karim Akbar next to Malin.

Impeccably dressed in a grey Zegna suit, with an expensive bright red tie that goes well with his baby-blue shirt. Karim's broad cheeks are freshly shaven, his brown eyes are expectant and his thick, dark hair is cut shorter than usual, making him look younger. Malin had expected him to take the job at the Migration Board, but he chose to stay, as if he had found some sort of mutual career satisfaction with his new woman, bitch prosecutor Vivianne Södergran.

Sven at the whiteboard.

Weary, incredibly weary, but he doesn't think we can tell, and his voice is hoarse and rough as he starts speaking: 'Well, this is what we've got.'

Malin hears her own words and those of the others as they go through the current position of the investigation into Woman X.

About twenty years old.

Subjected to abuse and serious sexual assault.

Then cut open and finally killed, murdered, probably by a blow to the head following her flight through the forest.

It seemed likely she had been lying in the forest since early December, when the cold first arrived, and her body had been preserved through the winter.

Knocking on doors hadn't given them anything.

The soldiers from Kvarn were busy searching the forest, together with some of the police's own dog-handlers.

Johan Jakobsson's sex offender from the register will have to be questioned.

He lives up near Stjärnorp Castle, and it might be worth asking there as well, and at the neighbouring estate, Sjölunda.

Rumours spread quickly through smart drawing rooms, and it might be worth talking to the seriously wealthy, see if they've heard anything, maybe they've still got the same overview of the area that they used to have.

The suggestion came from Waldemar Ekenberg, but Sven Sjöman said no. For the time being there was no reason to disturb the Douglas family at Stjärnorp, or Count Stålskiöld at Sjölunda.

Sven has had someone check all the registers for missing women.

No one matching their woman in either Linköping or the country as a whole. They'd be expanding their inquiries abroad now, if there was a possibility that they were dealing with a woman who'd been trafficked.

Which wasn't out of the question.

But the registers in the countries they usually came from were less than perfect, to say the least. Far too often the police themselves were involved in the trade.

'So don't pin your hopes on that,' Karim Akbar says. 'But obviously we'll be making a request.'

And once again Malin finds herself thinking of Kristina, but still can't conjure up her face, and instead hears herself as a child shouting 'Kristina the Slag', and the nickname echoes through her as if it had been shouted in a school corridor.

'She could be a girl who went off the rails,' Malin says. 'In which case it's far from certain that anyone would have reported her missing. She might have fallen below everyone's radar.'

'That sort of thing happens,' Waldemar says. 'I came across a girl in Mjölby once, from Stockholm, who hadn't had any contact with her family since she was sixteen. Abusive home life.'

The detectives fall silent.

And Malin knows that they're all quickly searching their memories, and in those memories will be girls like her own Kristina, lonely, ignored, mute, sexually precocious, the ones who fell pregnant, and then, as soon as they could quit school, just vanished.

'Anything else?' Sven asks when everyone's thoughts seem to have ebbed away.

And he looks at Malin as if challenging her to mention Maria Murvall.

So she makes up her mind, there's no point holding back, and she tells the others about the obvious connections to Maria's case, the location, the wounds, and she mentions the woman in Lund, but not her trip to Stockholm and her conversation with the prosecutor, Fredrik Kantsten. She doesn't want to muddy the waters with even more information, wants to maintain some sort of focus. She's not sure how the others are going to react, and, without quite understanding why, she also wants to keep something to herself, and not let everything she knows become other people's property, not yet.

'There are certainly similarities,' Waldemar says. 'Could we be dealing with the same perpetrator? A serial rapist? Serial killer?'

'It's impossible to say,' Sven says. 'We'll have to regard it as one hypothesis. Is there anything definite to go on in that line of inquiry, Malin?'

'No,' she says. 'Nothing definite. As far as I can tell, there might be similarities in the ages of our woman in the forest and the woman down in Lund, but we don't know if there are other similarities, and of course Maria is considerably older. And we don't have any idea how the presumed perpetrator came into contact with the women, how he chose them, do we?'

'No,' Sven says. 'We don't even know the identities of the other women, so it's not going to be possible to look for answers in their backgrounds.'

'We'll just have to keep it open,' Malin says. 'There's no denying that there are significant differences.'

She pauses.

'But the women's injuries are very similar,' she goes on. 'As if nature itself were intent on destroying them. The burns, cuts, the vaginal trauma. There are differences, of course, but we're basically dealing with a form of violence that seems to be both methodical and the result of blind fury.'

The others sit in silence, absorbing what she's said.

Seeing the women's violated bodies before them.

'I remember Maria Murvall's brothers,' Zeke says. 'Crazy bastards. Could they have anything to do with this? Their hunting cabin's not that far from where we found our woman.'

'I doubt it,' Malin says. 'Maria's their sister. And believe me, they love their sister. They'd never harm a hair on her head. They may not be angels, but they're not rapists. I'd have huge trouble believing that.'

'Malin, Zeke,' Sven says. 'You can keep that line of inquiry open, and look for more parallels, if there are any, but we'll have to treat it as an entirely separate investigation. After all, there's more than five years between the crimes. Go and talk to Arto Antinen as soon as possible.'

Sven falls silent, takes a deep breath.

'Any other ideas?' he asks.

Malin sees Börje Svärd purse his lips before opening his mouth to speak: 'It was the end of the hunting season,' he says. 'If she's been lying there since early December, we should probably check anyone who rented a hunting cabin in the area. I know that several of the farmers around here take payment for hunting rights these days. It might be worth looking into.'

'Good,' Sven says. 'You and Waldemar look into that, with Johan's help. And check anything else that was going on in the area around that time. Meetings. Contests, orienteering, anything at all.'

The door to the meeting room opens.

Karin Johannison walks in, her blond hair loose, wearing a full-length green floral-print dress.

You look like a hippie, Malin thinks. All you're missing is a joint. Just a few years ago you were dressing like an upper-class chick.

Karin stops in front of the whiteboard.

Looks more hesitant than usual, as if something's troubling her, but her voice is still strong, clear, and factual when she starts to speak.

'Woman X. This is her.'

Zeke, Malin thinks as she hears Karin's voice. What are you feeling now?

Karin takes a photograph out of her brown leather briefcase and holds it up to them.

'I've got other pictures.'

Karin has cleaned her face, closed her eyes, then taken a portrait shot, and Woman X looks as if she's asleep, as if she's finally getting some proper rest, and there's an indecent beauty in the picture, as if Karin had enjoyed making Woman X beautiful.

In some of the pictures her eyes are open.

A dead look in them, yet still full of something, like ultimate despair.

'We could release them to the media,' she says. 'That might give us something.'

'We can't release a picture yet,' Sven says beside Karin. 'We'll have to wait a while, see what the investigation comes up with, see if we can identify her and notify any family.'

'That could take a long time,' Karin says. 'Don't the circumstances demand that we release the picture at once? As far as I understand it, we have no idea who she is. And clearly there's a madman on the loose out there, and he could very well be busy committing or planning further attacks.'

It isn't Karin's place to comment on the investigation,

Malin thinks. She never usually does. But she can't help herself, that much is obvious.

Insight demands sacrifice, she goes on to think.

Is that how it is?

That everything really does have a cost?

Only now does Malin notice the children in the preschool playground outside the window, defying the rain. The sound of their noisy games finds its way into the meeting room.

That's why we're sitting here, Malin thinks, it's for your sake we have to solve this case, and she hears Karim say: 'We'll hold back with the picture, Karin. I agree with you in principle, but this time sensitivity has to come first.'

Karin nods.

'Anything else?' Johan asks.

'Yes,' Karin says, with a note of hesitancy and the same worried look as when she first started to talk. 'To my great surprise I managed to get a sample of someone else's DNA from the woman's body. The traces of semen that I found weren't as degraded as I first thought.'

'DNA?' Waldemar says.

'Semen, inside the deep wound to her stomach. So if the man who did this is in our database, we've got him.'

'We've got DNA from Maria Murvall,' Malin says. 'We can compare the sample from Woman X and see if we're dealing with the same perpetrator.'

Silence settles on the room.

'There's one problem,' Karin says. And now she's a scientist. Thoroughly professional.

'What?'

Malin can hear the aggression in her own voice.

'When Maria Murvall was last of interest in an investigation, the DNA sample found on her body was ruined during the analysis. An assistant managed to use the wrong chemical during one stage of the process.'

'What did you say?'

Karin repeats what she's just said, and goes on: 'I'm sorry. It happened here at the National Forensics Lab, and I've only just found out. No one informed me until now.'

'But for God's sake, we must have the sample in digital form? In some archive?'

Karin shakes her head.

'All the test was able to prove was whether the suspect in the old case was the right man. No more than that, and evidently barely that much. I could only give a positive/negative answer then. And the last remnants of the sample were destroyed, without my knowledge, as being unusable. So there's no complete analysis stored anywhere. The police in Motala never got that far in their investigation. And then it was too late.'

'But isn't that obligatory?'

'Not at the time, Malin, unfortunately. We had far fewer resources when Maria's case was first investigated, so no analysis was ever done unless it was absolutely necessary. And we didn't have a national database to match our samples against either.'

'So we've got absolutely no DNA from Maria Murvall's attacker? Someone who could also be Woman X's attacker?'

'I'm afraid so,' Karin says quietly, and Waldemar sighs loudly, then blows the air from his lungs in a way that almost reeks of contempt.

Idiots, Malin thinks. How useless could people be? The National Forensics Lab, and Motala too.

Fuck.

But no point looking back, crying over spilled milk. They have to move on.

And Sven summarises what she and the others have all realised: 'Things happen. There's no point lingering over it. We just have to brush ourselves off and move on.'

Grunts and nods around the table.

'The assistant was dismissed?' Börje says.

'No. But he's no longer with us,' Karin replies.

What did you just say? Malin thinks. Trying to focus on the facts they've got.

You said semen.

In the wound on her stomach.

'So you're saying,' Malin says, 'that he or they cut her open and then had sex with her through the wound?'

'It looks like it,' Karin says.

'He wasn't bothered about the risk of infection from the blood?' Börje asks.

'The sort of person who'd do that probably isn't thinking about the risk of infection,' Malin points out.

'He cut her open,' Karin says quietly. 'And burned or scalded her.'

Lost DNA.

But some new DNA.

And someone who cuts holes in women in order to fuck them in the hole.

A serial rapist? Serial killer?

Or something much, much worse?

Someone wants to cut a hole in you and fuck you through it, buddy.

Where have I read that? Karin wonders. Maybe it was from one of those art installations by Jenny Holzer?

The detectives in the room all breathe out at the same moment, and when they fill their lungs again they realise that the air is low in oxygen, that what they're all involved in, the experience they're sharing now, threatens to suffocate them, and destroy everything they are, everything that they believe in.

12

Arto Antinen.

What does someone like that believe in?

His own right to take what he wants? That his path is the right one?

His DNA isn't in the database, there hadn't been any reason to take a sample in the rape case for which he was convicted.

Another DNA failure.

Let it go, Fors.

He must be Finnish, judging by his name, she thinks as she knocks on the door of a little red cottage in a clearing surrounded by dense pine forest. According to the Tax Office, Arto Antinen owns the cottage, which is too deep in the forest to be worth much, at least a kilometre from the beaches of Lake Roxen, between Stjärnorp and Sjölunda.

The rain has stopped, the sky half-covered by hesitant summer clouds, and if it weren't for the cold wind it would feel like summer, as if the forest around them were full of blueberries ready to be picked and eaten.

Disgusting, Malin thinks.

Exposing yourself at a playground.

Raping your own girlfriend.

He'd tied her to the bed while drunk, according to the report, and then fucked her on and off for a whole weekend. He had evidently lost it when she threatened to leave him, and decided to show her who was boss in their world.

He had gagged her, stuffing a sweaty sock in her mouth.

And then violence, one flesh laying siege to and conquering another flesh, to show who's in control.

What's moving in the forest?

Light doesn't reach far between the trees, is that where you ran, Maria? Is that where you fled for your life?

Zeke is standing beside her on the unsteady little flight of steps, and the wind is brushing through the trees around the small clearing, and the door opens, and in front them stands a skinny little man with bloodshot eyes and breath that would make a teetotaller drunk in seconds, and which makes Malin giddy with thirst.

Arto Antinen raises his eyebrows.

And, his brow furrowed into a myriad wrinkles, says in a thick Finnish accent: 'Come in. I've been expecting you ever since I heard about that woman being found on television.'

Karim Akbar enjoys the flashbulbs, the cameras, the questions, the feeling of knowing something that no one else knows.

He once read an interview with the film director Stanley Kubrick, and when asked about his own greatness, and the myths surrounding him, he had said: 'Always act like you know something nobody else knows.'

And now I know more, Karim thinks, than this hungry pack of badly dressed hacks in front of me.

'For reasons relating to the investigation . . . no, we don't know who the woman is, and out of respect to her family we're not releasing a photograph . . .'

A good turnout.

The national press is there, as well as Swedish Television, radio news and TV4.

He adjusts his tie, the two-and-a-half-thousand-kronor Brioni that Vivianne had bought for him when she was at a prosecutors' conference in Milan. She's got good taste, Vivianne, and Karim can feel his mind wandering, he's so used to this performance now.

Question.

Answer.

Question.

He's just finished writing his book on issues of integration.

He's promoting the controversial opinion that demands should be made of anyone migrating to Sweden, serious demands to help them contribute to their own integration in return for receiving any social benefits at all.

Learning Swedish.

Learning about Selma Lagerlöf.

Passing tests.

Submitting to the education that will lead to a job. But also demands that they learn Swedish culture. Take part in it, submerge themselves in it. Hell, even go to the open-air museum at Skansen.

And they must apply for every job going, wherever in the country it might be, even if they happen to be a Muslim woman with sixteen children from central Africa with half her family in Södertälje.

The Swedish Democrats have exploited the silence on an issue that affects huge numbers of Swedes. Karim hates them, and as an immigrant himself he ought to be able to convey politically incorrect views without being called a racist, and take the edge off the Swedish Democrats' rhetoric, and get rid of the country's shame.

He's going to get a lot of press attention with the book.

And, if he had ever been considering a career in politics, that's all over thanks to the views he's promoting. Unless it isn't, seeing as he's writing exactly what people are thinking.

'Next question . . . no, I'm afraid . . .'

★ ★ ★

Johan Jakobsson is sitting at his desk in the open-plan office, searching feverishly through websites and forums, looking, clicking, looking further.

Neither Ljungsbro Football Club nor Stjärnorp Sports Club appeared to have held any competitive events during the period in question, and he hasn't yet found any hunting cabins available to rent in the area, or even any hunting licences.

But there are plenty of cottages to rent in the area around Sandvik, if that isn't too far? And they're not hunting cabins, more summer cottages. He'll still have to call their owners. Just to see.

Even further away is the old training centre run by the Social Democrats, or rather the Workers' Education Council. But that's been empty for years, hasn't it? He had forgotten it even existed.

He concentrates on hunting cabins.

He's checked the classifieds in both the *Correspondent* and *Folkbladet*, and Sweden's biggest online listings website.

There don't seem to have been any other large gatherings in the vicinity either. No big revivalist meetings at the Pentecostal Church in Stjärnorp.

Börje Svärd has, however, managed to track down one hunting cabin, and a few desks away Johan watches him call a farmer who, according to the advert, has a cabin to rent during the season, and hears him ask a few questions.

'I see, so it hasn't been rented out for the past few years, and you haven't noticed anything unusual? OK.'

Börje hangs up.

Shakes his head, first to Johan and then Waldemar Ekenberg, who's sitting beside him.

Arto Antinen's hands were shaking as he poured coffee for them.

His cottage consists of an old kitchen with yellow units from the fifties, and a messy little bedroom with pink wall-paper, the whole room full of empty bottles, cartons from ready-meals and overflowing ashtrays.

A stench of sweat and dirt and resignation.

Malin and Zeke are sitting on ladder-backed chairs on either side of a rustic old pine table, its top covered in burn marks, and on the kitchen worktop a jumble of knives surrounds a portable single-ring cooker.

Arto Antinen sits down opposite them.

'I was living here during the period you're interested in,' he says. 'I moved in when I got out in November, but I don't know anything about the girl you found in the forest. I've got nothing to do with that.'

'Why did you move here?' Malin asks.

'I wanted to make a fresh start,' Arto Antinen says. 'I'd lived in Kisa all my adult life, but I wanted to start again.'

In which case you weren't living here when Maria was raped, Malin thinks.

'So you don't know anything about the girl we found murdered?' Zeke asks in a calm, reassuring voice.

'No, why would I?'

'We're just wondering, as I'm sure you can understand. You do have, after all, a history of using violence against women, don't you, Arto?'

Zeke tries to make the words sound friendly, and the pupils of Arto Antinen's eyes contract, and Malin can feel his anger spread through the room.

'Fucking hell,' he says, glancing greedily at the half-full bottle of vodka on the worktop.

'She wanted it, the cunt,' he whispers. 'Then made up a load of crap about rape.'

'The court believed her,' Zeke says. 'You were convicted.

And it doesn't really seem very likely to us that she wanted to spend a whole weekend tied to a bed.'

'It's OK to feel ashamed,' Malin says. 'You took your punishment like a man.'

Arto Antinen's shoulders seem to droop slightly, and his undernourished body seems to deflate.

'I'm on pills,' he says.

'For depression?' Zeke asks.

Arto Antinen shakes his head.

'Antabuse?' Malin asks, already aware of what pills he's taking.

'The other ones,' Arto Antinen says. 'The ones that stop you having sexual impulses.'

Sexual impulses.

He uses the formal term, making it sound less real, Malin thinks. It makes what he did less true, the memory less unbearable.

'I know what I did. And I don't want to do it again. It's better for me not to feel anything. Better for everyone.'

'Did you have to agree to that?' Zeke asks. 'As a condition of your parole?'

Arto Antinen shakes his head.

'OK,' Malin says. 'But we'd still like to take a DNA sample from you, so we can clear you of any involvement in this case.'

Arto Antinen's pupils get even smaller.

He clenches his small fists so hard that the knuckles turn white.

'Like hell,' he whispers. 'I've paid for my crime. I'm trying to be a better person, doesn't that give you the right to be believed? I haven't got a damn thing to do with the woman you found in the forest. I'm not letting anyone have my fucking DNA. You're not getting a single strand of hair from me.'

'If you're innocent, it can hardly do any harm,' Malin says.

Thinking: I don't give a damn about your so-called integrity.

Arto Antinen flies up.

Overturning the table and sending their coffee flying, and Malin just manages to avoid the cascade of hot black liquid as she and Zeke quickly get to their feet.

'That's enough. Get the fuck out of here if you haven't got anything else to say!'

Arto Antinen is shouting at them from over by the cluttered sink.

Zeke holds his hands up.

'We're going,' he says. 'But don't you worry. We'll be back with a warrant from the prosecutor.'

There.

There's the advert.

It's ten past eleven when Johan Jakobsson reads the advert on the website of the *Swedish Hunting* magazine.

'Luxury hunting cabin available to rent for deer hunting on the Sjölunda estate, Östergötland. Call for pictures and rates.' Followed by a phone number.

Sjölunda.

The estate is owned by Count Peder Stålskiöld.

Johan Jakobsson had never heard the name before it was mentioned at the meeting. This Stålskiöld must keep a low profile.

The neighbouring estate to Stjärnorp, some ten kilometres further around Lake Roxen towards Finspång, from where they found Woman X.

Malin and Zeke.

Weren't they going in that direction? Wasn't that what was agreed at the meeting?

Now there's a good reason to pay a house-call.

He picks up the phone and calls Malin.

Malin's mobile rings as they're walking the short distance from Arto Antinen's cottage to their parked car.

Above them a grey, almost black covering of cloud is threatening to drown the world with its contents.

She answers.

Johan Jakobsson tells her about the count, the cabin, and that the advert was first listed on 1 November.

'We'll head over there. We're pretty close,' Malin says.

They hang up.

Zeke has the driver's door open.

'What do you think about the lunatic in there, then?' he asks. 'Has he got anything to do with this?'

'Who knows?' Malin says. 'We'll have to get that DNA sample sorted. Then we'll know for sure.'

'I'll call Sven,' Zeke says. 'He can take it up with the prosecutor.'

Maybe the request will end up being dealt with by Karim Akbar's prosecutor, Vivianne Södergran.

The career bitch.

The academic.

The beautiful and successful and interesting and enchanting woman who's clearly on her way somewhere in life.

Malin has disliked her from the moment she first set eyes on her.

But why do I actually dislike her so much? Malin wonders as she opens the door on her side of the car.

She hasn't done me any harm, but I still can't stand the sight of her.

A powerful gust of wind comes shooting out from the forest, as if a flat whirlwind were rushing through the trees, cold and hard, and hits her and Zeke with full force as they stand by the car, making them almost lose their balance in the sudden blast.

What was that? Malin wonders.

She feels her heart and stomach move closer together, as if a powerful jaw had grabbed her and were trying to bite deep into her.

Then the words come to her.

A lone woman's words.

'Save me.'

'Help me.'

And Malin knows that the woman is waiting for her, that she's somewhere nearby, waiting to be rescued.

It's urgent, Malin thinks.

We've got to hurry.

This comes down to me, me and no one else.

The words crackle through her body, like a shock from a dying cable.

13

A fox, perhaps two metres long, its coat glossy and slick, closes its jaws around the pheasant's long neck, apparently trying to press it into the ground, whispering in its ear: Can you feel the air vanishing?

You're the one dying, you're dying.

The old, varnished oil painting is hanging on a grey stone wall above an open fireplace that's two metres high and the same across.

A closely woven rug with a colourful Arabian pattern is lying in front of the hearth, and around it there are three worn, brown leather armchairs. And in them sit Malin, Zeke and Count Peder Stålskiöld, eldest son of the Stålskiöld family, heir to the whole estate of Sjölunda, no more, no less.

The large room is gloomy, and what looked from the outside to be a modest yellow-stuccoed eighteenth-century house surrounded by espaliered larch trees is on the inside something quite different, a gothic cave where dark, enclosed rooms follow one after the other, apparently without end, and what little daylight there is filters in through gaps in heavy, brown velvet curtains.

The count had asked them in.

Dressed in muddy jeans and a stained flannel shirt, he looked like an ordinary farmer, just back from the barn.

'Dreadful,' he said as he showed them into the sitting room after they explained why they were there. 'Dreadful.

It was just a few kilometres from my property where they found her, on Fridman's land, if I've understood correctly.'

They took their places in the sitting room, in front of the unlit fireplace.

The count was in his mid-fifties, and unlike a lot of tall men he seemed to be in full control of his body; lithe and sinuous, it looked as if it had been shaped by hard work. His face was the same, thin, bony, weather-beaten, but you could discern a long and unbroken line of beautiful women in his features.

'We're talking to everyone in the area,' Zeke says, lifting the glass of lemonade that the housekeeper had just brought in, three tall, slender glasses on a tin tray.

'So I understand,' Peder Stålskiöld says. 'That's how you do things, isn't it?'

'I assume you have a good idea of what goes on around here,' Malin says, trying to make it sound like a compliment.

'Worse than you, I'd imagine. People keep their distance.'

'Have you heard or seen anything, anything at all, that could have some connection to the murdered woman in the forest?'

The count leans back in his armchair, looks up at the painting of the fox, and rubs his hands on his jeans, picking at a bit of dried mud.

'No,' he says.

Appears to reflect.

'No. Nothing at all.'

'We saw an advert,' Zeke says. 'In *Swedish Hunting*. About a hunting cabin on the estate. Has it been rented out at all?'

'It was only rented once,' Peder Stålskiöld says. 'I've had very few enquiries, and they all thought it was too expensive. We're still going through hard times. People are careful with their money. But I don't want to lower the price, because then I'd just attract the wrong sort of people. So the cabin has stood unused.'

'It wasn't rented out in December, or at the end of November?' Zeke asks.

And Malin sees Peder Stålskiöld become restless, a hint of anger in his eyes, then he smiles again.

'Like I said, it's been standing empty. You can see it if you like.'

'That won't be necessary,' Malin says. 'We're just trying to find out who might have been in the area when the crime is thought to have been committed.'

'And they or he or she might have hired a hunting cabin?' Peder Stålskiöld fills in.

'For instance,' Malin says.

'Or just been passing through,' Peder Stålskiöld goes on. 'Anyone at all could have just been passing through, couldn't they?'

Neither Malin nor Zeke responds, aware of how broad their search is right now, as if they're shooting at a target from afar with a sawn-off shotgun, hoping that at least one piece of shot will hit the truth, and, if not actually bring it down, then at least slow it down enough for them to catch up with it.

'For the time being,' Malin says, 'we're not ruling anything out.'

And she curses herself for explaining anything to Peder Stålskiöld, seeing as they didn't exactly do that with Arto Antinen.

Equal before the law?

Hardly.

Justice doesn't exist.

Justice is an invention of the rich to keep the masses in check, make them believe in the concept, that the world is moving in that direction, when it's actually heading the opposite way.

'Peder! Peder!' a shrill voice suddenly cries.

Malin turns around.

In the doorway stands a slim, uptight-looking woman in her fifties, dressed in riding clothes and shiny, black leather boots.

Her skin is stretched tightly over her cheekbones, and Malin thinks she looks as if she's had a facelift. She must have been beautiful once, but now she mostly looks rather careworn.

'Have you sorted out the waitresses for dinner this evening?'

Peder Stålskiöld looks away from them and turns to the woman.

'It's all arranged, darling.'

Then the woman turns around and disappears into the darkness.

'My wife,' Peder Stålskiöld says. 'Victoria.'

'Charming,' Malin says, and the count's face doesn't move a muscle.

'The children are at boarding school in Sigtuna,' he goes on.

'My daughter's at Lundsberg.' Malin feels the words fly out of her mouth by themselves, doesn't want to say it, doesn't want to justify herself to this person.

Yet she still does so.

'I almost want to ask how that came about,' Peder Stålskiöld exclaims, then he smiles a crooked smile, and Malin is astonished at the insult, and Zeke says: 'Is there anything else you could tell us that you think we should know? Any vehicles you've seen? Any rumours you've heard?'

Peder Stålskiöld closes his eyes.

Opens them again ten seconds later, stares first at Malin, then at Zeke.

'No, I'm afraid not.'

Then he stands up.

'You'll have to excuse me. I've got a field to plough.'

The count slaps his hands together restlessly, and Malin feels like jumping on him, getting him in a stranglehold and teaching him a thing or two.

But manages to restrain herself.

'Well, I'll call if I think of anything.'

And Malin wants to ask him about Maria Murvall, if he knows anything about her, if he even remembers her, the woman who disappeared from life in the forests around here.

'Well, then.'

But she stays silent. Thinking that she'll have to ask about Maria on a later occasion, if it becomes relevant to the investigation.

They watch Peder Stålskiöld disappear into one of the large, yellow-painted barns over at the edge of the forest, and Malin imagines she can hear a thousand cows lowing, their pus-dripping udders full of infected milk.

Below them they can see Lake Roxen, calm and black, waiting for rain.

A man in overalls is heading in their direction across the farmyard, and Zeke waves him over, introduces himself and Malin, and wonders if they can ask a few questions.

A bearded face, shoulder-length hair, in his forties. The man introduces himself as Victor Johansson, as his gaze flits anxiously beyond them.

'You work here?' Zeke asks.

'Yes,' the man says. 'As a farmhand. A labourer, as people used to say.'

Victor Johansson has nothing to tell them either, about the murder in the forest, about the woman's body that was discovered by a father and his two children while they were out looking for morels.

'The hunting cabin,' Zeke says. 'Do you know if it's been rented out?'

'What did the count say?'

The question comes quickly, and Malin replies just as fast.

'We'd like your answer.'

'Not that I know of,' Victor Johansson says. 'As far as I know, it hasn't been used at all.'

Victor Johansson pulls out a pair of dark sunglasses. Puts them on, even though the sky is covered with cloud.

Blindness, Malin thinks as she sees her own reflection in the lenses. Are you one of the blind, Victor Johansson?

'Are you sure?' she asks.

'Was that all?' Victor Johansson says, before turning away and leaving them alone in the yard, as the first bloated, chill drops begin to fall from the sky.

Can you feel the rain?

I can't.

I can't feel things like that any more.

Have those men, Arto, Peder, or maybe Victor Johansson, got anything to do with how I ended up in the forest?

Have they got anything to do with Maria?

Have they got anything to do with the other mute woman?

Do you think you can save us, Malin? You think you can, don't you, and it seems to me that you're enjoying this cold rain, the way it hits your cheeks and trickles through your blond hair and down your neck, and Zeke is standing over by the car, yelling at you to get a move on, you're crazy to be standing out in the rain.

You're not crazy, Malin Fors.

I'm not crazy.

No other woman is crazy either.

Someone cut a hole in me.

Violated me.

It's the world that's crazy, Malin, the world is crazy. Completely fucking insane.

'Shouldn't we take a look at the cabin anyway?'

The rain is drumming hard and insistently on the car roof, the vehicle still stationary in the farmyard.

Zeke's question broken up by the noise.

'Yes, we should,' Malin says, digging out the count's phone number, and without a hint of emotion in his voice, without a hint of protest, he tells them how to get to the cabin.

'You'll find the key on a hook at the back, under the floor by the western gable.'

The rain is pouring down as they run from the car towards the little red wooden cabin, which looks as if it must have been lowered from a helicopter into a hollow between two dense sections of forest, and ground and sky seem to merge together in the hollow as the firs and birches sway to and fro in the rain, trembling in a damp, veiled mist.

'Bloody hell,' Zeke says.

They're both soaked.

Their clothes are clinging to their bodies, and they're coughing and swearing. The key is where it should be.

Malin grabs it, feeling the cold metal against her fingers, and she fumbles in the wet, but they're soon inside the musty cabin.

A small kitchen, with Gaggenau appliances, real oak parquet floors, the trademark blue squares of Hästens mattresses in the two double bedrooms.

A marble table, a low beige sofa and a massive flat screen television.

'Not much here,' Zeke says, and Malin has a sense of

being in the cleanest room she's ever been in, that someone with an unhealthy cleaning obsession has been at work in a vain attempt to disinfect the world. Control it.

But she doesn't say anything.

Breathes, sniffs, tries to see, hear, remember.

Tries to be present in the moment, to understand what's happened here, to hear the voices that she knows want to tell her something.

Was I here in this cabin?

Were we here, Maria and I?

Are our fates intertwined? Aren't all our fates intertwined?

But how should we know if we were here? You saw my injuries, Malin, Maria's injuries. Injuries like that erase everything else.

Someone misses me.

Unless I'm missed by no one?

What if no one misses me?

Remembers me?

But no one wants to remember me.

The rag doll.

Violated.

But you miss me, Mum, don't you?

But are you capable of missing anything in your current state?

I want to touch your cheek, Mum, I see you on that hard bunk now and I want to stroke your cheek, lie and say that everything's all right, that everything's going to be all right.

That nothing bad has ever happened to us.

That we can wipe out the past.

Then everything would be fine, wouldn't it?

14

They drove back in silence, towards the station, watching the edge of a rain-front drawn like a dividing line right across the Östgöta plain. The fields rippled back and forth in waves so vast that they seemed to have come from some distant ocean.

Zeke at the wheel, his eyes glued to the road.

First rain, then sun.

Then rain, then no rain again.

As if the world were changing from moment to moment.

Zeke didn't put any music on, and Malin was relieved not to have to listen to yet another German choir muttering some long forgotten chunk of Wagner.

She spent the drive resting.

Thinking.

Maria.

What happened in the forest?

Malin thought of the file she's got on the case in her flat. The folder is bulging, swollen with documents, notes, pictures, maps of the paths Maria might have stumbled on through the forest, possible routes for the cocoon of pain and violence that someone or something had turned her into.

Had the devil been waiting for her in the forest? An unknown, evil force for which we mortals have no name?

Malin had walked the various routes, following her marks on different maps, going back on her own to the place where Maria had been found.

Peering into a lot of buildings.

Drawing a line on the map to show how far Maria could have walked.

Map and compass in her hand, her own desire for certainty the driving force as she set out across country, through rain-wet moss and damp chill and isolation and fear of what could be hiding behind every tree trunk, every nest of roots, every rock.

She had walked in ten, twenty different directions, all points of the compass had carried her footsteps.

Sometimes she had felt that someone or something had been watching her, following her through the forest, trying to weigh her up before an attack, and she had vainly drawn her pistol out there alone in the vegetation, yelling into the black spaces, into the gaps between the tree trunks: 'Is there anyone there? Whoever you are, show yourself!'

But no one had shown themselves.

Nothing or no one.

And what had she been hoping to find? An entrance to hell? Beelzebub's lair, where an eight-headed human monster that devoured women was lying in wait for its next victim? A hidden hunting cabin, an unremarkable little red cottage with white gables where an unremarkable man sat waiting, ready to confess that he had lost control in the forest one day and done that to Maria Murvall?

Violated her.

Cut her open.

Cut her mute, dragging her away from life, to a space between life and death.

Zeke stopped the car outside the station.

The clock on the dashboard said it was a quarter past three, they'd stopped for lunch in the café in Ljungsbro.

He was heading home to be there when a workman

arrived, but she was planning to fit in a quick session down in the gym.

'Take it easy now,' he said as he dropped her off. 'I know what you're thinking.'

Malin nodded.

'You've got to let go of Maria Murvall. If you're ever going to find out what happened to her, first you have to stop thinking about it. You know that, don't you? Only then will you be able to see clearly again.'

He was right.

Obsession doesn't help anyone.

Clarity of thought, on the other hand, does.

'I'll try, Zeke. I'll try.'

Malin realises that she still hasn't told Zeke about her trip to Stockholm. Maybe he'll see it as a betrayal, but that can't be helped.

The addiction is always there.

And the madness.

If you can't drink, you need something else to occupy your mind, the innate restlessness of your being, nervousness or whatever the hell you want to call it.

That's how she chooses to see her obsession with what happened to Maria Murvall.

That's how Malin explains to herself the fact that she is once again standing in the corridor outside Maria Murvall's room in Vadstena Hospital, that she is here instead of at home with someone who loves her, longs for her, wants nothing more than to hold her in his arms.

She's still sweating from her hard session in the gym.

Maria's doctor, a consultant called Elena Kaczynski, has grown accustomed to her visits, and has said that she can go and see Maria whenever she likes, if nothing seems to be going on.

But what could possibly be going on?

Mute, she eats what she needs to.

Allows herself to be dressed. Wakes, sleeps, breathes. And breathes again and again and again.

Mutely she allows herself to be showered twice a week.

Goes to the toilet.

But throughout everything she is silent, registers nothing, her pupils occasionally follow the light, but it's as if they only absorb what Maria wants them to.

She reacts to noise, but doesn't seem to hear, unwilling or unable to understand words, words said by the voices that come close to her.

And who comes?

Her brother Adam. The only one of the brothers who seems able to handle seeing his sister sitting there like that.

Her mother Rakel had never been, and Malin saw the notice of her death in the *Correspondent* ten months ago.

Rakel Murvall.

The woman who tried to control her world with an iron grip.

Gone now.

Maria's door, the white-painted door in front of Malin, isn't locked, doesn't need to be locked, because Maria doesn't go anywhere.

She could come and go as she liked.

But she stays.

Winter, summer, autumn and spring. Sun, storm, rain, driving snow.

The passage of time has no meaning for Maria Murvall.

She lives in a season of her own.

A season in which everything is possible, yet simultaneously nothing. A season of inverted emotions. Dead emotions.

This season has a name, Malin thinks.

The fifth season.

'Are you there, Maria?'

Is she there?

She has blood, muscles, sinews and cells, a chemical process that refuses to stop.

Maria doesn't even try to commit suicide.

For the simple reason that she might already believe herself to be dead, Kaczynski had once said.

But no, you're not dead, Maria, Malin thinks as she gently pushes the door to Maria's room open and walks in.

Outside the window is an anonymous grey, two-storey hospital building with a red tiled roof, beneath a sky that seems ready to declare the day over.

'Maria, it's me.'

And Maria is sitting on her bed, wearing white hospital trousers and a faded, cheap pink cotton blouse, and she's sitting with her knees pulled up, her blond hair, neatly brushed, hanging down over her shoulders, her blue eyes staring out into nothing.

She takes no notice of me, Malin thinks, not that I was expecting her to.

Or was I?

What am I doing here? Why am I here again?

Had I been hoping that the woman we found in the forest, the woman I saw in Lund who's just like you, might have brought you back to life? That you might finally wake up, and come back from the strange place you're in?

In vain.

Seeking an answer to the mystery to which I'm seeking an answer is nothing but vanity.

And somehow I'm going to be punished for my vanity.

Malin takes a few steps forward, the room is warm and damp, smells of sweat.

She sits down on the end of the bed.

On a white crocheted bedspread.

Looks into Maria's eyes.

Blink, blink, blink.

Light breathing, automatic.

Blink.

Blue, blue, blue, and the way her hair is arranged covers the scars on Maria's forehead, and the thick red reminders on her neck.

'What happened?' Malin asks. 'Try to remember, Maria, what happened to you in the forest?'

She synchronises her breathing with Maria's.

The blinking of her eyes.

What do you see, Maria? What do you think, feel?

Where did your clothes end up? Who were you running from? Are there more women?

But presumably that's the whole point of this, that you don't want to feel anything, and you've perfected that now.

You're adrift, aren't you? Floating outside your own body.

You're the aura of light around a world condemned to eternal darkness, cursed by its own actions.

15

A cluster of flies is dancing in the last remnants of the daylight.

Malin switches on her mobile as she emerges into the car park at Vadstena Hospital.

Ten cars stretched out in front of the expanse of Lake Vättern, and a new front of cloud is on its way up from the south, a rolling wall that looks like storm clouds against the evening-dark sky.

There's a smell of sulphur and freshly lit barbecues.

One message.

She listens to it as she opens the door of her white Golf.

'Sven here. I just wanted to let you know that I've decided to release the picture of Woman X to the media. Karim agrees. We've got nothing to go on as far as her identity is concerned, nothing's changed during the course of the day, so we have to take the next step. I just thought you should know. It ought to be on this evening's news. And, for your information, the search of the forest today didn't produce any results.'

So quick.

She erases the message, thinking that this is the right move, the investigation has to move on somehow, they mustn't get stuck at the start or else they might never make any progress.

She thinks about the drifters.

Lonely souls.

Kristina.

The toilet, full of rutting, crowing teenage boys.

Kristina the Slag.

Always that name.

And if Woman X in the forest is a Kristina, then surely someone will recognise her picture in the media, and tell them who she is? Won't they?

Or can a young woman become completely invisible? Can derision and mockery and possibly violence and abuse, the shame of eyes looking away, make a girl invisible, forgotten for ever?

Malin wants to answer no.

But knows that the answer is yes.

We choose to forget.

Not to see.

Ignore feelings. Stick to facts, Fors.

You couldn't have done anything for Kristina, if that was even her name.

Method.

Motive.

Opportunity.

We don't actually have the answers to any of those. We don't know what sort of weapons the murderer used, we haven't got a bloody clue about the motive, or how he found the opportunity to carry out the murder, and I'm standing here, not a single step closer to any answers, in this god-forsaken car park.

A car pulls in.

Stops a dozen or so metres away in one of the few free spaces.

A rusty yet well-maintained blue Vauxhall, practically an antique, and Malin has an idea whose car it is, and then the door opens and a large man gets out and walks straight over to her with firm, almost threatening steps, his prominent chin emphasised by the cropped hair that he seems to have taken to cutting himself.

'You're here again,' Adam Murvall says, and his voice is gentle, careful, not hostile or aggressive, the way it can be.

He's dressed in shabby jeans and a green tracksuit top.

'How is she?' he asks, and Malin wonders what he means by his question. Adam Murvall looks like a thug, but Malin knows better than to underestimate him.

She shakes her head.

'Nothing,' she says.

Adam Murvall narrows his small, blue-black eyes, and seems to be peering off towards the waters of Lake Vättern.

'I heard you found another woman in the forest,' he says.

Malin nods.

'And now you think there's some connection between them? Between her and Maria?'

'I don't think anything,' Malin says.

'I know you. We haven't used the hunting cabin up in the forest for several years. Not since, well, you know. And it's a fair way from where you found the new woman, isn't it?'

He's talking about when our paths crossed a long time ago.

When he and his brothers blew up their half-brother with hand grenades out in the forest, but there was no conclusive evidence, and all they managed to pin on them was poaching and possession of illegal weapons.

'There's no need for you to worry, Adam,' Malin says. 'I don't think you, any of you, have anything to do with this.'

'No?'

He gives her a sardonic smile.

The weary smile of the incorrigibly lawless, which says: Don't trust the law, it's always treacherous, unreliable.

'You can still bear to visit her? After all these years?' Malin asks.

'She's my sister. If I abandon her she'd have no one.'

Malin swallows.

Feels like saying: She's got me, but knows that isn't true. I've got Maria, but she hasn't got me. I need Maria, and what happened to her, but she doesn't need me.

So you need her as well, Malin thinks. Unless you're afraid, Adam?

She looks at the thickset man in front of her.

He's no longer squinting.

Afraid of what Maria might say?

Is that why you come here?

Or do you feel guilty? Do you think you should have been able to protect her? Protect your little sister?

'I saw that your mother passed away. My condolences.'

Adam Murvall shakes his head.

'It was high time,' he says. 'The old bitch had done more than enough damage to last ten lifetimes. It was time she went to hell.'

They stand there facing each other.

She imagines she can hear Adam Murvall's heart beating, beating like a tightly clenched fist on a door that will never be opened.

It's banging, his heart.

Out of despair?

Fear? Something else?

'Thank you,' he suddenly says. 'Thank you, Malin Fors, for caring about what happened to Maria.'

Adam Murvall turns away.

Walks off towards the entrance to the hospital, towards his mute sister.

Malin stares off at the grey-black wall of cloud.

Closer now.

Greedy, starving.

As if it wanted to devour the whole world.

★ ★ ★

The *Correspondent*'s website.

Malin is sitting in the dark in her bedroom, looking at the front page of the newspaper's website, and there's the picture of Woman X, Karin's perfect photograph, which almost makes her face look alive, shamelessly beautiful.

An article, without a byline, saying that the police are appealing for information about the woman's identity.

Daniel Högfeldt hadn't called. Maybe he's got a new source in the police? It would be a relief if he has, Malin thinks. She can't handle his intense, persistent voice.

Peter.

She had expected him to be waiting for her in the flat, and didn't call to check, but it turned out that he was the on-call doctor that night and there'd been a car accident and one of the victims needed an immediate operation.

So now I'm sitting here alone in the darkness, Malin thinks. Then she thinks about the woman, the girl in the photograph in front of her, and the fact that someone, perhaps her mum or dad, is now looking at the picture and feeling their stomach clench, feeling all their faith in the goodness of life explode.

The picture is shown on the television news as well.

With a number to call if you have any information.

Woman X.

The hole in her stomach. Who would do something like that?

Penetration. The male newsreader doesn't mention any of the details.

Malin turns off the television. Wishes Peter could come home, that he's fixed that patient.

I could do with a fix, a big fucking drink, she thinks, and feels the itch in her bones, her whole body, and a voice inside her is saying: 'Just one drink, Malin. That wouldn't do any harm, just one shot of tequila, if you haven't got any in the flat there's some down in the Pull & Bear pub. They've got all you need to stop feeling anything.'

To stop her feeling that she's not getting anywhere with her life.

That she has a responsibility for Maria. The other women. That she has a responsibility to dare to do things, to feel things.

You can't live without feelings, Malin thinks.

Because that's no life at all.

That's why people don't really try to save children born before the twenty-first week of pregnancy. Because they're not capable of the most basic feeling, they haven't even developed the survival instinct.

But I have.

I have to get rid of this thirst.

Ten minutes later her heart is pounding and she's sweating hard.

She's racing along the bank of the Stångån River in the very last remnants of the day's light, in her second bout of exercise for the day.

She runs on.

Trying to run from all the thoughts and reach one single, simple feeling of here and now, in the moment.

16

The blue of the early morning sky is solid, as if someone had poured varnish across the whole of the firmament to preserve this particular moment of clear sky for the future, as a memory of how simple yet incomprehensible the world can seem at certain moments.

Waldemar Ekenberg and Börje Svärd are walking through the old military barracks that have been converted into flats. They do this occasionally, Waldemar picks Börje up from his house out in Tornhagen, and they leave the car there and quickly walk the two kilometres to the police station, talking about anything but work.

But this morning work intrudes.

And, as a cold northerly wind drives through the barracks and forces its way through Waldemar's shabby brown cord jacket and Börje's blue anorak, Waldemar says: 'I've never felt it this strongly.'

Börje sees a woman emerge from a door in one of the former barrack blocks. She's wearing a red coat, and she looks scared, as if someone is chasing her.

He knows what Waldemar means.

'If we get hold of the man who killed that girl, I don't know what I'd do. I just pray that I'm not the first person to catch him.'

Börje can hear the seriousness in his voice.

And doesn't feel like stopping him.

He knows that life sometimes makes unreasonable demands, and remembers how his wife Anna, desperately ill with MS, begged him to switch off the respirator several times towards the end, and how he had wanted to, but couldn't do it.

'I'll just have to make sure I get to him first,' Börje chuckles.

'I'm serious.'

'I know,' Börje replies. 'You'll just have to do what you have to do.'

Another door opens. Another woman, the same age as Malin. She doesn't even glance in their direction.

'Sometimes I get so tired of all the pissing about,' Waldemar says quietly.

'What pissing about?'

'The way we piss about with people who've done bad things. We both know that it doesn't do any good, trying to be understanding. Maybe we should do the opposite. Destroy them. There are certainly times when it would feel good, that much is obvious.'

'You know what?' Börje says. 'You're crazy, Waldemar.'

But this time he doesn't laugh.

And his partner doesn't smile either, and they lengthen their stride slightly, moving more quickly towards Linköping Police Station.

Malin got to the station early that morning.

Had a quick cup of instant coffee standing up in the kitchen. Peter had gone back to his own apartment to sleep after the operation had dragged out.

It's a quarter past eight now, and Malin is sitting at her desk in the office in the police station.

Waiting for the others to arrive. She's just said hello to Börje Svärd and Waldemar Ekenberg as they came in together, the way they sometimes do.

They've gone to get coffee from the kitchen.

Zeke's late, he's usually here earlier than this. Sven Sjöman is probably in his room preparing for the morning meeting at nine o'clock. Johan Jakobsson will be on his way after dropping the kids off at school and preschool.

Expressen's website.

They're leading with the woman's photograph.

Malin clicks to close the window.

No tip-offs have come in overnight.

Publication of the picture hasn't yet given them anything at all.

Maybe their victim is from some distant country.

Or a girl from here, someone no one wants to acknowledge, someone everyone has forgotten.

Malin sees the phone on her desk start to flash, the ring has been broken for three weeks now, and she rather likes this silent flashing, this gentle way of requesting attention.

'Malin.'

The receptionist, Ebba.

'Ebba here. There seems to be someone who's got something to say about the picture. A woman, I can't really understand what she's saying. Do you want me to put her through?'

'Yes, put her through.'

'Police, yes?' a voice asks in English.

A young woman on the other end of the line.

Malin holds the phone tightly to her ear as she sees Zeke arrive opposite her, looking at her inquisitively, and she hushes him, holding up her hand to show that the call is important.

The accent is strong, Eastern European.

'Police, yes. Malin Fors, Detective Inspector.'

'I call the police, yes, saw picture yesterday of woman on TV, woman found.'

Malin tries to sound calm and suppress her excitement.

'Do you know her name?'

'Yes.'

The voice scared, haunted, defenceless.

'You know her name?'

'I can't tell you, but I know. I have to go now.'

'Wait.'

'No, they will notice I am gone.'

And the line goes dead and Malin feels the fear drifting out of the phone.

'We need to trace that call,' Malin says, and sees Zeke dial a number and hears him give some technical details.

'Yes, now, I want you to check right away. OK? I'm not hanging up until you check.'

His voice rough as sandpaper.

And just as gentle.

'Thanks,' she hears him say after five minutes of silent waiting.

He looks up at Malin.

'The call was made from a phone-box in Skäggetorp. The Skattegården block. They're all rental flats out there, aren't they?'

Linköping has plenty of hidden sides.

But Skattegården is one of its darkest shitholes.

The most neglected part of the Skäggetorp mass housing project, with run-down flats owned by a slum landlord.

Nothing could be further from the doctors' villas in Hjulsbro, or millionaires' row in Ramshäll.

'It was a woman,' Malin says. 'She spoke English with a thick Eastern European accent. Said she knew Woman X's name. That they'd notice she was gone if she talked any longer.'

They're both thinking the obvious.

Some immigrant girl who recognises her friend, so: is there a brothel in Skattegården? One we've heard rumours about, maybe even one we've been keeping an eye on?

Some flat to which the city's randy men make their way when the mood takes them?

'We need to get out there,' Malin says. 'Take a look around, ask questions, see if we can get hold of this girl.'

'We can bring it up at the morning meeting,' Zeke says. 'There's only fifteen minutes to wait.'

The playground outside the preschool is empty of children, but Malin can see them at morning assembly as well, sitting inside in a big circle on the floor, singing, their lips moving without any sound being audible.

As if she has gone deaf.

The world mute.

A world trying in vain to make itself heard.

Sven Sjöman quickly summarises the state of the investigation: the search of the forest hadn't come up with anything, but would be continuing today; they are looking through the results of the door-to-door inquiries (nothing); that Arto Antinen had refused to give a DNA sample, but that the prosecutor, Jonas Riedel, thank God, not Vivianne Södergran, Malin thinks, is going to sign a formal demand for a sample.

That was how they got the Haga Man, Malin thinks. By forcing him to give a DNA sample.

But is Arto Antinen our man?

Malin sees Sven's mouth move, and she tells them about their visit to Count Peder Stålskiöld.

But she says nothing about Maria Murvall for the moment.

Not a thing.

And none of the others raises that line of inquiry in the meeting, so she has no reason to bring up her trip to Stockholm.

But why shouldn't I mention it? I have to get it out some time, so I can see clearly again.

And she asks for permission to speak, then tells them about Fredrik Kantsten, the prosecutor who was supposed to have hurriedly shut down the investigation, and her trip to see him in Stockholm while she was on leave.

The others listen attentively.

She looks at Zeke while she speaks.

He gives no indication of being disappointed or angry that she hasn't said anything to him before. He seems to understand, almost to have known about what she did.

None of the others reacts either.

They just let the information sink in.

'The way things are at the moment, the connection is still very tenuous,' Sven says. 'But we'll have to bear it in mind. Right now our best option is to focus on what we've got to do next.'

'There could be a link between Woman X, Maria, and the woman in Lund,' Waldemar Ekenberg says. 'Are we dealing with a serial offender? The MO is fairly similar.'

Börje Svärd and Johan Jakobsson say nothing, don't seem to have quite processed all the information.

'We'll bear it in mind,' Sven says. 'No more independent excursions off-duty. We can't go bothering prosecutors like that. And it would have been good if the rest of us had heard about it earlier.'

There's no real emphasis in Sven's words. As if he doesn't really mean what he's saying, but is obliged to say it, and she knows that's the last she'll hear along those lines.

She changes tack.

Brings the group back to the present and tells them about her recent conversation with the woman with the east European accent.

And Waldemar says: 'Could be one of Woman X's whore friends.'

The lack of respect in Waldemar's words makes Malin angry.

What evidence is there that Woman X was a prostitute?

And even if she was, what right did a man like Waldemar have to talk about her in such a condescending way?

Then Malin realises that he might be right: it could very easily have been one of Woman X's sisters in misfortune who somehow got hold of a phone, wanting to tell what she knows.

Telling us in order to avoid the same fate herself? Malin wonders.

And she's aware that Waldemar uses that sort of language to create distance between himself and the gruesome crimes he has to investigate.

'I could kill whoever did this,' he goes on, and no one in the investigating team takes him to task for the brutality of his words.

Malin sees Waldemar's knuckles turn white as he clutches the edge of the conference table with both hands. She's feeling impatient, wants to get out to Skattegården now.

'We haven't got any of the flats out there under surveillance,' Johan says.

'We just have to carry on without any preconceptions,' Sven says. 'Börje and Waldemar, you take the last of the door-knocking around the forest, and you, Johan, keep looking for anything that might have been going on out there at the time in question. Leave no stone unturned. And we'll see if Karin can come up with anything else. Malin and Zeke, you get out to Skattegården, have a poke about out there.'

Skattegården.

Three-storey brick buildings with flat brown roofs, the blocks laid out right on the edge of the plain, as if the architect wanted the wind to be able to torment the poor bastards who were forced to live there. Neglected gardens, overflowing bins, playgrounds where no sane person would let their children play, and satellite dishes on every balcony.

On the way there Zeke said, with a degree of anger in his voice, that Malin could have told him about her trip to Stockholm, that as partners they aren't supposed to keep things from each other, because it makes them less effective as an investigative team.

'Fuck, Malin, tell me everything!'

'I will,' she assured him, and Zeke let the matter drop. She knew that was the end of it, out of everyone she'd ever met Zeke was the least likely to hold a grudge.

And I'm the most likely, she thought.

There's a strong smell of cooking lingering around the houses.

And it's noisy and full of life even at this time of day, at half past ten in the morning, when most of the residential areas in Linköping are quiet as the Marianas Trench.

The people she and Zeke encounter.

Young women in headscarves and full-length, all-enveloping dark dresses.

Henna tattoos on their feet.

Some in black burkas.

Coloured men who are trying to look busy, snotty kids running loose around the buildings, kids that seem to be looked after by no one and everyone.

They stop one of the men.

Show their ID.

'Have you noticed any flats where there are a lot of men coming and going?' Zeke asks. Doesn't mention anything about the woman who called, doesn't want to risk putting her in danger.

The man shakes his head.

Blind.

'You're sure?'

The man shakes his head.

Mute.

And the pattern repeats itself. No one has seen or heard anything, and they ring on a few doors at random in the area around the phone-box where the woman made the call.

Almost all the occupants are at home.

All answer with the same shake of the head.

No, they're not aware of anything like that.

And plenty of them are afraid.

As if people in authority had come and knocked on their doors before, with anything but friendly intentions.

Best to mind your own business.

Keep your head down.

Lie low.

Otherwise maybe I'll be thrown out of the country?

Malin and Zeke get back in the car. Look out at Skattegården. They soak up the atmosphere, but there are no men who don't seem to belong, no men with an eager, randy look in their eyes. No taxis pull up outside any of the doors to let out a love-starved engineer or doctor or preschool teacher or car accessory salesman.

Nothing.

And yet.

They could both feel it.

Something has happened here.

A black girl, maybe fourteen years old, her hair covered by a green and orange headscarf, her ample frame concealed by vividly patterned yellow and green fabric, with fashionable sneakers on her feet, stops by their car.

Looks at Malin and Zeke with big brown eyes in a round face.

Hesitating, as if she wants to say something to them, and

Malin looks at her, into the dark eyes that radiate intelligence and warmth.

'I'll go out to her,' Malin says, and Zeke nods.

'Go ahead. Looks like she's got something on her mind.'

Malin opens the door, and the young woman, the girl, doesn't move from her spot by a lamppost in front of a neglected hedge.

'Hello,' Malin says.

The girl returns the greeting, they shake hands, and she doesn't seem scared or defensive, just curious and focused.

'There is one flat,' the girl says.

Perfect Swedish.

And it occurs to Malin that she should be in school, but I won't worry about that, not now.

Malin nods.

Feels adrenalin rising in her body.

Lets the shared silence foster trust, and it's lunchtime, all the men, women and children who were around earlier are gone now. Malin can hear the clatter of plates and realises that they are alone, apart from Zeke inside the car.

But a thousand eyes can still see us, Malin thinks.

They're looking at us from their windows, everyone here, aren't they? And they want to be left alone.

But you, you're not worried that they might see you as a traitor, are you?

'What's your name?' Malin asks.

'Fatima. Fatima Sheikiru.'

'So where's the flat?'

Fatima looks at Malin, as if trying to gain her trust.

'A lot of men go there.'

Then she takes several deep breaths before saying: 'Try number 3B on Skattevägen. The ground-floor flat. She might be there.'

17

Three battered, brown veneer doors, the same white concrete on the floor and walls.

And a fourth door, at the end of the hall, its handle almost glowing in the gloom.

The doorbell radioactive.

'I can show you the way,' Fatima had said, but Malin and Zeke had said that wasn't necessary. So she had given them simple directions and the address. The flat was just around the corner, maybe seventy-five metres away.

'You'll find it OK,' Fatima had said.

'Did you see her make the call?'

'Yes.'

'How did she seem?'

'Scared. Stressed out.'

'And she could be in this flat?'

Fatima had nodded once more.

'It's the sort of flat men go to.'

Zeke had got out of the car and given her a long look of gratitude, then Fatima had left them, vanishing among the white brick buildings, into a door that led to another country.

And now Malin and Zeke are standing in front of a perfectly ordinary door made of faded plywood.

They've already rung several times.

But everything's quiet. No sign of life.

A faint smell of sulphur, as if a fire were smouldering

somewhere in the building, or as if someone had lit a thousand matches and was waiting for them to burn out.

A peephole is staring at them.

And they don't know what's hidden behind that hole, they've tried looking in through the letterbox but didn't manage to see anything, there's no name on the door, no post on the floor, just silence, and behind them a flight of steps leading upward in the liftless building. The black handrail could do with a coat of paint.

'What do you think?' Zeke says. 'Was she talking rubbish?'

'No,' Malin says.

'Do you think there's anyone in there?'

Malin nods.

Hushes Zeke.

Then she carefully pulls out her key ring from the pocket of her jeans, finds the picklock, thinking, we're going in, we can come up with an official justification afterwards.

The picklock in the door.

And she sees Zeke draw his pistol, feels her own against her chest.

There's something behind this door, Malin thinks.

There's something. I know there is.

The door opens.

Crouching beside it, Malin pushes it open and Zeke goes inside with his pistol held out in front of him.

Scans the empty hall, then moves further in, and then they hear the cries.

Agitated cries, captive cries, finally gaining the air they need.

Women.

Men.

One man?

How many women?

What language are they crying in? The language of anger and fear.

Russian, Ukrainian, and Malin lurches forward as she draws her own pistol, and she sees the hall as a tunnel, with swaying grey textured wallpaper, lined with rooms, and she realises how defenceless she and Zeke are, wide open to whatever violence may be inside the flat, and she pushes past him.

Where are the bodies behind the voices?

The first door in the hall.

She kicks it in.

Open.

She has her gun in front of her. In the darkness of the room is a bed, a wastepaper bin, but no people, and Zeke has moved on, and she follows him past an empty kitchen with piss-yellow cupboards, and the voices get stronger, then she sees something metallic reaching out from the doorway at the end of the hall, and she yells: 'DOWN! DOWN, ZEKE, for fuck's sake get down!' And she ducks, throwing herself onto the plastic floor and the shots from the pistol ahead of them are deafening, and she sees Zeke snake across the floor.

He knows what it's like to be shot, and then the gun is gone from the doorway and they hear voices, and is that a door opening?

Zeke has reached the doorway from which the shots came, he's inside the room and now she's there as well, and there's an arm reaching in from the open terrace door.

Zeke takes aim quickly.

Shoots from a lying position on the floor, at the hand holding the pistol through the terrace door, and he fires three times, and is sure he hits his target. But before the hand in the doorway drops the weapon it manages to fire another two shots, and then there's a different sort of scream, the scream of direct physical pain, impossible to hold back.

Has Malin been hit?

No.

And then Zeke sees a woman, or is it a girl, huddled on a sofa, an ugly green thing covered with flannel cloth in front of a filthy white wall, and he sees the handcuffs on long chains tying the girl to the radiator.

She's wearing black silk underwear that makes her pale skin glow white, and the girl is clutching her stomach, silent now, and blood is pouring and she must have been hit by the bullets from the man's pistol, the two shots, and Zeke sees Malin carry on towards the terrace door, kicking the pistol away from her on the floor, then she vanishes through the door, focused, as if there's no possibility in her world that the man who just shot at them, who wounded this girl, who has somehow been holding her captive in this flat, is going to get away.

I'm bleeding.

Blood is pumping out of my stomach.

Am I going to die now?

I don't want to die.

Is this my punishment for making the phone call?

Is this my punishment for not being able to protect you, for us not being able to protect each other?

Katerina Yelena presses her hands to the wound in her stomach. Feels the warm blood flowing out of her, as if she were nothing but a great big hole, and she slumps to one side, her whole body hitting the soft green fabric of the sofa, and she thinks it's nice to fall, landing in a soft, cotton-wool world.

This ends now, she thinks. It does, doesn't it? It has to end, doesn't it?

And then she sees the man, an unknown man, his face above hers.

The handcuffs mean that her arms are at an unnatural angle, but it no longer hurts when the metal cuts into her wrists.

But her stomach is burning.

As if a red-hot millipede were wriggling about in there, trying to get out.

The man's head is shaved. But he looks friendly nonetheless. As if he means well. But can there be any men who mean well?

Don't hit me, she thinks. I'll be quiet. It hurts, but I'll be quiet.

I've been shot.

I'm burning now.

And the fog is coming from the forest.

Drifting in across my eyes, making the world hazy, blurring its edges, and this is where it ends, isn't it?

This is the end.

Stop.

No more.

The end, my friend.

The man is running, twenty metres ahead of Malin.

He hasn't looked back, but Malin knows that the jeans-clad figure is aware that she's there, that she's chasing him, that she's after him, the bastard.

He must have realised she's armed, and that she's contemplating stopping and shooting him in the leg.

But she doesn't stop.

Has to close in on the bastard.

Run, faster than him.

And she glimpses the drops of blood on the ground, he's bleeding, must be from his hand, and he's fast. He darts to and fro between the buildings, as if he is trying to shake her off and hide in the confusion of satellite dishes and clattering plates.

I'm not getting any closer, Malin thinks three minutes into the chase.

Lactic acid is making her dull with pain, her lungs are panicking for oxygen.

I might actually be losing ground.

I should be able to do better than this.

I know I'm fast, in good shape.

He's thirty metres ahead of her now, and she feels her body becoming unresponsive, screaming for energy, and she curses it for letting her down, feels like drawing her pistol and firing at random to stop the bastard, whoever he is, this pimp – this murderer?

Could that be the murderer running ahead of her?

Thirty-five metres now.

She hasn't eaten since breakfast. Her energy is gone.

Thirty-seven.

He's going to get away, Malin thinks, and makes a final effort to speed up.

Lets her will take command of her body.

Running.

Fighting.

Trying to master the exhaustion and the lactic acid that is making every last one of her cells feel sick.

But it doesn't help. He disappears around a corner.

And as she rounds the corner she sees him far away between two blocks, on a narrow gravel path, and that's where the miracle happens.

A body swathed in colourful fabric emerges from between two bushes.

A sneaker kicks out.

In between the man's legs.

Knocking him to the ground.

The man screams as he falls.

Bellows.

Sounding like an animal that knows it's been caught.

The human monster will be put in a cage, the swine will be treated like the animal that it is.

Four seconds later Malin is pressing her pistol into a perfectly shaven cheek.

'Don't move,' she yells. 'Don't move! Do not move!'

He moves, tries to get up, tries, and Malin quickly raises the gun and hits the man hard across the nose, and she hears the bone break beneath the thin layer of skin, sees blood run from both nostrils, and the man is crying in pain now.

And lies still.

Fatima is standing a few metres behind Malin.

She's smiling.

Looks at Malin, who says: 'I've got a pair of handcuffs in the inside pocket of my jacket, you can help me put them on him if you like.'

Fatima moves towards Malin. Feels the headscarf tight around her head. Wants to put the cuffs on the man.

18

You're lying on a white sheet in a blindingly white room.

Chained by transparent tubes.

A transparent plastic mask covers your face all the way up to your closed eyelids.

You were my friend for a few short days.

We both know what fear is.

What dirt is, what it means to be deceived, to want a different life, but ending up with a feeling of being one of the living dead, or of actually being dead.

Because I'm dead.

But you, you're still fighting.

The wound in your stomach.

Can it ever heal? All your blood seemed to want to pour out of you, as if it were finished with your body, with oxygenating what turned out to be your life.

But you were also finished with that life, weren't you?

But perhaps something new lies ahead now.

I hope so.

For your sake.

But also for my own sake.

How could I bear it otherwise?

It has to be possible to change things, like your mechanical breathing and the life you're trying to hold within your flesh, the life you're desperately clinging onto, even though it wants to drift off and join me.

But you're not welcome here, not yet, and the man standing by your side in a white coat can keep you there.
He can do that.

Peter is standing beside Katerina Yelena's hospital bed, checking the pressure of the machine supplying oxygen to the young woman's breathing mask, and feeling satisfied with the job he's done. He can detect the smell of surgical spirit and blood lingering around her body like an invisible mist as he adjusts her nightdress and feels the soft white cotton between his fingers.

She's probably going to make it.

He didn't think she would when they brought her in, unconscious and almost drained of blood, with a gunshot wound in her abdomen where a nine-millimetre bullet had torn through her small intestine in several places before coming to rest deep inside her liver.

He spent three hours operating on her, they had to give her eight litres of blood, and her heart had stopped three times, but they got her back each time.

Liver.

Intestine.

Arteries, capillaries, nerves.

Everything could be repaired.

Foreign Minister Anna Lindh had died of injuries to her abdomen.

But he wasn't about to let this one, his patient, die. She was too young for that.

Peter strokes her arm, trying to instil calm through her anaesthetised state.

She can sleep a while yet, even if the police, his Malin, want to talk to her.

Evidently they've found the girl's passport, Ukrainian, in

the flat in Skäggetorp. It had been in a bag in the bathroom.

Malin had called when he got out from the operation and at that moment, as the tension and concentration dissipated, it had been good to hear her voice, even if she had started pressing him almost at once about when they could interview her.

The pimp hadn't started talking yet.

Russian.

Malin had chased him, and had been helped by a young immigrant girl.

She had told him all this over the phone, as if she'd been describing a trip to the supermarket.

And she had also described holding her pistol to the pimp's face.

'Is she going to make it?'

'Yes, probably.'

'Sure?'

'In all likelihood, yes. But she needs rest.'

He had heard in Malin's voice that she really cared, that this wasn't just a job, but somehow personal.

In front of him lay a recently operated woman whose life he had saved. And she was transformed before his eyes when he heard Malin speak: from a patient and a body to a human being, and it's as a human being that Katerina Yelena is lying in front of him now.

He strokes her arm again, and says: 'You can do this. You'll see, you can do this.'

Something warm on my skin.

A warm current in my ears.

My darkness is light, and I can sense that there's an angel here with me, unless it's something else? A gushing warm stream of heat, giving birth to my breaths for me, and I can see even though I'm blind, unless I'm asleep?

Everything's going to be fine.

I believe that.

And that's why I carry on, that's why I can't feel any pain, and just let the warm stream bubble deep into the core of me.

From her place in the observation room next to the interview room, Malin can see Waldemar Ekenberg and Zeke trying to work on the man she managed to capture out in Skäggetorp, with Fatima's help.

It's almost four o'clock now.

They found his passport in an old Adidas bag.

Andrei Darzhevin, thirty-two years old.

Russian.

His bandaged hand is resting on the grey table top, and the glow of the halogen lamps set into the black ceiling of the room make his face sharp and hard, as if he has been carved from a piece of flaming marble. His plastered nose juts into the light like a fragile, forgotten peak, and the eyes set deep in his skull are black, full of an almost instinctive defiance, but something else as well.

Sorrow? Resignation?

They know he can speak English, he swore at them, yelling as they put him inside the police van.

Patched up now, ready to be interrogated.

He's bloody lucky, Malin thinks, that it looks as if she's going to be OK, the woman in the hospital.

Otherwise we'd have him for premeditated murder, Malin thinks.

What if he wanted to kill her to shut her up, if he didn't hit her by mistake when he was aiming at us? That could be the case, even if it was unlikely. But we've still got him on attempted murder of a police officer and resisting arrest.

Sven Sjöman hadn't let her conduct the interview herself.

She's presumed to be too wound up after the chase out in Skäggetorp.

Instead she sees Waldemar silently hold the picture of Woman X up in front of the Russian pimp's face, because he is a pimp, the flat was set up as a small brothel, complete with condoms, diary, sexy underwear and bondage equipment.

Whips.

Studded belts.

Underwear with spikes on the inside.

Handcuffs, gags and nylon rope.

God alone knows what fantasies the men of Linköping indulged in that flat. What liberties they took. What power they gave themselves over other people, people presumably hardly worth even pissing on, in their opinion.

On the table of the interview room there are three other pictures.

Of a girl, some seven years old.

Portraits.

Cut out with a shaky hand. They found the pictures in the bag, and now Malin is wondering: Is that Andrei Darzhevin's own child, or, God forbid, a child who has been kidnapped to work for him?

But he's refusing to talk.

'Who is the child?'

Zeke's voice the sound of a rattlesnake.

'Where can we find her?'

Waldemar, on his feet now: 'You tell us everything! What do you know about this woman?'

And now what she's been waiting for happens. Waldemar loses patience and roughly grabs the back of the pimp's head, and Zeke doesn't move a muscle as Andrei Darzhevin's head is forced hard onto the table, and Malin puts her finger to the button on the wall in front of her, shutting off the noise, doesn't want to hear, but she does want to watch.

The tape and plaster on the pimp's nose bloody now.

Think of him as the pimp, not as Andrei.

Again and again, Waldemar Ekenberg presses the pimp's broken nose down onto the table, and Malin looks away, but knows what's happening, and part of her wants to cry out: STOP! while another part wants to shout encouragement: BEAT THE TRUTH OUT OF THE BASTARD!

In the end there's just a bloody mess of tape and plaster and possibly flesh, and Waldemar and Zeke give up and leave the room.

Waldemar is seething with adrenalin as he opens the door to the observation room.

'Bastard,' he snarls at Malin.

Zeke is right behind Waldemar.

'He's not saying a word.'

And Malin watches Waldemar's back as he disappears into the darkness of the corridor outside. Thinks about their Woman X. And the fact that she had evidently worked at the brothel, perhaps the young woman in Lund had been in the same profession? Maybe they had all encountered the same insane client? Was it the same rapist and murderer, and had he found his victims by posing as a customer?

But that doesn't fit with Maria. She was a perfectly ordinary social worker.

But among her clients?

Could there be something there?

Malin thinks, I've been through the list of her clients a thousand times. Nothing, there's nothing like that there.

I'm grasping at straws, Malin thinks. Seeing connections the way a madman has visions.

Sven Sjöman is sitting in his office, looking out over the car park in front of the hospital, enjoying the sight of the afternoon sunlight embracing the white and yellow façade, and the way the wind seems to be coming from above and rustling the crowns of the large birch trees as if they are tousle-headed urchins.

The people in the car park are walking steadily from or towards pain and anguish, and seem badly exposed to the world and all its evils.

The young woman who was shot is fighting for her life in a room inside the hospital.

Katerina Yelena.

With a serious gunshot wound to her stomach.

And presumably an even greater wound in her soul.

He doesn't want to be down in the basement and the interview room right now, doesn't want to know what's going on down there.

Let them do as they see fit. I'm tired of this now. Let them do what they have to do.

Karim Akbar thinks much the same.

Sven knows.

But Karim has to stay even further away from any misbehaviour, and a scandal would break if the media found out what went on in their interview room from time to time.

We, Sven thinks, the entire police force, are a distinct space.

And society needs that sometimes. A space where anything can happen, for the sake of results.

Most citizens understand that.

Most police officers.

But we have to use that space wisely.

Use our judgement, and seriously work out when to apply pressure. Believe that we have the capacity to work out when a bad act is good. As President Truman said when he gave the go-ahead to drop the atomic bomb on Hiroshima.

Two years left to retirement. Or more, if I like. But I want out now.

Everything's fluid.

I can't distinguish between events any more. My unshakeable certainty is gone.

You don't get wiser as the years pass, Sven thinks. You resign yourself to the fact that the world is completely grey, yet simultaneously black and white.

And you yourself – no one else, no collective – set the standard, the tone.

A boil full of pus, he thinks.

This case is a boil full of pus, it has been ever since Maria Murvall came staggering out of the forest like a dark woodland spirit, maybe even further back in time, but we still haven't seen anything of what could be coming, the forest might well be hiding the worst it's got from us.

He's sent a request to National Crime. To find out if they have any ongoing investigations that could be connected to theirs. To see if they know anything about the brothel, anything at all that could be linked to their work.

And he's just spoken to the prosecutor, Jonas Riedel.

The legal warrant against Arto Antinen is going to take a while. Jonas Riedel said he needed to check the space for manoeuvre.

19

Peter.

His open white coat looks like angel's wings by his sides; tired wings drooping to the ground as he walks towards her along the hospital corridor of intensive care ward nine.

The corridor is dimly lit at this time of the evening, but she can still make out the dimple in Peter's chin, his smile, and she's running now, Malin, wants to sink into his open embrace, let herself be enveloped by him, his scent, and the warmth that seems big enough for so many people.

Then she's there, and they hug, and his scent merges with the acrid smell of disinfectant, the sound of his breathing merges with the bleeping and hissing of all the machines keeping the ward's patients alive.

Keeping Katerina Yelena alive.

They kiss.

Peter tastes metallic, with a hint of coffee and cinnamon buns, and the presence of his hard, soft body brings her to life, makes her forget how long the day has been, and for a moment she wants to drag him into the nearest toilet, and let him fill her up the way that only he can.

Bleep.

Hiss.

People fighting for every breath.

That would be undignified.

Instead they let go, move a metre or so apart, and Malin asks: 'Is she conscious?'

The question means: Can I talk to her?

Peter shakes his head.

'But you can go in and see her, she's in room nineteen.'

'OK,' Malin says.

'You go ahead, I've got some final notes to dictate today, then we can go home together after that, OK?'

Katerina Yelena is lying in bed with an oxygen mask over her face.

Her abdomen is covered by a large bandage, and Malin can see her ribcage move up and down, up and down, and there's something calm about her breathing, as if she finally feels safe.

Her eyes are closed.

Sedated, still.

Malin takes a step closer to the bed, and sees that there's a cactus with downy thorns and a little red flower bud on the windowsill behind it.

She thinks of her brother, and Maria, and all the mute people she's trying to get closer to. And she wonders what this Katerina must have been through. And what false promises must have brought her here, to a brothel in Skattegården, where middle-class men from Linköping lived out their perverse fantasies on her as if she were their own private toy.

How many beatings?

How much pain?

How much humiliation?

You can help us get closer to the truth, I know you can, you can be a step on the path towards knowledge about what happened to Maria and the others, even if you don't know it yourself.

It was you who called us.

Wasn't it? About Woman X.

Is she from far away, like you? Or is she from around here? And ended up in the flat via a different route?

Fuck those men and all their fucking self-justifying desires.

Fuck them.

Who the hell do they think they are?

And Malin touches Katerina Yelena's arm, stroking it to indicate her presence, but as she touches the arm it's as if electricity, an unfamiliar arc of life, fills the room, and even though she's sedated, Katerina Yelena opens her eyes, and her hand jumps and she pulls off her mask, opens her mouth and tries to scream, but no sound emerges from her lips.

A rapid, intensive bleeping.

The alarm on the machine that's supposed to be giving her oxygen through the mask.

No one's breathing any more, the machine seems to think, and is panicking.

Malin tries to soothe Katerina Yelena, holding her arm and putting the mask back on her, but Katerina's muscles are cramping, her hand refuses to let go of the mask, and the soundless scream goes on.

Is that your scream? Maria's? The nameless woman in Lund's?

Woman X's?

You know who the dead woman is. Don't you?

The door opens behind Malin and she knows it's Peter and possibly someone else, and he gently moves her aside, checks the apparatus beside Katerina's bed, turns a valve and her cramps ease, her eyelids close and, just as quickly as she woke up, she's gone, in a deep, chemical sleep that no longer seems to give her any real rest.

'That shouldn't be possible,' Peter says, turning to Malin. 'Did you do anything?'

They're alone in the room, the nurse who assisted Peter has gone.

'I didn't do a thing.'

'She's heavily sedated, so that really shouldn't be possible,' Peter says again. 'She didn't really wake up, she was still asleep.'

'She seemed awake,' Malin says.

'She couldn't have been,' Peter says. 'Let's go, she needs peace and quiet.'

The lift down from the ward smells of rubber and dill sauce, and a body that you want to throw yourself at, hug so hard it becomes yours.

Peter is standing beside Malin in a pale blue shirt and jeans, a quick change, and they're going from the ninth floor down to the hospital lobby.

At the third floor, oncology, the lift stops and a mother gets in with two children, a boy and a girl of about five.

The boy, small and blond with serious blue eyes, smiles beseechingly at Malin, and she wonders if it's his dad who's ill, lying in a single room with cancer.

Daddy.

You mustn't die.

You mustn't die.

You've got to stay.

You're not supposed to abandon your children.

Then Malin has an idea.

Once the lift has stopped and they have got out she takes Peter's arm and stops him as he is about to stride off towards the hospital car park.

'I have to go to the station,' she says. 'I need to go.'

And he looks at her, seems to want to plead like the little boy in the lift, shout, curse, force her to put him first, put what they've got ahead of work.

'Bloody hell,' he says. 'It's nine o'clock, for God's sake, can't it wait till tomorrow?'

'No.'

'Please? I want to go home and relax. With you.'

'I've got to go,' Malin says, and he takes a step back and throws up his arms.

'In that case, what can I do?'

The look in his eyes unfathomable as he says those words.

Are you accepting it?

Or are you just pretending? Are you having doubts?

Have to get to the station.

They reach Peter's black BMW in the car park, then go their separate ways.

Malin sets off to walk the short distance from the hospital to the police station, where a few illuminated rooms glow like predators' eyes in the approaching night.

Where are the pictures?

Of the pimp's little girl.

Malin finds them in a folder on Waldemar Ekenberg's desk. She makes copies, then, with the copies of what might be Andrei Darzhevin's daughter in one hand, she goes through the underground passageways that lead to the detention cells adjoining the district courthouse.

She's soon standing outside the door of Andrei Darzhevin's cell.

A uniformed guard with a full, bushy brown beard puts a key in the lock.

Then remembers that he's forgotten something and doesn't turn the key.

Instead the guard looks through the spyhole, and says: 'Bloody hell. I can't see him.'

20

The guard tries to push the door open.

Shoves.

It won't open, and Malin joins in.

'Could he be lying out of sight of the spyhole?' she asks. 'Is there a blind spot?'

The guard sighs.

'Theoretically, yes, but you should still be able to see part of him.'

Andrei Darzhevin is big, Malin thinks, remembering how Waldemar had hit him, and how a doctor had come to patch up his nose for the second time that day, they said he'd tripped, exacerbating the injuries he suffered during the chase, and the doctor had looked disbelieving, but didn't appear to care overmuch about the well-being of the pimp.

Perhaps Andrei Darzhevin is lying dead behind the door.

Malin forces herself to think, knows the problems the pimp's death would cause, the missed opportunity to ask important questions, but she also realises that she wouldn't give a damn if they found him lying behind the door, choked on his own blood.

Fuck him.

She doesn't want to think about her emotional coldness, and how evil deeds make her cynical, because if evil really is contagious, what does that make her? She's worked as a police officer for fifteen years.

The pictures of the child.

She's still clutching them in her hand.

What if he is her father?

In cases like this, the child has a right to their father, no matter who he is. And she probably loves him regardless.

Andrei Darzhevin.

Make a human being of him.

Use his name.

And what do I really know about him?

Please, don't let him be dead.

And she and the guard push, shoving the door open, and they hear a grunt and then the resistance disappears and Malin sees Andrei Darzhevin crawl towards the bunk in the cell, its sheet bloodstained, his nose bandaged in white compresses and tape.

He looks at Malin.

Nods.

What does the look in those brown eyes show? Hatred? No. Anger? No, not that either, something else. Is that tiredness I can see, a longing for sleep?

'You can wait outside,' she tells the guard, and he leaves them alone, locking the cell door behind him, and Malin picks up the acrid smell of sweat from Andrei Darzhevin's body.

'I'll be outside,' the guard says through the door. 'I can hear if anything happens.'

I'm not the one who's scared, Malin thinks. Darzhevin, on the other hand, is probably scared of getting another beating.

Malin crouches down in front of Darzhevin, who is now resting on the bunk, lying on his side, the whole of his big body seems to have decided to retreat, yet somehow still not quite ready to capitulate entirely.

She puts the pictures of the girl in front of him.

The blond girl with the wide eyes, full of an apparently

boundless anxiety. A girl struggling in a world she can't make any sense of.

Malin talks calmly, in English, as best she can.

'This is your daughter, yes?'

No reaction.

Darzhevin just puts one hand over his nose, as if to stifle the pain.

'This isn't a girl you or anyone else has kidnapped. This is your child, Andrei.'

Andrei Darzhevin groans, seems to want to look away, but in the gloom of the cell he meets her gaze, determined to maintain his silence.

'I don't know where you live, or where you come from, but I know that wherever this little girl is, she wants to be with you, her daddy, and you want to be with her.'

Malin falls silent, feels her knees start to ache, as the lactic acid flows into her muscles because of the unnatural posture.

'You know,' she begins, and for a moment feels ashamed of the lie she's about to tell, but the ends, the damned ends, justify these bastard means.

And she says: 'If you want a new life, I can arrange for your daughter, your family, to join you here, and you can all have a new identity here in Sweden. You can move on, free from all the shit that your life must contain. You want out, don't you?

'But you have to talk to me, Andrei. Tell me who the woman we found in the forest is, because you know, don't you? Even if she was never in the flat in Skäggetorp, you know who she is. Maybe you know where she comes from as well? And who brought her here, who killed her?'

The look in Andrei Darzhevin's eyes becomes dull, as if he is trying to suppress everything he knows.

She leans closer to him and can smell his cloying, heavy

breath, can hear him breathing through his mouth.

'This is your daughter, isn't it? I can arrange for you to be with her.'

Andrei Darzhevin stretches out his bandaged hand and pushes the pictures off the bunk.

'We found her in the forest,' Malin says. 'She must have been tortured to death by the devil himself. I can't begin to imagine the pain she must have suffered. What if it's your daughter next time? Or when she gets bigger? This has to stop, doesn't it? This evil shit has to stop. I, we, don't believe you had anything to do with her death, because no pimp would do something like that to one of his assets.'

Darzhevin shuts his eyes again.

'Andrei,' Malin says. 'The woman we found in the forest was someone's beloved daughter, and you know that, even if I understand that in your job you sometimes have to pretend that women aren't human beings. Just to be able to survive. And I know that you have real bastards, dangerous, violent men above you in whatever organisation you happen to be part of. But I'm promising you a way out. Here and now. A way to a life with your family. Whoever you are, wherever you're from.'

Andrei Darzhevin opens his eyes again.

A weary, almost amused look in them.

Do you think you can fool me so easily?

'I don't believe a word of what you're saying,' he whispers. 'You can't give me anything, and we both know that. But I'll tell you her name.'

Andrei Darzhevin coughs, tries to stifle a sneeze, but fails, and blood starts to drip from the compresses covering his nose.

'Her name was Jenny Svartsjö. She was Swedish. That's all I know about her. All I'm saying. She was in the flat for a short while at the end of October. Then she was taken away. I had nothing to do with what happened to her in the forest.'

'Who took her?'

'Where?'

'Why?'

'Why did someone take her?'

'Where did she come from? Here?'

Malin can hear her questions, the way they rumble around the cell, dissolving and reforming as unfamiliar noises.

Was Jenny Svartsjö, our Jenny, my Jenny in the forest, one of the lost girls? One of the neglected ones? And why hasn't anyone remembered her?

But she might have disappeared long ago.

From God knows what domestic circumstances.

From God knows what forgetfulness and blindness among those who might have been able to rescue her.

'Where?'

'Why?'

But Andrei Darzhevin gives her no answers.

He's shut himself away again. As if he is waiting for something inevitable.

Jenny.

That's my name, was my name.

That was the name my mum called when she wanted me to come in from the vegetable patch she had on her little scrap of land out in the country, next to the cottage she inherited from her dad. The devil, as she always called him.

Jenny.

Jenny.

That's still my name. It's the lonely name all the invisible people around me in this space call after me when I try to ignore their pleas for help.

I'm dead.

I'm just as helpless as they are.

Only you, Malin, can help me now, Jenny Svartsjö.

You have to help me, Malin, you have to help all of us.

There have been, there are, and there will be far too many like us.

PART 2

Refugees from a Dream

[In the darkness]

This is happening now.

This is happening to me.

I remember the basement, the others, the way we didn't say a word to each other, I remember the car, the hands, the glimpse of forest, the way it reached out to me, then the silence.

Someone, something took me, placed an order for me, brought me here to use me.

Opening a case that contained the whole of hell.

The predator, concealing an even worse beast.

Is that the devil I can hear, feel, the devil whipping me, over and over again?

Burning me, cutting me?

I bite the cloth in my mouth, try to scream, but it's impossible, I can't even scream, and where am I?

Why is this being done?

Why is this being done to me?

Why?

What if there isn't a why?

My arms are fastened above my head. A blindfold over my eyes. My feet shackled to the floor.

My whole body hurts.

When will the fear and pain change into something other than a burning present moment? Never, I know that now, and red-hot irons are pressed hard into my breasts and I try to scream, smell the stench, the smell of my own flesh being charred to black ash and it stings, burns, and I am turning to steam, want to turn to vapour, but then he stops, because it is a he, isn't it? And then I feel cold, a burning cold and a cudgel on my shoulders and spikes tearing the insides of my thighs, rose thorns that make fresh warm blood flow out of me, and my arms are chained, aren't they?

My arms are stretched up towards the roof of this infernal lair, and I'm breathing, it would be nice to stop breathing and I can see nothing but black and the blindfold is greasy and then a syringe, a prick in my armpit, liquid being injected under the skin, and soon, soon I will be allowed to sleep.

But before that a waking dream in which greedy millipedes wriggle into me, eating me, boring their poisonous barbs into my innermost walls and eating from my wounds, making them ooze pus, and then hands moving over my flayed legs.

Faces.

How many faces does the snake have?

Where does it get all its faces from? All its teeth, all its poison, all its apparently insatiable desire for more of me, more of my flesh, more of the very essence of me.

Is there anything at all left of me?

And I'm sleeping now.

I have to sleep.

Let me be sleeping now, let all this have been nothing but a dream.

Maria Murvall is sitting on her bed, her back straight under her pink and white nightdress.

Muscles tense, become a movement and she stands up, goes over to the window, looks out into the dark night, and the landscape of the moon is shifting tones of ochre and grey, a waiting, all-encompassing tundra where lonely flags hang limply in the void.

She blinks.

Blinks again.

And there is thunder inside her, blinding white lightning explodes with each breath, and what is it that's moving, sparking inside her?

What face? What snake? What beast? What remnants of me? Of that which is me?

She doesn't know, but she sees her hand against the windowpane, feels pulses surge through her body like a whisper to her soul, to that which is her, deep inside, beyond blood and flesh.

'Maria.'

'Maria.'

She is searching for herself.

'Maria.'

The voices are shouting, and she recognises the forest, the branches, the barbed bushes creeping up her legs, wanting to force their way inside her, but this time she doesn't run, she stays, lets it happen, lets what has to happen move into her.

Fear is somewhere else.

Then Maria formulates a thought.

I am not fear.

I am no longer afraid.

Fear exists, but not here.

Am I afraid?

I, Jenny Svartsjö.

Is there anything for me to be afraid of? Or has fear passed for me, here where I drift freely, beyond, yet still in the world.

I am close to the woman who is hanging from chains attached to the ceiling in an isolated room, her naked body is bleeding and burned, just like mine, and I circle around her in her loneliness. Try to whisper beautiful words into her dream.

I see Maria standing by the window of her room. She's

blinking, blinking, blinking, trying to find a code that can bring her back to life.

I encourage Katerina. You have to go on breathing, I urge. You have to.

Just like our nameless sister in misfortune is doing in the hospital in Lund.

Malin.

Awake now, she's sitting in her kitchen drinking tea, before going to lie down in bed next to the doctor who's dreaming of the woman whose life he saved.

The women.

All the wordless women, somehow taken out of time and cast into a season of their own.

Heat becomes cold, snow become warmth, rain makes the ground dry and warmth fills the sewers with amputated heads and maggots, the forest is carving its own signs into the bark of the trees, opening its own veins in the hope that all this will come to an end.

I am beyond time now.

That's the only way everything can be put right.

21

It's going to work.

Everything will be OK.

It has to work.

The forest closes around Malin.

The crowns of the pines are vibrating in the sun's rays, reflections raining down like polished diamonds onto her white skirt, her black blouse, the jacket concealing her pistol.

The ferns seem to want to clamber up her legs, wrap around her muscles, fell her to the ground and find their way inside her, tear with their rigid fronds, cut up all of her inner spaces.

The plants want to make her theirs, and she fights an impulse to run away, and stands motionless in the clearing where they found Jenny Svartsjö's mutilated body, and sees her come staggering through the clearing, from every direction, and there's the same sulphurous smell then as now, and Malin wants to hear her whisper her story on the warm breeze flowing through the trees.

What do I actually think I'm going to find here? she thinks. It's just gone midday and her stomach is screaming for lunch.

She takes ten steps forward, and stands on the exact spot where they found Jenny's body, looks down at the ground, at the ants that have made a path across the place where she was lying, marching over the yellow cordon tape that has blown to the ground.

There's nothing here, Malin thinks. How are we going to make any progress?

They've found Jenny Svartsjö in the passport database. One single passport, issued when she was five years old.

She grew up in Tranås. They've confirmed her identity using dental records held by a dentist there.

It didn't take long for them to build up a rough outline of her history.

Parents divorced when she was eleven. Her dad moved to France, but isn't registered there any more.

As if the ground had swallowed him up.

Her mother had no fixed address, but was known to social services in Tranås. Severely alcoholic.

They had looked for more relatives to inform of Jenny's death, and during those intense hours of searching Malin had once again wondered about the fact that no one had recognised Jenny earlier, surely someone must have recognised her from the past? Or had shame really managed to blind everyone who had ever crossed her path? Were they ashamed at having abandoned her? At not bothering to help her?

They still knew too little about Jenny.

Certain things were available in official databases.

They had got more information from people they managed to find at her old school, and from social services in Tranås.

It looked as if Jenny had pretty much left school in the seventh grade.

She had had 'problems'. Nothing more specific than that.

Her mum drank, her dad had left his family.

Jenny had ended up in a children's home.

Then was sent home.

And evidently disappeared, while the authorities thought she was still living with her mother. And then she was eighteen, no one's responsibility, no one's problem.

But where had she gone?

What path had led her here?

She was twenty-one years old when she died.

God knows how she ended up in this forest.

I'm going to find out, Malin thinks.

I'm not going to abandon you, Jenny.

I'm not going to let any of you down.

And she thinks of the mother who abandoned her daughter. Why?

Tove, Malin thinks.

Lundsberg is in a forest like this, and what would I do if some colleagues knocked on the door one day and told me you had been found dead?

I'd go to pieces.

But first I'd track down whoever did that to you, Tove, and I'd kill him, or her, or it, with my bare hands. I shot a woman once when she was trying to kill you. And that feels good to this day.

A sparrow flaps its wings on a pine twig close to Malin, and the world is beautiful here, it's teeming with life, smells of life, but all I can think of is death.

I have to get away from it, Malin thinks. I have to get away from death, and you, Katerina, you, Maria, you, nameless woman in hospital in Lund, you're my ticket away from it.

She had come out here during her lunch hour. Alone, after their efforts to find out more about Jenny Svartsjö.

Katerina Yelena was still sedated after being shot, and was still unable to be questioned.

Andrei Darzhevin had refused to say anything else.

He hadn't said anything about his associates. Nor how

Jenny Svartsjö had ended up as a prostitute in the flat in Skattegården, or out here in the forest. If he knew anything that could help them, he was keeping it to himself.

The flat in Skattegården had been leased out by a blissfully unaware student who they had managed to talk to by phone in Sydney. And the landlord hadn't received any reports of problems.

Karin Johannison's examination of Jenny's body hadn't produced any more leads. The military's search of the forest had been completed, and hadn't come up with anything that could be linked to their case.

Jenny didn't have a criminal record. And her disappearance had never been reported.

No one had missed her.

No one had recognised her.

No one.

There's a sudden snapping sound, just to the left of Malin.

She spins around.

Did she see someone behind a tree?

No.

I'm alone out here, she thinks.

Jenny had been in the flat in Skattegården until October. They knew that much.

After that she disappeared.

Where to?

To Arto Antinen's house?

The DNA test would give them a definitive answer to that.

But it could hardly have been him, could it? Even if it was undeniably a remarkable coincidence that he just happened to have settled in the area at roughly the same time that Jenny ended up in the forest, raped, mutilated, and murdered.

She had been picked up from the brothel. By whom?

Malin prods at some ferns with a stick, watching the dewdrops clinging to the underside of the fronds fall to the ground.

As many questions as there are leaves on a tree.

Maria Murvall.

The woman in Lund.

Katerina Yelena.

Jenny Svartsjö. There has to be a connection.

It must be possible to piece all of this together to form a whole, a coherent narrative.

There's no silence in the forest.

Cracking sounds, whispers, the quivering wings of a bumblebee, and it's warm here in the clearing, improbably warm, hot, and now the ferns are moving, trying to wrap themselves around her, and, against her will, Malin starts to run, eager to get away, rushing through the forest, breathless and breaking into a sweat, until she sees her white Golf on the forest track.

There.

Calm down, Fors, calm down.

The key in the ignition.

All the women, all their faces, my own in the rear-view mirror, getting older by the day. Soon twice as old as them.

How can I ever bring any clarity to this? Malin wonders as she heads out across the Östgöta plain towards Linköping.

Malin.

Hurry up.

Work out what happened to me, there's a woman lying on a hard bunk in the filthiest of rooms.

Love your daughter, Malin.

Don't let anything come between your love.

Rise about any evil of that sort.

Kill that evil.
Kill it.

Her mobile rings just as she's crossing the bridge over the E4.

The cars like slow bullets beneath her.

Skäggetorp and Tornby in front of her.

Ikea's blue and yellow box.

Like a monument to overgrown dreams. Tax avoidance.

The huge supermarkets with their wretched panelled façades and oversized fading signs.

Zeke's voice: 'Social services have found Jenny Svartsjö's mother. She's supposed to be here.'

'In Linköping?'

'Yes,' Zeke says calmly. 'Pick me up from the station and we'll see if we can find her.'

'How did social services know?'

'Don't ask me. You know how it is. Same as with Maria Murvall. There are a few dedicated social workers who keep more of an eye on their clients than they have to. Maybe she can explain how Jenny ended up where she did.'

Half an hour later, in a harsh but hesitant afternoon light, they pull up beside a shabby grey caravan parked next to an abandoned factory on the outskirts of Tallboda, some ten kilometres east of Linköping.

The factory is set slightly apart from the other seven small units on the industrial estate.

Beyond the car park and caravan the forest takes over.

They get out of the car.

Walk heavily towards the caravan.

There's light inside.

The flickering glow of a candle.

'Does she know what's happened?' Malin wonders.

'She might have recognised the picture in the paper?'

'Maybe.'

'She ought to have been in touch if she did.'

'Don't be so sure.'

Zeke shakes his head. Steps forward determinedly and knocks.

No one answers, and Malin puts her head to the door, and hears heavy snoring.

She pushes the handle and the door opens, and they are hit by a stench of urine, rubbish and vomit.

But they steel themselves.

Go into the mess, into the dirt and damp, and under a stained blanket on a cushionless bunk lies what must be Britt Svartsjö.

They shake her awake.

Slowly.

Muttering.

'What the hell? Who the hell? Fuck,' and the smell of alcohol is overwhelming.

But Britt Svartsjö wakes up.

Sits up, and her lean grey face is bruised around one eye, and the thin skin is stretched tight and covered with little red blisters. She has sparse, matted grey hair, glossy with grease, and everything about Britt Svartsjö reeks of neglect, as if she and the world agreed to give up caring about each other a long time ago.

She looks at them, and Malin can tell that she knows.

'You don't have to say anything. I know why you're here.'

Britt Svartsjö's grey-green alcoholic's eyes turn black.

'You can go away again,' she says. 'I've got nothing to say to you.'

Malin sits down on the bench next to Britt.

'She was murdered,' Malin says. 'In the most brutal way. We have to find out what happened.'

Britt Svartsjö seems to be trying to organise her thoughts, to anchor herself in the present.

To work out if the police are here to help her this time.

'It's five years since I last saw her. And even then she spent most of her time in Stockholm.'

'You haven't seen her since then? Did you hear anything about where she might have been?'

'I don't even know where I've been. Does it look like I do?'

And Malin sees Tove in her mind's eye, and suddenly feels sick with shame. Knows that she neglected her daughter, but not like Britt Svartsjö, not like that. That's right, isn't it, Tove?

I can't have been that bad a mother?

How could anyone let themselves go to that extent?

But I came close, Malin thinks. I was on my way down to this swamp and turned back.

'What about her dad?' Zeke asks.

'The last time I heard from him, he was in Australia. Then I heard he'd died.'

'Died?'

'Yes, vanished. Probably murdered, because I daresay that's what they do to people like him down there. See that they disappear in the desert.'

'People like him?' Zeke wonders.

'He was a paedophile, Jenny's dad.'

Britt Svartsjö says the word without emotion.

'He abused her. I saw him, and I left in the middle of the night, taking Jenny with me. But nothing was ever right after that.'

'Could he have had anything to do with Jenny's death?' Malin asks.

Britt Svartsjö shakes her head, and one of her legs begins to twitch, before she goes on without pausing: 'He's long since dead. Gone. I could never forgive myself for letting him get away with what he did. For not seeing anything. I couldn't even stand to be in the same room as Jenny. So I ended up hitting her when I drank. But we had a little cottage for a while, I think she was happy there.'

'Did she have any friends who might know anything? Anyone you're aware of?'

'They avoided her like the plague at school in Tranås. There might have been a few boys who helped themselves, what do I know? It was a long time ago. Then she disappeared, and I don't know where she went after that.'

She's telling the truth, Malin thinks. Wants to get it all out.

If I'd let a paedophile get hold of Tove my guilt would know no bounds. Maybe I'd have pushed her away out of utter shame as well? And she thinks about Kristina. In her school. Her own Jenny.

Kristina the Slag.

And how vast would the shame be if it were your own daughter wandering those school corridors, confused and broken and tragic and abandoned and without any faith in the world, in men? Who knows what they can do to a woman, a child.

'How did you end up here?' Zeke asks.

'It's a friend's caravan. She's doing time in Hinseberg. But I can drink anywhere.'

'We'll arrange for the undertakers to contact you,' Malin says.

Britt Svartsjö shakes her head.

Then she says: 'You haven't got a hundred-kronor note I could borrow?'

Drink yourself into the darkness of shame, Mum. Drink yourself to death and meet Dad in the flames.

I wasn't happy in the cottage, nor in the open meadow surrounding it.

But I did glimpse a few short moments of freedom, a freedom that was never mine.

You have to dare to love, Mum, to become bigger than the pain.

You abandoned me.

Did you know that?

A mother should never abandon her child.

No matter what happens.

They laughed at me in the school corridors.

Spat at me.

Even the teachers laughed, and you drank and drank and drank because you felt so sorry for yourself.

I moved on, Mum.

Straight into a different sort of darkness.

And now, Mum, I'm leaving you on your own.

Johan Jakobsson's elbow aches. He's taken a couple of different painkillers, but knows he ought to get some stronger anti-inflammatory pills to deal with this new flare-up.

Click, click, click.

It gets to your elbows.

What am I looking for?

He looks out across the open-plan office.

The room looks almost foggy through his tired eyes. The uniformed officers over by the kitchen are dark-blue silhouettes with smooth faces and mouths like black holes.

Zeke isn't at his desk, probably at home having lunch. Börje Svärd and Waldemar Ekenberg went off to Snodda's fast-food kiosk in Ryd, asked if he wanted to go with them, but he'd rather work.

Looking for something, anything, that might have a connection to their case.

Yesterday evening he sent out a request to the ten officers

around the country that he was on a course with in Los Angeles last winter, where they learned how to search efficiently in various databases around the world without transgressing any privacy regulations.

A two-day course, three free days in Los Angeles, but he had felt homesick on the flight out. Los Angeles was a seething, unfathomable caldron, and he had realised that he really was a family man, a man suited to contexts of a more manageable size.

Such as being a police detective specialising in information retrieval and analysis.

In Linköping, possibly the most manageable of all provincial cities in Sweden.

In his request he outlined their case, and referred to Maria Murvall. His question was open: Does anyone know anything? Has anyone seen or heard anything that might be connected but which I can't find in the archives?

Not everything ends up in the digital world.

Almost everything, but not absolutely everything.

His inbox flashes.

An email from Hasse in Hälsingland.

Urgent.

One of the ten.

Johan clicks to open it.

And a new line of inquiry into the murder of Jenny Svartsjö opens up.

22

The tapping of keys.

Phones ringing.

Voices squawking familiar words.

The sound of breathing and a dishwasher rumbling in the distance in the communal kitchen, the ping of a microwave oven.

And a focused male form.

Johan Jakobsson heads towards Malin the moment she and Zeke appear through the door of the office in the police station.

The look in his eyes is expectant and guarded, but he can't hold back a smile, the sort police officers allow themselves when they make progress in the investigation of a crime that urgently needs to be solved.

He stops Malin just before she reaches her desk.

'We've got another one,' he says. 'A case that resembles ours, as well as Maria and the woman you saw down in Lund, at St Lars.'

'Another one?'

Malin can feel her heart contract and she wonders how many women like hers there are, women dumped in the country's forests like fallen, unwanted stars in a growing darkness.

What pattern do these bright points form?

Is there even a pattern?

I have to find the pattern, she thinks. I'm going to put a stop to this.

'Yes, another one,' Johan says. 'A Jessica Karlsson. In Hälsingland. The police in Ljusdal found a girl, a young woman, wandering aimlessly in the forest one morning, raped, cut, and severely abused. Looks like she'd also suffered severe burns to her mouth.'

'That certainly matches some aspects of our case with Jenny. And the woman in Lund. The use of violence resembles ours, as well as the forest, the rural setting, and her age,' Malin says.

Thinking: But it doesn't match Maria.

'OK, where's the woman now? Can I see her?'

'You'd need supernatural powers.'

So she didn't survive, Malin thinks, this Jessica Karlsson didn't survive, and the office becomes a tunnel of sounds and light around her.

Will it never end?

Another dead woman, another one beyond salvation.

Malin pushes past Johan and sinks onto her chair.

Zeke comes over to them from the kitchen, a mug of coffee in his hand, and he looks at her and nods.

'You heard what Johan just said?'

'Yes, but not all of it.'

Johan goes on: 'It happened four years ago. In the autumn. Jessica Karlsson was a perfectly ordinary local girl from a settled family background. She was seventeen years old, and worked at a hotdog kiosk. One night she didn't come home after shutting up. And four days later she was found wandering along a remote forest road. Naked. Covered in cuts. Raped. Just like Maria Murvall. And the woman in Lund. And like we might have found Jenny Svartsjö if she'd managed to escape whoever was tormenting her.'

'There are still a lot of differences,' Zeke says. 'For a start, there's the distance between the locations. Some of the women's ages are similar, but Maria is rather older.

And this Jessica didn't have problems with her family, which Jenny Svartsjö did, to put it mildly.'

'Why these particular women?' Johan asks.

'Why not?' Malin says. 'They're women. Young. Maria a bit older. They probably looked pretty attractive. At least one of them was going off the rails, which is basically the stereotype for women who end up as victims of male violence.'

'The degree of violence is the same,' Johan says.

Malin and Zeke look at him, waiting for him to go on: 'Jessica's mouth was ruined, apparently her lips, oral cavity and even her tongue had been burned off with acid.'

'How?' Malin asks.

'It was as if someone had stuffed a rag soaked in hydro-chloric acid in her mouth.'

More and more insane, Malin thinks. And knows she must suppress her empathy, and respond coolly to the suffering Jessica Karlsson had to endure.

'Was she able to say anything about what happened?'

'No, nothing,' Johan says. 'Not a damn thing. She couldn't talk because of her injuries, but she didn't write anything either.

'She was mute,' he continues. 'Didn't say a word, and ended up in a hospital up there, in a ward for chronically ill psychiatric patients.'

Muteness.

What sort of violence do you have to suffer for words to disappear? Malin wonders.

What sort of evil? And what's at the core of that evil?

'Then what?'

Malin sees Zeke close his eyes and take a sip of his coffee, trying to put himself somewhere else in his thoughts.

'She killed herself. They didn't think she was suicidal, then they found her hanged in her room, she'd tied the sheets to the radiator to make a noose. She hung herself by lying on the floor and letting herself be suffocated by the weight of her head. She was nineteen.'

'And they're sure it was suicide?' Zeke asks.

'I assume so,' Johan says. 'That was two years ago. But before that she hadn't made a sound since she was found, and the case had been dropped much earlier.'

'What do we know about her?' Malin asks. 'And why don't we know more about this? Surely this ought to have been a big story in the media?'

'Apparently the extent of her injuries was hushed up. And, according to our colleagues up there, it happened at the same time as a sex scandal involving some union bosses, and when news was leaking out about the torture of American prisoners in Afghanistan. So it got lost in the noise, just another violent rape out in the sticks. A pin-prick in the statistics.'

'So what do we know, then?' Malin asks again.

'Not much,' Johan replies. 'She's buried in the cemetery in town. Looks like her mother was her only family.'

'And the investigation didn't get anywhere?'

Johan shakes his head.

'Our colleagues in Ljusdal didn't find anything. As Hasse Eriksson up there put it, "it was as if she ended up in the forest of her own accord".'

'Are they sending us a copy of the investigation?'

Johan sighs.

'The investigation was declared confidential by the prosecutor, so we can't have it. Hasse Eriksson told me everything he felt he was able to.'

Zeke rubs his elbow.

'What the hell are we dealing with here?' he says.

'I don't know,' Malin says. 'But I'm going to find out.'

★ ★ ★

Sven Sjöman is leaning back in his chair in his office.

Behind him Malin and Zeke can see the hospital, the car park in front of the yellow and white panelled building, the people like ants down among the cars, busy living their lives, and the sky above them shades of blue and white like a vast, rippling flag draped across the seats in a football stadium.

They've told him about their meeting with Britt Svartsjö. That they basically didn't find out anything new, and Sven has called to request information from the Australian authorities about an Ingvar Svartsjö.

Then they moved on to Hälsingland.

'We have to go up there,' Malin says. 'Talk to the detectives, find out what they know, what they remember, see the place for ourselves. Even if the case is confidential, they'll talk to us.'

Sven shakes his head.

'The circumstances look similar to our case. And, to an extent, the associated cases as well. I agree with you on that. But going up there? You know how things are with the budget. We can't afford that sort of luxury on such thin evidence. You'll have to talk to them over the phone.'

Zeke leans forward in his chair.

'That's not the same thing, Sven. You know that.'

'But there isn't any money.'

But this isn't just about money, Malin thinks.

You don't really believe in this yet, do you? Haven't really got the energy for this any more, the last thing you want is an investigation that spills over regional boundaries, across the boundaries of what we can understand and make sense of.

The wrinkles in Sven's face just make him look tired now, they don't give him intellectual authority the way they used to.

Almost forty years investigating violent crime. Longer than anyone could cope with, really.

And it's taken its toll on Sven. Maybe he's ill? Malin thinks, then forces herself to focus on the case.

So what do you think then, Sven, about this case?

Where did Jenny Svartsjö spend those years when she was off the radar? How did she end up at the brothel, among Russians and Ukrainians, and then out in the forest?

Do you think it was Arto Antinen? Or some Russian involved in the brothel who lost control and left her to die in the forest after first torturing the life out of her? Andrei Darzhevin? Was he the one who killed her? But if that's the case, what about the links to the other women?

He could hardly have had anything to do with them, they were found far away, a long time ago. And he hasn't been in Sweden that long. It could hardly be Arto Antinen either. Although we can't be absolutely certain.

Do you think Jenny Svartsjö's murder is an isolated case? That it isn't connected to the others?

That could be true, but Malin knows, feels that there's a link.

'You have to see the connection here, Sven,' Malin says. 'We need to look under these stones. That's what the investigation's voices are telling me.'

Sven's own mantra.

Which he drummed into her when they first started working together, long ago.

'Listen to the investigation's voices. Hear what they have to say.'

'That'll have to wait, I—'

Malin interrupts him.

'I'll pay for the petrol and hotel, if we need one, out of my own pocket. If you give me and Zeke the time to go, I'll pay the cost myself.'

And she sees Sven capitulate.

He smiles.

Probably wanted this all along.

He looks first at Zeke, then at Malin, then Zeke again, and the wrinkles in his face transform in front of Malin's eyes, and become a sign of authority again.

'Is that OK with you, Zeke?'

Zeke nods.

'Go whenever you like,' Sven says. 'Right away or first thing tomorrow.'

He leans forward towards them: 'Be careful. Who knows what we're dealing with.'

Andrei Darzhevin has sat down on the floor of his custody cell. He's trying to tie the sheet, testing various knots. The little window up by the ceiling of the cell must be made of reinforced smoked glass, and at this time in the afternoon it lets in a fuzzy light that reminds him of the poisonous water in the stream close to the house he grew up in, in a village just outside St Petersburg.

His friend Ilya drank some of that water one summer.

He got cancer from the mercury and died a year later with his stomach eaten away by the burning larvae of the illness. He screamed with pain throughout the whole of July and August, the morphine the hospital was supposed to provide had been sold as drugs on the black market.

What illness has been eating away at me?

He sees his daughter in his mind's eye, hears her laughter as she runs across the yard, jumps on the sofa in the only room of the flat, hears her scream when he shouts at her mother, pushing her into the radiator as hard as he can.

'Bitch.'

'Whore.'

And her mother bled and cried, and he held his daughter

afterwards, wanted to comfort her, but she was nothing but fear, fear of him.

Why not *Crime and Punishment*?

He knows as much as Raskolnikov about regret and self-justifying violence. He knows that there is no forgiveness for some things.

How do you make a noose?

If I tell them everything, they'll kill my daughter, I'm in no doubt about that. Unless not even they are that cruel? If I don't say anything, many more will die. I didn't mean to shoot Katerina. And I shouldn't have dragged Jenny off, I knew deep down what was going to happen to her.

So what's the best option?

Andrei Darzhevin buries his head in his hands, and feels his bandaged hand touch the compresses and tape over his nose.

Barriers covering the skin. As if love were no longer possible.

I know what's best, he thinks, and recalls his daughter's laughter and her mother's screams, the fear as she wriggles away from him across the floor of the flat, and everything else he's guilty of.

You can never remove one part of yourself and let the rest live. I will always be all of me. I will always be the evil contained within love.

He sees his daughter.

She's running beneath a blue sky over an unfamiliar meadow, wearing a white nightdress that gets caught by the wind.

You'll never meet the same fate as them.

Never.

But I know what my fate must be.

If only for your sake.

★　★　★

'Your brother,' Zeke says as they walk down the yellow-painted corridor away from Sven Sjöman's office. 'He's in Hälsingland, isn't he?'

Malin nods.

She can see her brother in his room, surrounded by posters of cheesy pop stars.

'We could visit him,' Zeke says. 'If we're going to be up there anyway.'

Malin nods again.

'It can't be far out of our way,' Zeke says.

'We'll have to see,' Malin says. 'We'll see.'

Tove.

Her face in the glass of the door leading to the open-plan office.

It's there all of a sudden, in Malin's own reflection, and Tove seems to be calling to her.

Lundsberg is on the way to Hälsingland.

But we haven't got time for that detour, and Malin feels like calling Tove, to say that she and Peter and everyone she wants will be coming to her end-of-year concert, to say that everyone wants to see her onstage, singing in the chapel where the concert is taking place.

She feels the weight of her mobile in her jacket pocket as she pushes the door open to escape the image in the glass.

Shall I call?

No.

I'd have to tell her I was heading in her direction, otherwise I'd feel like a liar, a traitor, and if I tell her Tove will be disappointed that I'm not calling in on the way, so it's better not to call, not to start anything off, not create a load of disappointment and worry.

Jenny Svartsjö's face.

Her mother.

Thank God there's nothing like that between us.

Malin doesn't call her daughter.

And in Lundsberg, in the forests of Värmland, on the second floor of the hundred-year-old stuccoed building of the student residence, in a single room, on a single bed, lies Tove Fors, seventeen years old, trying to conjure up an image of her mother. She wants to call her, but doesn't want to nag, doesn't want to ask her for yet one more thing that she's bound to think is a huge nuisance.

Mum hates nagging, when you try to tell her what she ought to do.

So it's best not to call, Tove thinks, so I don't start anything silly and feel embarrassed afterwards.

23

They had decided to set off immediately.

Even though the sky was darkening to the south and the radio was warning of an approaching thunderstorm.

Malin and Zeke had worked out that they could be in Hälsingland by ten o'clock that night.

They could find a cheap hotel on the way.

Before they left they received an update on Katerina Yelena. Her condition was stabilising. The gunshot wound wasn't infected, but she was still sedated and couldn't be questioned yet.

Malin had called Peter.

His voicemail clicked in, she knew he was at the hospital, probably in the operating theatre.

She had left a message.

'Hello darling. Something's come up in the investigation. I'm going up to Hälsingland this evening. It can't wait, and you know how important this case is.'

Then silence.

'I miss you, I think about you all the time. I'll call when we get there. I'm going with Zeke.'

And now, with her hands on the wheel and Zeke beside her in the passenger seat of the white Golf, now that dusk has settled over the forests of Närke and she can hear the thunderstorm chasing the car, occasionally illuminating it with lightning, she's thinking about Peter, and how hard she finds it to know what she really feels for him, even if it's fundamentally a pure, clear feeling of what she imagines is love.

But you can never know for sure, she thinks.

She hears Zeke snore.

Turns down the volume of the stereo, no German choral music, thank God, but she doesn't feel like listening to any more of Billie Holiday's far too beautiful voice, can't deal with any more twilight just now, and tries to clear her thoughts instead, concentrating on nothing but tarmac, oncoming traffic, fir trees, pines, scrub and ferns that split into multiple heads, snapping at naked women's legs fleeing from a powerful force that wants to destroy them, make them blind and silent, and then kill them, carry them far from life as we know it.

I see the car moving through the forest.

You, Malin, and Zeke, are sitting in it. You're heading into the coming night, towards a darkness that is beyond comprehension.

There are snakes here.

Millipedes.

One hundred thousand singing Aborigines raising their voices and singing lines across the landscape, creating the patterns that form the basis of our lives, of all the death we are obliged to have around us, the price we have to pay for our breathing, for our love.

Do you imagine that anything is free, Malin?

Nothing is free.

Nothing at all.

What do you imagine that Jessica Karlsson, her spirit, other people's memories of her, will be able to tell you?

You are stubborn and curious, Malin, but most of all you're scared, aren't you? Scared that you, or Tove, will become one of us?

That you will end up like your brother, as good as mute, and unaware of the world in a small room in a hospital in an utterly insignificant place.

Feel the fear.

Meet the demons.

Wrestle them to the ground, vanquish them, and they'll disappear.

How ridiculous!

I know how the fight ends.

Jessica knows. Maria knows. Katerina knows, my mum knows, and the young woman in hospital in Lund.

None of us has any illusions.

We're not hoping for justice.

But it feels good, Malin, it feels good to know that you care, that you're prepared to sacrifice your life for our sakes.

Because you are, aren't you, Malin?

There are some things worth dying for, aren't there? And some things you have to kill for.

Some crimes must be punished by death.

You still have to earn the right to be human. Both in life and in death.

I have felt Jessica close to me at times. We comfort each other. Floating free in a space that is ours alone.

We help each other to conquer the terror. The loneliness, the longing to be alive again.

Something's dying, Malin thinks. And it will never come back.

Hälsingland.

The sign marking the border is at the edge of a small community, just a few houses spread out along the road.

White asbestos panelling on shabby façades.

Greying red wood stain, a few wrecked cars, an oil tank, rusty, and then forest again.

Her mobile rings.

Janne's number on the screen.

She hasn't spoken to him in weeks, and she feels nothing as she takes the call.

Polite introductory phrases.

'I've just spoken to Tove,' he says. 'She's worried you're not going to make it to the end-of-year concert.'

'She doesn't have to worry,' Malin says.

'You're sure?'

'Yes.'

'Have you booked the time off?'

'This is some serious bloody nagging.'

'Malin, I want to be able to say to—'

'I'll be there. We can go together, OK?'

Janne falls silent.

'OK. How are you?' he eventually says.

I can't do this now, Malin thinks. I just can't.

'Listen, I'm working. It's difficult to talk. I'll call nearer the time of the concert.'

A deep sigh at the other end of the line.

Janne hangs up without saying goodbye.

Quick to take offence, Malin thinks.

Then she reflects upon what he's seen seeing with the Rescue Services Agency in Bosnia and Rwanda. What he told her on the few occasions she got him to open up, when he woke up in a cold sweat, screaming after fevered dreams on dark nights in the house out in Malmslätt.

He told her about women with burned genitals. Women who had been systematically raped in order to destroy their societies and tattoo the shame into the communal soul. How collective hatred expressed itself in violence towards women, so vile that even she couldn't bear to hear the words that came out of his mouth that night.

Because what could she say?

That everything would be all right?

That no woman would ever again be punished for being a woman, because men, bloody men, need her in their power games?

'They screamed and cried and hit us when we tried to help them,' Janne whispered. 'They looked at me like I was one of the men who had raped them, hurt them. I never did anything, ever, but still, in a way, they were right. I was somehow part of that violence, and they hated me for it. Even if some of them wanted my help. And I wanted to help them. But how could they trust me? How could they know I wouldn't behave like the other men who had come out of the forests and jungles and ruined their lives?'

'You're not like them,' she had whispered. 'You're not like them,' and she had stroked his back, feeling the sweat of shame, and hoped that there was a way out from every-thing she couldn't understand and comprehend, just sense as an anger and a never-ending pain.

It's already half past ten, and they've agreed to stop at the first motel they find.

Zeke hasn't nagged any more about going to visit Stefan.

She doesn't want to visit him.

And knows that she ought to.

And she does really want to, I really do want to.

They drive another ten kilometres, straight into the forest, and now they aren't far from Sjöplogen, the village where Stefan's care home is.

She can feel his presence now.

His loneliness.

His sorrow at having been abandoned, without ever being able to understand it, his sorrow at his mother turning her back on him, his stepfather, everyone who ought to have felt and acted out of a duty of love.

She thinks about her father.

And she gets angry, thinking it would be best if he died,

and the first time she felt that she was ashamed, but then she accepted it, because it was true and genuine, just like the message she had left on Peter's voicemail.

What her dad had done when he hid her brother's existence from her was unforgiveable.

If she were to forgive that, not only would she be betraying herself, but every child that humanity has managed to produce.

Black or white.

Forgiveness not possible, not desirable for everything.

Not for those of us living in the grey zone.

They drive through another small village.

A sign by the road says its name is Svartvik. 'Black inlet.'

Black. Black inlet. A world painted black. A church painted white. Houses painted traditional red. Wrecked cars in gardens, battered caravans.

The Swedish countryside.

A grey three-storey building clad in asbestos panelling. A canvas sign saying: 'Rooms 300 kr. / night.'

Perfect, Malin thinks, and stops the car in the gravel yard in front of the building.

They knock, and it takes almost five minutes for an old woman with a grey, cloud-like face and a thin frame concealed in a pastel green towelling dressing gown to open the front door, with the safety-chain on, and peer out at them through a fifteen-centimetre-wide gap.

'We were wondering if you've got two rooms for the night?'

Zeke must have picked up on the woman's hesitancy, because his voice is full of boundless calm and reassurance.

The woman nods and opens the door.

'But I've got no breakfast except for a bit of bread I could toast.'

'That's fine,' Malin says.

'But the rooms are clean, I can promise you that,' the woman says, and ten minutes later Malin is sitting on the edge of a soft double bed in a pink room where an excess of lace covers every imaginable surface: the bedside table, the top of the television, the windowsills, as well as the bed in the form of an enormous, carefully crocheted white bedspread.

It looks like someone's dream of home, Malin thinks, lying flat out on the bed.

It's gone eleven o'clock.

Peter must have finished work by now, he'll be at home, in his flat, if there hasn't been an emergency.

She gets out her mobile.

Calls, feeling a pang of conscience and thinking that she ought to be with Peter instead of here, in this strange room that smells flowery and musty from the presumably mouldy floorboards.

'Malin.'

His voice.

A crackling jolt of heat inside her.

'It's me.'

'Where are you?'

'In Svartvik, in Hälsingland.'

And she explains what brought them here, five hundred kilometres away from him, and he listens, murmurs, and Malin detects a hint of impatience, almost irritation, and he wants to say something, she can feel it, but what?

'You want to say something.'

'Maybe.'

'What is it?'

'Some other time.'

'Why not now?'

'It's not something we can talk about over the phone,' and now, Malin thinks, he's leaving me now, another chapter in my love life is over before it's even begun, he's fed up with me always putting work first, he's found someone else, someone educated, with style and money and a nice name that suggests lovely fucking genes.

He's leaving me.

And what the hell would he want with me? Who am I? An alcoholic fucking cop who's past her prime, who has to exercise like a lunatic every day to stop her body going to pieces.

I'm going to be an old spinster, a fucking lovelorn old spinster.

'Tell me now.'

Her police voice.

Don't, whatever you do, argue with me.

Tove. She remembers now, Tove had something she wanted to say the last time they spoke, but decided to keep it to herself.

'OK,' Peter says.

'OK?'

'Yes, I'll tell you what I want to say. Because you seem ready to listen.'

Silence.

Malin waits, hears the sound of her own breathing echo around the room, and gets the impression that every last bit of lace is going to dissolve in all her used air.

'I'm thirty-nine,' Peter says. 'You're thirty-seven.'

So that's where he's going. She breathes out, I can deal with this, he's probably feeling lonely there at home, but I can't go there, I don't want to, I really don't want to.

'I know how old we are,' she says.

'We can't go on like this.'

'Are you leaving me?'

'That's not what I mean, and you know it.'

She can't say the word 'child', can't bring herself to utter the word, and it's as if she can feel her coil scratching inside her again.

'I want to have a child, Malin. I want us to try properly.'

A noose around my neck, but also a longing.

She can't say anything, her entire being is in violent disagreement.

'Say something,' he says. 'Don't you see how much I love you, I've never loved anyone the way I love you.'

Mute.

Now I'm mute, and she feels herself burst, as tears start to run down her cheeks.

'I want us to have a child,' he says again. 'You know that, Malin. I've said it before, and now I'm saying it again. I want us to try to have a child together. Because if we don't do it now, it might be too late. We're neither of us young any more. I want us to try properly now. Not later.'

She wants to shout yes.

Wants to shout no.

What shall I say? A child? Me? In this bloody world, in my bloody life?

A wonderful little boy crawling over the tiles in a newly bought villa.

'Don't you want to?'

I'm not the sort of person who can be a good mother, she thinks.

'I want to,' she whispers. 'I want to.'

'A little Malin and Peter clone.'

'Yes.'

'I'll make an appointment to have your coil removed.'

'Yes, do.'

My sobbing, he must have heard.

'Are you upset, Malin?'

'No,' she says.

'But you're crying.'

'I'm so happy, I'm crying. I know you mean it.'

'You're crazy, Malin,' Peter says. 'Of course I mean it.'

And she tries to find something else to say, and she wonders why she's crying, and she sees herself in this damp, silent, godforsaken room, and realises how ridiculous it is to be here, alone, talking about having children.

She ends the call.

Dries her eyes.

Do I even want a child? Is that even fair?

And she wishes he'd stop nagging, because in his desires she has to confront her inner self.

Their words vanish like echoes into the darkness of the forest.

Spinning on their own axis and becoming dreams of a better life, dreams of the very simplest but simultaneously most difficult sort.

People who know what they want.

Who know they can get to where they want to be.

Malin has got up from the bed.

She's standing by the window of the room, the thunder and lightning haven't made it this far north. She's drawn the lace curtain aside, and is looking down at the forest that takes over where the small, fussily neat garden ends.

Fir trees.

Pines.

A few sparse maples, and the darkness grows denser the deeper into the trees she tries to see.

Something's moving among the trees.

Something that's making the ferns and bushes tremble.

Something that's always lived there in the darkness.

What is it?

A monster that believes it has the right to take what it wants, no matter what the cost to the next person, and the next, and the next?

An engorged monster? With a charming, polished smile? A man? Something beyond what the rest of us would regard as human?

The same creature that rapes women to destroy communities in the Congo. That practises genital mutilation on women in a hundred countries.

That forces a little girl to her knees in front of its groin while a video camera whirrs in the background.

That uses and uses up, discards and dumps once it's had its pleasure, its whims and lusts.

This creature is a man, Malin thinks. A man beyond men, yet still in all men, in all human beings.

Then the forest changes before her eyes.

Becomes a single woman's face.

Not a particular woman's face, but all women's faces, somehow distilled into one form.

And the mouth of the face opens.

And she hears the woman's scream, unfamiliar, distant, again.

'Rescue me.'

'Help me.'

And she knows it's urgent. That there's no time to lose.

Because the woman is real. A different woman, not Jenny Svartsjö. Not Jessica Karlsson.

This woman is still alive.

She's out there somewhere.

Malin moves away from the window. Undresses and gets under the covers, and soon she's asleep, dreaming forth her life.

24

Friday, 20 May

You're going to have a child, Malin.

You're going to have the son you never had.

You're going to give birth to all my unborn children, give birth to them for me.

Let me see him run over dew-damp grass on a mild summer's evening.

Let me hear him sing forth my life, and in the dream Malin hears the exhortations, thinks, I'm going to give birth to a child, I'm going to carry a child in my body, let it grow inside me, give life to a child, an unspoiled life that the world can't get at, I'll defy everything that's happened, she thinks secrets beyond secrets beyond secrets.

I shall give love.

I shall do everything right.

I shall be a faultless person.

What am I doing here?

She's standing outside her brother Stefan's room in Norrgården care home in the village of Sjöplogen. The home looks like a shrunken manor house from the outside, with pinnacles and towers and carvings adorning the small, white, wooden three-storey building. Even inside there is no institutional atmosphere. Rag rugs cover the scratched parquet floor, and the armchairs and sofas could have been picked up second-hand anywhere.

Zeke is standing just behind her, he insisted over breakfast that they come out here, and that he would come in with her and meet her brother.

She said no to start with.

Both to coming at all, and to Zeke coming in with her.

'He's your brother, Malin. I want to meet him, I want to know what it's like for you when you come up here.'

'I don't come very often.'

'Well, we're here now, aren't we?'

And why protest? Where does this instinct come from, always to say no to anything that might be difficult, that might offer resistance? As long as that applies to me, that is. It's the opposite with other people's pain.

Isn't that the instinct that stops most people from developing at all?

Which locks people inside themselves and in what they are expected to be?

So no became yes, and now she's standing here, nervous as usual before seeing her brother, and she can feel Zeke's breath on her neck.

How many doors like this am I going to have to stand in front of? How many people who are somehow beyond themselves am I going to have to meet before I reach any sort of peace?

They're like stars, these people, Malin thinks. Like still, burning globes in a sky, happy just existing.

Possibly the only sane people out of all of us.

'Well, let's go in then,' she says, thinking that she'll never get used to this, and her legs feel weak and she wants to walk away. She misses the boy, the man behind that door, but she still wants to run.

She opens the door.

And he's sitting in a wheelchair by the window, up already in spite of the early hour, and he turns around as they enter the room, smiles at them, but says nothing, makes no sound, and his blue eyes are empty, but not lifeless.

'This is Zeke,' Malin says. 'I work with him,' and her brother looks out of the window, at trees whose crowns are swaying gently in the wind.

She and Zeke sit down on chairs next to him, and Malin talks to him, asks him how he is, what he's been doing since she was last there, but his face doesn't move at all, and Malin wonders if that means she somehow doesn't exist at this particular moment.

She looks at Zeke.

He smiles, then she strokes her brother's arm.

She looks around the room.

At the posters of the singer Carola.

At the dust dancing in the dull sunlight. And she stops asking questions and starts talking about herself, about Tove, about Copenhagen, and after a quarter of an hour she gets up, signalling to Zeke, kisses her brother on the cheek and says goodbye, and promises it won't be long before they see each other again, thinking: Have we ever actually seen each other? But perhaps we meet in feelings, somewhere we're reaching out our hands to each other, comforting each other.

'He's like you,' Zeke says.

'How do you mean?'

'In loads of ways. Where do you want me to start?' Zeke replies with a smile.

Ljusdal Police Station.

A brown-brick, overgrown two-storey box with a green-panelled roof, located in the centre of town, just a hundred metres from the Ljusnan River. When they crossed the bridge over the river a short while ago, the arched supports made Malin feel as if she was behind bars. That she was wrong and was doing something bad, instead of right and doing good.

A police car was parked outside the station, and there weren't many people on the streets. In front of Malin and Zeke, in a sparsely furnished office, sits Detective Superintendent Hans Eriksson, a man in his late forties with uncombed, curly brown hair and a face grey from smoking, his cheeks furrowed and drooping, like a toad's.

But Hans Eriksson's eyes are full of life, and those green spheres seem to belong to another face entirely. Those eyes, Malin thinks, watch over this community, notice everything that doesn't quite fit, that could therefore be a sign of danger.

'A tragic story,' he says with a hoarse voice. 'Gruesome too. So gruesome that the papers up here didn't actually write about it. Her injuries were impossible to describe in print. And at the time there was a lot of other stuff for the papers to write about instead. Jessica Karlsson was found stumbling along a road out in the forest, on a seriously cold, late-autumn morning. She was bleeding, cut to pieces and had been raped with a blunt object. And her mouth, her lips. Bloody hell. You know?'

Malin nods.

'We never got anything out of her, and after a couple of years in a psychiatric hospital she hanged herself.'

Malin listens intently.

Recognises the pattern, the situation, the cold, early morning that almost seems capable of giving birth to women that the forest has violated.

A tornado that I find myself at the centre of.

'A local girl,' Hans Eriksson goes on. 'Liked by everyone. She disappeared when she was on her way home from work at the hotdog kiosk. No one saw anything, and we never found out what happened. We didn't really make any progress at all. To this day her friends still leave flowers on her grave.'

'Nothing?' Zeke wonders, as Malin stifles the same question.

'We questioned a few outsiders who had rented a hunting cabin in the area,' Hans Eriksson says. 'Big shots. But it didn't lead anywhere, I don't think they had anything to do with it.'

A hunting cabin. So they'd had the same thought as us.

'What do you think happened to her?' Malin asks.

'I don't know. Maybe someone in the area had an isolated attack of madness and then came to his senses again. In which case he's still here. Just as you must have thought with your case, I wondered if it could have been someone who was travelling through. A lorry driver, someone like that, a tourist, but we didn't get anywhere with that either. And there were no known sex-offenders in the area.'

'Could we have the names of the men in the hunting cabin?' Malin asks.

Hans Eriksson leans back with a frown.

His eyes darken, become less alive.

'That was the only odd thing,' he says. 'We had a young prosecutor up here at the time, and he wanted to drop the case early, quickly, as if someone were putting pressure on him from above. And, when we didn't make any progress, he got his way.'

'What was the prosecutor's name?'

'Jimmy Kalder.'

'Doesn't mean anything to me,' Malin says. 'Is he still here?'

'No, he's in Umeå now. Wanted something bigger.'

'The men's names? Can't you let us have them?' Malin asks again.

'I've got them in my head, but I can't let you have them. The prosecutor declared the case confidential specifically to protect the identities of those concerned.'

'But you told Johan the girl's name?'

'I wasn't thinking when I got his email. I just answered straightaway, and now I've already said more than I should.'

'Just between colleagues,' Zeke says. 'What were their names?'

Hans Eriksson shakes his head.

'It was a mistake even to mention them.'

Then he looks at them and smiles.

Not mockingly, but in a pointed way.

It wasn't a mistake, Malin thinks. You knew exactly what you were doing, and then the look in his eyes changes and she sees something like fear in them.

Are you afraid of the men behind those names? Malin wonders. But the fear in Hans Eriksson's eyes is more of an introspective fear, as if he were afraid of himself and the way he has perhaps been forced to see himself reflected in those men.

'But there's probably a way to find out the names, isn't there?' Hans Eriksson goes on. 'I've got my principles, though. You know, if even we in the police don't practise as we preach, why should anyone else? We have to set an example, don't we?'

The look in his eyes inscrutable now.

As if he were seeking an invisible boundary. As if he wanted to make the right choice in a world in which every choice is both right and wrong.

Jessica Karlsson's doctor.

A Viola Lagerberg.

She agreed to meet them in her lunch hour. Informally and off the record.

They were given her name by Hans Eriksson, he was able to tell them, seeing as the doctor wasn't named in the case file.

The restaurant in Åhléns, on the second, top floor of a department store that must have been built in the sixties, and whose ventilation system seems to date back to then. The smell of frying hangs heavy over the worn chairs with their sagging cane seats and the plastic flowers in cracked terracotta pots. They're surrounded by mums with babies.

Salmon with hollandaise sauce. Ham and potato hash.

The woman opposite Malin and Zeke is unremarkable, with a small button nose holding a pair of red glasses in front of her grey, watchful eyes. Grey, steel-wool hair and a thin frame hidden by baggy blue knitwear, a sense of withheld strength, hidden but not invisible.

'I was the one who found her,' Viola Lagerberg says. 'After two years, we didn't regard her as a suicide risk. We hadn't decreased her medication or anything. And I don't think she was in any pain from her injuries any more. Her oral cavity had healed, so even if her lips and teeth had been burned off, and her gums were mostly just scar tissue, I don't think she was in actual pain. Apart from in her soul.'

'And she hanged herself from the radiator?' Malin says, and Viola Lagerberg nods.

'It doesn't take more than that. I've seen it before.'

'So have I,' Malin says.

A female student in a flat in Ryd.

A blue face drained of oxygen, bowels that had opened, bloodshot eyes, scared but at peace.

Was that how it was?

Then a thought strikes Malin, a thought that's been lurking on the edge of her consciousness: 'Are you sure she hanged herself? Could anyone have sneaked in and done that to her?'

Viola Lagerberg pauses. The forkful of salmon stops halfway to her mouth.

'We never got a word out of Jessica. She never wrote anything. But she had tried to harm herself before, several times. With a fork, and a pair of scissors. She cut open the scars where her lips had been. Whatever she experienced out there in the forest, it finished her. She didn't want to live. I'm quite sure of that.'

'So there's no doubt at all?'

Viola Lagerberg shakes her head.

'Visit her grave. There are bound to be flowers there. She was very popular, and people remember her.'

On the way to the cemetery they call Sven Sjöman.

As they drive past the sparse buildings of Ljusdal, matchbox villas with asbestos panels and the occasional block of flats, Malin hears Zeke outline what they've found out and talk about how to get hold of the case file, and how they didn't get the names of the men who rented the hunting cabin.

There's no question that they want to get hold of them, it might be a long shot, but there could be a connection, somehow. And the prosecutor, Jimmy Kalder, why did he want to close down the investigation, just like Fredrik Kantsten in Lund?

Malin recalls her meeting with him in Stockholm. It was only a few days ago, but it feels like several ice ages have passed since then.

The way he had seemed so dismissive of her, and perhaps had something to hide. People in this country have no idea how much power prosecutors have, Malin thinks, and how fucking cowardly they are when it comes to handling sexual offences.

They get out by a small, white-rendered church, and

behind a metre-high wall they can see a well-kept church-yard fringed by big old maples that have witnessed plenty of people come and go.

Christenings, weddings, and funerals.

People are born, people disappear.

Malin and Zeke head towards the northern corner of the churchyard, where they've been told Jessica Karlsson's grave is.

A grey stone cross.

Jessica Karlsson, born 2 July 1990, died 1 December 2009.

You were just a couple of years older than Tove.

Bouquets of white roses.

Red tulips.

And a card.

Laminated to withstand the wind and rain.

A picture of a girl who must have been Jessica.

Before the forest.

Before the rag soaked in hydrochloric acid in her mouth.

In her school graduation cap. Shoulder-length blond hair, rosy cheeks and inquisitive, sparkling blue eyes.

'We remember you, Jessica. Always in our hearts.' Signed Sofia, Lina and Cornelia.

Malin closes her eyes.

Women as warm, human stars.

Shall I give birth to your child as well, Jessica, the child you might have had one day?

Stina Karlsson adjusts her bleached hair and holds out a photograph of Jessica towards Malin, apparently keen to rearrange her features so she looks happy, optimistic.

It's not really working, Malin thinks.

The wrinkles are still there.

The sadness in your eyes.

The picture: A little girl running over dew-damp grass beside a cottage one summer evening.

'She's six years old there,' the friendly but subdued woman says, standing next to Malin by a stripped pine coffee table. 'Jessica was a sweet child, everyone loved her, she was so pretty. She was nineteen. I had her for nineteen years.'

Stina Karlsson is in her sixties, retired early from her work as a nursing assistant because of her back, and a widow for many years, 'long before the terrible things that happened to Jessica'.

She's offered coffee and home-baked raspberry buns.

Her rented flat is on the outskirts of Ljusdal, by the edge of the forest, in a red wooden building that contains four flats in total. Stina Karlsson's living room is furnished with a mixture of heirlooms and things from Ikea. She's put a big pile of photographs from her dead daughter's childhood on the coffee table, and is keen to show them all to Malin.

Zeke is waiting in the car.

'You go ahead,' he had said, she had realised he had had enough for the day, and couldn't handle the mother's grief.

'Jessica's dad died in a car accident. So I'm on my own now.'

Another picture.

A girl in a football strip, red shorts, green top.

'She showed a lot of promise. Then she got tired of it.'

'Do you have any idea who might have hurt her?' Malin asks.

Stina Karlsson puts the picture back on top of the pile.

'I think it was the forest,' she says. 'It must have been the forest. And her mouth, her lips and tongue, it must have been hell itself that burned her like that. It couldn't have been done by a human being.'

Malin nods.

Stina Karlsson picks up yet another photograph.

A little girl queuing to go on the merry-go-round at Liseberg funfair in Gothenburg.

'You should have seen her. She loved merry-go-rounds.'

As Malin is leaving, Stina Karlsson says: 'Can't you stay a bit longer? Look at some more pictures with me?'

25

The photograph of Tove.

It's on Malin's bedside table.

Tove with a book, sitting on a bench down by the river.

It's just after ten o'clock on Friday evening, and Malin has just arrived at her flat and found Peter in bed, asleep, exhausted after operating on a young man who was injured in a motorcycle accident.

He told her over the phone that the operation took nine hours, and that there hadn't been another surgeon available to relieve or assist him.

'Peter,' she whispers in his ear.

He can't hear me, Malin thinks.

She looks at him, noting how his usually so masculine cheeks look boyish when he's asleep.

He's lying on his back, and she curls up beside him, thinking that she'll book an appointment with the gynae-cologist tomorrow to get her coil removed. It's a Saturday, but I'll get hold of someone to make an appointment.

Or was he going to book an appointment? Yes, that was it.

What's Tove going to say if I get pregnant and tell her she's going to have a brother or sister?

She's bound to be happy.

She has to be.

Malin hasn't got the energy to think about it.

And Peter is warm, and in his sleep he moves closer to her, puts his arm around her and he's all muscles and humanity, something to orbit in a world where everything seems to lack any point of anchor.

'You're home,' he whispers, into the darkness of the room, the words refugees from a dream of having her close and being there for each other.

The next morning, at three minutes past nine, the detectives of the Violent Crime Unit of the Linköping Police gather around the white table in the meeting room. Just a few days have passed since Jenny Svartsjö was found.

During the night a low, dark grey cover of cloud has swept in from the south and is now throwing rain at Linköping and the preschool playground.

Johan Jakobsson, Börje Svärd, Waldemar Ekenberg, Sven Sjöman, Malin, Zeke.

Everyone's there, working on the murder case on a Saturday, everyone but Karim Akbar, who's busy on other matters.

Sven is sitting at the end of the table, not using the whiteboard today. His attempts to sound firm and decisive can't conceal his tiredness, and Malin thinks he must be sleeping badly, has picked that up.

'Let's start with Arto Antinen. The prosecutor still hasn't managed to get authorisation for a DNA sample,' Sven says.

'What's taking so long?' Waldemar snaps. 'It shouldn't take several days.'

'You know what prosecutors are like,' Börje says. 'They're a bunch of cowards. Maybe he's scared Antinen will kick up a fuss if he's innocent?'

'Kick up a fuss about what?' Zeke says, and Malin can tell that he's tired as well, maybe he's had a row with Gunilla?

Maybe she got jealous about his trip to Hälsingland? Wondering if he was really up to no good with Karin Johannison.

'I'll keep trying,' Sven says. 'Sooner or later we'll get permission. They're always cautious when it comes to matters of personal privacy.'

'Now we know Jenny Svartsjö's identity,' Johan says, 'shouldn't we check to see if they ever met? He's from Kisa, she's from Tranås, not that far away. They might have come into contact with each other.'

'Do you believe that?' Zeke says. 'There's a big difference in their ages, and Jenny Svartsjö hadn't lived in the area for a very long time.'

'I can do a quick check,' Johan says.

'We can ask when we take the sample,' Sven says. 'It's worth bearing in mind.'

He sighs before going on: 'And as far as Andrei Darzhevin is concerned, he's been arrested, formally charged on suspicion of the attempted murder or manslaughter of Katerina Yelena, and for procuring. Börje and Waldemar questioned him again yesterday, but he's clearly decided not to say another word. He seems to have withdrawn into himself, if you ask me. We could do with knowing the names of his contacts, but I doubt he's going to give us anything.'

Sven fails to suppress a yawn.

You can get sleeping pills, Sven, Malin thinks.

He goes on: 'Katerina Yelena is still sedated, but her condition is regarded as increasingly stable. I've sent a request to National Crime to get any information they may have about our brothel, in case they've got an ongoing investigation that could be linked to our case, but so far we haven't heard anything, and our regional colleagues aren't conducting any investigations of that sort at the moment. That much is clear.'

'So we're not going to get any further with that unless we can make Darzhevin sing,' Waldemar says, pushing his chair back so he can stretch his long legs out under the table.

'OK, Malin,' Sven says, choosing to ignore Waldemar's insinuation, 'I'd like you to tell us what you and Zeke managed to find out on your trip to Hälsingland.'

Malin tells the others about Jessica Karlsson.

About the similarities with the cases of Jenny Svartsjö, Maria Murvall and the woman at St Lars in Lund.

About the similarities in the violence.

In their ages.

About the differences in geographic location.

That they don't know how the victims fell into the perpetrator's hands. As far as that's concerned, the four cases appear to be very different. One prostitute, possibly two, one ordinary girl with an ordinary life, possibly on her way home, and one social worker. Their appearances also vary. Blonde, brunette.

And as she talks a thought begins to formulate in her head, gradually taking shape, but she's unable to articulate it. It's a simple, obvious thought, like when you've spent a long time looking for something only to discover that it was right in front of you the whole time.

She can't put it into words yet.

She goes on instead.

About the men in the hunting cabin whose identities it would be difficult to get hold of, because of the confidentiality ruling, unless they can come up with more evidence to compel disclosure. And about the prosecutor who was keen to drop the case.

She looks around at her colleagues in turn as she summarises her findings, as if to convince herself that there is a connection, that it isn't just a random product of her own overheated imagination. But at the same time she feels that there's something that's still evading her and the others.

And she remembers Hans Eriksson, the detective in Ljusdal. The ambiguous look in his eyes as he talked about the men in the hunting cabin.

Johan.

Alert, no doubt about that.

Börje. He's trying to piece together what she's saying. Waldemar, who seems to be waiting for her to say something that might give him the chance to use force in the near future.

Zeke.

Calmness personified, not even pitching in when she related what Hans Eriksson had said, he seems entirely happy with her account, and she's surprised that none of her colleagues seems to doubt the connections she can see, but perhaps they're too obvious to question. Even if the incidents may be separated by time and geography, they're linked in other ways.

The time of year.

The reluctance of the prosecutors.

The women's age, albeit with Maria a bit older than the others.

The violence.

The apparent lack of motive.

The injuries.

The scars.

And the forest, the way nature itself seems to have come to life and attacked the women, as if to wipe out their consciousness and wrench them away from any form of human belonging.

'So that's where we are,' Malin says as she concludes her account.

And Waldemar drums his fingers on the white table top.

'It shouldn't be that bloody difficult to get the case file

from Ljusdal, the one in Lund wasn't even declared confidential, for fuck's sake.'

'That's the prosecutor's decision,' Sven says. 'There's not much we can do about it. The prosecutor in Malmö wanted to drop the case, but didn't think it necessary to declare it confidential. Whereas in Ljusdal a young, punctilious prosecutor seems to have gone to the trouble of doing that.'

And in her mind's eye Malin can see Prosecutor Fredrik Kantsten, the amiable look in his eyes concealing his arrogance. It would be perfectly in character for a man like that not to bother declaring a case confidential. As if to show who had the real power. He could always declare the next case confidential, just because.

Conscious capriciousness.

Playing games with matters of great seriousness.

Unless Fredrik Kantsten is hiding something else. But if that were true, surely he would have ruled that the investigation into the girl in Lund was confidential?

Malin feels her thoughts bite their own tails.

Tries to focus on what's being said in the room.

'Even so,' Waldemar Ekenberg is saying, 'it must be possible to find out the names of the men who rented the hunting cabin. I'd like to have a word with them, and whoever rented it out.'

Bloodthirsty now, Malin thinks. And if they've got anything to do with any of this, you're welcome to beat the crap out of them for all I care. And she sees a deep hunger in Waldemar's eyes, as if this whole thing has somehow become personal for him.

'I'm afraid we'll have to manage without them,' Sven says, and Malin gets the impression that he doesn't sound disappointed or upset enough, and maybe it's finally happened, Sven Sjöman has grown far too tired to be a good police officer.

I never thought that would happen, Malin thinks.

They go on to discuss possible motives, a conversation that revolves around sadism, desire, power, sending messages to other women, revenge, a conversation that brings no clarity at all, and Malin finds herself thinking once again about the warlords in the Congo who use rape just like any other weapon.

They discuss whether to have a perpetrator profile drawn up. But they decide to wait, aware that such profiles can lead them to focus on particular issues.

Then Sven sums up the meeting.

And in the middle of the summary he pauses.

'By the way, I've heard from Australia. An Ingvar Svartsjö entered the country five years ago, but there's no sign of him ever having left. Nor any other sign of life. So what Britt Svartsjö says might well be true.'

The detectives nod.

They can all recognise the smell of a dead line of inquiry.

Then Sven allocates new tasks. Says: 'Right, let's hunt down the bastard who did this.'

And when he says the word 'hunt' something clicks inside Malin and she finally manages to formulate her thought: 'There is one more connection, the most obvious one: all the murders and assaults took place in the hunting season, and there seem to be hunting cabins popping up everywhere. In Maria's case, in our case out at Sjölunda, in Ljusdal, and who knows, maybe down in Skåne as well, even if there was nothing mentioned in the case file. But it could well mean that hunting and the hunting season have got something to do with this.'

The others sit in silence.

Looking at her. They know she's put into words something they should all have seen at once. But they're not reproaching themselves, that's just what can happen when a case is developing fast.

The way you see things gets distorted, the way you think
as well.

Everything blurs and becomes an amorphous mass,
impossible to get any sort of overview.

But what to do with this similarity that connects all the
women: the timing?

'Good,' Sven says. 'Very good. We'll bear that in mind,
and keep an eye out for anything connected to hunting that
crops up during the course of the investigation.'

And with that the meeting is over, and as they're about
to leave the room Sven tells Malin that Karim wants to see
her in his office, it's something urgent that can't wait, and
Malin feels her heart skip a couple of beats.

What the hell have I done now?

Sven sees how worried she is.

'Calm down, Malin,' he says. 'You're going to like this, I
promise.'

Karim Akbar is wearing a grey Corneliani suit that fits
perfectly.

White shirt.

A formal red tie, and he looks like a leading politician or
an overpaid businessman, Malin thinks. The head of a
company in some unexciting industry.

Insurance, perhaps.

Karim is sitting behind his walnut desk, bought in spite
of their restricted budget, as if he wanted to indulge himself
after turning down the prestigious job with the Migration
Board.

Malin knows he paid for his black leather chair himself.

She's sitting on one of his visitors' chairs, and the thin
cotton seat does nothing to conceal how uncomfortable it is.

'You need to go and talk to Vivianne,' Karim says. 'I can't
tell you why, but you need to talk to her.'

'About what?'

Vivianne Södergran. Karim's flirtatious, stroppy squeeze of a prosecutor.

Malin can't hide her scepticism.

She hates the career bitch who thinks she's so bloody wonderful, and Malin knows that she and Karim have started to enter Linköping society, that they've been invited to dinner by the District Governor, and that Karim's been invited to join the Freemasons.

'Go and see her in her office at two o'clock.'

Will she be there then? Malin thinks. On a Saturday? Surely that's when she gets her nails done.

'Why? I've got enough paperwork to last me half a lifetime. And plenty of other work.'

Karim smiles.

'Malin. I know what you think of Vivianne. But you know as well as I do that it's best not to have preconceived ideas about people. That you have to give them a chance or two to show who they are.'

'I don't have any preconceived ideas.'

And Karim leans forward and smiles even more broadly, then he starts to laugh, and his laughter turns into a drawn-out chuckle.

'Malin,' he groans, gasping for air. 'You're very funny, you know that? Two o'clock in her office. That's an order.'

26

Three, four, five . . .
　Up.
　Obey me, muscles.
　Now.
　Push. For God's sake.
　Think. One, two, fuck you.
　One, two.
　Fuck you.
　The rougher, the stronger, the harder the better.
　Pump, push, push everything from your muscles, make yourself stronger to deal with all the shit this world throws at you.
　The gym in the basement of the police station stinks of sweat, and the vomit-green walls make her feel sick, like a veil over Malin's eyes as she pushes the weights up towards the ceiling.
　One,
　two,
　three.
　Peter called, he'd booked a time with the gynaecologist at three o'clock that day, and at first she felt annoyed, even though she had agreed to it, how the hell could he arrange a gynaecologist, surely she could do that for herself? Then she realised that her anger was ridiculous, you help each other out in a relationship, and this involved them both. When he mentioned the gynaecologist's name, she had been taken aback.

Ärendsson.

She recognised the name at once from the investigation down in Malmö, the expert who claimed that the woman in St Lars could have inflicted those injuries herself.

At first she had protested.

This was too close.

'He's the best,' Peter had said.

And she hadn't felt like arguing, and couldn't tell him that Ärendsson had cropped up in their investigation. She blanked out the thought of herself half-naked in a room with the man.

Maybe she just shouldn't go?

But of course she would.

She could check him out, if nothing else.

Don't want to go, want to, don't want to . . .

I'm superwoman, I can handle something like that.

The meeting with Vivianne Södergran won't take long, whatever the hell that's about.

Alone down here. Mustn't drop the weights.

No more now, just one more.

She pushes the bar up, slips it into the rests and the whole world shakes.

The shower is cold at first, then hot.

And she pulls on her underwear, jeans and the plain white blouse, then her holster, pistol and jacket, and combs her hair with her fingers. Her cheeks look red in the mirror.

Soon she's standing in front of Vivianne Södergran's ellipsis-shaped desk. She has the same self-important manner as Fredrik Kantsten in Stockholm, and it strikes Malin that she reminds her of Karin Johannison a long time ago, when Karin thought she was something special and dressed far more smartly than she does these days.

But much worse.

Vivianne Södergran, with her suntanned, made-up skin,

perfect hair, her long eyelashes and tight checked suit and shiny tights, is far worse than Karin Johannison ever was.

'Welcome.'

Several octaves too high. Unbearable. And Malin wonders what Karim, who is deep down a rational and decent bloke, sees in this over-made-up grasper at the back end of her thirties.

We're the same age, Malin thinks. But I'll never be as much of an old crone as she is.

'Malin,' she says, and her voice is lower than usual. 'Sit down.'

What the hell does she want?

And obviously the chair Malin sits down on is comfortable, a bit too soft, too ingratiating against her backside.

'We don't know each other,' Vivianne Södergran says once Malin has sat down.

The walls around them are covered with bookcases bulging with law books and folders.

'No, we don't,' Malin says. 'You wanted to see me?'

'Yes.'

'Can I ask what about?'

Vivianne Södergran looks Malin in the eye.

The prosecutor's own big brown eyes in that over-made-up skull are full of a deep seriousness that Malin thinks clashes badly with her glossy, consciously formal exterior, and she is surprised by the look, almost taken aback.

'Can I trust you?' Vivianne Södergran says, and Malin feels like saying that it depends on what it is about.

But something in Vivianne Södergran's manner has changed, and makes Malin say: 'You can trust me. Whatever you want to say will stay between us.'

'I'm afraid it probably won't. But I know you're very keen to get hold of information about a confidential investigation up in Hälsingland. That's right, isn't it?'

Is she threatening me? Malin wonders. Is she trying to trap me somehow?

'Relax,' Vivianne Södergran says. 'I'm one of the good guys.'

Bloody hell, Malin thinks.

And then she begins to understand what this meeting is about.

And feels ashamed.

Ashamed of what she's been thinking about Vivianne Södergran. I ought to know better than to judge a book by its cover, I of all people ought to know better.

'I belong to a network of women who hold positions in society that give us the opportunity in our professional roles, through our contacts, and in the fields in which we have a particular competence to combat all forms of violence and oppression against women and children. We might not always be able to make much of a difference, but we do what we can, and we're not afraid to look the other way when we have to.'

Malin nods.

Thinks about the detective in Ljusdal, Hans Eriksson, and how he must have planned this so they could get hold of the case file in a safe way.

Suddenly feeling humility towards Vivianne Södergran.

Malin relaxes in the chair.

And then she looks down at her jeans, her blouse, and thinks how unsophisticated, how plain she looks, and that people actually have respect for a woman like Vivianne, who makes an effort to show that what she's doing is serious, and that it's important to her.

'One of the women in the network works in the prosecutors' office in Gävle. And she's been able to arrange this. Someone in the police up there has spoken to her as well.'

Vivianne Södergran holds a black folder out to Malin, then puts it down on the desk.

Some of the photocopied pages seem to want to fall from the file, to be read immediately.

'As you understand, you haven't received this. And if you have to act on the information it contains, which I believe you will, you'll have to come up with a reason, anything at all, I really don't care, but nothing must lead back to me. Or anyone else. And be very careful when you share its contents with your colleagues.'

'No problem,' Malin says. 'I'm good at that sort of smokescreen. Thank you. This is astonishing. Sorry if I sounded . . .'

'Get the bastard who did this. That's all I want. OK?'

'Do you believe that the name of that person is in here?'

'To be perfectly honest, I don't want to believe that it is.'

The black folder on the desk. Suddenly it seems to glow in the dim light.

'Be careful,' Vivianne Södergran says. 'Some of the names in there. They could burn you, they could burn you very bloody badly.'

There's a slight tremor in her voice.

She looks away for a second.

'I can promise you one thing,' Malin says, as she picks up the black folder from the desk. 'I'm going to get to the bottom of this, if it's the last thing I do.'

The names. The men.

The names in the scorching hot file.

And she realises now, as she sits in her white Golf in the car park, that what she saw in Vivianne Södergran just now, apart from determination and decision, was fear.

Fear in its very purest form: the fear you feel when you detect the smell of the monster, seconds before it shows itself.

She's already called Peter.

Told him to cancel the gynaecologist and make an appointment with another one, a female gynaecologist, she couldn't lie there with her legs open for Ärendsson. Even she isn't that much of a superwoman.

Once again, Peter wanted to know why. 'He's the best.'

'I can't tell you why. Just say I can't make it. I want to see a woman.'

'I'll sort it out.'

It's burning.

The gynaecologist, Emanuel Ärendsson, the most experienced in the University Hospital, and quite an authority, according to Peter, was one of the names in the folder.

He was one of the men in the hunting cabin in Hälsingland.

And cropped up in the investigation in Malmö.

And that was only the start.

27

The names.

She has to get to the others in the station, has to show the names to Sven Sjöman and Zeke, she has to, has to what?

She shuts the folder.

Puts it down in her lap, she can still smell her and Zeke's tiredness after their trip to Hälsingland in the car.

Sven knows how she got the folder.

Zeke doesn't.

But he won't ask any questions, he'll just absorb the information, and won't care where it came from.

The others?

Waldemar Ekenberg will wonder, Johan Jakobsson too, and even Börje Svärd. But they won't really care.

Malin notices her hands shaking, as if they belong to another body, and feels that a large, cool, neat tequila would put a stop to the shakes.

But she needs to keep her head clear now.

Needs to make sense of this.

The names.

How does it fit together?

The afternoon light outside the car is sharp.

Blinding, dazzling.

Then women's screams inside her. Which women are screaming? Crying for help?

They're in chains. Another woman is lying bleeding on a cold floor.

Malin shakes her head.

The car feels like a medieval dungeon, and the day, or what remains of it, is full of millipedes crawling towards her soul, and she feels the air inside the car running out, opens the door and runs towards the police station with the folder clutched in her arms.

Sven Sjöman seems to have been expecting her.

He's sitting at her desk in the office, chatting to Zeke, and he sees the folder in her hands, and how agitated she is, and then he gets up and says: 'I've forewarned Zeke, we'll talk around at my house. Just the three of us.'

Sven Sjöman's living room.

New green leather sofas, bought from a furniture chain known for being a cut above Ikea.

They look horrible, Malin thinks. Sven's wife must have chosen them, Sven has better taste than this.

But taste has never been this home's strong point.

Lace tablecloths. Swarovski figurines on the windowsills. Dreadful prints by someone called Madeleine Pyk.

The three of them all took their own cars, and before they set off she could see that the pair of them were practically bursting with curiosity. Sven evidently didn't know the names yet either, but he must have heard that they were important to their ongoing case, and that discretion was needed.

The folder on the living-room table.

Malin opens it and finds the document that shows the names of the men who were in the hunting cabin.

Zeke and Sven lean forward and read.

'Bloody hell,' Sven says, and in his voice is none of the tiredness that's been there recently.

'Bloody hell,' he repeats, and Malin thinks: How many times have I heard him swear over the years?

A handful?

'Christ!' Zeke says. 'You can't help wondering what the hell this is.'

Peder Stålskiöld.

The count from Sjölunda.

Owner of the large estate not far from where they found Jenny Svartsjö, and in the same belt of forest where Maria Murvall was found.

Emanuel Ärendsson.

Consultant gynaecologist at the University Hospital, the man Malin was supposed to be seeing now about the removal of her coil.

And there, at the bottom of the document: Fredrik Kantsten. District prosecutor in Stockholm. The prosecutor in charge of the investigation into the nameless girl at St Lars in Lund. Who put pressure on the police to close the case prematurely.

Connections.

In geography, time, events. Lines crossing and meeting, not evidence in themselves, but forming the points of light that detectives look for and follow into the darkness.

Unless the whole thing is a coincidence? It doesn't have to mean anything. There are a lot of differences between the various cases.

The men are friends who rented a hunting cabin.

They must be hunters.

But the count?

The location of his estate. And Malin recalls the hunting cabin on his land. Which had supposedly always stood unused.

The gynaecologist lives in Linköping. And he examined the woman in Lund.

The prosecutor in Stockholm.

And Malin thinks about the young prosecutor, Jimmy

Kalder, who shut down the investigation into Jessica Karlsson. Could he have been subjected to pressure from above? Competition is ruthless within the Public Prosecution Authority, and you need friends in order to advance.

'We can all see the connections,' Sven says. 'But this doesn't necessarily mean anything. And, as far as the rest of the world is concerned, we don't even have this information.'

'The connections are there,' Zeke says. 'Fucking Christ!'

'You can't help wondering,' Malin says in a low voice, and outside the window a gentle rain starts to fall on the flowering apple trees in Sven's garden, making the white petals droop under the weight of the drops.

'What the hell do we do with this?'

Sven swears for a second time, and then he looks at Malin as if she were head of the preliminary investigation rather than him, as if he were informally handing over responsibility to her as of now.

'I don't know,' Malin says.

'Shall we keep it within our little group?' Sven wonders.

'Why?' Zeke asks.

'It's sensitive. These are respected members of society, the press would have a field day.'

'And if they have got something to do with it,' Malin says, 'we really don't want them finding out what we know. The more people know, the greater risk there is of leaks. And we have to think of the people who have supplied us with this information.'

'OK, let's not say anything to the others yet,' Zeke says. 'Not until we've got more. Even if I trust them implicitly, I agree that it makes sense to keep these names between ourselves.'

'Karim knows,' Malin says.

'Don't be so sure,' Sven says.

Malin realises that Karim probably doesn't know the

names, that it might not even have occurred to Vivianne
Södergran to tell him about the contents of the folder she'd
managed to get hold of.

'I think we should agree that Zeke and I will carry on
working on this on our own for a few days, and not tell
anyone except Johan. We need his specialist knowledge to
be able to dig out information about these men. Their connections to each other, their careers, family circumstances,
anything that could make things clearer and take us forward.'

Sven nods.

'That's what we'll do. Malin, you talk to Johan. But be
extremely cautious.'

'Should we talk to Karim? Before we proceed?'

A hint of doubt in Zeke's voice.

'Like I said, we need to be cautious,' Sven says. 'I'll talk
to Karim.'

Malin gets up from Sven's sofa.

Her hands are shaking again as she goes to pick up the
folder from the table.

Sven notices and smiles: 'No tequila, Malin, no matter
how good it might taste.'

Once Malin and Zeke have left Sven, he goes over to the
living-room window. Looks out at his garden, at the hundreds
of little white flowers on the plum tree.

He planted that tree the year they bought the house.

How many years ago is that?

He can't be bothered to work it out, just knows that his
wife makes very good jam from the plums the tree produces
each year.

At the far end of the garden, almost at the compost heap,
is a small fountain. A concrete angel that squirts water from
its mouth.

Or used to squirt water.

The pump stopped working years ago.

Broken.

Somehow or other. Just like he's felt for the past six months or more.

He gets his mobile out and dials Karim's number. Karim answers on the second ring.

A short summary.

To judge by Karim's agitated murmuring, Sven realises that he knows what they've found out, which isn't really surprising considering his relationship with Vivianne Södergran.

'I want Malin and Zeke to go on working with this,' Sven says. 'With extreme caution, because in a strictly judicial sense we've got nothing on these men. Just a few connections, and tenuous ones at that.'

Karim falls silent at the other end of the line.

Sven can hear him breathing, reflecting again, because he must have considered everything already.

'Do what you have to do,' he says. 'The nature of the crimes justifies it. If there's even the slightest chance that these men know something, then we've got a justification to pursue this line of inquiry. We can deal with any problems later.'

'Good,' Sven says. 'Thank you.'

'You know, Sven,' Karim says, 'all evil is actually one and the same. It was the same evil that we're seeing here that drove my family out of Kurdistan and drove my dad to his death. It's just different faces showing themselves. And this one has got a particularly ugly face.'

Then he hangs up.

He looks around his office in the station, thinking about Vivianne, and his son, whom he sees all too rarely.

Then he sees Jenny Svartsjö's body in his mind's eye.

He sees his father's face, swollen and blue in the noose

he had made of the shower hose. Karim had been the one who found him.

He was eleven years old at the time.

His dad's empty, bloodshot eyes. With something of his look still in them, full of fear, but also relief.

There was no relief in Jenny Svartsjö's eyes in the images in Karim's mind.

Just despair.

He knows that his detectives are working flat out now.

It's time to stretch the limits of acceptable police work.

The way things stand, the world demands that.

Johan Jakobsson gets impatient when Malin briefs him in the meeting room, out of sight and earshot of Waldemar Ekenberg and Börje Svärd.

He seems to want to throw himself at his computer.

His aching mouse-arm seems to have vanished, and he looks as if he'd be prepared to take morphine to be able to carry out this task.

'I did a few quick checks,' he says. 'I couldn't find anything to suggest that Arto Antinen had any connection to either Jessica Karlsson or Jenny Svartsjö. But I'll keep looking. Who knows what he might have come up with?

'From what I've been able to find out in various official registers, there's no evidence that Jessica had any sort of secret life that could have brought her into contact with a murderer.'

'There wasn't in the Ljusdal police's investigation either,' Malin says. 'She was a perfectly ordinary girl. I'm convinced of that.'

'So, hunting season is the clearest connection,' Zeke says.

When Johan has left her and Zeke they remain seated in the stuffy room, staring at the blank whiteboard and trying to figure out how they're going to move on from here.

How does it all fit together? If it does even fit together.

What have they got?

Some men who rented a hunting cabin. A seasonal connection.

Are they just being paranoid, making a mountain out of a molehill?

What about the brothel in Skattegården?

Katerina Yelena?

Andrei Darzhevin?

Jenny Svartsjö?

Is the brothel in any way linked to the men, and, if so, how? Or is it just a coincidence that they both feature in the same investigation?

The young woman in St Lars in Lund? Who is she?

How does all this fit together?

They write on the board, without using the men's names, noting every man, every woman, every location.

Trying to see a different pattern, but no clear picture emerges.

Sadistic sexual violence.

Torture.

Murder.

Young women murdered, violated, raped.

Men, prominent men, appearing in different places. Why?

'This is big,' Zeke says. 'I can feel it.'

But Malin can hear doubt in his hoarse voice.

'Maybe we just want to see a big conspiracy with sexual brutality in the upper echelons of society?'

'Do you believe that?'

'With this case, I honestly don't know,' Malin says. 'There are too many possibilities in each line of inquiry, it's like a fucking hydra with loads of heads, but somewhere all of this comes together in one single body, one overarching context, I'm absolutely certain about that.'

'You can't kill a hydra,' Zeke says. 'You know that, don't you?'

'Of course you can,' Malin says. 'You have to burn it, then bury it, otherwise it comes back twice as strong.'

'The DNA on Jenny Svartsjö's body,' Zeke says. 'There isn't a hope in hell that we're going to get samples from Stålskiöld, Kantsten or Ärendsson. Neither Karim nor any prosecutor would go that far, not the way things stand. Regardless of how serious the crimes are.'

Malin shakes her head.

'We've got nothing on them. Other than suspicions. And don't forget that formally we don't even know that they were in Ljusdal. We've hardly got enough at the moment to even talk to them. We'll have to hope Johan finds something.'

Malin shuts her eyes.

Feels exhaustion paralyse her brain, putting a stop to any sensible activity, and the more she thinks about the case, the less clear everything gets.

But perhaps the truth exists, nonetheless, among these three men?

'I'm tired,' she says, weighing the folder in her hand. There isn't really much more of use in it. The farmer who rented out the hunting cabin in Ljusdal had a watertight alibi, he'd been hosting a party at home on the night in question.

'Me too,' Zeke says.

'Let's sleep on it.'

Peter, Malin thinks. I hope you're home. I hope you're waiting for me in the flat, that you're not on standby and have been called in for an operation, that misfortune is resting this evening.

He is waiting for her in the flat.

In the kitchen, as she stirs a pan of chicken sauce to go

with the pasta, she tells him that they might have made a breakthrough in the investigation into Jenny Svartsjö's murder.

'I cancelled the appointment with Emanuel Ärendsson today, like you asked,' Peter says. 'I'll make a new appointment with him. When would suit you?'

'Any time. But like I said on the phone, I don't want to see Ärendsson. I want to see a woman.'

Peter looks bemused as he breaks up a packet of spaghetti by banging it hard against the worktop.

'That's what I don't understand: why can't you see him? He's an authority in his field. Coils are perfectly routine for him. And gynaecologists are usually men.'

'I've heard some less than flattering things about him. A colleague thought he was creepy.'

Peter raises his eyebrows.

'He's a perfectly ordinary fifty-six-year-old.'

'Can't you book me in to see a female gynaecologist?'

'It's just a routine procedure, does it really matter?'

'I'll book it myself, then, if it's that bloody difficult.'

'Calm down, Malin, I'll sort it. It's no problem, I mean, I do work there.'

She nods.

It makes sense for him to book the appointment. Of course it does.

And she wishes she could tell him details about the investigation, about why she can't see Emanuel Ärendsson. The thought of standing naked in front of him, regardless of whether he has anything to do with the crimes against the women, makes her feel nauseous.

Peter goes out into the hall and she hears him talking on his mobile.

He comes back into the kitchen and stops in front of her with a smile.

'I've got you an appointment. Tomorrow, at two o'clock. With Helena Popova. She's coming in on a Sunday just for you. Does that suit madam?'

'I'll have to see if I can make it,' she says.

And Peter puts his mobile down on the table, hard, and throws out his hands.

'You really don't want to, do you?' he says. 'What do you really want?'

'I do want to.'

She stirs the pan of pasta to stop the spaghetti sticking together. Feels the hot steam rise up to her cheeks, and she looks at Peter, his impotence and disappointment.

'I can leave if you'd rather,' he says calmly. 'I thought you'd realised this isn't a game for me.'

'I'm scared,' Malin says. 'You have to understand that. And, please, stop all this bloody nagging.'

'Scared of what?'

'I don't know,' Malin says. 'Everything to do with having a baby, absolutely everything.'

'There's nothing to be scared of.'

He goes over to her at the cooker, puts his arms around her, and she feels anger bubbling up inside her.

'There's a hell of a lot to be scared of. You're not the one who has to deal with all the crap that goes with being pregnant.'

'I'm here for—'

She wriggles out of his arms, takes a step back and shouts: 'I'd be dealing with it on my own, don't you get it? I'd be on my own. How fucking stupid are you?'

Peter backs away.

'You wouldn't be alone.'

'Get out,' she says, following him as he retreats into the hall, and without even thinking about it she shakes the spoon at him.

'You're always alone. If you can't understand that, you might as well go.'

'Calm down, for God's sake. I'm going.'

A look of fear in his eyes.

Fucking coward.

'What, are you frightened I'm going to hit you?' she yells.

He opens the front door.

'You've got a fucking weird way of expressing your love,' he says.

'Who the hell said anything about love? You can fuck off with all your bloody baby ideas. I've got neither the time nor the inclination to have a fucking kid.'

The words are streaming out of her.

She wants to press stop, but can't. Perhaps she really does want to say these words?

'You're even crazier than I thought,' he says as he pulls on his ridiculous grey, mid-length jacket.

'Crazier than I thought,' he says again before leaving.

Closing the door gently behind him, and she shouts: 'And you wouldn't want to have a kid with someone this crazy, eh?'

Then there's just the echo of her shout, and the sound of a saucepan full of pasta bubbling over, the hissing as the hot water hits the even hotter hob.

She sinks to the floor in the hall.

Digging the nails of her index fingers into her thumbs.

She feels like running after him, begging him to stay, saying sorry, sorry, sorry, but how do you do that?

I do want to have that baby.

I don't.

I do.

How the hell am I supposed to know?

She gets up.

Looks out of the kitchen window.

Sees him walk across the grass by St Lars Church in the darkness.

His shadow is long in the hazy light of the street lamp, and he doesn't turn around, just disappears into the night, becoming a blinking star among millions of others in a crystal-clear night sky.

Resistance, Peter thinks as he hurries over Trädgårdstorget. She's made up of resistance, contradictions.

He sees the young immigrant kids hanging around outside the uninviting McDonald's. The girls with bleached hair waiting for the bus. Couples on their way home from the cinema. A homeless man rooting through a bin.

Peter is still breathing hard.

Like walking into a storm, into the wind.

Fighting to move forward.

Not giving up.

Malin's a person lashed to two different horses that are pulling in opposite directions.

He feels like running back to her flat.

Taking her into his arms. Holding her tight, tight.

Get her to realise that he's for real. That he's not going to disappear, no matter what gets dragged out of the swamp. That she isn't alone. That the best way to show her love this evening was to walk away.

I'm here. I can handle it. I want you.

I can handle it.

Can't I?

Of course I can.

He crosses Drottninggatan. Continues towards his own flat. Thinking that it can all wait, sometimes the best way to move on is to move sideways, not lose your footing.

★   ★   ★

Malin has opened her file about Maria Murvall, spreading the papers over the floor and table in the living room.

The file on the nameless woman in Lund is lying jumbled up on the kitchen floor.

Malin is sitting on the coffee table in the living room.

Staring down at the documents.

At the list of Maria's clients. She's questioned all of them. At the medical officer's report. At the maps. At the transcripts of interviews.

What is it I'm not seeing? she wonders.

What am I blind to? She's got the same feeling now as she had earlier today before she realised the connection to the hunting season. But the feeling is much deeper now. So she lets go of it.

Peter.

She finds herself thinking about Rudolph, his father. The hunt they conduct down there. The deer on the estate. The relative proximity to the place where the girl in St Lars was found.

Could he have organised a hunt? Could those three men have been there as his guests?

Paranoid, Malin thinks. Fending off the thought.

The files.

The whole flat is a mess of paper, whose essence I just don't understand.

So what am I being blind to?

28

The draining board.

Blinkers on when I see it.

See all the mess, all we couldn't do.

The remains of the previous evening's emotions are still lingering in the room, like the smell of something left in a frying pan, burned, and then thrown away.

Anger.

Longing.

A desire to bring all the threads together.

Coffee.

Warm and soothing and beige with milk heated in a noisy old microwave.

Malin has woken from a night oddly free of dreams.

It's just past seven o'clock.

She's standing by the draining board in the kitchen, trying to gather her thoughts, the feelings that are sparking through her body like fallen power lines.

I'm not going to throw this away.

I can't, I mustn't let my own insecurities lose me Peter.

She had felt in need of a drink last night.

Wanted to go down to the pub on the ground floor. Empty a whole bottle of spirits, she didn't care what, escaping into the wonderful no-man's-land of alcohol.

Don't think about that now. But she knows that the only

thing that can save them is if they really try for that baby, if she tries.

Nothing less, otherwise their love is over, regardless of how many times they say sorry. Over before it really got going.

Sunshine today, patchy, cumulus clouds covering part of the sky.

The row.

Their first real one, about important things. She had been expecting him to call her when he got back to his flat and had calmed down, and had herself wanted to call, but she hadn't. She realised that she was the one who needed to calm down.

He hadn't called.

Neither had she.

Like cats circling each other. But now Malin is standing in the kitchen, and knows she has to approach him, knows she has to swallow her hurt and her pride, change part of her nature and actually approach him.

Otherwise?

The end.

And he has to accept me.

He has to.

Sven Sjöman had called, though. He'd changed his mind since yesterday, having thought about things overnight, and said that Karim was giving them a free hand, that they could tell the others in the team about the new information, not keep anything secret, the whole of his detective's soul was telling him that, and Malin knew that they were suffering a sort of minor panic, not acting rationally or correctly.

The passion in Sven's voice.

Soon time for the meeting of the investigating team.

Other meetings.

And she sees the wind catch the tree tops over by the church, as a crow settles on one of the red tiles of the church roof.

It sits there for a while, then flies off again.

Maybe, she thinks, Peter has been testing me, and is gone now? How do I know he's thinking the way I am? Maybe our relationship is over now, and the feeling is overwhelming and she'd do anything for a glass full to the brim with tequila.

Only drink can help on occasions like this.

Against feelings like this.

But there's no drink in the flat.

Instead, she takes a deep gulp of coffee.

Thinks about the names.

The men behind them. The darkness she needs to go into. The light she hopes to find beyond it.

The whiteboard.

The names of the men in the hunting cabin in red.

The women's names, the nameless woman in Lund identified as 'St Lars woman'.

One column of similarities. Another of differences.

DNA found only on Jenny Svartsjö.

Maria's samples ruined by the National Forensics Lab.

No point wasting time on that now.

A sombre mood sitting like a heavy weight on the people around the table.

Dense anxiety and fear in the room. Frustration. The realisation that they need to make progress.

Karim Akbar.

Impeccably dressed as usual, even though it's Sunday. He's called in everyone on the team, agreed to pay overtime. Malin had expected him to back off, thinking about the consequences for his own career if they started to dig into these men's lives in connection with crimes like these.

Shameful, terrible, vile crimes.

So all police officers must work. Free time and rest can come later.

And the men.

If your name shows up in a case like this in a way that can be described as relevant, you might never be clean again, not in your own eyes, but above all not in other people's.

But the meeting had started with Arto Antinen.

The authorisation to compel him to supply a DNA sample had arrived.

Börje Svärd and Waldemar Ekenberg would be heading out to his cottage after the meeting to get hold of the sample, and then the National Forensics Lab would rush it through. Everyone was hoping the result would be positive, but none of the detectives in the room actually believed it would be.

This was bigger.

A deeper wound, right into the body of Swedish society. A pus-filled boil caused by something that must have gone awry a long, long time ago.

A black cyst that had spread through every limb of the body, a hydra with an unknown number of heads.

They agreed, once again, that Johan Jakobsson should dig out everything he could find about the men. Their backgrounds, their links to each other, to other people. Unearthing something with which they could confront one of them.

So far he hadn't found anything.

For the time being they're not going to question any of them, not show their hand until the time is right. Fear can be their best weapon for making someone talk. And the more they know, the easier it is for them to make someone feel afraid.

Malin had wanted to confront Fredrik Kantsten about the fact that he had rushed the investigation in Skåne, and that his name had cropped up in the case of Jessica Karlsson, which was also dropped quickly by the young prosecutor, Jimmy Kalder.

But Sven Sjöman said it was too soon.

Andrei Darzhevin.

Katerina Yelena. Still sedated in hospital, and Sven says: 'I'm convinced this is all connected, somehow.'

'Time for a bit of serious police work,' Waldemar says, and Malin thinks about what she's got ahead of her, what they've all got ahead of them, and the sort of force that might be needed, and she wants to talk to Peter, to call him and say sorry, but that will have to wait, actions speak louder than any words now.

'Take care, be cautious, but not weak. Do what you have to do.'

With these words Karim concludes the meeting.

Vivianne Södergran, Malin thinks, as she sees Karim's determination. She's making you a better person. Isn't she? And that must be the point of what we call love.

She tells Zeke she has to go to the dentist for a routine check-up, for the first time in two years, and she doesn't want to cancel at such short notice because she'd still have to pay up in full and that would sting because the greedy bastards get paid so insanely well as it is.

'On a Sunday?'

'Mine's open on Sundays. If you have an appointment.'

'Sure, Malin. Come back when you're done.'

The gynaecologist, Helena Popova, is a middle-aged woman, friendly and formal, and she doesn't mention Peter. She gives her a happy smile of understanding, as if she is going to help the pair of them, her patient and her professional colleague, by doing something beautiful.

But can anything beautiful happen in this room? The pale

grey wallpaper has a deathly pallor under the fluorescent lights, and isn't there a faint smell of sulphur? Disinfectant, perhaps? Or the thin paper covering the examination table?

Helena Popova is sinuous, small and slender. Neat blond hair framing an angular, intelligent face, with still more intelligent brown eyes behind round metal-framed glasses.

She probably has children herself, Malin thinks, grown up now, and as she undresses in the examination room she can't help wondering how Popova's etiolated body managed to produce children. But what do I know, perhaps she hasn't even got any?

The chill of the room envelops her body, the white tunic she puts on is made of scratchy nylon.

And Malin thinks about Karin Johannison, who wants nothing more than to have a child to look after. Who's planning to adopt. Who wants to give her excess of love to a small human being.

Who am I to doubt? To hesitate?

What right do I have not to want this?

I have to, don't I? Otherwise I'm mocking all childless women, all those whose love is desperately trying to find somewhere to go.

But still.

I know nothing about the woman who is about to push a cold instrument inside me.

And Malin starts to feel sick, thinking that this is wrong, have I no shame in my body? But she gets into the gynaecologist's chair and puts her legs up, and is it possible to feel more open, revealed, exposed?

It is, Malin thinks.

Oh yes, it's possible.

And she shuts her eyes, feels the metal inside her, and hears Doctor Popova's calm voice explaining what she can see, saying that everything looks absolutely fine.

Like a shock through her body.

Malin tenses up. Every muscle goes rigid and a violent pain shoots through her, up through her stomach, stabbing her heart like a thousand darts, and she sees a naked woman in chains in a dark, underground lair.

The woman is covered in wounds, her face is cast down and she is groaning, pleading for help, for mercy, for someone to rescue her, and then Malin sees a black shadow approach the woman and she knows that this is happening, it is happening now, and it's real, this isn't just something happening deep inside her, in this examination room, under the segmented lamp's shimmering lemon-sliced light.

The woman is screaming.

More women are screaming.

Malin has to fight not to let the women's screams become her own, and she feels sweat break out on her forehead as her muscles almost go into spasm.

A hand on her brow.

'Relax.

'Relax, we'll soon be finished, this is a very simple procedure, nothing can go wrong.'

Malin opens her eyes, unless perhaps they were already open? The world is there, and Doctor Popova, but the tortured woman in the lair is gone, and the screaming women, if they ever really existed.

But Malin knows that she exists.

That they exist.

That it's happening now.

That it hasn't stopped.

'There, all done,' Doctor Popova says. 'Now there's nothing to stop more little people coming into the world.'

What would they want with this world?
To end up like me?

But I'm sure you're a better mother than mine, Malin. That your child will have a better father than mine, because what he did to me was unforgiveable.

So he must burn.

He shall burn for the entirety of his eternal death.

Screaming and tormented, the way I was in life.

But believe in the world, Malin, believe that love is possible.

That there is something worth hanging on to, beyond all the misery.

29

How am I going to deal with this bastard?

Arto Antinen.

Something in his wizened appearance makes Waldemar Ekenberg want to throw up, ashamed of being human, of being born as one. This bastard's worse than his dad.

His whole being reeks of hopelessness, of giving in to his desires, an acceptance of them, of allowing himself to cross the boundary.

Revolting.

And now this man, this rapist, is sitting in front of him and Börje Svärd, on a ladder-backed chair in his stinking cottage, and the bastard's crying. He says he's had his punishment, that he's taking medication to suppress his urges, that it isn't right that they can force him to give a sample, that he hasn't got anything to do with the murder of Jenny Svartsjö, that he's never even seen her.

'I'm completely innocent.'

Waldemar adjusts his blue shirt and pulls up his brown gabardine trousers before taking a step closer to Arto Antinen.

Asks: 'Did you know Jenny Svartsjö? Or a Jessica Karlsson in Ljusdal? Have you been travelling around the countryside to get hold of women? Young ones? Huh?'

Arto Antinen shakes his head.

He's not going to answer, Waldemar thinks.

I'm going to get the sample from the bastard now.

'If you're so innocent, why the hell didn't you let us take the sample of your own free will? And stop blubbing before I smash your head in.'

'It's not right.'

'Do you really think that this is about you?' Börje says. 'This is about murdered women, raped women, and you're bleating and crying about your rights.'

Arto Antinen hesitates, clenches his jaw, then looks Waldemar in the eye and opens his mouth.

Börje puts the swab in his open mouth, smelling his breath, a stench of yesterday's alcohol and unbrushed teeth, pieces of food rotting in cavities and hidden gaps.

He wipes the swab under Antinen's tongue.

Hard, Waldemar thinks as he sees Börje poking about in the rapist's mouth. Bloody hard, but Börje doesn't have the same sadistic streak as him.

That word.

Sadistic.

He doesn't like it, but knows that's what he can be sometimes. He sometimes likes to cause real pain when he crosses the boundary in the hunt for information, pressing a bit too hard to hear them scream, hear the human sound that only comes from genuine, deeply felt pain.

But this cunt in front of them?

How much fucking pain has he not inflicted?

Revolting fucker.

It would be better if we found him dead in the forest. And Waldemar sees the bottles of vodka on the kitchen counter, two full bottles of Explorer that must have cost a fortune for an unemployed ex-con.

He goes over to the sink, and behind his back hears Börje say: 'All done.'

And he hears Arto Antinen blubbing as he picks up one

of the bottles, unscrews the lid and empties the contents down the sink.

'For God's sake, Waldemar.'

Waldemar turns around and stares at Arto Antinen.

'You don't need that, you never know what someone like you might get into your head when you're drunk.'

'Stop it!' Arto Antinen calls from his chair. 'This isn't fucking fair!'

Waldemar Ekenberg picks up the second bottle.

Tips out the contents, then grins at Arto Antinen.

'And who the hell said that anything in life was ever fair?'

Arto Antinen is lying on the floor in his cottage, no longer able to stand upright, it's as if all the energy in his body has drained away.

He breathes air into his lungs, lets it out, feels the warmth of his innards hit the hand he's holding out in front of his mouth, feels the cool of the floorboards beneath him.

It never ends, he thinks.

His mouth is still sore.

It's going to go on and on.

The test.

What are they going to find out about me that they don't already know? The smell of alcohol from the sink. He feels like getting to his feet and licking up the last remnants of vodka before they evaporate.

Sadists.

They're sadists.

A psychologist once told him that he was a clinical case of sexual sadism, and that he needed to learn to control his sexual impulses.

Air in, air out.

The lonely, exhausted warmth of life against his ageing hand.

Arto Antinen shuts his eyes.

Will it ever end? he wonders. Or is desire eternal?

Börje Svärd watches Waldemar Ekenberg get into the car outside the cottage. The green of the forest frames his tall, thin but strong form, lending it a glow it doesn't deserve.

He hates Waldemar's predilection for violence, for going too far.

But he knows that it's sometimes necessary.

And he's a good friend, he took me on after Anna's death, asking me home to meet his wife in their villa in Mjölby, taking me along to Mantorp to watch the horses and motor-races.

Waldemar shuts the car door, starts the engine, and Börje gets in beside him.

'Vile bastard,' Waldemar says.

His body seems somehow wrapped up in itself, every muscle slightly tense.

'I'm sick of dirty old men,' he says. 'Especially the ones who don't reveal everything. I want the birds to sing.'

And Börje thinks that violence can be justified, but only as a means to get at far worse forms of violence.

He thinks about how the boundaries dissolve on the fringes of human behaviour, and the distinctions, the precious impressions we all carry inside us about good and evil, melt away and are replaced by something else.

By good violence.

Sometimes directed against the innocent.

But necessary violence.

And Waldemar is tailor-made for that sort of violence.

'Let's go,' Waldemar says.

And as he says the words a fly starts buzzing in the car, loudly, persistently, as if it comes from a different world.

★ ★ ★

Malin got dressed, thanked Doctor Popova, and then made her way through the hospital corridors. She realised that she had forgotten to ask Popova about Emanuel Ärendsson as she had intended.

But perhaps it was just as well.

Some things should remain separate, private.

She took the lift up to ward nine, hoping that Peter would be there, not busy with his round, not sitting in a meeting or operating; she knew he was on duty this weekend.

She knocked on the door of his office.

But he wasn't there.

No one at the nurses' station knew where he was.

She wandered around the ward a few times.

Feeling the memory of Helena Popova's metal instrument inside her.

Cold in the heat.

The pain was still there.

Maybe they had passed each other? Missed each other by chance?

The previous day's row.

It had been an argument about life and death.

And it struck Malin that the whole of her life was about such extremes.

That the boundaries of everything were the same, just as clear, that the search for the truth was the common denominator in everything she did.

She cursed herself.

Felt sick at her own inability to realise what was important in a person's life, and her own fear of realising it.

Then she went past Katerina Yelena's room.

For a few short minutes, in her self-absorption, she had forgotten that she was there.

She hesitated outside the door, wanted to go in, but what would she find? An oxygen mask, the bandage over the wound to her stomach, bleeping sounds, loneliness, vulnerability.

If Katerina Yelena knew something, was she actually in danger? Ought they to put a watch on her?

No.

Women who were the victims of trafficking rarely knew anything about the men behind the trade. They might recognise a face, but they never knew any real names or identifiable places.

She didn't go in, carried on towards the lifts, and the lift door opened and there was Peter.

At first he looked surprised, then hesitant, and he didn't move from the spot.

The lift door started to close again.

Malin's foot in the gap.

Quickly, as though thrust out from her body, and the door opened again and he got out, took her in his arms, but she kept hers limp by her sides, letting herself be suffused by his warmth and she felt tears welling up in the corners of her eyes, and felt like a very small girl, and she felt ashamed again, fighting back the tears, and then she said: 'I've seen the gynaecologist today. Just now.'

'I love you,' Peter whispered in her ear. 'Everything's going to be fantastic. Isn't it? I'm convinced everything's going to be really fantastic.'

Andrei Darzhevin feels the blow hit his head.

His sleep ends abruptly the moment the clenched fist lands on his skull and he throws the blanket off and tries to sit up, but is being held down by an almost unbelievably determined frame that reeks of cigarette smoke.

Brown fabric.

Grey?

Then he feels the steel against his nose, the pain as what must be the barrel of a pistol is pushed up into his nostril, and then he screams, but knows instinctively that it's pointless, because even if anyone could hear him, nobody actually wants to.

The crazy policeman's face.

What was his name?

Waldemar?

And Andrei Darzhevin knows what's coming, he's encountered far crazier cops at home in St Petersburg, and he knows that he can get this far but no further with silence, because otherwise he might be found hanged in this cell.

Hang me.

I want it, he thinks.

Do it for me.

And he sees his daughter in his mind's eye, running across the meadow, and wants to thrust the image aside and let this policeman beat him to death, because that would be for the best.

Wouldn't it?

Soak up the violence.

He feels the policeman hitting him, but he could beat anyone he liked. He feels the force in the blows directed at his own shortcomings, and his unbearable memories.

Why should it be any different here to home?

Had he ever believed that?

And the blanket is pulled from his body, and he wishes he had worn his trousers as he had thought, feels naked in just his underpants, and Waldemar says, in broken English: 'Now you talk, you bastard. Tell us everything you know, anything that might be important.'

And Andrei knows what he can say.

But still.

He shakes his head, feels the barrel of the pistol scrape the fragile blood vessels and the blood start to trickle under his bandage and over his upper lip.

Waldemar falls silent.

Isn't he tougher than this?

But Andrei Darzhevin knows that the man who has come to his cell is one of the really tough ones.

'Don't move.'

He feels his underpants being pulled down.

'You fucking bastard.'

Another cold object.

A knife against his testicles now.

'Give me something, or I'll cut your fucking balls off, and then you'll talk with a squeaky voice for the rest of your life, like a fucking eunuch for your mafia friends to piss all over. I'm sick of people like you. I'm prepared to take the consequences of cutting your balls off, get that? I'm done with this. Who are your fucking contacts?'

Don't you get it? Andrei Darzhevin thinks. I'm not scared of you, but at the same time he realises that this is what his life is going to be like, for ever, one way or the other.

'So I want to hear you squeak, you understand?'

And he feels the knife begin to cut into him.

He stares into Waldemar's eyes. The fear in them, the fear that the only language he has won't be understood.

Andrei Darzhevin blinks.

It doesn't matter any more.

And when he speaks his voice is flat, as if he were already dead, letting the words be carried out of him on the air of his last breath.

'Paul Lendberg. Check him out.'

Then he falls silent.

30

Help Johan Jakobsson.

That's all we can do right now.

Both Zeke and I.

But once she got back to the police station Malin didn't have time to do anything before Johan and Zeke called her over to Johan's desk.

'We've found a few things,' Johan says. 'It might be enough to motivate a very cautious talk to one of the men.'

She leans over Johan's shoulder and looks at the screen. 'What have you found?'

'They were at university in Uppsala at the same time,' Zeke says. 'They all lived in the same residence, belonging to the association for students from Småland. Don't ask me why.'

He clicks to another window.

Black, with old-fashioned, swirling red lettering.

'The Skulls Society.'

Some sort of student association supposed to have existed since 1898. Just two links.

One with a brief history.

'The Skulls Society. An association for the most prominent male students in Uppsala, those expected to be future leaders of the Kingdom of Sweden. To this day, members are only accepted after thorough examination and testing.'

Then a page of pictures from meetings in the forest, some black and white, some colour, where the members,

young men, seem to be at some sort of scout camp, but
without uniforms and always ready for drinking and
partying rather than acts of charity.

'Look here,' Johan says.

A black-and-white photograph, undated, of three young
men in a forest clearing, dressed in dark suits.

Beneath the picture are three names: 'Honourable
members Fredrik Kantsten, Emanuel Ärendsson and Peder
Stålskiöld.'

'Friends,' Zeke says. 'Bloody weird society. Children
playing at being important. They must have kept in touch.
Could that be our way in? What did they do in this society?
Is there a constitution? We could ask. The website doesn't
say anything.'

Malin nods.

But is this really enough?

Enough to talk to the men, as things stand?

The Skulls Society.

Could something have started back then, if anything had
actually started?

'I want to talk to Ärendsson,' Malin says. 'See what that
throws up.'

'Why would this society publish pictures of certain
members, identifying them by name, if it's supposed to be
so secret?' Johan wonders.

'Who knows?' Zeke says. 'But you can see that they're
more kids than adults. They probably haven't even considered the contradiction, and just wanted some pictures on
the website. I mean, they shouldn't even have a website.'

'It makes people curious,' Malin says. 'And mystery is the
mother of curiosity. They probably want to be mysterious
and famous, otherwise what's the point of any association
or society? There's something called Skulls and Bones at
Yale. Secret but very well known. Several US presidents

have been members. The Skulls Society might be a small-scale Swedish version. Even if I've never heard of it.'

'We haven't managed to find any more information online. Nothing on Wikipedia or any blogs. Nothing at all so far,' Johan says.

'But our friends in the hunting cabin up in Hälsingland were all members of the society,' Zeke says. 'That sounds to me like a good enough reason to ask a few questions.'

'We'll have to check with Sven. But considering the nature of the crimes, I think we ought to be allowed to question anyone we like,' Malin says. 'And that hunting trip is bloody weird. As is the fact that both Ärendsson and Kantsten cropped up in the Lund case.

'Anything else, Johan?'

'That's all so far, but I'll keep looking. I'll see if there are any more links to the case in Skåne, where Kantsten was the prosecutor. I ought to be able to get something out of the registers.'

Malin walks over to Börje Svärd.

He tells her that getting the DNA sample from Arto Antinen passed without drama, and that Waldemar went off on a cigarette break fifteen minutes ago, and has been seriously agitated.

Malin calls Sven.

Tells him what they've found, and he falls silent.

'A society in Uppsala?'

'I know it's not really much, but we have to move forward somehow.'

'OK.'

'OK to what?'

'Get hold of this Emanuel Ärendsson. See what he's got to say. Just the fact that he's a gynaecologist and crops up in this sort of context makes me feel very uneasy.'

★   ★   ★

The grand 1920s villas by the old cemetery are white and grey mini-palaces in the neoclassical style, incomprehensibly luxurious and large for all-things-in-moderation Linköping.

Tall lime trees shoot up towards the blue sky inside the two-metre-high stone wall that surrounds the house where Emanuel Ärendsson is supposed to live. Well-maintained white stucco, with the branches of the surrounding trees providing angular shadow.

Fifty-six years old.

He probably isn't home, seeing as he's an eminent physician, and respected doctors are probably at the hospital or university at this time of day, but on the other hand it is Sunday, so he might be at home after all.

But he was prepared to let me have an appointment on a Saturday, Malin thinks.

A strong wind sweeps down behind the wall and the trees move like snakes, their crowns becoming black heads backlit by the blazing sun.

They left the car in the car park by the old cemetery.

The gate wasn't locked.

The gravel is crunching beneath their feet, announcing their arrival.

And the trees lean over them, and Malin can hear a woman scream. Is the sound coming from the basement?

Are they getting close to something without realising? And she looks at Zeke, but his face is calm, he doesn't seem to be able to hear the screaming, and Malin realises it's only inside her.

Someone being tortured.

Behind the basement windows?

Behind the panes of smoked glass at ground-level?

They knock on a solid door of stained oak.

Beating a ring in a lion's mouth hard against the wood as if to wake the devil himself.

Malin.
I remember myself now. Was I once where you're standing now?
I daren't say.
Instead I want to remember who I was.
The little girl that I was, full of dreams.
Dreams about love.
Warmth.
Children.
A good man.
I had dreams like that.
But I got something else, one of humanity's greatest curses, all the self-justifying male violence against women, against children.
You knocking on a door with a lion, Malin.
But what are you?
The violence has to end, Malin.
My grief has to end.

The blood on Waldemar's brown trousers could be wiped off, and the custody officer pretended not to have heard anything when he let Waldemar out of the cell.

And that fucking little pimp Darzhevin wouldn't say anything either.

He knew better. Who would believe him, take his side?

No, he was all alone in his cell, and he knew it.

Waldemar Ekenberg had gone to the gym changing room.

Tidied himself up after the tussle in the cell.

Taking deep breaths to get his adrenalin down as he sat for a long time on the toilet, crapping out every last bit of his wife's beef stew from the day before.

Three large helpings of a rather good sludge flavoured with bay leaves and peppercorns.

But his heavy breathing didn't want to calm down.

Am I starting to get old? he wondered. Losing my edge?

Then he remembered the barrel of the pistol hard in the pimp's nose, under the bandage, the blood, and the blade of the knife against his worthless scrotum, and remembered the power in every fibre of his body.

Old.

Me?

Like fuck.

I can do much worse.

And he felt the blows to the pimp lingering in his body. The blows to his father's stomach when it was full of cancer.

The pain he caused, the vengeance. The feeling that enough was enough. No more abuse and torment for Mum.

And he felt his breathing return to normal, and he became the calm version of Waldemar Ekenberg. Then his conscience started to creep up on him, his doubts over whether he'd done the right thing.

Was he one of them now?

Where's that boundary?

Bollocks to boundaries.

Do what needs doing.

The others must have been wondering where he'd gone, especially Börje Svärd.

And he had gone back up again.

Malin and Zeke had gone off to see that fucking gynae-cologist who'd been in the hunting cabin.

Damn.

He'd have liked to do that.

Then he had gathered Johan Jakobsson, Börje Svärd, and Sven Sjöman around his desk.

Told them what Andrei Darzhevin had said. The name he had given him.

He had seen the look on Sven's face.

Sven had realised what he had done to get the cunt-merchant to sing.

And he could see that Sven had long since accepted that the boundary between right and wrong is fluid, multi-dimensional, and impossible to capture with word, or thought, or even deed.

It just is, Waldemar had thought. That boundary. It's different for every individual at every moment.

Good.

Evil.

As fundamental and difficult to explain as the fact that we human beings manage to breathe.

Malin.

I wish Malin was here, he had thought. She'd have appreciated the value of some honest, old-fashioned police work.

But she's probably where she needs to be right now, trying to lure evil out of its very darkest lairs.

31

Is she here?

The woman I can see inside me, Malin thinks, the one being tortured in a dark lair.

Unless it's light?

Do they want to see their victims in bright light?

Emanuel Ärendsson opened the door to them.

Not working on Sunday. A short man with thinning hair and dark rings beneath watery grey eyes, sagging cheeks, a round head on narrow shoulders, and a gently protruding stomach that made him look like two pears on top of each other, past their best. An insecure boy of less than obvious charms, Malin thought.

Standing in the hall, which was furnished with dark, heavy wooden furniture from the twenties, as well as a modern standard lamp with a pink gauze shade, Emanuel Ärendsson tried to be welcoming.

At first he had seemed surprised when he saw Malin and Zeke. Then scared as they showed their ID, and then exaggeratedly polite.

But Malin wasn't falling for that, and realised that it was obvious he didn't want them there.

And when they followed Emanuel Ärendsson from room to room, she was full of a peculiar feeling of being somewhere completely different from where she actually was. That the discreetly patterned wallpaper, the colourful lithographs, the traditional rugs and old furniture were all just props in a confused film that was really about something else entirely.

As if Emanuel Ärendsson had a home other than the one that was on show.

And he himself gave the same impression.

He didn't quite seem to fit his own life. Like someone desperately seeking membership of the upper middle class, but who got no further than a skilful imitation.

If he recognised Malin's name from the appointment Peter had made to remove her coil, he didn't show it.

He responded curtly when she and Zeke commented on details of the furnishings on the way to the drawing room, where he had decided they should sit. He explained that his wife was in Mallorca, playing golf with friends.

Golf and literature, Malin thinks, as she and Zeke each sit down in a blue, upholstered Howard armchair, in a room whose walls are covered with bookcases, mostly fiction.

Emanuel Ärendsson is expansive as he tells them about a table he bought while he was at a medical conference in Bali, and had shipped home by container.

'It was much more expensive than I expected,' and Malin sees his fingers clasp a brass electric fire-lighter, and sees the lighter become an organically shaped gynaecological instrument, sees him in a white coat, can feel the instrument pushing inside her, sees the bags under his eyes, thinks: You enjoy it, don't you? You enjoy it, and then she hears Zeke ask: 'You must be wondering why we're here?'

And it strikes Malin that they haven't said anything, and Emanuel Ärendsson hasn't asked, just accepted their appearance and let them in.

He knows what they want.

Or else he has nothing to hide.

Everything can mean anything.

'So why are you here?'

Zeke explains the case they're working on.

What they know.

About the connections between Peder Stålskiöld and the forest where Jenny Svartsjö was found, Prosecutor Fredrik Kantsten who was in charge of a similar case in Skåne, where Emanuel Ärendsson himself was called in as a medical expert.

The links between them. The Skulls Society.

They lay almost all their cards on the table.

To provoke a reaction.

'And then we saw that you'd been in Hälsingland together with the others. In a hunting cabin at the time when Jessica Karlsson was found raped and abused in the forest up there. In the same way as Jenny Svartsjö, and the woman in Skåne in the case you were involved in, for which Fredrik Kantsten was the prosecutor. You were both in Hälsingland. I'm sure you can appreciate why we as police officers might be wondering about these connections?'

Emanuel Ärendsson crosses one leg over the other and clicks the brass lighter.

'So that's what you in the police call connections? If I as a scientist were to see any connections on such loose evidence, I'd have been thrown out on my ear.'

'We're not scientists,' Malin says, and Emanuel Ärendsson smiles in response to her declaration.

'How did you come to be called in as a medical expert in Skåne?' Zeke asks.

'Through my old friend Fredrik Kantsten, who was the prosecutor there. He needed a second opinion.'

'And you thought she could have inflicted those injuries on herself?' Malin wonders out loud.

Emanuel Ärendsson nods.

'Absolutely. I've seen women demonstrate the most astonishing capacity to self-harm. They want to harm themselves.'

'Women?'

'As a rule, men never harm themselves.'

Another click of the lighter. A flame appears at its end.

'What were you actually doing in the hunting cabin?' Zeke asks.

'I thought the documents in that case had been declared confidential?' Emanuel Ärendsson says, rubbing his free hand over his balding head. 'How did you get hold of them?'

'What were you doing in the cabin?' Zeke asks again. 'Do you have any explanation as to why you and your friends, who happen to have cropped up in the police investigation into the woman in Lund, should happen to have been in Hälsingland at that precise time?'

'Tell us,' Malin says.

She tries to make her voice sound threatening, knows she can't show any sign of weakness to this man.

'To be honest, I really don't understand what you mean when you mention connections. Fredrik and Peder and I have been friends since Uppsala. Since then we have gone hunting together every so often. And now that there are a few crimes involving women, we're suddenly under suspicion? Coincidence, that's all I can say.'

At least you're not making excuses, Malin thinks.

You're not saying: I've got nothing to do with violent attacks on any women.

So she asks: 'Were you in the city in late November and early December last year?'

Emanuel Ärendsson thinks.

'I wasn't away anywhere, no. Why?'

'That was when Jenny Svartsjö is presumed to have been murdered.'

Make excuses, she thinks.

Asks: 'Have you been out to visit Peder Stålskiöld, at his new hunting cabin? The one with the nice fireplace?'

'I didn't even know that he had a hunting cabin. We've never hunted on Peder's land.'

'Did you know Jenny Svartsjö?'

'What an absurd question. Of course I didn't know her.'

'No?'

Emanuel Ärendsson falls silent.

'The flat in Skattegården. The Russian women. The prostitutes. Have you ever visited them?'

'I don't know what flat you're talking about.'

And Malin changes tack, asking earnestly: 'What's your friendship like? Take it from the start. I know you were in the same society in Uppsala.'

'Yes, we were members of the Skulls Society. Like a lot of others. Since then we've kept in touch over the years, mainly through hunting trips some time each autumn, like I said.'

'Just the hunting trips?'

'Yes, that's our shared interest. Occasionally in the course of our work as well.'

'And you and the count, Peder Stålskiöld,' Zeke wonders. 'You never socialise otherwise? He does live in the same city, after all, so I was thinking . . .'

'We don't socialise otherwise, no.'

'You've never been hunting in Skåne?' Malin asks.

'No, never.'

'Do you know Maria Murvall?' Malin goes on.

'Should I?'

And Malin sees his pupils dilate, the clearest sign that someone's lying.

Then Emanuel Ärendsson leans back in his armchair, looks out of the window at the grey wall, half covered by glossy ivy.

'Is this what the police do? See a tiny conspiratorial link and then disturb law-abiding citizens as they go about their business, linking them to all manner of grubby affairs and making them feel violated, without sparing any thought for what you're doing?'

'Are you feeling violated?' Malin asks.

Emanuel Ärendsson doesn't answer.

Instead he gets up from his armchair, the smaller grey pear of his head appears to be lifting the large pear of his body.

'It would take more than that for me to feel violated.'

Then he looks at Malin, holding her gaze for ten seconds, and seems to be wondering whether to utter the words that are on the tip of his tongue, and Malin can see the uncertainty in his eyes, as if he wants to do the right thing by his friends. She's thinking: Behind your polished façade you're nothing but a hanger-on. You do what the big boys say, so you can tag along and play, don't you? You're weak, and you know it.

And she considers the man in front of her, and Fredrik Kantsten and Peder Stålskiöld. Could it have been them who hurt her women so badly? Are these men really capable of that sort of violence?

Maybe, she thinks. Or maybe not. Maybe there's another man, a fourth man, someone else beyond the others.

Is it possible to be a well-regarded member of society and commit such crimes?

Is it?

Maybe, Malin thinks. It's probably perfectly possible.

'We went hunting in the Hälsingland forest. No more than that. We're old friends. I've got nothing to do with anything that you're investigating. And I can't imagine that either of my friends has.'

Now you're making excuses, Malin thinks.

'What we're investigating is the torture, rape, kidnap and murder of young women,' Malin says. 'I acknowledge that our connections are vague and may not mean anything, but we have to follow any lines of inquiry that arise. That's what our scientific method looks like. You know: test, move on or abandon.'

The corner of one of Emanuel Ärendsson's eyes twitches twice, and his scalp is shiny through his thinning hair, glinting in the sunlight.

'Have you ever been hunting in Skåne?'

'No, I've already said that.'

'And you've never had any prostitutes with you on your hunting trips? For a bit of fun among friends?'

As she says 'fun among friends', Malin draws quotation marks in the air.

Emanuel Ärendsson's eyes are expressionless.

'You'd do anything to be allowed to be with your friends, wouldn't you?'

His eyes remain expressionless, but the corner of one eye is twitching again.

'You're clearly under great stress,' he finally says. 'People always are when they have to open themselves up the way they must to remove a coil they've had in place for a long time. Remember that stress is never good if you want to get pregnant.'

You bastard.

Zeke's eyes widen.

Malin is first to leave the room.

She listens for the women's screams, but there are no women here.

On a door that must lead down to the basement is a brass sign with the words 'Treatment Room' engraved on it in black lettering.

On the way back to the car Zeke asks: 'Malin, what the hell was that last bit? Anything I should know? Anything else you're keeping from me?'

'It was nothing. I didn't get it either.'

Zeke sighs and says no more, but the vibrations from his body make her realise that he knows exactly what the hell happened in there just now.

He opens the car door by the old cemetery.

Squints.

A flock of grey sparrows like a shower of gunshot against the sun behind him, a single bird like a wild shot that could hit anything, destroy everything.

'OK, Malin,' Zeke says. 'Fine.'

He smiles.

'Bloody hell, that's the best thing I've heard in ages.'

32

Persistence. Endurance.

A cooperative elbow, Johan Jakobsson thinks.

Plenty of anti-inflammatory pills.

That's what you need to work on a case electronically.

The new name that Waldemar Ekenberg had been given by Andrei Darzhevin.

Paul Lendberg.

There were nine Paul Lendbergs in Sweden.

The whole lot of them seemed to be perfectly ordinary.

Then he had an idea.

And typed in the name Paul Lendberg alongside the names Ärendsson and Kantsten.

Could there be another connection?

Search.

Bang.

He had hit upon a list of all the students in Uppsala during the academic year 1975–1976.

And Johan started to drum nervously at his keyboard when he realised that the men from the cabin in Hälsingland and a man with the name supplied by Andrei Darzhevin had studied in Uppsala at the same time.

Unlike the others, this Paul Lendberg hadn't finished his degree.

No telephone numbers listed.

He opened the website of the Skulls Society.

No Paul Lendberg in any of the pictures, if the captions were to be believed.

Nor in the register of the Småland Association, nor in any other context that linked him to the other three men. At least not from what Johan could find online.

He found several Paul Lendbergs in various official government registers.

One convicted of fraud, who had been in Kalmar Prison for the past three years. It could hardly be him. Another one caught speeding in Malmö.

In the register of companies, another Paul Lendberg was listed as living in Stockholm, at 36 Skogsvägen.

He ran an import business under the name Eastoria Trading, which appeared to do most of its business with the former Eastern bloc. A property on Skogsvägen was registered as belonging to the company.

Eastern Europe.

Russia, Ukraine.

Darzhevin, Yelena.

Svartsjö.

Swedish.

But she had been at the Russian brothel. Swedes were in no way immune to involvement in people trafficking and the sex trade.

Was that the sort of business Paul Lendberg was involved in?

Johan checked the date of birth of the Lendberg who was listed as the proprietor of the company. 1956, the same year as Fredrik Kantsten, and one year younger than Emanuel Ärendsson and Peder Stålskiöld.

That could be their man.

He could be linked to the others, but unlike them he only appeared to have studied in Uppsala for a short while, just as tens of thousands of other young men had done that year.

But still.

A small connection, if somewhat tenuous.

His fingers drummed on the keyboard against his will.

Make them stop.

More typing.

He tried Google.

Nothing.

Their own registers.

Nothing.

The passport database.

No picture of Paul Lendberg.

He ought to have a passport, considering the fact that he does business abroad.

But if he's involved in trafficking women, he could be working under a false identity.

Google Images.

No picture of Paul Lendberg.

Where's Malin?

Johan rubbed his elbow, and thought that he should call her.

She and Zeke must have finished with Ärendsson now, and could well be on their way to see the count.

They might find this new information useful.

Waldemar Ekenberg is standing outside the back door of the police station, smoking.

He looks out across the car park and the cars shimmering in the sun, towards the premises of the National Forensics Laboratory, based in what used to be the mess block of the old regional regiment.

Still no results from Arto Antinen's DNA sample, but they've only had it a couple of hours, and even the most basic analysis takes a day or two.

Applying pressure.

It pays off.

He hasn't been able to concentrate since his visit to see Andrei Darzhevin in his cell, but he knows that Johan Jakobsson is working as hard as he can to dig out more information about this Paul Lendberg.

They're going to find him.

It's going to mean something.

Something's going to happen.

And Malin and Zeke will definitely have found out something from that cunt-doctor.

They're getting somewhere with this now, he feels sure of that.

Doubt has never been Waldemar's strong point.

Malin gets the call from Johan Jakobsson just as they turn off by the church in Vreta Kloster, past the locks at Berg.

The first yachts are in the series of locks leading down to Lake Roxen now, their bare masts like feelers reaching up towards the sky. A few gulls are circling high above, looking as if they want to shit on the doctors' villas that line the canal.

'Johan here.'

And he tells her what he and Waldemar Ekenberg have uncovered, and urges her to ask the count about Paul Lendberg if they're going to put him under pressure.

She presses the button to end the call.

Feels the air being sucked out of the car as she gasps for breath.

She can hear the woman screaming again, and grimaces, wants to stop it, but it goes on ringing inside her like a signal born of fear.

What is this? she wonders silently to herself.

★   ★   ★

Count Peder Stålskiöld asks them in, and his exaggerated calm suggests that he knew they were on their way.

Soon Malin can't help wondering why he went to the bother of even letting them in.

In the spacious hall of the manor house, dressed in a dark blue suit with a pink bow tie, he tells them that he's spoken to his friend Emanuel Ärendsson, that he knows they've just been at his house, 'snooping about'.

Then he walks ahead of them through the enormous house in silence.

In an airy dining room whose ceiling must be six metres high, he pulls aside a heavy red velvet curtain, and the room goes from gloom to brilliant light in a second, and Zeke sees a halo appear around Malin's head in the sudden transition from darkness to light.

The count opens a large glazed door behind the curtain and steps out into the sunshine, and the sudden glare makes it look as if he's disappeared until they follow him.

They find themselves on a large terrace, some hundred square metres in size.

White-painted, wrought-iron furniture with plump blue and white cushions, and a shiny stainless-steel Weber barbecue waiting for warm summer evenings.

The count doesn't invite them to sit down, and helps himself to something that looks like port from a carafe, not offering them anything: 'You're on duty, after all.'

A broad patch of gravel, a garden, and Malin can smell new-mown grass, lush and potent, and five hundred metres away the waters of Lake Roxen shimmer in the sunlight, the reflections like little stars in their eyes.

She sees Victor Johansson the farmhand disappear on a ride-on mower into the sunlight down by the water.

The count takes a sip of his drink.

Straightens his back, then, with the angry voice of the

insulted narcissist, he begins to speak: 'I know why you're here. You have no right at all to come and ask a load of questions on such flimsy grounds. I'm not going to comment on what I know you're calling connections. I have the right to do as I please.'

Zeke raises his hand towards Peder Stålskiöld, and Malin can feel herself instinctively adopting a defensive posture in the face of the count's inherited authority, as if all her determination and focus vanish when confronted with his fucking heritage.

'We'd like to—' Zeke begins.

Peder Stålskiöld clenches his jaw before interrupting: 'There's nothing you could ask to which I can imagine replying. I let you in for one reason alone, to say thus far but no further. Now you can leave. Understood? And don't come back.'

Malin looks at the man in front of her.

Little beads of sweat on the faint wrinkles on his high forehead.

Are you going to get your whip out next? she wonders.

Then her courage returns: 'Did you have whores with you on those hunting trips? You could tell us that much, surely? Did the count buy a bit of fresh meat for himself? What does your wife say about that?'

Peder Stålskiöld shakes his head.

Drains the glass of port.

Then he leaves them.

They see his blue-clad back in the doorway, and the curtain, almost black beyond him, becomes a monster's maw around his figure.

'What about Paul Lendberg? Do you know him?' Malin shouts after the count, but gets no answer.

In Stockholm, twenty minutes later, District Prosecutor Fredrik Kantsten is sitting in his office.

He has just put the phone down.

Buries his head in his hands.

That bloody police officer.

That woman.

The fucking bitch who showed up unannounced.

Malin Fors.

Why the hell should an insignificant little bitch like that be allowed to get away with it? Does she have any right to exist at all?But it's coming now.

This is too big.

So it's coming now.

Unless perhaps it isn't?

There must be a way, but how the hell am I going to work it out?

Everything I, we, have suspected but done nothing about. Passivity is complicity, that's what I've always said in my lectures on equality. Anyone who doesn't work actively for equality contributes to inequality.

What bollocks.

What could we have done?

I'll do what I can to save myself.

Paul.

How the hell did they manage to get hold of his name?

He shuts his eyes.

Feels that this unknown darkness he's had close to him for so long is soon going to reveal its true face.

Something's going to change.

Something's going to shatter.

Whatever will be, will be. I'll be OK.

33

What rights does a person have?

A man?

A woman?

They certainly don't have the same rights, nowhere near, Malin thinks.

Eyes closed.

Late afternoon now.

Zeke at the wheel, they're on their way back to the station.

The men.

Their faces.

The way she, Malin, had always wanted to be like them in one respect. Unquestioning assumption of their rights, their violence, unafraid of their own lack of shame.

Janne. Her ex-husband.

Daniel Högfeldt.

Peter.

And they're among the good guys. Who know that their rights have limits, who know about thus far but no further.

Plenty of other men. The ones who aren't as good.

The hydra's heads.

Janne had told her he had seen a member of staff at a hotel in Bali kill a poisonous snake that had found its way into the pool area.

First he had hit it in the head with a pool rake.

Several times.

Then, when he was sure the snake was dead, he had

stamped on its head, again and again, with the heel of his sandal.

Then held the snake up to the guests with a sad smile: 'Plenty more out there,' he had said, pointing at the jungle behind them.

Is it possible to chop off all the hydra's heads, kill all the snakes that emerge all over the world?

Malin can see Jenny Svartsjö making her way through the forest, already abandoned by herself and everyone else, wounded and bleeding, trying to escape her killer.

To what sort of life?

Maria Murvall mute, the girl in St Lars mute.

Jessica Karlsson.

Who committed suicide.

Four women. The same fate. The same perpetrator? The same evil? The same snake?

Evil men, Malin thinks. The ones who take what they want from women, from children. Who believe they have the right to whatever they want.

A twenty-five-year-old girl who's gone off the rails? Terrified, but I don't give a damn, I'm having her. A girl on her way home from a hotdog kiosk late one night? Sure, she's mine. A few more whores, sure, a neighbour's girl, my daughter, sure, why not? I've got such an itch in my pants, I want this throbbing in my groin to stop, and it's my fucking right to do it whatever way I want.

Cocks.

Snakes with heads.

The sperm could land on any face at all. A Maria? A Katerina? An unknown woman? An Eastern European slut? A junkie? A teenage girl who's run away from home? A nameless whore in a flat in a suburb I've never been to before?

You see. I'm a man. I've got money. I want to fuck now.

And I've got the right. They get my money. I'm handsome, the sort women dream of. You're lucky to get me, if you don't show your gratitude you've only got yourself to blame.

Maria's suffering.

She's suffering for all of us.

My father, the betrayer of love, without even realising it, he joined the ranks of the self-justifiers.

Do the men under investigation belong to that group?

Malin is sure.

She just needs to work out how.

The gynaecologist, Emanuel Ärendsson.

The prosecutor, Fredrik Kantsten.

Count and landowner, Peder Stålskiöld.

The rapist, Arto Antinen.

The pimp, Andrei Darzhevin.

Paul Lendberg, an unknown, new dark star who seems to orbit around them all.

And many more men, faces, names, bodies, feelings, all mixed up, making it impossible to tell them apart, their bodies a single entity, their faces dragons rising up from an impenetrable darkness.

Someone, more than one person, being tortured in a lair.

Malin knows it's happening.

Who's bleeding?

Who are you bleeding for?

It's liberating to let your thoughts and feelings roam freely, Malin thinks, even if I am heading towards the edge of the abyss, staring straight into my own and others' darknesses, the story that keeps us shackled to our lives.

Karin Johannison is sitting with her feet up on the footstool that matches the wine-red Josef Frank armchair that she managed to claim in the divorce.

Her feet are buried in thick yellow socks, almost dirty

yellow in the approaching evening light outside the leaded windows.

The flat on Drottninggatan isn't big, two rooms plus the kitchen, but it's nice, with high ceilings and wood panels dating back to when the building was constructed in 1911. And the striped brown wallpaper matches her Miró prints perfectly.

The television is on.

But Karin can't summon up the energy to watch. She's got her eyes closed. She can see Jenny Svartsjö's corpse in her mind's eye, first in the forest, then even more cut up in the mortuary at the National Forensics Lab.

She thinks about her colleague's mistake with the DNA sample from Maria Murvall.

How embarrassing it had been to have to admit it to the detectives, how tragic that her former colleague had messed up like that, and that the others had hidden the mistake from her until she needed the sample again.

Are they scared of me?

Surely I'm not the sort of person anyone would be scared of?

None of the detectives seemed to hold her responsible for the ruined sample, still less criticise her or go on about it.

They had just been looking ahead, and still are.

Just as I want to do.

Malin has to catch the bastard who did that to her.

I'm getting more and more like Malin, Karin thinks.

I live in a two-room flat in the city centre, I work in the criminal justice system, and I've no fixed plan for my life.

But she's got a boyfriend. A daughter.

I've got none of that.

But that's going to change.

The adoption papers are in the hall, filled in and ready to send.

I'll post them tomorrow.

Karin inhales the smell of the flat through her nose, and feels how it smells of her and no one else, and thinking that she likes how big the room feels when she knows it's hers alone.

A quickly convened meeting of the investigating team at a quarter past six.

Sunday evening. No rest now, no respite. Push on. Save the city's inhabitants from anxiety and insecurity. Work until their hearts and souls are bursting with exhaustion.

They're all there. Even Karim Akbar. His suit crumpled now.

No response from the National Forensics Lab about Arto Antinen's sample.

Large, grainy enlargements of passport photographs on the whiteboard, and the whirr of the decrepit overhead projector.

Outlines of men, faces, wrinkles, noses and mouths.

Johan Jakobsson hasn't managed to find anything else significant to the investigation.

Katerina Yelena still sedated in the University Hospital.
Paul Lendberg.

They have to try to get hold of him. Money for a trip to Stockholm must be found, they don't want to let their colleagues in Stockholm take over that line of inquiry.

'I'll sort it out,' Karim says.

The detectives in the room.

All somehow full of confidence, but tired after almost a week's work on the case, and aware that the coming days will bring more hard work.

But, in spite of their experience, they're also scared of what they think they might be getting closer to.

A tree with a million roots, mother of a snake with a thousand heads.

The pictures on the whiteboard stare down at them as they sit around the table, trying to see the connections more clearly, advancing theories of how things might fit together, trying to fend off their own doubts.

The heads in the pictures are bigger than the detectives' heads.

As if they are looking down on naïve peasants who thought they could hold these powerful, bloodthirsty bandits captive.

34

I'm finished, Andrei Darzhevin thinks.

He sees his daughter drift across the summer meadow, her blond hair rippled by a light breeze, her white nightdress like a smoky mirror for all that is good in this world.

He suppresses the image.

Scared of what it might do to his sense of purpose.

There's a lot these people aren't going to know about me, he thinks as he pulls the sheet from the bunk in the cell.

There's a lot I don't want to know about myself.

I'm going to take my secrets with me. Erase those deeds from the world's memory.

I want to forget everything I've done, all the pain I've caused other people, but of course I was forced to.

He was right, that cop, Waldemar, who wanted to cut my balls off.

I wish he had shot me.

They see me as unscrupulous, he thinks as he carefully and as quietly as possible rips the sheet into three pieces.

My child.

Nicola.

You'll be better off without me, because what have I got to offer you? And I hope she survives in the hospital, Katerina.

I hope she survives.

I have nothing to say in my defence.

I'm one of the heads of the hydra that must die, and in order for the hydra to die, I must die. My corpse must burn.

He feels like screaming.

Howling all his grief, his memories of children's homes and young offenders' institutions and knives stuck into unknown stomachs on someone else's orders, of women beaten and taken against their will by him and others. Crying out his shame at his daughter's terror when he hit her mother.

He wants to ask for forgiveness, but knows it's too late. That there aren't any excuses, that it's better for everything to end, here and now.

Better for everyone.

For Nicola, for her mother.

He loved her once, he thought he did, but how do you love someone? Without hitting them? Abusing them?

I never managed to learn that. So you do one thing, then another, and then you do everything.

Beating.

Wounding.

Kidnapping.

Raping.

Selling.

And you convince yourself that you're right, that it's your fucking right to do what you want, and that you have to beat and sell and threaten and wound, because otherwise the men up above, higher up in the organisation, will come after you.

They'll cut your throat in an unfamiliar bathroom and dump your body in unknown waters, and there's your wretched excuse, Andrei Darzhevin.

Paul. I let them have him. He was the one who kept us supplied with fresh goods. But there are dozens of others. Immediately above, further up, and alongside. The monster

I am a part of can't be killed. We're all over the surface of the world, have existed in every age.

He ties the three parts of the sheet together.

Fastens it to the gap between the thermostat on the radiator and the water pipe.

Tries it out.

It will hold his weight. He wonders if any woman has ever done this, to try to escape what a man has done to her?

They must have. No question.

The child.

His daughter.

He's doing this out of love for her, however strange that might seem.

He has reached the end, knows that nothing good can come of going on living, it will be a relief not to have to be the person he has become.

He knows how to fashion this noose, he tied one once before at the young offenders' prison outside Novosibirsk.

On that occasion it was for someone else, angry and scared, mad at the fact that his time was up long before he would have chosen.

Two names.

That's all these people will get from me, about me. A balance between truth and honour.

They'd come after me as a traitor, but what have I said? Two names.

I can die with that.

Nicola.

Nicola.

We'll meet again. In the meadow where you drift now, for ever clad in white.

Andrei Darzhevin goes down on all fours and puts his head through the noose.

Lets his upper body relax.

Remembers injustices, violence, and brief moments of warmth, the times he was loved for who he is, the few times love wasn't feigned because he had scared someone.

He lets his muscles go limp.

Lets himself fall.

Falling straight into a rapid electric darkness where tiny fire-coloured lights welcome him as a lost friend.

Malin is lying in bed.

Peter is beside her, and she wants to try, he wants to try, but they say nothing to each other about it.

It's the right time of the month.

It might work.

It has to work.

It has to not work.

And he is big and hard and warm and the sheet is like a second skin to them, and loving words emerge from deep inside them.

She is warm.

Hot damp and soon I shall overflow, soon soon and he's coming and the noise, the words of the dead are with them, talking to them of life.

And now I'm exploding, Malin thinks, and she hears Peter, feels him mutter, whisper, yell, and the world dissolves and reforms in the same breath.

He sinks away.

Out.

Lies down next to her.

'Bloody hell,' he says. 'Bloody hell, Malin,' and for the first time in a very long time she likes the sound of her own name. It's no longer alien to her.

Something's moving in the darkness.

Something that wants more than anything else.

There's someone new here now, isn't there, unless he's somewhere else, somewhere much warmer?

A single piece of shot in a melting world of lead.

I see the two of you sleep and hope and dream about silvery stars far off in galaxies full of unknown life.

I see your daughter Tove, Malin.

She's in her room in her student residence in Lundsberg.

She's thinking about you.

She's worried that the question is going to make you angry, the simple question she wants to ask you.

She misses you.

Never stop longing for her, Malin.

Tove curls up in the corner of her bed in her room in the student residence. Over on the desk, in front of the poster of Billie Holiday she bought off eBay, a candle is burning.

She closes the book she's been reading, a stupid thriller by an overambitious, hard-boiled author from Linköping.

But even though she thinks the book stupid, she can't stop reading it.

It's like a poison.

A lovely, harmless, stupid poison.

No one here reads anything but thrillers.

No Fitzgerald, no Austen, the boys don't even read Hemingway.

Bah.

But they can be sweet sometimes.

Like Tom.

My boyfriend. That is what he is, isn't he?

He is.

Not as uptight as a lot of the other boys. He's in the second year, comes from Stockholm, his family lives in an enormous apartment in Östermalm and owns several big companies, or, to be more correct, his extended family jointly owns the companies.

What's Mum going to think of Tom, of his family? She hardly said a word when I told her about him, didn't seem to want to take on board the fact that I can actually meet boys up here.

And she misses her mum, it looks as if she's not even going to have time to come to the end-of-year concert. Tove has tried to tempt her with the fact that she'll be singing on-stage, but not even that seems to have helped. And I know she'll refuse when I ask her about dinner with Tom's parents.

But Dad's coming, I know that, so in that sense it will be business as usual.

Dad there when Mum lets her down.

But at least she's not drinking these days, and Peter's nice, but whatever they do, they mustn't have a child.

And Mum? She's not really capable of being a proper mum, for someone who is genuinely helpless.

Her and Peter.

They mustn't have a child.

And Tove knows it's silly, but she wants to have her mum to herself, even if they hardly ever see each other.

She ought to realise how much effort it's taking to dare to go up on that stage, even if I do actually quite like it.

And Tom's parents want to meet her.

She's waiting for Tom to come to her. Boys are strictly forbidden from visiting the girls, but once the housemother has gone to bed he creeps in through the window, once they're sure Mrs Groberg is asleep.

Tom.

Mum's going to die, if and when she meets his family.

His dad set up an airline, then sold it and made a fortune.

Now they live on the Riviera, his parents, when they're not in Stockholm.

Something's moving outside the window.

It must be him, and she feels the tingle in her stomach, and even lower down.

If they get found out they'll be expelled.

Seeing as she's on a scholarship, she certainly would be. Instantly.

And, God, she'd miss this school, she's already grown to love this place, the peculiar sense of freedom and being special, a bit better than other people.

She's ashamed of liking that feeling.

But appreciates that it will be good for her in the future.

One way of describing it is self-confidence, and that's a good quality to have.

Then she sees his blond hair, his long nose, and the horn-rimmed glasses that make him look intellectual, even though he isn't at all.

Expelled.

You have to make sacrifices for love.

You have to dare to.

35

Monday, 23 May

I don't want to see, Malin.
　I don't want to see what I know I'm about to see.
　The blood. The pain. The violence.
　I want to be blind.
　Deaf.
　I want to sew my eyelids shut and let the space around me become nothing but memories.
　I don't want to see those open, bloodshot eyes of his, the man hanging from the sheet tied to a radiator.
　I don't want to see the woman lying tied up on the floor in the corner of a dark room.
　But I can see everything from here.
　And that is my curse.
　So is this hell?
　I don't want to believe that.
　I tried to do nothing but good as long as I lived.
　Now I don't want to see any more.
　Make me blind, Malin, make me blind.
　Like all the living. The ones who don't want to see.

Peter.

He's fast asleep, and she'd like to kiss him but doesn't, because she doesn't want to wake him, and kisses the air above his head instead.

Malin gets out of bed.

It can't be more than three o'clock in the morning.

Going to Stockholm today. To see Fredrik Kantsten.

But there's something else that I need to do first.

And what was it that happened yesterday, last night, when Peter and I made love?

Inside me, outside.

She gets up, in spite of her tiredness and longing for more sleep, more dreams.

She puts on a pair of jeans and a T-shirt, packs the essentials in a case, then creeps out of the flat and drives to the police station.

She says hello to the night receptionist, a young woman in her mid-twenties whose name she doesn't know.

She picks up the case file from her desk, checking that the copies of the men's passport photos are inside.

She'd have liked to have a picture of Paul Lendberg.

But that can't be helped.

She goes back out to the car, then drives the thirty-five kilometres to Vadstena Hospital.

The moon is hanging above Lake Vättern, forming a perfect beam of light across the dark night sky and down across the lake; a horizontal pillar of light pointing straight at her as she locks the car and goes inside the hospital.

The corridors are silent and still, and she's holding the enlarged passport photographs in her hand now, has left the rest of the file in the car. She nods to the night nurse. They're used to her, let her come and go as she likes. They know she wants the best for Maria. For them. And what harm can it do? No one has managed to get through to Maria, bring her back to the world.

Maria's room.

No staff in sight, and it's as if they're alone on the planet, she and Maria, alone beneath the moon and all the winking stars and hungry black holes of the galaxy.

She opens the door carefully.

Expects to see Maria asleep in bed, but instead sees a figure silhouetted in the chair by the window, a face raised towards the flood of moonlight.

Malin goes up to Maria.

Doesn't touch her, stands off to one side of her so that she can see she's there from the corner of her eye.

No reaction.

Malin sits down on the bed, and then she puts the photograph of Emanuel Ärendsson in Maria's lap.

'Maria, do you recognise this man?'

Maria doesn't move, doesn't blink.

'Do you recognise him?'

Then Maria looks down at the photograph, seems to study the image, closes her eyes.

'Have you ever met him? Do you know who he is?'

And Maria looks up again, gazing out at the sky.

Malin takes the picture from her lap.

You recognised him, didn't you? You remember him, don't you? I know he didn't examine you after you were found in the forest, his name doesn't appear in the file on that case.

'Tell me, Maria. Tell me you remember him, tell me what you know.'

Malin puts the photograph of Peder Stålskiöld in her lap.

And she seems to look down, unless that's just wishful thinking?

The photograph of Fredrik Kantsten.

And Maria looks down again, and Malin asks: 'Were they in the forest, was it these men who hurt you?'

Maria's gaze fixed on the sky now.

The room silent, and Malin finds the sound of her own voice strange, but she has to go on with her questions: 'Do you recognise this man?'

'Have you ever seen him before?'

Maria's head droops, her whole body seems to slump and shrink in front of Malin's eyes, and then she raises her shoulders and seems to nod. You're nodding, aren't you, Maria? Aren't you?

'Was that a yes?'

'Do you want to tell me something, Maria? Was he in the forest?'

And without wanting to, Malin raises her voice: 'Was he in the forest? Was he one of the men who hurt you?'

Maria lifts her head.

And as a cloud passes in front of the moon and makes the night black, Malin sees Maria's jaw muscles start to cramp, her legs jut forward, and her feet, her bare feet hit the metal radiator beneath the window with full force, and Malin can't help wondering if every bone in them is broken, shattered, and Maria's cramp spreads through her body like the poison from a snake bite, as if the poisonous fangs of a millipede had punctured her skin and her body has triggered an allergic reaction.

Maria's face is contorted.

Her fingers are entwined around each other, and she's shaking, and froth is dribbling from the corners of her mouth, foaming its way out, and tear after tear is trickling from her eyes, and it's as if Maria has been struck by a bolt of electricity that's eating her up from inside, as if she is running jerkily through the forest at night, trying to escape the honed knives that want to cut her from inside, then drag her down among the roots of the trees.

What have I done? Malin wonders.

The photograph of Fredrik Kantsten is on the floor, the other pictures strewn across Maria's bed.

What should I do?

And Maria's face changes colour. Goes from white to

red, to pale blue, and Malin realises that she can't breathe.

The alarm.

Where the hell is the alarm?

There.

On the table.

And Malin presses the red alarm button, and just fifteen seconds later two white-clad women are in the room, lifting Maria's rigid body over to the bed, and Malin watches as she lands on the photographs, crumpling them, as the men's faces disappear from view and become invisible.

One of the women runs out.

The other one looks at Malin, and Malin knows that they recognise her, and there has been no reproach, no curiosity about what she's doing there or if she's done anything to put Maria in this state.

'It's urgent.'

And the nurse comes back after another fifteen seconds.

A syringe in one hand, an oxygen mask and canister in the other.

Malin helps hold Maria still.

Then the nurse inserts the needle, the bite of a millipede, and the cramps ease after just a few seconds, and then the nursing assistant puts the mask on Maria and she sucks in air, greedily, as if she wants to stay with them for a while, as if her life still has meaning.

The nursing assistant pulls the pictures from beneath Maria's body, and picks up the one that has ended up on the floor.

Holds them out to Malin, and the three women stand silently in the room.

The moon is shining again.

The room is dark, but still light.

'Does she usually seize up like this?' Malin asks.

'She's never done it before,' the nurse says. 'Never.'

'Those men . . .?' the nursing assistant says.

'I don't know anything yet,' Malin says. 'Maybe. Something's happening.'

Then the two nurses look at Malin, and one says: 'I want you to know that we appreciate all your efforts here. Anyone who does the sort of thing to women that he did to Maria can't be allowed to go free.'

'Thank you,' Malin says.

'We should be thanking you,' the nurse replies, looking almost cheerful, a quiet, restrained joy, possibly the joy of friendship.

36

Conny Nygren, Detective Inspector and acting head of the Violent Crime Unit of the Stockholm Police, was pleased to hear from Malin Fors, even though it was very early in the morning.

He was looking forward to meeting the hot-tempered, brittle, talented detective inspector from Linköping again. Fifteen years younger than him, but at least as wise. He had met her and her colleague Zeke Martinsson before, towards the end of a case involving the kidnapping of two young children.

He had been hoping for an opportunity to try to persuade her to come and work for them up in Stockholm.

He takes a sip of his bitter coffee.

Switches on his computer and looks out across the deserted room he shares with six other detectives. At the adjustable desks that the union negotiated hard to obtain, the cables dangling from a hole in the false ceiling, the black computer screens. At his colleagues' family photos, the unwashed mugs. Thinking that one police station is much like another. More or less. Here, and throughout the civilised world.

It's no more than six o'clock, so he's alone in the office. Up early, as usual, never needing more than five hours' sleep, and his flat on Södermalm always feels far too empty.

Paul Lendberg.

A Russian pimp at the brothel where the murdered Jenny Svartsjö is believed to have worked had mentioned his name.

He had checked with his colleagues.

No one knew anything about a Paul Lendberg.

But he knew the address on Lidingö. A large, isolated yellow wooden building with a fantastic view across Mölna.

It had once been owned by a music producer. A bloody successful one, back when Conny was in uniform, and they were called out there on several occasions to sort things out when parties got out of hand.

Then the music producer moved to Florida and calm had prevailed again.

Conny Nygren's stomach has spread over the years – along with his smoking-induced wrinkles and receding hair-line – even if he has managed to shrink it during the past year thanks to less beer.

But why should he hold back from drinking beer, something he enjoys so much? You never know which beer is going to be your last.

The furrows in his brow.

Worry lines.

Because if he has one shortcoming as a police officer, it's that he genuinely cares. About abused women, drug-addicted kids, even the dogs beaten by alcoholics. He's never been able to stay detached. From anything.

Except possibly that spoiled, partying music producer.

But perhaps the calm that had settled over the building on Skogsvägen is deceptive, he finds himself thinking.

Custody officer Nina Negroni didn't bother with one of her duties overnight.

Instead of making her usual round of the six cells and checking on their inhabitants through the hatches in the doors, she had concentrated on her course literature and her Snickers bar. She shouldn't eat that sort of thing, considering her spare tyre, but who can resist them?

The exam in economic science.

It was next Saturday, and she was behind.

And nothing ever happened at night anyway.

Someone might be awake, there might be a bit of shouting. If they were Muslims they could be a bit loud with their prayers, but generally things were always quiet.

But there's no way of skipping the morning round, before the day shift shows up.

So she gets up from her chair in the guards' office.

Undoes the two locks in the first door, goes into the airlock, locks up behind her, then opens the second door and goes into the custody corridor.

Locks that door behind her.

The men in the first three cells are asleep.

A Muslim is praying in the fourth one.

Is he facing the right way?

Nina Negroni has never bothered to work out which way Mecca is, even though she's been asked several times by inmates.

They had to work that out for themselves.

They should have thought of that before they fucked up, shouldn't they?

The fifth cell empty.

Only the sixth one left now.

That Russian pimp.

Thirty points left on her course.

Then she'll be a qualified economist, with a focus on economic science.

Paul Krugman is a god.

No question.

The banks needed to be regulated, the state had to take responsibility for society, the market couldn't handle everything, and it certainly wasn't remotely self-regulating.

But a custody unit like this would probably benefit from being privatised.

I could probably run it better than it's being run now.

She puts her hand on the cold metal hatch in the door of cell number six.

A purely routine check.

And she pulls the hatch open and looks inside the cell, and sees a shade of blue that she's never seen before, and smells the sharp tang of excrement, and then she screams.

Sven Sjöman's call reaches Malin as she pulls up outside Zeke's house to pick him up for their trip to Stockholm.

Zeke's house glows red in the morning light, freshly painted, well maintained, like all the others in the neighbourhood.

Mature plum trees.

Neat flowerbeds.

Plants.

As if a bit of external order were all it took to keep a grip on the chaos of life.

'He's killed himself,' Sven said in an infinitely weary voice.

'Who?'

'Darzhevin.'

Malin is silent.

He must have hanged himself.

What the hell did Waldemar do to him in that cell to get Paul Lendberg's name? Malin wonders.

I know what he did.

No, I don't know.

'He hanged himself during the night, tied his sheet to the radiator. Evidently the custody officer skipped her rounds, so he was only found this morning. But at least she was in her office the whole time, so there's nothing funny going on. But obviously there'll have to be an investigation.'

And Malin has an urge to drive back to the station. Ask Waldemar some serious questions.

But stifles the urge.

Nothing funny, you said, Sven.

Someone hangs themselves while in their custody, and there's nothing funny about it.

Sven.

What's going on? Maybe you need some time off? Just like you're always saying I do. Or is it time to retire?

Blossoming fruit trees.

Tulips.

A quiet Linköping morning, and a far too tired Sven on the phone.

'He must have been ashamed,' Malin says, 'and he was probably scared.'

'I'm sure he was,' Sven says, 'and maybe he was tired of the person he'd become.'

And Malin wonders how many more people will have to die before they get to the truth.

Then she suddenly feels angry and blows the horn three times to let Zeke know she's there, to make it clear to the sleeping, dreaming inhabitants of this smart neighbourhood that nothing is as peaceful as it looks on the surface.

Two and a half hours later they're standing outside Paul Lendberg's villa on Lidingö. The house is at the far end of Skogsvägen, surrounded by lush gardens hidden behind high wooden fences, and between the trees Malin can just make out the water of Värtan harbour. Even the tarmac on the pavements looks clean here.

On the way up she called Johan Jakobsson and asked him to fax the pictures of the men to Peter's sister's girlfriend at St Lars, with instructions to show them to the mute, nameless woman down there. See what the reaction is.

Conny Nygren is already in position outside the house, standing beside his car, and Malin and Zeke greet him.

Malin notes that he's lost weight since she last saw him, that his nylon shirt isn't quite so tight across his stomach.

'You're looking well,' she says.

'Thanks.'

'What's your secret?' Zeke asks.

Conny Nygren laughs.

'I'm smoking more than ever. It makes me less hungry, I suppose. But mostly I've been drinking less beer.'

He tells them the story of the house, and says he hasn't managed to find anything on Paul Lendberg, officially or unofficially.

'You've got a messy one this time,' he says to them.

'Serious shit,' Zeke says.

'But that's why we get up in the morning.'

Conny states this as a fact rather than a question.

Then he leads the way up the wide, paved drive to the large gate in the fence surrounding the palatial yellow wooden house, with its bay windows and ornamental gables.

They ring the entryphone.

No answer.

Malin tries the gate.

Locked.

She gets out her picklock and tells the others to look away.

It takes her thirty seconds to unlock the gate.

'Look! The gate's open!' Zeke says.

'So he doesn't mind having visitors,' Conny Nygren says.

The garden is still and silent, and the house beyond the bushes even more tranquil, as if nothing bad could happen in this place.

Bars over the cellar windows, but none on the other windows.

Can I hear women screaming? Malin wonders.

I can hear a woman screaming, can't I?

What are we getting close to?

Conny and Zeke are calm. Don't seem to have heard anything.

Am I mad?

But then she hears the screams again, louder as they get closer to the house.

Can you hear that? she feels like asking.

But they can't hear anything, she can see that from their faces.

The world is silent.

As quiet as only hopelessness can be.

37

What's your name?

Where are you from?

What happened to you?

Why have you given up, because you have given up, haven't you?

Senior physician Sara Markelberg approached her patient cautiously, the way she always did, keen to show respect even though she seemed neither to demand nor even want it.

Outside the window the day was smiling at people, warmth reminiscent of late summer had swept in over Skåne and Lund from the continent, confusing nature, and the rooms of the secure ward were too hot for May.

The fax from Malin.

The pictures.

She was in no doubt that showing them to the girl was the right thing to do.

If something could rouse her from her almost vegetative state, it might help explain what had happened to her, and bring the guilty to justice.

Sara spread out the enlarged pictures of Fredrik Kantsten, Emanuel Ärendsson and Peder Stålskiöld on the bed.

Moved her hand in front of her patient's eyes.

Downward, trying to get her to look at the men.

She seemed to stare at the photographs.

In silence.

A plane from Sturup Airport went past across the sky.

And now the young woman looks up from the pictures. Staring ahead of her again, and Sara looks at her, and concludes that the pictures haven't provoked any reaction at all.

She gathers up the pictures.

The black and white faces of the men.

Then she goes out. Leaving loneliness to itself.

The stickers from the security company on the front door of the house could hardly shout any louder.

Leave.

Go away.

No one gets in here.

Beware of the dog.

A sharp but sweet smell of freshly blossoming flowers, drying grass.

But no barking.

Malin, Conny Nygren and Zeke are standing outside the door of the house on Skogsvägen. The garden is peaceful behind them, and all three are surprised at the tranquillity, at the isolation the house and garden offer even though the property is situated in one of the suburbs closest to the centre of Stockholm.

They knock.

Malin knocks with the lion's paw.

Cold in her hand.

No one answers, the house in front of them seems to be empty, but Malin can feel a presence here, feels that they need to find out what lies behind the façade of the house, behind the pretention.

'We have to get in,' she says, and Conny Nygren nods, then he bends down, picks up a large stone from the flower-bed by his foot, and throws it through the nearest window, and the three of them expect the crash and tinkling to be followed by a persistent alarm, but all that follows is an even more persistent silence.

'Christ, it couldn't be any quieter,' Zeke says.

Women screaming.

Malin can no longer hear them.

An alarm would have given them an excuse to go inside.

Break-ins must be investigated.

But the broken window also gives them that opportunity.

And when Conny Nygren puts a picklock in the three locks in the front door, Malin imagines she can hear screaming, whimpering women again, and a tree top close to them is shaken by ten strange white birds taking off into the mottled sky.

Why?

Is something coming through the vegetation of the garden? And Malin turns around and sees for the first time how neglected the garden is, no one's done any gardening here for a long time, not even the bare minimum.

Wild grass. Unpruned trees.

Is someone coming?

Was that why the birds took flight? Is someone creeping up on us, and, if so, who?

But behind them, around them, is nothing but silence and the gentle sigh of the invisible waters of Värtan harbour, then Malin hears the click of the third lock and the door opens.

A dark hall lined with shining mahogany panels, a huge room with a high ceiling, opens up before them.

A musty smell of stagnant air and drifting dust particles.

One staircase leads up.

Another down.

The silence even extends in here, Malin thinks.

★ ★ ★

They go from room to room on the ground floor.

Something makes all three of them draw their weapons.

Dust swirls on the air, unused rooms succeed each other, furnished like Carl Larsson paintings, only more expensive, with all the furniture against the walls. Heavy Chinese carpets, outsized oriental cupboards, lamps that appear never to have been lit.

No one seems to have used these rooms in a very long time.

A huge, sparkling white kitchen, new, German, and they walk through it, and Malin thinks that here, in the midst of all this nationalistic-romantic pomp, this kitchen looks as if it's from a spaceship, utterly out of place.

They go upstairs.

Following in each other's footsteps as they ascend the creaking steps.

The rooms up here are in use.

Filthy clothes hanging over armchairs. Dirty plates and pizza boxes on a table, a Loewe home entertainment system in front of a deep sofa, then a bedroom with a huge, round bed covered by a violet satin sheet.

A full ashtray on the floor.

And they look through drawers, carefully, to hide the fact that they've been here, and they lose track of time, not noticing as seconds become minutes that become hours.

But they find nothing.

Nothing in any wardrobe or drawer. Nothing unusual, just ordinary things, bank statements, receipts from various restaurants.

'What are we actually looking for?' Zeke asks quietly.

'Anything that might explain why Darzhevin mentioned Paul Lendberg's name.'

And in her mind's eye Malin can see two custody officers cutting Andrei Darzhevin down from the radiator, his body falling heavily to the floor of the cell, his eyes staring out at nothing.

Guilt.

Shame.

Fear.

And Malin is filled with those feelings here, but also a rare sense of power exerted, that she, they, are exercising sovereign power as they hunt through Paul Lendberg's life.

They carry on downstairs.

To the basement.

There are passageways leading off in three directions from the room at the bottom of the stairs.

'Let's split up,' Zeke says. 'We've probably been here long enough. We have to speed up.'

And then they hear a bang from upstairs, and all three of them stand still, listening for sounds in the house, raising their weapons to show that they're ready.

One minute.

Two.

Three.

Four.

Five.

But nothing happens, and Conny Nygren whispers: 'Probably a bird flying into a window.'

Malin nods.

During those silent, focused minutes she has been trying to work out which way the windows with bars face, and has decided that they must be at the far end of the corridor straight in front of them.

'I'll take this one,' she says.

'OK,' Zeke hisses, and they each disappear into their own passageway, and all three get the feeling that they are in a mine. In contrast to the generously high ceilings on the floors above, the ceilings of this underground level are oppressively low.

An electric cable has been strung along the ceiling, and from it hang bare light bulbs.

Malin makes her way deeper along the corridor.

There's a smell of damp, of earth, and a peculiar smell of washing detergent, as if someone had switched on a powerful air-purifier somewhere.

But the purifier can't conceal the strong smell of sulphur lurking behind the detergent, almost strong enough to resemble ammonia.

A wine cellar, just a few bottles on racks with space for a thousand.

A sauna.

Then a laundry that seems to date from the fifties, and light filters in through the cellar windows, no bars yet, those rooms must be further on.

Then a locked door.

A heavy steel door painted white.

Can I hear women?

The first locked door in the house, and far behind her she hears Zeke shout.

'All clear.'

'Here too,' Conny Nygren replies, and Malin gets out her picklock.

The lock opens.

She pushes the white door aside and enters a huge washroom that makes her think of pictures she's seen of the showers at Auschwitz.

Bars on the windows.

Another door directly ahead.

White.

Steel.

Another lock.

And she picks this one as well, and hears Zeke and Conny approaching from behind, unless it's someone else?

A room without windows, like the airlock in a prison, but when she sees the padded walls she realises that this was once part of the recording studio, and in front of her is a rusty door, locked with three heavy steel bars.

Who's that coming?

She turns around.

Zeke and Conny Nygren behind her.

One minute passes, two.

None of them says anything, and Malin puts her ear to the door but can't hear anything, unless perhaps she can? And they pick the three locks on the metal bars, one each, and push the door open and a stench of urine and excrement and fear hits them like tracer bullets.

The women.

All three of them hear them now.

First they whimper.

Then they whisper.

Whispering words in many different languages, and then several women's voices scream at them at once, and Malin slowly begins to make out the women, one two three four five six seven eight nine woman dressed in soiled clothes and chained to the insulated walls of this whitewashed room, their bodies hanging down on the filthy white-tiled floor.

Bars on the small black windows beneath the ceiling.

Metal rings drilled into the walls. Chains attached to them.

Nine women. But ten rings, one of them empty, the chains in a heap on the floor.

Women.

Women's bodies, in chains.

As if someone owns them, as if they are possessions.

'You don't have to be afraid any more,' Malin hears

herself whisper, as she finds herself thinking that whatever Waldemar Ekenberg did with Andrei Darzhevin in that cell, it was entirely justified.

38

The women.

Their filthy bodies, their eyes flitting about, as if incapable of seeing anything.

Quiet now.

As if they have screamed enough. Lost faith in words.

Zeke had rushed out of the room the moment after he went in. Malin had heard him throwing up in the next room, then he had come back in, pulled himself together, and whispered to her: 'However vile this is, we have to stay focused.'

Malin had nodded.

Female uniformed officers and detectives are helping the women now, everything male has been banished from the room.

Malin, Zeke and Conny Nygren had given them water.

Warmed them with the blankets Conny Nygren fetched from the bedrooms upstairs.

Spoken gently in English.

They could have done with being able to speak Somali, Ukrainian, Russian and several other languages. One of the women, a young girl of Jenny Svartsjö's age, had whispered in perfect Swedish: 'Help me, help me.'

Malin had approached the women cautiously, the way you do a dog that's scared of being kicked, and she had sat down beside one of them, holding her, whispering soothing words, and the stench had disappeared, leaving nothing but closeness.

And it had struck Malin that the room looked like a store-room. The goods neglected, but not so badly that they couldn't be scrubbed up and sold to the highest bidder. Because these women were no more than merchandise in Paul Lendberg's eyes, merchandise that could be bought and sold to the highest bidder, and if no one wanted them they could always be disposed of.

Bodies, human beings as a commodity.

Everything can be bought with the right money. And if you've paid money for something, you can do what you like with it.

Rape, cut, kill. Control. Use it to become a god. Or the devil.

It had felt like several thousand years, the whole of human history, before reinforcements arrived, before other officers could take over. Malin and Zeke and Conny Nygren had just wanted to get out of there.

But these women weren't mute.

They hadn't yet fled into themselves, away from themselves.

And at last backup had arrived, like a longed-for mountain-rescue patrol, and Malin had felt ashamed when she left the women she had found, ashamed as they reached out their arms to her.

Outside the house, below a window, a wounded bird was flapping on the ground, unnoticed.

Now she's standing beside her white Golf on Skogsvägen. She can just see the shimmer of open water in the distance. The media haven't arrived yet, but it can only be a matter of time before the flashbulbs and television cameras greedily come to suck up the fresh blood.

She feels the call of drink, then a faint nausea as her stomach lurches.

Hunger.

She hasn't eaten in hours.

'I'm seriously bloody hungry,' she says, and Zeke replies: 'Let's go and get a burger.'

And she can see Zeke's hands shaking, knows he's talking about food to take his mind off the women, and what they've just seen.

Malin's doing the same, but it's leading her astray.

A burger, she thinks.

And feels an urge for something else.

You mustn't let your desires get the better of you.

Mustn't even take the first step in that direction, Malin thinks.

Like those men, some of those bloody men, appear to think.

Just this once I can help myself to forbidden fruit.

Just this once I can get a woman to suck me off if I pay her for it.

Just this once I can penetrate her.

Next time tie her up.

Next time . . .

Women chained to walls. Buried in unknown locations. Eighty women, one of them Swedish, were tortured and kept as sex-slaves in brothels in Murcia in Spain, and the story made scarcely a ripple in the world's newspapers.

Why do some men assume they have that right?

Do Fredrik Kantsten, Peder Stålskiöld and Emanuel Ärendsson assume that?

The men do it because they can, Malin thinks. Because the rest of us choose to turn a blind eye, to look the other way.

And in the distance she and Zeke can see Conny Nygren directing more newly arrived police officers, uniformed and plain-clothed alike, and Malin feels a sudden longing for Stockholm, for doing what so many do and moving from Linköping to the capital, to get a larger stage on which to grow.

Peter.

There's no reason why he shouldn't be able to find a post in Stockholm.

He came second in his year at Lund, and even the prestigious Karolinska Hospital in Stockholm ought to want him, and now that Tove's moved there's nothing tying me to Linköping.

Or is there?

Have I got so old that I'm stuck in the Östergötland mud? And she looks at the wealthy suburban splendour around her, the huge stone buildings behind the neat walls and freshly painted fences hiding verdant gardens and a wealth of life. But they hide much more than that. There's crap all around us. Like the case they had the previous summer, when a woman killed her husband after finding pictures on his computer of him sexually abusing their two young children.

He ended up with a hammer in his skull.

All of it taking place in the smartest part of Linköping.

There's filth everywhere.

But also light, Malin thinks as she sees the first of the women being led out, under an orange health-service blanket, to one of the ambulances on the drive in front of the house.

Then she turns to look down the road.

Sees a black BMW approach the house, and thinks that it must be one of the neighbours, then the sunlight shines through the tinted windscreen and she sees a face, and then the glass goes dark again.

Calm turning to panic, then determination, all in the space of a second.

Paul Lendberg.

It must be him.

She's certain.

And first he slows down and Malin draws her weapon,

takes three steps out into the road, but the man who must be Paul Lendberg puts his foot down and drives past them, and she wants to pull the trigger.

Shoot straight through the windscreen.

But she knows she can't do that, and Zeke has started their car and she throws herself into the passenger seat, yelling: 'That was him! Drive, for fuck's sake!'

The flashing light on the roof now.

The siren.

And they see the black BMW disappear around a leafy hedge and Zeke drives after it and the tyres squeal as they take the same bend as the car they're chasing.

Are there children here?

Hedges, walls, houses.

Adrenalin gives Malin tunnel vision, and suddenly the smart suburb comes to an end and they drive past three grey tower blocks and over the radio she calls Stockholm central control.

'Pursuing black BMW along . . .'

Where are they?

'Lidingöleden!' Zeke yells.

'All available cars . . .'

She shouts the registration number into the radio, gets the answer: 'No vehicle of that number registered.'

And ahead of them Malin sees the black BMW, heading out onto the Lidingö bridge, swerving between the cars, and Zeke accelerates, but gets caught behind a car towing a caravan that refuses to get out of the way, in spite of the siren, and Malin wonders if the driver is deaf.

Is that why he's not moving?

But then it pulls aside, and Malin can see the black BMW a long way ahead of them, and it turns off towards the tarmac desert of the Värtan harbour district, and then it's gone.

'Shit!' she yells. 'Drive, for fuck's sake!'

Zeke takes no notice of her anger, pulls off where the BMW left the main highway, and his hands are no longer shaking, adrenalin has calmed him and made him more focused.

A harbour.

A maze of grey concrete and car parks and cars, and then an underground station.

Ropsten Station, at the end of the line.

And the black BMW is parked outside a newsagent's, the door open, and how much of a head start has he got? A minute?

I can catch him.

'Stop!' Malin yells.

And moments later she's out of the car, pistol drawn, racing up the steps leading to the platform.

A train is standing at the platform.

And she rushes along it, past blue carriage after blue carriage, and people stop when they see her adrenalin-fuelled body race past, when they see the gun in her hand.

Two carriages left.

And the doors close.

No Paul Lendberg.

The last carriage.

And there, behind a window in one of the doors, there he stands.

The train begins to move.

He sees her.

She sees him, the monster, the man, the human being, disappear, and he waves at her, with a smirk, and she wonders if there's an emergency brake, some way to stop the damn train.

But how?

The blue train vanishes into the tunnel.

Becomes first a blue dot in the darkness, then just darkness in darkness.

And Malin screams.

'Fucking bastard shit! Fuck!'

Zeke behind her: 'They might be in time to get him at the next station. They can stop the train there.'

39

When Malin and Zeke arrived back at the house on Lidingö there were vans from Swedish Television and TV4 outside the gate, along with cars from the evening tabloids, with photographers and journalists hovering like attack helicopters ready to strike and destroy.

The train had been stopped at Karlaplan underground station, the third on the line, but the exits hadn't been blocked in time. Or he could have got out at the second station, Gärdet.

Paul Lendberg had been able to get away from the scene, and they would have to start back at square one with their hunt for him.

Sara Markelberg had called as they were driving back in the car. Her patient hadn't shown any reaction to the pictures.

Malin and Zeke had pushed their way through the reporters.

The eighth and ninth women had just been taken away from the house, and a team of forensics experts was going through every centimetre of the basement. They would carry on through the whole house and garden, who knew what might be there, what horrors Peter Lendberg's house might be hiding.

Everything impossible was possible, and it's with that thought in mind that Malin, Zeke and Conny Nygren, visibly shaken, are now sitting around a dusty dining table on the ground floor of Paul Lendberg's house, trying to make sense of the investigation. Conny Nygren had only been given a brief summary when Malin called that morning, but now he needs, wants to know everything, trying to put his own puzzle together, to make a whole out of the various fragments.

They know they have to set aside the image of the women, their empathy for them, and fix their attention on the path ahead, make themselves emotionally cold. They can deal with the crap later, in all likelihood mainly in their dreams.

So they focus.

Malin begins with Jenny Svartsjö.

Explains that they're still waiting for the results of the DNA sample from Arto Antinen, the convicted rapist.

That a woman named Katerina Yelena had phoned, and seemed to know who Jenny Svartsjö was.

That had led them to Skattegården in Skäggetorp, where a small brothel had been uncovered.

And so on, up to today's raid.

'And we know how that turned out.'

Paul Lendberg's escape.

The women.

One of them Swedish. Perhaps, like Jenny Svartsjö, drifting about in Stockholm, when she got caught up in the trade that Paul Lendberg was evidently engaged in. Had Jenny once been in his basement?

'There's one thing about this case that I can't escape,' Malin says, fixing her eyes on Conny Nygren's.

'That none of us can escape,' Zeke adds.

'More than five years ago another woman was found in almost the same patch of forest as Jenny Svartsjö. On a forest road not that far away. Her name is Maria Murvall, and she too was badly abused and raped.'

'Is?'

'Yes, she survived,' Malin replies. 'But she either hasn't

been able to or hasn't wanted to say anything about what happened to her. She's in a psychiatric hospital now. Mute.'

Conny Nygren's eyes narrow.

'Go on,' he says.

'I've been working on Maria Murvall's case in my own time,' Malin says.

'Obsessively,' Zeke adds.

Conny Nygren smiles.

'I can imagine.'

'But I haven't got anywhere.'

'And?' Conny Nygren says. 'No DNA from her?'

'No. It was ruined during an investigation a while back. So we didn't get anywhere there. And we found no DNA on the others.'

'Others?'

She explains about the case in Lund, quickly shut down by the prosecutor.

'That sort of thing happens,' Conny Nygren says. 'There aren't resources to stretch to everything. Supposedly.'

'I actually spoke to the prosecutor, a Fredrik Kantsten, he's here in Stockholm these days. He said much the same thing. Resources were needed elsewhere.'

Conny Nygren frowns, and his eyes fill with distaste.

'So it was Fredrik Kantsten? I've had plenty of dealings with him. I didn't know he'd been in Malmö. A career man. He'd rather do nothing than take a risk. But sometimes he shows a surprising willingness to act.'

'More about him in a bit,' Malin says. 'Anyway, we sent out an informal request for information to a whole load of police districts, to see if anyone had had a similar case. And one appeared. In Ljusdal, up in Hälsingland.'

Malin pauses.

'A Jessica Karlsson was found in a similar state four years ago. Beaten, raped. On a forest road, early in December, she'd gone missing on the way home from work in a hotdog kiosk. She later committed suicide in hospital.'

'And this is where it starts to get really interesting,' Zeke says.

'We managed to get hold of the case file on Jessica Karlsson, even though it was declared confidential.'

'And?'

Conny Nygren sounds impatient now, he's leaning forward, lower arms resting on the dusty table. He seems to have sorted out all the details of the case: similarities, differences, and has reached the conclusion that this really is extremely interesting.

'To begin with, the detective there said that the prosecutor was eager to drop the case.'

'Who was the prosecutor?'

'A Jimmy Kalder. A young buck.'

'Have you spoken to him?'

'No, but we ought to. Apparently he's up in Umeå now. But what we did find out from the file was this: three men had rented a hunting cabin not too far from the place where Jessica Karlsson was found.

'A gynaecologist called Emanuel Ärendsson.

'Prosecutor Fredrik Kantsten. The one who wanted to put a lid on the Lund case.

'And Peder Stålskiöld, who owns an estate adjoining the forest where Jenny and Maria were found.'

Malin sees Conny Nygren's eyes widen, first in surprise, then interest.

'It gets better. Or rather, even more intriguing,' Zeke says.

'Before the investigation in Malmö was shut down, Kantsten called in a second gynaecologist to evaluate the woman's injuries. The gynaecologist claimed that they could have been self-inflicted. And that gynaecologist was Emanuel Ärendsson.'

'Bloody hell,' Conny Nygren says.

'But we haven't got anything definite, really,' Zeke says, and he goes on to explain about the Skulls Society, and how the men got to know each other in Uppsala when they were students there, and that Paul Lendberg also seemed to have been there at the same time.

'You have to admit,' Malin says when Zeke's finished, 'the whole thing's bloody weird.'

She tells them how Maria reacted to the photographs.

'Obviously it's all connected,' Conny Nygren says. 'We just don't know how. Have you got anything to link the men with Jenny Svartsjö? Or the other victims?'

'Not yet. But there might be something. We've tried digging into her background but it's hard to get anywhere. No one paid her much attention, she seems to have been abandoned by everyone,' Zeke says.

'Those men were more than just friends at university. They've been on hunting trips together over the years,' Malin goes on.

'And maybe more than that,' Zeke says.

'Maybe,' Conny Nygren says. 'I don't suppose it's particularly unusual for men off the leash to use prostitutes. Perhaps they knew Lendberg from Uppsala and got their prostitutes that way?'

Malin takes a deep breath.

Looks at her colleagues.

'Maybe. We'll have to confront them. Ask straight out.'

Conny Nygren's eyes widen again, and Malin can see hesitation in them.

'We need more,' he says. 'We don't know how they met the victims, if they are actually guilty. And the victims are fairly varied. As well as the geographical locations, obviously.'

'They could have gone hunting in different parts of the country. And had fun wherever they were, getting hold of girls, then losing control,' Malin says. 'That would explain the different locations.'

'Have you tracked down other hunting cabins that they've rented?'

'No,' Zeke says. 'Peder Stålskiöld's got one, but it's supposed to have stood unused.'

Conny Nygren nods.

'We need to establish clear links between them and Paul Lendberg if we're going to be able to go after them for this. They belong to society's elite. We can't and shouldn't just march into their lives any way we like. Because, after all, what you've described is really nothing but a series of remarkable coincidences, isn't it? And the fact they studied in Uppsala at the same time isn't enough. For that to be remotely fair, we'd have to question at least another five thousand men. And no matter how sorry I might feel for Maria Murvall, her reaction doesn't necessarily mean anything.'

He's right, Malin thinks.

But, on the other hand, Conny has no influence on what Zeke and I do.

The investigation into Paul Lendberg and the women in the cellar is Conny's case, but Jenny's murder and the cases of Maria and the other women are mine.

'We can talk to the prosecutor in the Ljusdal case,' Zeke says.

'Yes, you can,' Conny Nygren says. 'And just hope you find more connections, more links. Maybe Kantsten put pressure on Kalder? The Public Prosecution Office is full of ambitious people who'd step over corpses to further their careers.'

Malin nods.

'But you think we should leave our prominent gentlemen alone for the time being?'

Conny Nygren smiles.

'That might be the smartest move. Wait until you've something else to confront them with. As far as my case is concerned, I've got nothing on them. But yours? Maybe you've got someone who could apply a bit of pressure?'

Conny Nygren smiles again.

A smile full of energy, a detective inspector reluctantly finding pleasure in the most hideous misery.

Malin can feel that things are on the move, that they can say what they like in this room, but it isn't in their power to decide what happens next, as if every act were pre-determined and impossible to influence.

40

'I saw it on television,' Peter said. 'The four o'clock news. That was where you were going this morning, wasn't it? To see him?'

His voice seems almost unreal on her mobile, as if he belongs to another world, where there's no place for any of what's happening now.

Malin makes herself more comfortable on the bed of her room in the Hotel Oden in Odenplan. The yellow textured wallpaper could do with painting, and the mattress squeaks and protests under her weight. No smoking. Yet the lacquered wooden top of the bedside table is full of burn marks.

But what can you get for five hundred kronor a night these days?

The television is on. The evening news is reporting on their case. The chief executive of Save the Children, Sten Dinman, is criticising the police's efforts over the phone: 'Several of these girls were underage. The police have to find a way of stopping this trade. They need to be more efficient.'

Even the chief executive of ECPAT, Sylvia Vogel, is upset.

We're doing our best, Malin thinks, as she listens to Peter's voice down the line.

'Be careful.'

She and Zeke had decided to stay, to find a couple of rooms and get to grips with things the following day; it had got too late to call Jimmy Kalder at work, and calling him at home would be intrusive.

Wouldn't it?

She had wanted to call, but Zeke had stopped her.

She had spoken to Sven Sjöman and told him what had happened. That they had no leads on where Paul Lendberg might be.

Sven had told her that Johan Jakobsson hadn't yet managed to find any more connections or relevant information, nor had Börje Svärd and Waldemar Ekenberg, even though they had spent all day on their computers, requesting information from all manner of archives.

Sven's budget could handle one night in a hotel.

No more.

Malin hadn't told him she was planning to talk to Fredrik Kantsten and Jimmy Kalder tomorrow. No matter what happened. No matter what anyone thought.

It had to happen.

Arto Antinen's results still hadn't come back. Something had gone wrong, and they had to do it again. Not the test itself, but the chemical analysis.

Karin Johannison had been very apologetic, according to Sven.

Malin had suggested getting DNA samples from Kantsten, Ärendsson and Stålskiöld, but Sven had dismissed the idea.

'We're not there yet, and you know it. It takes a lot of evidence to justify that sort of invasion of privacy.'

'Can't we request to see a list of Ärendsson's patients? To see if there are any missing women on it?'

Sven had said no to this as well. It took time to extract that sort of list, and it wasn't yet justified. 'And surely he wouldn't be so stupid, if he is actually guilty of something as serious as this, as to attack his own patients?'

You're right, Sven, she had thought.

And now she can hear Peter's breathing through her mobile.

The voice from another world.

'You can't imagine what it looked like,' she says.

'No, I can't. Do you want to tell me?'

'I'd rather not.'

'You don't have to. How are you feeling otherwise?'

'You mean since yesterday? Since I saw the gynaecologist?'

'I mean any way at all.'

'I'm feeling better just from hearing your voice.'

'It looks like Katerina Yelena's going to make it.'

'I'm glad,' Malin says, but hears that the words don't ring true, even though they are. It's just that she has so much else on her mind at the moment.

And then Peter's dad, Rudolph, comes into her head. The archetypal patriarch giving his speech at the party, his eyes caught by the flickering light from the sconces. What are those eyes saying?

And she can't help it.

Asks Peter: 'Do you know if your dad ever arranges hunts at Martofta?'

Silence on the line.

A deep sigh.

She's expecting him to say: 'Malin, you're being paranoid.'

But instead he says: 'I can see what you're thinking. But Dad never organises any hunts. He regards that sort of thing as the height of idiocy, that sort of macho behaviour. And he hasn't got a hunting cabin that he rents out. I know that for certain. He manages the game on the estate with the help of contracted gamekeepers. So you don't have to worry about that.'

And Malin feels a knot in her stomach that she'd previously been unaware of unravel. But she still asks: 'Did he study in Uppsala?'

'He was at Lund, Malin. Where else would he have gone?'

What's this case doing to me? she wonders. I'm seeing demons everywhere, but they aren't everywhere, are they?

'You must think I'm being completely paranoid.'

'No, just a bit paranoid. What kind of man do you think my father is?'

'Maybe a reincarnated silent movie star?'

They both laugh, then Peter is silent for a few moments before he says: 'But I can understand your brain being overheated. What you're looking for is pure evil. People have been driven mad by less.'

Then they talk about nothing much for a while before hanging up.

And Malin looks out of the window, at a bland art nouveau block opposite, its white render grey with exhaust fumes. She looks down Västmannagatan, past the swollen white backside of Gustav Vasa Church towards the Mecca of middle-class dreams, the blocks between Odenplan and the Central Station.

Her phone rings again.

Tove's number.

'Hi, Mum.'

'Hello darling.'

'What are you doing?'

'I'm in Stockholm. For work.'

'Oh. But everything's OK?'

'Fine. Can't complain.'

And Malin wishes Tove was there with her, wants to tell her that, but knows she won't be able to make the words sound genuine, they'll sound hollow, the way the whole world feels right now, hollow and inhospitable, like a place with too little oxygen in the air for anyone to survive on.

Paul Lendberg's mocking grin as the train pulled away.

Fuck him.

They had seized his car, but a quick search of the BMW hadn't given them anything.

And Malin hears Tove talking, but can't bring herself to take in any of what she's saying.

'The end-of-year concert. My singing. Dinner with Tom's parents at the inn. Is that OK with you?'

Hang on.

What's Tove saying?

Dinner with Tom's parents? Sitting and eating nicely with the upper classes? No, that's the last thing I can handle.

'What did you say?'

'You mean dinner with Tom? I haven't wanted to bother you with it before.'

So that's what she didn't want to say before.

Her initial anger subsides.

And is replaced by shame.

But Tove. Of course you could tell me.

Are you really that scared of me?

'Of course I'd like to have dinner with them,' Malin says. 'It'll be fun.'

The relief in Tove's voice. 'You don't have to exaggerate, Mum.'

Then she asks: 'Mum. Are you and Peter trying to have a baby?'

How the hell could she know? Has Peter said anything? No. And no one else knows.

'Do you want a brother or sister, is that it?'

As soon as Malin has said the words she realises she should have thought before saying anything at all, and she wants to run away from the disappointment in Tove's voice.

'So you are trying?'

How to get out of that one?

'No,' Malin replies. 'No,' she repeats emphatically. 'We're not trying to have a baby.'

And Tove sounds satisfied.

And drops the subject, and Malin can feel the hand holding the phone shake, and feels grubby all over.

Then she manages to ask Tove what she's going to do this evening, but doesn't listen to the answer.

She can't bear to hear or think about anything to do with Tove or her question about babies.

Instead Malin does what she always does.

Throws herself in a different direction.

She says goodbye to her daughter, thinking about Prosecutor Jimmy Kalder, and when Tove has hung up she gets up from the bed and dials his home number in Umeå.

'Hello, Jimmy Kalder here.'

A young man's voice, trying to sound older. A man with ambition but low self-esteem, Malin thinks. The sort who drives an expensive car to show how important he is.

'My name is Malin Fors. I'm a detective inspector with the Linköping Police.'

The sound of children in the background.

The clatter of saucepans.

'I'm busy at the moment, as you can probably hear. Can I call you back?'

No hesitation, no curiosity. He knows why I'm calling, Malin thinks. He knows.

'I'd rather deal with it now. It's important.'

To hell with sensitivity and tiptoeing around.

She explains why she's calling, not giving him a chance to interrupt her, hearing the noise of the children but ignoring it.

'So why did you drop the investigation into what happened to Jessica Karlsson? Do you have a good answer to that?'

'I didn't want to drop it at all. That's not true.'

'I'm having trouble believing that.'

'You're on thin ice now. Why are you calling me at all? These are pretty serious allegations you're making against me.'

He knows, Malin thinks.

Change tactic.

'One woman is dead. Two others are in psychiatric hospitals. Another committed suicide. We've just found nine women chained up in a basement. This has to end, don't you think?'

Silence on the line.

Jimmy Kalder must have gone into another room.

'What exactly do you want from me?'

'You're young,' Malin says. 'In the middle of your career. And I know how it works. My question is simply whether anyone put pressure on you from above? For instance, did Fredrik Kantsten ask you to push for the case to be dropped? He was one of the men in the hunting cabin. Did he imply that he would sabotage your career if you didn't do as he wanted? Anything like that?'

Silence on the line again.

'I'm not expecting you to answer,' Malin goes on. 'But if we both count to ten and you hang up when we get there, it's a yes. OK?'

No answer.

'I'm counting now. One, two . . .'

She falls silent.

Counting in her head, inhaling the smell of smoke in the room, and thinking how wonderful a cold beer would be.

'. . . eight, nine, ten.'

Click.

The line goes dead.

You bastard, Malin thinks. You bastards. Who the fuck do you think you are? But Fredrik Kantsten is a man of action, she has to give him that.

★ ★ ★

Malin puts her mobile down.

The clock on the television says it's a quarter past eight.

She calls Zeke's room and tells him about the conversation, and he reproaches her, but not wholeheartedly, he was probably expecting her to call.

They decide to rest, get some much-needed sleep, and Malin realises how tired she is after her early start, showing the pictures to Maria, and everything that has happened since.

It's been a hell of a day.

It feels as if it's lasted longer than a lifetime.

Time is short, yet still feels endless, and she lies down on the bed, shuts her eyes and hears the gentle rumble of noise outside, the city crackling and grinding, banging and crashing and huffing and puffing and crying out its rage and delight at its own existence.

A few blocks away someone is cutting the throat of a man sitting tied to a chair in a bathroom entirely lined with sparkling white mosaics.

Death has crept up on the man slowly, waiting for him, standing outside his house, following his car, watching his passage across the earth, waiting and biding its time, but now death has grown tired, and the man must go along with it.

Malin can't hear the man's throat come apart, but the act sends echoes into dreams that will soon be hers.

41

The hydra with its throat exposed, its neck bent back.

Those gaping blowtorch heads with acid-spraying mouths. The millipedes, their legs clinging to the darkness of dreams. Hissing: Can you feel your own darkness, Malin? Does anyone feel their own darkness?

In the dream she is the girl running around in a house, running from room to room looking for people who don't exist but have always existed, she is the child looking for secrets within secrets within secrets.

Something is revealed and the answer is a new mystery, another person lying alone in a bed in a room, breathing, and unable or unwilling to accept love.

Flies buzzing.

Their bodies grow fatter in this peculiar season, their silver-splinted wings are sharpened scythes, striking again and again, cutting off the women's arms, legs, heads, but new faces keep on growing out, as if to demonstrate a new, unfamiliar fear each time.

Fear within fear.

Stories without meaning are screamed into Malin's dream.

A man killing himself in a car crash one summer's day.

A three-year-old daughter and a pregnant wife in her seventh month waiting in vain in the garden of their house.

Oppressive heat.

A man cycling with his son. The son wobbles. A truck drives past. Eternal grief.

Sun, rain, snow. Eternity.

A woman on a beach.

The water is coming in, closer and closer with each wave.

The woman sees her children play at the water's edge.

Then she sees herself. Sees her father coming into her room at night. She's five, six, seven and he's a doctor and he examines her.

Shows her how you have to examine a little girl to stop her getting sick.

The woman screams.

In Malin's dream she remembers the fear that was hers. She remembers what happened, how her father forced himself on her, time and time again.

Sleepless, warm nights in the fifth season, when life hits back, all those nights are Malin's in the dream, lifelong stories flicker past, an ocean, perhaps the Atlantic at night, beats over and over again at the threads holding her life.

Then the barb, a fly's vomit, a poison injected directly into the space of the dream, making it freeze to warm ice, and Malin cries out, screams, but what is she screaming for?

The hydra's heads, the snakes' bodies eating their way into the chained women's genitals, who are the men?

Emanuel Ärendsson.

Fredrik Kantsten.

Peder Stålskiöld.

Paul Lendberg.

And another man?

A body is dumped in water, is it happening now or then? In the dream, time is skewed, and Maria and Jenny flee through dark forests at night, the trees lunging after them, knocking them to the ground, hollowing out their humanity, forcing them to submit.

Malin wants to get out of the dream.

But she isn't in control, the dream is stronger than sleep itself, and she screams to herself.

Stop it

Stop it.

Give up.

But then Tove is there, Peter, Janne, and an unknown face, a little boy's, and behind those faces, in a dense, lightless jungle, the hydras are squirting their acid, heedlessly wanting to destroy the world, assuming they have the right to take, take, take and take.

A young man who's hanged himself from a radiator.

A male body curling up on a bed, a hydra's sharp teeth eating the flesh from the man's ankles and he stares up at Malin, scared, alone, and he is her brother, then the body slips out of focus, becomes four bodies, four beds, and she walks up to Maria's cramping body, to Jessica Karlsson who has hanged herself from a radiator, Malin walks and walks until she is staggering through an open landscape, easy prey for unfettered evil and all the forces that really own the world.

She has been left behind.

Alone in the world.

She is the very last human being.

Then she sees an unfamiliar woman on the plain ahead of her.

And the dream lets go of Malin, but she wants to stay now, run and get the young woman who is stumbling forward, trying to find herself. Looking for the person she was and ought to have become. The person she would have been if she had been left in peace as a child, if no one had come to her at night, the emissary of lust and self-justification. If she had been allowed to feel, for more than just a few seconds, from more than just one person, unconditional love.

But then the woman is gone.

Malin doesn't know who she was.

Then the dream turns black.

And Malin hears a woman's scream. She has heard it before and the dream becomes restless, because the woman does not belong in dreams.

Her blackness is real.

'Save me.'

'Come now. Because soon it will be too late.'

But the dream fends off the woman's voice.

Doesn't want to know.

The world distorted for ever. Her, distorted for ever. All of us distorted, the dream whispers.

You, me.

We must all learn to live with the grief of becoming something other than what we should have become, what we could have become.

We must leave anger and violence and grief and hatred and fear and pain behind us.

Otherwise we are lost, the dream whispers.

I want to be with you, Malin. To comfort you when you wake and wonder where to go, what to do, because you can feel that it's urgent, without quite being able to put words to that feeling.

But I am with the body that's floating in the water.

I still hate him.

I thought I would lose that feeling, but I hate him.

Hate.

And he is floating naked in the water.

With his head down, but the blood has long since stopped flowing, gushing from his throat.

I saw when he was cut open.

I know what did it.

You're not close yet, Malin, not even remotely. And the man floating isn't in my space, his space is different, and I will never meet him, he is a wingless bird shot through a world of fire, a skinless bubbling screaming burning mass of pain.

I have met Jessica.

She is still resting.

Wondering why things turned out the way they did. Why she ended up where she did, in the noosed end of a torn sheet tied to a radiator in a Swedish hospital.

Västmannagatan, outside the window of Malin's hotel room. She's taken all her clothes off in the stuffy room and has opened the window, and can feel the cold air streaming in.

A man in the window opposite is watching a porn film, intercourse on the swimming-pool blue screen clearly visible in the darkness.

In and out.

In and out.

The porn industry.

It isn't entirely unbearable, possibly not even wrong, Malin thinks, as long as it's adults with adults. But the lies, the self-justification, the compulsion.

The falseness.

The rotten stench that spreads through society when someone takes and takes and takes.

We establish rules, tacit agreements for how to live together, and we follow them. But there are yet more tacit agreements, so quiet that they can only be heard by very few people, and followed by even fewer, and people are lost in the name of those agreements.

Sacrificed.

Women.

Children.

Their dreams.

All their potential life.

The clock says it's four in the morning. And nocturnal Stockholm is achingly calm, but Malin knows that calm is illusory. Events and incidents are swallowed up by the city, by its capacity to forget and forgive almost anything.

A woman staring at a computer screen.

Light behind a drawn blind.

Dark rooms, plants in the windows, curtains open.

You mustn't drink, Malin thinks. Because then you go under.

We're born with a noose around our necks. And later we feel it being tightened.

I think I'm breathing, but I'm really gasping for breath.

I'm fighting against myself and against the world, and all that comes of that fight is melancholy, an awareness of how weak and pointless and tiny I really am.

In the sounds of the city she can hear the patter of her feet over the floors of a house.

Room after room after room.

Person after person.

Feeling after feeling.

Breath after breath.

And she wants to hug the girl that was once her, tell her that everything will be all right, tell her I'm going to put everything right, but when she looks down there's nothing but the worn floor of the room.

So Malin begins to run again.

Running straight into the thunderous wave that is her life.

42

Tuesday, 24 May

Darkness is pouring in over me.
I can't stop it.
What am I now?
Fear?
Anger? Loneliness?
Perhaps I myself am the torrent of darkness.
I look down on all the wandering people who have become my story, the little girl who was me at my mum's cottage.
We were alone there.
Dad was never there.
That was why I loved those days.
And later, when he had disappeared, Mum sold the cottage and poured the money down her throat.
I look down on Malin.
She's sleeping uneasily in a hotel-room bed where thousands of people before her have tried to make sense of their dreams.
Zeke.
Lying with his eyes closed in a bed a few rooms from hers. Trying to find a way into sleep, but his thoughts refuse to rest. He's thinking about his wife Gunilla, about Karin Johannison, about the realisation that no one can have it all, that you have to make choices, and then live with the happiness and the pain that those choices bring.
For him.

And for others.

And his wife is asleep, dreaming of her son Martin, about her grandchildren, but also Zeke, and she sees him run away from her in an unfamiliar field, she's calling him back, wants to scream that she forgives him, but instead only curses come out of her mouth, oaths of love, the self-righteous anger of trust betrayed, and in the dream she wants to hit him, make his nose bleed for hours, colour the whole world with the red of love.

There is also hatred in the dream.

The evil of love.

Blood red.

Just like Karim Akbar's sweaty brow, cheeks. The blood rushing to his head as he rolls off Vivianne, at first she received him with groans, then screams, as if she wanted to let go of everything connecting her to herself, to the expectations of the world, and he gave her what she wanted, hard and quiet and efficient, and he likes the encapsulation of those moments. The power of silence and darkness, and the two lonely bodies that could be the two last human beings left on the planet after the great catastrophe.

Börje Svärd.

Johan Jakobsson.

One alone with a woman, asleep in the bedroom of his house. Unsure of the future. Doesn't he really need proper love?

Johan curled up beside his daughter, she woke up an hour ago, scared after a nightmare, and he wants to comfort her, soothe her, show her the goodness of the world with the warmth of his body, silence the monsters that have taken up temporary residence in her soul.

Waldemar Ekenberg.

Sitting naked on the bench in his kitchen.

Smoking and noting the accelerating decline of his body. Not with horror, but interest, feeling the way his body itself doubts the point of going on.

He's thinking about me.

About violence.

The women Malin found in that basement.

His mother. The black knots of cancer.

He's thinking about Jessica, who took her own life. About the woman in Lund. He's thinking about them, and then he feels that it's good, so good, that he, they, never had children, because what does this world want with children, with girls, with women?

He feels like sticking a pistol up God's arse and pulling the trigger.

Or maybe the devil's arse? Unless the two of them are one and the same? Either way, Waldemar is thinking, I want to blast this world in the right direction, but which direction is that?

He pinches the thin white skin of his stomach, takes a deep drag on his cigarette, then coughs.

Sven Sjöman has made his way down to his carpentry workshop.

He went to the doctor's earlier in the day. Finally underwent the tests that might show why he's been having trouble sleeping.

'At your age,' the doctor told him, 'men sometimes suffer from an excess of oestrogen.'

The lathe is spinning at high speed, the sound muffled by the egg boxes fixed to the walls.

The smell of freshly turned wood.

The concealed freshness of the forest makes him feel like taking deep breaths. Like feeling that he's alive.

I know what I am.

I'm dead.

The feelings that were once me are gone for ever.

They ought to clean up better, Margaretha Baldersson thinks as she crosses Norr Mälarstrand, at the junction with Baltzar von Platens gata.

Rubbish litters the streets for weeks.

And in Stockholm's parks it's even worse. They look like rubbish dumps most of the time, and smell like them as well. The austerity tax really should be abolished, she thinks. Why should hard-working, well-off Stockholmers pay for flowerbeds in Karlstad? In Kalix? Let them pay for their own geraniums, and use the money for the capital's own parks instead.

Buster wanted to go out early today, and had started licking her feet, forcing her to wake up, and she had cursed him when she looked at her Georg Jensen watch and saw that it was only six thirteen.

But Riddarfjärden is always beautiful and peaceful early in the morning, and sometimes she gets to see the fog rising from the water like restless spirits, dancing gently across the surface, as if it were nothing but a large, black dance floor for the dead.

And she hadn't wanted to wake her husband, he had been up until two working on the accounts, so she had got up, made herself a quick cup of coffee in the Nespresso machine, and gazed out through the windows of the luxury apartment, and had seen the fog, the spirits.

So she had put Buster's lead on and now the small, white, rheumatic terrier is pulling her along Norr Mälarstrand with surprising force, but she manages to hold him back, even if her shoulders ache sometimes after sixty years of faithful service.

The Mälar Pavilion is deserted.

The pontoon where the gays and lesbians drink their disgusting rosé wine is bobbing in the water, and seems to be relieved to escape those unnaturally cheerful homosexuals and their irresponsible attitude to life.

Partying.

Having sex with complete strangers.

Spreading diseases like rats.

But she has to admit that sometimes she and Jan had walked past on late spring evenings and had jealously gazed upon their uninhibited rosé-drinking, realising how much fun homosexuals had.

More fun than us, she thinks now.

More fun than our circle of friends, most of them more dead than alive.

Best not to think about that.

Because we have a good life. We have everything we could wish for.

Buster is pulling her along, and he does his business at the entrance to Rålambshov Park, and she leaves the sausage of shit where it is, couldn't be bothered to bring a bag with her at this early hour.

Remarkably quiet.

She usually sees other dog owners, or at least an early morning jogger, but this morning everything is quiet.

In the park she lets Buster off his lead, and at first he races off ten metres across the grass, then seems to remember how old he is and stops abruptly, turning towards her with a sad look in his eyes, waiting for her to catch up with him.

Then, when she's caught up, he gets the scent of something and runs down to the water, in under the large willow that hangs over the little beach where the children usually paddle when the water has warmed up enough, in August.

And he starts to bark.

He doesn't usually bark, or run off anywhere like that, but she can see his hunched white frame through the trees, and he's barking insistently.

A dead bird, perhaps?

A bag of rubbish?

A homeless person, asleep?

She feels curiosity get the better of her, driving out any tiredness she feels this morning, any sense that she has seen this view far too many times.

What has Buster found?

She walks, then jogs over to him, and hears the water, smells its sweet, salty tang, and she has to bend over to get under the branches, but still gets leaves in her eyes.

Buster's stopped barking.

He's sniffing at something, and she can hear the sound of licking.

'What have you got there? What have you got there, Buster?'

And then she sees the body, the naked, slightly swollen male body, and her dog, her little white terrier, licking, nibbling at a large open wound in what looks like a cut throat.

She doesn't feel scared.

She reaches in her jacket pocket for her mobile phone.

PART 3
The Last Woman

[In the darkness]

I don't want to be afraid any more.

I don't know how much more I can take. I don't want to take any more.

I want the case to become a coffin.

I'm done with this life, with my body, everything that is me, I refuse to accept this.

And he, because it is a he, has taken me down from the chains in the ceiling, and has chained me to a wall instead, and he's covered me with a thermal blanket to stop me going into shock.

I understand that.

And my body has long since run out of adrenalin, and I know he's injected me with morphine to ease the pain, but the drug has stopped working and now there is only agony, agony that never ends, and even though I don't want to live any more, I want to run, run from the situation I'm in, the life that has been mine, I want to run from death and life alike, into a soundless, colourless, scentless nothing.

I want to hibernate.

And wake up one day and kill him, the man who made me his.

Kill the man who has cut, burned, penetrated, torn, mocked and violated me, the body and the person that are me.

Why is he doing it?

I know that question is pointless now.

His evil has no explanation.

Needs no explanation.

It's as obvious as breathing. It exists and is of itself enough, only psychologists and religious people need an explanation of evil.

I can't do anything about it. Just kill its incarnation when I see it, when I get close enough.

But I'm bleeding now.

I'm dying now.

And I hear him approach. And how can I kill him, when I'm tied up with barbed wire, chained to a wall in a dark, cold room?

Evil does what it wants with me.

It owns me. Has made me its own.

If I can't kill it, perhaps I can escape. Escape from death, life, pain, into nothingness.

The scream, it woke something inside me, slowly slowly lifting the fog of death and life, and I saw a face reflected in a window and I recognised that face as my own, although it wasn't me, it was a different woman, a different Maria.

I was old. I was newborn.

I didn't want to see myself, I wanted to stay in my empty white cave, not leave my emotionless world, I didn't want to leave in order to kill, but the time has come.

The woman who was here. There was a woman here, wasn't there? She will have to kill for me, she will have to kill the evil for me, I'll whisper, shout it to her, because I know the evil's name.

Maria Murvall is sitting on her bed.

Holding her hand in front of her eyes, moving her fingers, and they are dark trees moving in a strengthening wind. She sees eyes beyond the fingers and she opens her mouth, blows the air from her lungs, feels her vocal cords vibrate and she moves her tongue, trying to say the words that come to her, trying to say the name of the evil.

Sounds.

She hears the incoherent sounds coming out of her mouth.

The noises.

The ancient prayers, as old as humanity itself.

The prayers are coming from her.

But there is no solace in those noises, just a babbling, gurgling invocation that reeks of fear.

Why have I come back? Maria Murvall wonders.

She knows.

The case must be closed, for good.

She must assist death and rescue life.

Who is the evil, who is the evil?
We must destroy him.
We, all of his victims, are screaming that.
Destroy him!
Cut off his thousand heads, burn his body, bury the corpse.

43

Malin recognises the man lying naked with his throat slit in front of her on a shiny aluminium table in a basement room of the Karolinska Hospital, waiting for a post-mortem.

There's no smell in the room, just a scentless wintery chill.

The body, pulled out of a refrigerated unit with sixteen compartments, has a grey glow beneath the subdued fluorescent lighting, and rigor mortis makes the muscles look tense, as if the dead man were expecting an attack, the wound on his neck a stitched-together blue-black line.

'Here's our Paul Lendberg,' Conny Nygren says. 'We found a few photographs of him with his name on the back out at the house. It can't be anyone but him.'

Malin nods, recognises the face from the window of the underground train, smirking at her, and looks down at the man's hands, thinking that they're not going to wave mockingly at anyone again, they'll never chain a woman to a wall again, and she concludes that it is just that Paul Lendberg is lying dead before her, Zeke and Conny Nygren, waiting to have his torso cut open and his entrails, every single damn organ removed and examined.

Just like an animal that's been hunted and brought down.

Like an animal in the forest.

Before they went into the pathology lab, Conny Nygren told them that a woman had found Paul Lendberg with his throat cut in Riddarfjärden, at Rålambshov Park. That they had no idea how the body ended up there, no witnesses have contacted them, and they have no suspects either. They basically knew nothing about Paul Lendberg's affairs; he must have been incredibly skilful at putting up smoke-screens to hide his activities.

'But it's quite clear,' Conny Nygren had said, 'that this neither begins nor ends with him.'

And now the three detectives are standing around his body and feeling their eyes itch in the poor lighting, and all three of them are wondering: What are we dealing with here?

A murdered pimp, a torturer of women, a man mixed up in trafficking, a murderer? Perhaps. Their murderer? The man who took Jenny Svartsjö's life? Who rendered other women mute or drove them to suicide?

They've taken a sample of Lendberg's DNA. The National Forensics Laboratory has promised to prioritise it.

The women in the basement.

They're currently being questioned. In so far as that's possible. They're all scared, and many of them are too weak, too shocked, to be able to say anything comprehensible.

Some of them are in hospital, others in secure women's hostels.

'He got what he deserved,' Zeke says.

'He did,' Conny Nygren says, and ordinarily Malin might perhaps have asked them to show respect to the dead, saying that no one deserves to have their throat cut and then be dumped in cold, unwelcoming water.

But not this time.

The bastard who chained those women in the basement had used up all of his right to life. Intellectually she doesn't believe that, but every emotion in her body is screaming it.

Like paedophiles.

Eradicate every last one of them.

They do not enjoy Kant's good will.

They've broken the human contract.

So kill them.

'The wretched little dog that found him evidently helped itself to a snack,' Conny Nygren says.

'What breed?' Zeke asks.

And now Malin has had enough.

'It doesn't matter what fucking breed it was,' she whispers.

Zeke looks at her, knows he's gone too far, then looks back towards the body on the table in front of him, and Conny Nygren says: 'A white terrier. He was eating from the wound in his neck. The rich old bag had to drag the damn thing away once we'd finished talking to her.'

They've pushed the body back into the fridge.

Are standing next to each other, inhaling the room's cold air.

Their breath is fogging slightly as it rises from their mouths, but none of them feels the cold. Instead their minds are working feverishly to find any way to take the investigation forward.

'We're checking through all the databases, all the archives,' Conny Nygren says. 'If we've got anything there, anything to link Paul Lendberg to the other names that have cropped up in the case, anything at all that might have anything to do with this mess, we'll find it. We don't actually know anything about Lendberg yet, but we're bound to find something, some thread we can follow.'

Malin presses the nail of her forefinger into her thumb, hoping that the pain will lend her voice extra urgency.

'We have to talk to Fredrik Kantsten. About what I got from Jimmy Kalder, if nothing else.'

'We have to?' Conny Nygren says.

'Malin's right,' Zeke says, and Malin wonders why Conny Nygren is hesitant, why does he want to treat Fredrik

Kantsten with kid gloves? Could Conny himself be mixed up in this somehow?

But she knows that's an absurd thought. She's just being paranoid. She's rarely encountered a more straight and honest person than Conny. He just doesn't want to infringe anyone's privacy unnecessarily.

Conny Nygren smiles.

A confident, determined smile.

Then he says: 'Yes, I suppose it's time. Put him under pressure. See what you can get out of him.'

Put him under pressure, Malin thinks.

Yes, we shall.

And Conny Nygren turns around and walks out of the pathology lab, and Malin and Zeke follow him out, leaving the peculiar cold behind them, and emerging into an equally peculiar warmth.

Fredrik Kantsten switches on his computer.

Checks his email.

Looks out of the window of his office in Stockholm Courthouse, at the brown modernist blocks climbing up the slope of Kungsklippan. He knows that the City Hall is hidden somewhere in that direction, would dearly have loved a view of its turrets and gilded tower, pretending it was a castle that belonged to him. He had always imagined himself living in a castle or an estate, just like Peder, and why shouldn't I become a lord of the manor?

He had lunch with a friend yesterday, the head of a small public body examining whether the country ought to have a register of cats.

The National Hubcap Evaluation Authority.

The Inquiry into the Nutritional Value of Poo.

The Committee for Monitoring the Sexiness of Women's Underwear.

There's a bloody authority for everything in this country, Fredrik Kantsten thinks.

As soon as there's a change of government and people in the previous administration are out of a job, new public bodies are set up so that the people turfed out by the electorate have something to be in charge of.

'Do not disturb' messages on both door and phone.

He needs to think.

But can't think right now.

They've been to see Peder and Emanuel.

But my old friends sounded calm when I spoke to them.

And now the police have found Paul in Riddarfjärden.

Presumably his business associates, protecting their own backs.

And what the police found in his basement. Never had any idea it was that bad. Sure, the women were commodities, but treating them worse than cattle?

Why should I have seen that?

Didn't want to see, didn't want to know anything about it, because if I know and see, it can lead back to me.

It mustn't lead back to me.

The women.

Maybe that was still the best they could have expected? How many of their sort are murdered each year around the world?

Murder.

That's what this is about.

It's only a matter of time before the police come knocking on my door again, here at the Public Prosecution Office for fuck's sake, to ask 'a few questions'.

They're going to see the connections.

And wonder.

Can they find any link between me and Paul?

Or can they find out even more?

I managed to hush it up in the investigation in Ljusdal. Managed to persuade that youngster, Kalder, that his career was over if he didn't do as he was told.

Have I been seduced?

By the intoxication you can only feel in the proximity of a sort of total autocracy? By total ruthlessness?

No. Someone like me can't be seduced.

I seduce.

It's always been that way, even if not all girls have always grasped that. Particularly when I was a teenager and over-flowing with hormones.

It was good with the Skulls. You could just help yourself to what was on offer. The others paid for it, so why shouldn't I? And the girls wanted it, that much was obvious. I wasn't exactly an ugly old man.

My career must not be over.

This little storm must be stifled until it's no more than a gust of wind.

Fredrik Kantsten leans back in his office chair. Puts his feet up on the desk, looks at his brown Church shoes, and thinks how nice they are when they're as well polished and well kept as his.

District Prosecutor.

A guy with connections, worthy of respect in important circles, particularly from the left. Or closet right.

Sure. It's ridiculous to think of yourself like that, as an important person, especially if you're not yet fifty-five. It's almost a bit immature, almost childish.

But still, Fredrik Kantsten thinks, looking at his indistinct reflection in the office window.

Still.

I've earned the right to feel pleased with myself, to take what I want with impunity.

What woman, for instance, wouldn't enjoy a man like me, even if only to look at?

His face is reflected faintly in the window.

District Prosecutor.

Possible future member of the Court of Appeal.

A man who is the friend of the truly powerful.

Handsome for his age. Lithe, full of energy.

Possibly undersecretary of state in the Justice Ministry next time, if only the right-wing parties would get out of the way.

Fredrik Kantsten runs his hand through his hair, and wishes he could see himself more clearly in the window.

44

Cheap suit, Malin thinks. Doesn't he ever look at himself in the mirror?

But he probably does.

Often.

But he doubtless sees something very different from what I can see.

Barely a week since she was last in this room.

It feels smaller now, as if the man in front of her is shut in a box.

His suit is probably expensive, but it looks cheap, shabby, almost, like the world outside the window.

It's just before noon, and the sky above the angular brown façades of the modernist buildings is a mess of weather.

Rain from a heavy grey cloud over to the west, and high above the rooftops a summer sky with an expanse of magical blue dotted with small, feather-light clouds. To the east the sky seems almost to collapse, turning grey and autumnal.

Clear sky replaced by grey, sun turning to rain within an hour, warmth turning to cold.

An umbrella? Sunglasses? Warm top?

Fredrik Kantsten had been in his office, and agreed to see Malin and Zeke.

It was as if he'd been expecting them to show up, and now he's sitting in his office chair, leaning forward, and his face is even less distinct than Malin remembers it.

His sharp nose doesn't manage to draw your attention

from the acne scars on his cheeks, and his lips are full and wet with saliva.

What woman would want a man like this, would want to kiss that bloodless mouth?

Malin and Zeke are sitting opposite Fredrik Kantsten. She's wondering where to start, how they might be able to shock him into telling them something that can move them forward.

It's in the nature of the investigation that they don't know. They merely suspect. And that there are pieces of the puzzle missing.

Fredrik Kantsten is leaning forward to show his interest.

But also to dominate proceedings.

They've looked more closely into his background. Divorced, with two grown-up children, both living in London.

And Malin thinks that he has the smell of someone who uses prostitutes, and she can see him sitting in the front seat of a Mercedes in a grotty car park in an even grottier industrial estate being sucked off by some tart who takes no more than three hundred kronor for the trouble, or presumably the 'pleasure', if you were to ask Fredrik Kantsten.

He's staring at Malin.

What do you want now? Surely last time you were here was enough?

'As you know, I'm investigating the case of a woman who was raped, badly abused and finally murdered. You remember the parallels I mentioned when we last met? With the case in which you were the prosecutor? Now more parallels have cropped up, with a case in Ljusdal, concerning a Jessica Karlsson. Do you have anything to say about that?'

Fredrik Kantsten sighs.

'I have nothing to say about that.'

'We know,' Zeke says, 'that you were in a cabin in the area where she disappeared, when she disappeared. With your friends Ärendsson and Stålskiöld. We know that beyond any doubt.'

'Yes, we were questioned by the investigating officers at the time about it, that's true, but as I understand, the case was declared confidential. And we were only there to go hunting. I'm aware that you've spoken to Emanuel and Peder, we're good friends from our time in Uppsala. We usually go hunting together, once a year or so.'

You knew we would be coming, Malin thinks.

Do you know what we're going to ask? Do you know that I've spoken to Jimmy Kalder?

'What I find strange,' Malin says, 'is that you put pressure on the prosecutor in the case in Hälsingland, to drop the investigation and declare it confidential. And that you were also in a hurry to shut down the investigation in Malmö.'

Fredrik Kantsten leans back.

His eyes turn black.

'Those are serious allegations, you know.'

'But I know for certain that you put pressure on Jimmy Kalder.'

'I don't even know who this Kalder is. There are nine hundred prosecutors in the Swedish judicial system, and the idea that I would know them all is absurd. And the notion that I would put pressure on anyone within my own profession is equally absurd. Has this Kalder claimed that I did? If he has, he's being deeply immoral.'

Malin doesn't respond to the question.

Kalder, she thinks instead.

He had hung up at the count of ten, but hadn't dared say anything.

'Do you have any proof whatsoever to back up these allegations?'

'And Emanuel Ärendsson,' Malin says. 'You brought in your own friend as an expert in the case in Malmö. Got him to claim that the girl's injuries could have been self-inflicted. And, to be honest, I'm seriously fucking interested in why you were so keen to have that investigation dropped so quickly, and why you did so.'

'Did what?'

'Shut down the investigation in Malmö prematurely.'

'That's quite enough. I needed a second opinion. And Emanuel is a recognised authority. And the investigation wasn't making any progress.'

'Was it you who attacked her?' Zeke asks. 'Who subjected all those women to torture?'

'You're mad,' Fredrik Kantsten says, shaking his head. 'You can leave now. Are you suggesting that I, one of the top prosecutors in Sweden, would do something like that? Or could even be mixed up in something like that?'

'We've got you for pressurising a colleague,' Malin says. 'For misconduct in office. You won't get away with it. So you might as well lay all your cards on the table.'

'What cards? What evidence have you got? A few words, perhaps. My word against someone else's. I'll report you for harassment.'

They sit facing each other in silence for a moment.

Each sitting out the other.

'Are you in the habit of using prostitutes?' Malin finally asks, surprised at her own audacity, and glances at Zeke, who blinks slowly as if to give his approval.

'I have no intention of dignifying that question with an answer. The idea that a man like me would pay for sex is utterly absurd.'

Fredrik Kantsten puts the palms of his hands down on the mahogany desktop and lowers his eyebrows in a way that seems calculated to instil respect and a sense of power.

'You need to answer all our questions,' Zeke hisses. 'So answer. Do you use prostitutes?'

'As I said, I won't dignify that question with an answer.'

'And now Paul Lendberg has been found murdered in Riddarfjärden. He was at Uppsala at the same time as you and your friends. Did you know him?'

Fredrik Kantsten's mouth cracks into a toad-like grin.

'I don't remember a Paul Lendberg. What happened to him?'

'Yesterday,' Malin says, once again choosing not to answer his question, 'as I'm sure you must know through your work, or from reading it in the papers or seeing it on television, nine women were found chained up in the basement of his house out on Lidingö. And this morning he was found murdered in Riddarfjärden, with his throat cut.'

'I'm not working on that case. I don't see what it's got to do with me.'

And that's the problem, Malin thinks. We don't know either. We've got nothing but suspicions, vague hints of connections and links.

'Were you in the habit of using prostitutes on your hunting trips?' Zeke asks.

Fredrik Kantsten bites his lower lip.

Seems to be trying to swallow both his anger and the impulse to scream, then answers perfectly calmly: 'There's no point in your asking any more questions like that, because you won't get any answers.'

'We decide what questions to ask,' Malin says, and the look on Fredrik Kantsten's face clearly demonstrates that he knows they haven't got anything on him that could come anywhere close to them being able to press charges.

Yet he is still nervous.

'Maybe you used prostitutes back in your Uppsala days? In the Skulls Society? Was it Paul Lendberg who got hold of them?'

'What exactly are you getting at?'

'We can see an awful lot of connections,' Malin says. 'As, I'm sure, can you. Perhaps you could explain some of them to us? For instance, were you in Count Stålskiöld's hunting cabin last autumn, towards the end of November? And, if you were, was Jenny Svartsjö with you?'

'I wasn't. So obviously there was no whore there either.'

'Is there anyone else who usually takes part in your meetings, or has done in the past?' Zeke asks. 'Anyone we don't know about?'

Fredrik Kantsten's pupils dilate, then he raises his eyebrows.

'No,' he says. 'Just us. The idea that we might take prostitutes with us is ridiculous. We're all respectable men. I might be divorced, but Peder and Emanuel are married. We all have important positions in society. Why would we risk all that for a bit of meaningless sex?'

Then the phone on Fredrik Kantsten's desk rings.

He answers.

Says yes, yes, yes.

Who is it? A secretary?

A prearranged call to give him a reason to get rid of them?

He hangs up.

'You'll have to excuse me, duty calls. I'm sorry I can't help you. And as far as your misguided accusations about my alleged professional misconduct are concerned, I suppose you'll just have to lodge an official complaint.'

Malin looks into his face, into his eyes.

Businesslike now, as if their insulting questions were a minor inconvenience, an insignificant difference of political opinion, but there's nothing insignificant about this.

Abuse of office. Undue influence.

Dead women.

Mute women.

Tortured, raped women.

Chained, kidnapped women.

And Malin feels like twisting the nose of the arrogant man in front of her. But she holds back.

Instead she sees Zeke stand up, grab hold of Fredrik Kantsten's red tie and pull him up from his chair, and snarl: 'This isn't a fucking game. Got that? This is about murder, rape, kidnap and torture. All at the same time. You know things, I'm convinced of it. And if I have to shove a soldering iron up your arse, I'm going to drag you down into the shit with me. You fucking bet I will.'

Zeke lets go of the tie.

Fredrik Kantsten slumps onto his chair.

No smile on his face, just a look full of utter uncertainty.

And Malin feels scared.

Looks around the room. What if there's a camera in here, and their suspicions have misled them, what if Fredrik Kantsten is just a hunter who was in the wrong place at the wrong time, and just happened to know people in the same situation?

But then she sees the look in his eyes.

His big, black, lying pupils.

A man protecting other men and thereby protecting himself.

Malin takes a step forward and stares into Kantsten's small, close-set eyes.

'You're finished,' Malin says. 'You do know that, don't you?'

Hantverkargatan gets narrower down towards the City Hall, and seems to lose itself in a sequence of failed buildings.

The traffic is thundering past Malin and Zeke, the fumes lying heavy between the buildings.

They walk past a travel agent and health spa, and the pictures in the plate-glass window are clearly aimed at the very wealthiest. Villas with private pools, overblown, palatial hotel rooms.

I could do with a month with Peter in a villa like that, Malin thinks, and stops to admire the grandeur.

And considers what she and Peter are trying to do.

Feels inside.

Into herself.

Tries to feel if anything is growing inside her. If she is two lives now instead of just one.

When she was pregnant with Tove she could feel it right from the start.

But now she feels alone, and sees no one but herself beside that pool in the travel agent's window.

Don't think about that.

Focus.

She has to cut every single fucking head off the hydra they're hunting.

One of those heads is Fredrik Kantsten's.

She's sure of that.

But how does it all fit together?

Zeke is also looking in the window, at the villa with the pool. 'I'd like to be there right now.'

Then he turns to Malin and says: 'Well, that didn't really leave us much the wiser.'

But aren't you a bit wiser?

I'm drifting upward now.

Up and into Fredrik Kantsten's office.

He's sitting with his hand on the telephone.

Wants to call someone, but whom should he call, what would conference calls with his friends lead to, how are they going to find a way out of this?

You know, I whisper into his ear. You know, and you have to talk.

Your only chance is to talk.

Is there another man? Was he the one who killed me? Or was it you? One of the others? I have no idea.

I am eternal cold, I am all the fear your flesh can feel, I am drifting into you now, I can make you scream as you sit there with the phone in your hand.

I have that power.

And I shall use it.

Fredrik Kantsten feels an ice-cold fist take hold of his heart, and an electric pain courses through his chest, then he hears a woman's voice whisper in his ear: You killed me.

You killed me.

And with a grimace he moves his hands up to his heart, but realises that isn't where the pain is, it's a force inside him, and he tries to get rid of it but it's screaming in him, screaming in an unknown language, and he looks out at the modernist buildings, tries to pretend that they're the City Hall and the Palace of Nobility, sees his face vaguely reflected in the glass, and then he screams, and in his scream he can hear the voices of all the women he's hurt in his fifty-five-year-old life.

45

People and shrieking commerce.

Drunk Finns from the ferries, shoppers from the suburbs, a tangible feeling of cheapness. Androgynous boutique chains shouting out their names from backlit signs, enticing the rabble with 'come and buy, come and buy, if you do your lives will be happier', handicapped beggars holding out bowls in shaking hands, immigrants with signs advertising cheap steak and Béarnaise sauce outside the gaudy glass box of H&M's new head office.

Commerce is thriving.

No doubt about that.

Malin and Zeke are walking up Drottninggatan towards Hötorget, looking for somewhere to get a cheap, late lunch.

Three different pharmacies.

Unfamiliar names in the wake of deregulation. Billionaires behind the companies. Billionaires who can scent new billions like hyenas smell carrion.

As they pass the pharmacies Malin feels her stomach contract, feels something happening inside her as her hormones fight each other, but she pushes the thought, the feeling away, she hasn't got time for that now.

They go past a McDonald's.

I'd rather starve than eat that crap, Malin thinks. Excrement from cow intestines has been found in the meat, in the US a child died from it. When will the same thing happen in

Sweden? There ought to be warning signs outside those hideous places.

They get hotdogs from the kiosk outside the Concert Hall, and eat them on the steps in front of the sickly blue façade as Malin listens to the cries from the stalls on Hötorget.

'Madame!'

'Cheap, just for you!'

'Asparagus. Very cheap.'

Her mouth is full of chorizo when her mobile rings.

Conny Nygren's name on the screen.

'Malin.'

'Conny here. I've got something.'

A red bus goes past on Kungsgatan, and Malin sees a man get his hand caught in the revolving door of the Kungshallen restaurant complex on the other side of the street.

People eating behind the aquarium-like windows.

'Paul Lendberg was married to a Zara Zengman. We've just found her name in the register of people whose addresses are protected. She lives on Kungsholmen, so I presume they weren't living together, even though we haven't been able to find anything about a divorce.'

'We can talk to her,' Malin says.

'This is our case, really, but go ahead. Woman to woman. And, just so you know, it's OK to notify her of his death.'

'Understood,' Malin says.

The sausage.

The chilli is making her cheeks feel hot, and the sky is bright blue now.

Zeke has gone back to the kiosk to get another hotdog.

Conny Nygren gives her an address, then they hang up.

The building where Zara Zengman is supposed to live is next to the Karlberg Canal, at the far end of Kungsholm Strand, opposite the gleaming, white Karlberg Palace, where a couple of black cannons are pointing out at nothing, towards an enemy who has long since become invisible.

Zeke had protested at first.

If Zara Zengman was even at home, Malin shouldn't go on her own. Who knew what they were getting into? Maybe she was involved in what her husband was doing? Maybe she had something to do with his murder? Then again, maybe she didn't even know he was dead? They had no way of knowing.

But Malin had insisted.

I'll do this alone. What's the worst that could happen? I'd be surprised if she were threatening, had a gun in her flat, and when Malin is about to go inside the building she is confronted by a coded lock, but a little man with a beard and a beret is just coming out and lets her in.

I'll be OK if I have to inform her of the death. I've done that sort of thing before.

A small lift with a metal gate. Typical of buildings from the thirties.

Quite rightly, there's a Zengman listed as living on the seventh floor, and Malin goes up, closes her eyes, resting for a moment in white nothingness.

There.

And she rings on the door, and feels herself observed through the peephole.

Then she hears footsteps inside the flat, away from the door. Through a window in the stairwell Malin can see out onto a roof terrace that must belong to the flat. It faces the inner courtyard, with no view of the palace.

A shadow falls across the terrace.

Someone's climbing up a ladder towards the roof.

Malin runs the few steps to the window and tries to open it.

She sees a pair of bare woman's legs vanishing up the

ladder. And Malin shoves her elbow through the window and a shower of glass rains down over the tiles, and she reaches the lock on the other side without cutting herself and the window is open, and Malin carefully steps out onto the narrow ledge between the terrace and the window.

Shit.

At least fifteen metres off the ground, and she looks up.

A woman on the roof. Dressed in a lacy white nightdress, with loose blond hair. The wind grabs at the white fabric and her hair, making them look like a scared butterfly's wings against the blue expanse of the sky.

She is trying to escape across the roof, clambering slowly as the nightdress catches around her legs, but nonetheless making steady progress up the black tiles towards the ridge of the roof.

'Stop!' Malin yells. 'Stop, for God's sake! I'm from the police. I just want to talk to you.'

But the woman carries on.

Malin looks down.

I'll die if I fall.

Then she takes aim, and jumps the two metres to the terrace railing, grabs it and clings on before swinging onto the terrace and climbing up the ladder to the roof, after the woman who must be Zara Zengman.

'Stop, for God's sake!'

But the woman carries on.

She's up at the top of the roof now, sitting astride it and edging her way forward.

She turns around, and Malin catches sight of the woman, beautiful but past her prime, like a model who never quite made it because her features were too perfect, because there were no blemishes for people's imaginations to grab hold of.

Malin's reached the ridge now. She looks across at the palace, which now houses the military academy.

Quicker, braver than the woman.

'Zara,' she calls. 'Stop!'

And she's right behind the woman now, how to do this? Without the pair of us falling into the abyss. Should I grab her nightdress? The woman's hair is flying, and the fabric is caught by the wind again, looks like angel's wings now, and Malin reaches out to her, dazzled by the light, feels herself fumble blindly for the woman, but she's not there.

Am I falling now?

I'm falling.

No, I'm not.

The woman in sight again. Within reach.

No longer an angel.

Threaten her with my pistol? No. Wrap my arms around her? Then we might both fall.

So Malin puts one hand on Zara Zengman's shoulder, and she turns around and grabs Malin by the wrist, twisting it in an attempt to make her fall, but Malin parries the attack and throws herself at Zara Zengman, pushing her towards the side of the roof facing the terrace, so that if they do fall, they fall no further than that.

Does Zara Zengman want to fall? She may be a seriously deceived woman, or a hardened criminal, but the angel in front of me must love her life, mustn't she, just like I do mine? Mustn't she?

We aren't going to fall, tumbling through the air towards the ground like paralysed butterflies.

Zara Zengman twists Malin's wrist again.

And they both have to cling on to stop themselves falling the other way, away from the terrace, towards the abyss.

Then Malin jerks, stumbles, pulls with all her might in the right direction, and the two bodies tumble, tightly entwined, down the roof, the tiles scraping their skin wherever it's exposed, and then they fall the two metres to the hard wooden decking of the terrace.

Malin lands on top of Zara Zengman.

No pain.

Nothing broken.

And she gets up, hears groaning from the body on the decking, then Zeke's familiar voice: 'Don't move. You're under arrest. Don't move. Are you OK, Malin?'

She sees him hold his pistol to Zara Zengman's head, sees the white nightdress, the fabric flecked with dirt from the tiles, and then her blond hair, its roots quite black.

Zara Zengman has been examined by a doctor.

No bones broken.

No serious wounds, just scraped arms and legs, and now the thirty-five-year-old is sitting, patched up, in front of Malin and Zeke in a dimly lit interview room in Kronoberg Prison.

Hard chairs, a metal table. A tape recorder flashing next to Malin.

The green and beige prison clothes are hanging off Zara Zengman, and her blue eyes look tired under the cold fluorescent lighting, but even under these circumstances her face looks perfect.

High cheekbones.

Full lips.

A few crows' feet at the corners of her eyes, and a blank expression.

She already knew that Paul Lendberg had been found murdered, but didn't seem exactly grief-stricken by the news.

Malin has just asked her to tell them what she knows, has said she must have known something about her husband's business activities, and at first Zara Zengman hesitates. Then she looks into Malin's eyes, and it's as if the blank expression fills with meaning, a sort of shame and regret, but also a longing for something else.

Maybe there's grief in that expression after all. She must have loved this Paul Lendberg once, this man who has been found with his throat cut. Maybe he was the kindest, most considerate man in the world towards her?

There's no shortage of split personalities.

The notorious Haga Man was an ordinary family man.

Who tidied his children's bedrooms, felt the damp chill of the stainless-steel draining-board beneath his hands, who presumably nuzzled his children's hair and inhaled the little miracles' scent.

Paul Lendberg.

Destroyer of women. And seducer. Presumably the soft skin of his palm gently caressed your back, Zara, and he must have whispered sweet nothings in your ear, giving you a glimpse of all that this world has to offer.

Zara Zengman raises her head, and begins to speak in a slurred voice.

'I met Paul when my modelling career was beginning to stall. I was in Milan on a job. To start with I had no idea what he did, but I gradually realised. And then I left him, that was three years ago, and I didn't want to know anything about his business. At first I believed he was in import/export. And then I convinced myself that he was. That's how he himself used to think of it.

'I never got a divorce. Because he paid me one hundred thousand a month, to stay married and keep my mouth shut, I suppose. But I didn't know anything more than that about what he did. We had a tacit agreement.'

Zara Zengman shuts her eyes and pauses before going on.

'I swear to God I didn't know what he was doing to the women. I knew nothing about the basement.'

'What did you know about his activities?' Malin asks.

'Like I said: I didn't want to know. I persuaded myself that I didn't know anything. But I'm aware he used to provide prostitutes to high-flyers. For conferences and business trips, that sort of thing.'

'Hunting trips?'

Zara Zengman nods.

'But I had no idea he kept the women locked up, or any of that nonsense. I just thought he used his contacts in Russia and Ukraine to get hold of prostitutes for wealthy men.'

'How did you find out?' Zeke asks.

'I realised gradually.'

'How?'

Zara Zengman shakes her head. Looks down, evidently ashamed. Aware of what her good life has cost others.

'The things he used to say about his work didn't add up. And a woman knows.'

'But you never saw his dungeon in the house?'

'He must have put that in later. After I'd moved out. You have to understand that he was always kind towards me. Gentle. He was devoted to his work. To him, everything was business. He used to say he negotiated services. The only thing he was really interested in was money, and I think he actually liked the fact that he was paying me to stay married. Owning me in that way. Knowing he'd found my weak point and could exploit it.'

'But you never went to the police with what you knew?'

'I'd never actually seen anything. I just wanted to get away from him, from all of it.'

You deceived yourself for your own advantage, at the cost of your sisters, Malin thinks. I hope there's a place for you in hell.

With women like you, we don't need heartless men, she

thinks. But she also feels a measure of sympathy for Zara Zengman. For failing to find a way out, and feeling terrified when reality crashed in on her life, threatening to destroy it.

'And that was why you ran, when I showed up?' Malin asks. 'You'd heard that Paul Lendberg had been found murdered, you'd seen the women on television, and you thought one of his business associates from the East wanted to get hold of you?'

Zara Zengman nods again.

'You're right, I was terrified. I didn't know what to do. I should have shopped him at once. All those suspicions. I realise that now. But what proof did I have? I didn't want to know what he was mixed up in. I didn't want to. He was still kind to me, almost always. He listened, he cared, in a way no one else ever had.'

'It seems likely that he was deeply involved in trafficking,' Malin says. 'Did you know about that? Trafficking in people?'

'I didn't know anything. You have to believe me. All I had were vague suspicions. And what use were they? Better to take the money and run, live a carefree life and forget the whole thing. Anyway, who would have listened to me? You lot in the police? I don't think so.'

'We would have listened,' Malin says, without actually believing it. Zara Zengman would have been dismissed as a vengeful nutter. No one would have even tried to get a warrant to search the house on Lidingö on the strength of her word alone. Especially if she contradicted herself the way she is doing now, saying she didn't know anything, then giving a fairly clear impression of her husband's 'business interests'.

Just look at the way the prosecutor dismissed the statements of several witnesses in the case of Police Chief Göran Lindberg, up to his neck in a prostitution racket.

'You wouldn't have listened. And you know it. You'd rather not see either.'

And this, Malin thinks, is the mantra of the selfish.

The closest associate of evil.

Don't want to know.

Don't want to see.

Because then there is no evil. There are no paedophiles, no fathers raping their daughters, men abusing young girls from countries no one gives a damn about. No one like Jenny Svartsjö, and if someone doesn't exist, then nothing bad can happen to them, can it?

That's just the way it is.

If you shut your eyes, the reality you don't want to see disappears.

The women.

The ones in the basement.

All other women who have met a tragic end.

They do exist.

And you're feeling sad that those hundred thousand kronor aren't going to show up every month from now on, Malin thinks.

But on the other hand, you'll inherit what he had, if there is any money. Is that a motive for murder? Could you have murdered him?

No, Malin thinks.

The woman facing me is no murderer.

'Did you know about his clients?' Zeke asks.

'No. Like I said, I didn't want to know anything. I used to leave him to it.'

'Yet you still seem to know a fair bit about his affairs?'

The look in Zara Zengman's eyes grows foggy, distant, and she says: 'How do you mean?'

Malin shakes her head slightly in Zeke's direction, as if to say: There's no point.

Yet she still mentions Fredrik Kantsten, Emanuel Ärendsson and Peder Stålskiöld, but Zara Zengman doesn't react at all, clearly doesn't know them.

'Did you know about your husband's contacts in Russia? Ukraine? Anyone who might have had anything to do with the women?'

'No.'

'Did you know Jenny Svartsjö?'

Malin puts down a picture.

'No. But I've read the papers over the last few days. Was she one of his women?'

'We think so,' Malin says. 'It seems very likely. But it's very hard to get an overall impression of networks like this. They're often made up of small cells that don't know about each other. And our main priority is to find Jenny Svartsjö's killer.'

Zara Zengman closes her eyes.

Rubs her hands over her perfect cheekbones, her eyes.

'I feel ashamed,' she says. 'You've got to find the men who were helping him, the ones he was working with.'

'That's actually a different investigation,' Malin says.

And suddenly she feels sick. Nauseous in the face of this woman who, when it came down to it, was prepared to sacrifice other women for her own comfort.

'You despise me,' Zara Zengman says, looking at Malin.

'You're aware that you're going to be charged with protecting a criminal, and violent conduct against a public official?' Zeke says.

'I ought to be charged with far worse than that,' Zara Zengman says, her eyes suddenly crystal clear. 'I could have stopped those women being chained up in his basement. If I'd just bothered to open my eyes. Thought less about myself. God knows what I might have been able to prevent.'

May that realisation torment you, Malin thinks, torment you until it vanishes into a rush of denial.

Malin can see Jenny Svartsjö's body in the forest.

Cut open.

Violated.

As if raped, murdered by the forest itself.

Alone, abandoned, far from the place where she ran through meadows as a little girl.

She looks Zara Zengman in the eye.

Says nothing.

46

Malin, Zeke and Conny Nygren are sitting in the canteen of Police Headquarters, each waiting for the others to speak, wishing that one of them could quickly bring this to an end.

The trellis screens Malin remembers from her previous visit are gone, replaced by transparent folding screens with some sort of Asian pattern. They do little to relieve the institutional feel of the room, but the coffee from the machine is good, just a hint of bitterness. The whole room smells of old meatballs, packet sauce, and powdered mash.

Malin shuts her eyes. Her body feels tired, the way it always does when an investigation switches to top gear. She blocks the others out and concentrates on what is inside her, and hears a faint voice. It's trying to formulate words, but all she can hear is an irregular jumble of sounds.

But she wants to hear the voice, understand it, knows she has to listen to it. She has an idea whose voice it is. But how could that be possible?

'Malin, time to stop daydreaming.'

Zeke calls her back.

She shakes her head. Smiles at Conny Nygren.

'Emanuel Ärendsson,' she says. 'He might be the weakest of the three. He must be. That's the feeling I got when I was there, that he's the type of man who needs some sort of advantage over other people, otherwise he might snap. He seems very proud of being friends with

Peder Stålskiöld and Fredrik Kantsten, it means a lot to his self-image.'

They've discussed various possible ways to take the investigation forward.

But each time the discussion always comes back to the same three men.

Emanuel Ärendsson.

Fredrik Kantsten.

And Peder Stålskiöld.

Their motivation had seemed unclear at first, yet somehow isn't. Power, belonging, entitlement, desires that need sating, games to be played. Boundaries that were crossed a long time ago, and which continue to shift.

Is the missing piece of the puzzle beyond any moral compass? Someone at the outer limits of human behaviour?

Malin had thought this to herself without saying anything.

Maybe one of the three men really had committed those acts against the women in the forest? But was any of them so lacking in self-restraint? All three of them seem vain, with vastly inflated self-images, yet at the same time they grow worried when asked about their actions, insecure little boys who've lost their mothers.

Perhaps there is another man? One with no limits, one the others somehow look up to, want to be like, want to be close to. Perhaps they even want to be him? A man who never plays games, who never really satisfies any desires, who is just one vast lack of restraint, and therefore almost a superhero for whom everything is possible.

A man who can't grasp the concept of morality, and who therefore can't be immoral.

So far they hadn't managed to find anything linking Paul Lendberg and the men apart from their time at Uppsala. Nor anything that might lead them to his contacts in Eastern Europe or within Sweden.

They had made inquiries internationally, but hadn't yet received any responses, and Forensics was busy working on his computers and tracking his activities on his mobile.

But the three detectives feel that they have to move on right now.

And when they can't make logical sense of things, when their mental energy starts to flag and hopelessness threatens to take over, that's when violence rears its head.

'You've got nothing you can use to put pressure on Ärendsson?' Conny Nygren asks. 'To scare him?' And Malin can feel a steady ache from where she scraped her leg, but it's not a bad pain, more a reminder that she's alive.

She hadn't hesitated before climbing up onto that roof.

Wasn't scared for her own life, or anyone else's, not for a moment.

'Waldemar,' Zeke says. 'Send Waldemar around to see the gynaecologist and do his thing. He could make him say something.'

'Maybe Waldemar could find the piece of this damn puzzle that I know is missing,' Malin says.

'Waldemar?'

A questioning look on Conny Nygren's face, hopeful.

'A colleague with a very specific way of working,' Malin says, thinking that she doesn't care what he does now, she's sick of this, they need to make progress on the case, no matter what the cost. It's war now, and wars can't be won without sacrifice. Wars aren't just fought between states and factions, but here and now, in daily life, between the forces of good and evil, fighting for supremacy of the world.

So go ahead, Waldemar. Do what you have to. It's urgent.

There's a woman screaming.

We have to save her.

And against her will she finds that the thought of one of these men being tormented cheers her up.

Duty, Malin thinks. Where's the boundary of my duty? Our duty?

Where are the boundaries?

What have I become blind to?

'In that case I think you should call Waldemar,' Conny Nygren says. 'Let him do whatever he likes, because they've got things to hide, and they'll never tell us anything.'

Malin picks up her mobile.

He answers on the third ring.

'Waldemar,' she says. 'I've got a job for you.'

The sound of his breathing on the other end of the line.

Smouldering with anticipation.

Apply pressure.

He loves doing that.

He's going to do this on his own. He sneaked out without Börje Svärd noticing, and now's the time to fucking well show what we do to men who get in our way when we've got important things to find out.

He's walking across the gravel drive towards the gynaecologist's outsized villa, and feels the white walls close up behind him.

Waldemar Ekenberg looks at the ridiculous door knocker shaped like a lion as he adjusts his brown gabardine trousers.

He changed his shirt before heading out here. Took off the white one and put on the wine-red one he keeps in his locker in the changing room, along with some cable ties he keeps for occasions like this.

Sometimes he forgets about the shirt.

Like when he put pressure on the pimp.

Before he got out of the car he released the safety catch on his pistol. Just in case.

Emanuel Ärendsson.

Gynaecologist.

What kind of fucked-up person did you have to be to want to do that job? Looking at cunts all day long but never being allowed to have any fun with them.

But that sort probably think poking about with bits of metal is fun.

Probably makes them hard.

Now Waldemar can feel adrenalin pulsing through his body, and he likes the feeling.

Loves the rush.

The promise of violence.

The oldest form of human expression.

He takes hold of the ring in the lion's mouth.

And knocks.

Malin is standing in an aisle in the pharmacy at Fridhemsplan.

She approaches the shelf in the corner slowly. She comes close to turning back several times, focuses on other shelves, the massed ranks of medicines for the slightest ailment, the green signs hanging from the ceiling, the queue-numbering system by the prescription desk.

But she can't escape.

She takes the final step towards the shelf, bends over, and now she's holding a pregnancy test in her hand, the sort that turns blue if it's positive.

She had persuaded herself that she was here to buy headache pills and deodorant, but she knows the truth is somewhat different.

To buy or not to buy?

Pee and see?

But could anything really have happened that first time? So easily, at her age? In spite of her resistance to the whole idea?

But isn't there a microscopic suggestion, a hint of life deep within her?

Tove.

You're going to have a brother or sister.

Peter.

You're going to be a father.

Malin.

You're going to be a mum again.

You're going to hold a baby in your arms and feel the warmth of its skin, its strong, rapid breathing, the smell of the child's cheek as it sleeps, the intoxication of those sweet particles.

Your child.

Malin.

More sleepless nights.

More tired mornings.

Colic.

Nappies.

Hanging around playgrounds.

She looks out of the big windows towards Fridhemsplan. Sees the pub opposite, feels her whole body start to long for tequila and cold beer, and she feels like throwing the test on the floor, rushing across the busy street and drinking herself far from all her doubts.

She shuts her eyes.

Tries to control the desire, the impulse.

A swing, flying up into the air. Chuckling laughter.

An implacable will.

A toyshop with a thousand sounds and garish colours.

She puts the test back on the shelf.

The top shelf of the built-in oak bookcase.

Tove needs a ladder to reach the book she wants.

The student residence has a good library. Former students have left books behind, and donate money to the residence as well.

She reaches for the white spine.

The words on the spine.

Nabokov. *Lolita*. And she feels the sun on the back of her neck, feels hot, grabs the book in her hand and climbs down to escape the heat.

Alone in the library. Or is she? The other students don't come here much, they're not interested in fiction, like pretty much everyone her age.

She turns around.

And behind her stands the housemother, Klara Groberg, a woman of fifty or so who manages to seem unpleasantly strict even when her face looks friendly.

'Tove,' she says. 'I'd like a word with you.'

And Tove feels her stomach lurch.

Now this dream is over.

She knows about Tom's visits, I'm about to be expelled.

'Let's sit down in here.'

They sit down in a pair of armchairs in a corner of the room untouched by the sun.

'You know I see everything, don't you, Tove?'

Tove nods.

Feels one hand trembling, tears welling up.

'Absolutely everything.'

Tove nods again.

'And we've got rules.'

'I—'

'Don't say anything. I know it can't be easy for you, coming here on a scholarship. And I'm sure you know more than most students here, about most things. You're a sensible girl, aren't you? Careful? Who knows how to stop things getting out of hand?'

Tove nods.

Says nothing.

'As long as you're careful, then it's OK,' Klara Groberg

says. 'But only for you. People like you and me have to stick together here.'

Tove nods again.

'But don't let anyone else see or know.'

Then Klara Groberg gets up.

And leaves the library, leaving Tove alone in the shadow of the room.

The bastard opened the door, and Waldemar Ekenberg walked in without being asked, Malin had said the wife was still in Mallorca when they spoke earlier.

He showed Emanuel Ärendsson his ID, and wondered if he had a treatment room at home, said he wanted to see it.

And now, in the hall, he repeats the question, but not as a question this time: 'I want to see your treatment room.'

Malin had told him about it.

'What right do—?'

The man's weak chin annoys Waldemar.

Fucking pathetic.

'This right.'

Waldemar takes a step towards the gynaecologist. Grabs his shirt and pushes him up against the wall.

'Your worst nightmare has just arrived,' he says, then he lets go, and the gynaecologist catches his breath before leading Waldemar deeper into the house, and beside a staircase leading to the basement is a sign saying: 'Treatment Room'.

They go down the stairs, then into a large room with a small waiting area next to a door leading outside, Waldemar assumes it leads to some basement steps.

What's the best way to start this?

Start asking questions, then use force when the answers aren't good enough?

Or use force from the outset, and see if the answers come of their own accord?

He knows what works.

Apply pressure from the start.

Forget about pleasantries and logic.

Cause pain in a startling way.

Everyone's scared of pain.

Everyone understands it. Not everyone understands violence, but they understand how it feels.

Emanuel Ärendsson opens the door to his treatment room.

What's he hiding in there?

Textured yellow wallpaper. Narrow windows, frosted glass, up by the ceiling. A desk with a computer, the air scented by an air freshener hanging from the desk lamp.

A gynaecological chair.

Shiny, well polished, metallic.

The gynaecologist turns around.

Curious, with just a hint of fear in his eyes.

Because the man in front of him is still a police officer.

'Get undressed,' Waldemar says. 'Take all your clothes off and sit in the chair.'

47

A cable tie is fastened around the bastard's testicles.

His arsehole like an empty eye socket as he lies there squirming, with his eyes wide-open in terror, his white, mottled, hairy legs and his bulging stomach, even whiter.

His testicles hairy and red, swollen with blood because of the plastic tie around them.

Am I going too far? Waldemar wonders.

Feels a pang of conscience. Ignores it.

But it's still there, that pang, like a tension in his chest, just below his heart.

Ignore it. This needs to be done, are you losing your nerve, Ekenberg?

No.

This is war, a very quiet war that goes on every day, and in situations like that you can't go too far. You have to win, sometimes humiliate and eradicate the enemy, using whatever methods are necessary.

Abu Ghraib.

Guantanamo.

Secret torture chambers in Lithuania, Morocco, Poland and Germany.

We torture you, otherwise you blow us up. Even the good guys can and must inflict pain, it's no more complicated than that. Even if a load of soppy lefties don't get it. They can be fucking sensitive at times.

But someone has to go out onto the front line.

Do the dirty work.

Someone has to get their legs blown off so that Afghan girls can go to school.

Someone has to be tortured, tormented a bit, so that women are left in peace.

Someone has to say no.

I'm doing good. Just like I did when I punched Dad's cancerous stomach, somehow I know that the fucker's pain helped Mum get better.

Goodness has a price.

Only morons think any different, Waldemar reckons as he moves his lighter towards Emanuel Ärendsson's laughable testicles.

Let him sweat. Be like Hitchcock, never let the bomb go off, hold the lighter far enough away so as not to burn him, hold the pistol to his arsehole, but only gently, cold and careful, and now Waldemar Ekenberg strokes the gynaecologist's cheek, scratching him slightly with one of his nicotine-yellow nails, and says: 'What a lovely stomach you've got,' and pats the white fat.

'What do you want?'

The tone of the words contains the essence of fear, but also shame and guilt.

'You know what I want.'

'How should I know?'

'You know. Do you want me to pull tighter on your balls? Talk. Tell me what I want to know.'

'But how should I—'

Anger.

Tiredness.

Sinking adrenalin.

He's as helpless as Dad, and just as deserving of pain.

You don't attack women, you don't exploit them.

And maybe your pain will help Maria Murvall to get better.

Waldemar Ekenberg lights a cigarette, looks at the man in the chair, as defenceless as the women he's doubtless shamelessly exploited, and he's got the nerve to play innocent. Another one of those doctors who think they can hide their lack of emotion and responsibility behind a white coat.

Fucking hell.

And he feels like pushing the burning tip of the cigarette up Emanuel Ärendsson's arsehole, to hear the sizzling sound of burning flesh, taste the peculiar smell, then the scream, the plea, the nonsense.

'One woman murdered,' Waldemar says.

He holds back.

Stubs the cigarette out on the floor.

'One who committed suicide.'

He lights another cigarette and touches it to the gynaecologist's cheek, and Ärendsson's scream echoes around the treatment room, but Waldemar is sure his pain can't be heard outside the house, and anyway, who knows what sort of noises have emerged from this house before?

'Two women mute, raped, tortured. Nine chained up. What do you know? I'll burn you, I swear.'

'I know . . .'

'Tell me.'

'What?'

'You don't see them as human beings, do you? Just as patients, as cunts?'

Emanuel Ärendsson's gurgling voice, his bad breath, the cloying smell of something that died a long time ago, his plump cheeks and dead eyes.

Dad's eyes.

Carrion, Waldemar thinks.

'Tell me how it feels to be lying there in that chair, tell

me how you think your patients feel, how you think all the women you and your mates exploited on your hunting trips felt. Tell me about that.'

Emanuel Ärendsson is silent.

Says nothing.

Just gurgles and shuts his eyes, and then he opens them again and flashes a look of hatred at Waldemar, as if to say: You're naïve, stupid, us men should take what we want and what we have a right to. Who the fuck are you to think otherwise? Look at yourself.

Then Ärendsson says: 'Everything is about trust. Win someone's trust and you can do anything.'

Waldemar takes a few steps forward.

Looks down into the gynaecologist's face, the hate-filled eyes, and then he smiles.

'You knew Paul Lendberg in Uppsala, didn't you? He was the one who got hold of the whores you had with you. He's dead, so you can talk. He won't be coming after you.'

Emanuel Ärendsson is silent.

Shuts his eyes again.

He opens them when he feels hard pressure on his nose. He sees a blurry image of a scalpel in a heavy hand. He has to get free, free, free.

'You cunt!' Waldemar yells. 'I'll cut your nose off. Get it? You have no right to anything. Now talk, you bastard!'

Pain, blood.

A cut, deeper and deeper.

'I'll talk!' Emanuel Ärendsson eventually cries. 'I'll tell you everything!'

Waldemar pulls the scalpel away from Emanuel Ärendsson's nose.

'If I find out you've held anything back, I'll come back and I'll kill you. That's a promise.'

★ ★ ★

How does my voice sound?

Weak.

Scared.

Like the coward I've always known I am, deep down.

I, Emanuel Ärendsson, am a weak person.

I have never had to face any danger, I have never been faced with an impossible dilemma, have never had to take the consequences of anything.

But I have taken everything else.

And why shouldn't I help myself to the women he could get hold of for us? And it was cheap, like buying pork chops in the supermarket, and I had to help myself, otherwise Peder and Fredrik would have been cross and might not have let me go with them.

And what would he have said?

If I'm going to hold anything back, it's his name.

They don't seem to know that he exists, so if I'm going to get out of this with any dignity, I shall withhold his name.

The case in his hand, I can see it now.

So here I am, lying in my own examination chair, naked, the whole of my travesty of a body exposed, with a crazy policeman prepared to cut my nose off, as if I were an unfaithful lump of female flesh in Afghanistan.

He'd do it.

And I'm talking now, telling him what he wants to hear: 'We met in Uppsala. We were all members of the Skulls Society. Then we went on meeting up, mostly for annual hunting trips.

'We got to know Paul Lendberg in Uppsala. Even back then he could get hold of things. Marijuana, girls, they were free back then, but later, as we got older, there was no question of them being free. Too difficult, too many complications. He loves business. Loved business, that was just who he was.'

He's standing over by the wall, the policeman.

I can only sense him from here. He's smoking. I can smell it.

He stinks of sweat.

Unless that's me?

'And we let Paul sort out whores for our hunting trips as well. Swedish, and from abroad. He would deliver them in person to the cabins we were staying in, and then he'd collect them as well. And yes, I'll admit that we were in the count's cabin in November last year. And that the Svartsjö girl was there, with us in the cabin before she vanished, and he picked her up again afterwards, so we had nothing to do with that. I don't know anything about the one in Lund. Nor that Jessica in Ljusdal either. I swear.'

'What did you do with Jenny?'

'What did I do with Jenny?'

Silence.

The sound of a lighter.

Is he coming closer?

'I used a dildo in her anus.'

'Go on.'

'But Paul always picked the girls up. Always. We had sex with them, in lots of different ways, I'll admit, but we never did anything else. I swear by God that we never did anything else. I don't know anything about any of them being raped, or murdered, even. We didn't do that sort of thing. Absolutely not. And I don't know what Paul did with Svartsjö after he collected her. But I never got the impression that he hurt the girls, because that would have been bad for business.'

'More names.'

'There aren't any more names.'

Does he know?

Is he toying with me?

I have to say his name as well, I have to tell him, say it. But no.

I'm stopping at this.

'Was there anyone else in your gang? Were there four of you?'

I'm not sure now.

Not sure.

Buying sex is one thing.

But I'm a better person than this policeman.

Weak, perhaps, but better, and he's not going to win.

And I don't want to see anything beyond the obvious, that's why I chose this career. Seeing, but not seeing. Touching, but not touching.

Living, but not living.

'No. No one else. Just the three of us.'

'Sure?'

I nod.

'Did any of you stay longer?'

'No.'

'And Paul Lendberg always collected the girls?'

I nod, the policeman is practically desperate now, and I tug at my fastened arms, my ankles, and my penis has shrunk to nothing.

'And you have no idea who might have murdered Jenny Svartsjö? Could Lendberg have done it? No, why would he kill his livestock? So who? Do you know? And who could have killed him?'

I close my eyes before I reply.

I don't want him to see my pupils.

Then I say: 'I have no idea. I don't know who hurt all those girls. Paul seems to have become a real monster, but why would he ruin the source of his income? He was obsessed with money, even at Uppsala. I presume plenty of people might have wanted him dead, I, we had no idea what he was involved in, that business in his basement, I never went to his house. He was a good-time contact, and Fredrik was always the one who got in touch with him.' I go on talking, talking myself away from the hunting cabins, towards ignorance, towards myself as a weak, cowardly man who just went along with things, went along with the unwritten rules of the group, obeying orders, and nothing in this society would work if other people didn't do the same as me, the rules and morals of groups like this are what holds society together.

And the policeman seems to follow me, seems to be getting tired, as if he thinks he's found out everything, as if my fear is greater than his intellect.

'How does it feel?' the policeman asks. 'Lying there?'

'You want to know the truth?'

'Yes.'

'It feels nice to escape the illusion that we have any control over our lives at all. Because we don't, do we?'

48

Karin Johannison has the results of Arto Antinen's DNA test in her hand.

She puts it down on her overloaded desk and looks out at the corridor through the glass doors.

The concrete floor is hard and cold beneath her feet. Kalle took the Kurdish rugs she used to have in the office in the divorce. She hadn't felt able to protest seeing as he'd bought them on a business trip to Istanbul.

Must call Malin and give her the test results.

She wanted to have them as soon as they were available.

But she doesn't feel up to talking to Malin at the moment. Can't quite cope with her intensity.

Involved, but not quite. That's how Karin usually feels in their investigations.

On the margins.

Sometimes alone, but always respected by the team of detectives.

She's posted the adoption papers.

The decision as to whether she's been accepted will take months.

Then what?

She'll have to wait and see.

She picks up the phone on her desk and calls Sven Sjöman.

'It wasn't Arto Antinen's DNA in the hole in Jenny Svartsjö's stomach,' Sven Sjöman is saying, and Malin holds her

mobile close to her ear as she roots about aimlessly for a
blank sheet of paper on Conny Nygren's desk with her free
hand.

Feels disappointment clutch at her stomach.

But that would surely have been too straightforward?

'Karin called just now. So we can close that line of inquiry.'

'OK,' Malin says. Wonder why Karin called Sven first,
she usually always calls me if I'm involved in the case?

'That was all,' Sven says, and hangs up.

Before Malin has time to put her phone down it rings
again, an angry ringing far too close to her ear.

Waldemar Ekenberg's voice sounds steady at the other
end, as if he's trying to control the world through strength
of character.

'Malin, Ärendsson confessed that they got to know Paul
Lendberg in Uppsala. That he supplied girls for their meetings. He also admitted that the three of them were in the
hunting cabin on Peder Stålskiöld's estate in November last
year, and that Jenny Svartsjö was there. I called the farmhand you and Zeke spoke to out there. Victor Johansson.
He reluctantly conceded that his employer and a few other
men had used the cabin. I'll take it up with Sven. He can
sort out a warrant, then we'll be able to examine the house
where Jenny was last seen alive.'

Waldemar sounds clear and focused.

She'd had a feeling that Victor Johansson wasn't telling
everything he knew when she and Zeke spoke to him.

A feeling that she couldn't articulate at the time.

All police investigations consist of feelings like that.

Conny Nygren is out at the house on Lidingö to see how
work there is getting on, and Zeke is sitting next to Malin,
listening intently to her conversation with Waldemar.

They've been waiting to hear from him, but don't want
to know what he had to do to get the information.

So Fredrik Kantsten was lying. When he said they'd never even been in the cabin.

'And the other girls? Lund, Ljusdal, Maria?'

'Nothing. Nothing else at all.'

His voice hoarse from smoking, and the earlier excitement. Did he go too far?

But now they can confront Prosecutor Fredrik Kantsten with lying, get him to tell them if he knows anything else, and they'll be able to get all three of them for paying for sex. Possibly more than that. And what happened to Jenny Svartsjö? She wants to ask Waldemar, but lets him go on. Thinking: Why did Kantsten want to shut down the case of the girl in St Lars?

'What did they do with the women they paid for? Did you get anything more out of him about that?'

'Obviously he's denying they did anything to them except have sex. Albeit in pretty perverted ways. According to Ärendsson, Paul Lendberg delivered and collected the girls to and from the door. In one piece, both on delivery and collection. And you know what? I believe him. I think Lendberg picked Jenny Svartsjö up from the door, and that something happened after that.'

Waldemar's cool statement of fact in that last sentence. With the unspoken clarification: After what I did to him, he wouldn't have dared say anything but the truth.

Malin falls silent.

It must have been them, losing control. Kantsten, Ärendsson and Stålskiöld.

Why else would all these women with connections to them have met such terrible fates? Was there any other explanation?

Their sexual games must have got out of hand, and they had raped, hunted and murdered them. Unless Paul Lendberg had lost control even more catastrophically, even worse than he had with the girls in his basement?

The search of his house and garden is still going on. So far no bodies have been found buried outside or bricked up in the walls.

The women are still too shocked to be questioned.

Ten metal rings. One of them empty. Chains on the floor.

What if it's still going on? Malin wonders. What if there's one woman missing? And that the last woman who was in the basement is being tortured right now? Is it her screaming I can hear?

No.

No, no.

But there's a piece of the puzzle missing. And that piece is what happened to all these women after they escaped the clutches of these feeble men, and were perhaps sold by Paul Lendberg to an even more unbridled evil.

There's something else, something I, we're not seeing.

Thoughts are bubbling in her head now, refusing to settle and form a logical chain.

We still don't have any firm evidence against the three men.

Nothing, really, but circumstantial evidence and the accusation that they paid for sex with a murder victim, probably not even enough to get DNA samples from them.

Malin would have preferred it if Paul Lendberg were still alive. She's convinced he knew the truth, convinced that he didn't kill or rape either Maria, Jenny, Jessica or the woman in Lund. It would have been bad for business. After all, the basement resembled nothing so much as a storeroom.

But he's lying in a mortuary fridge with his throat cut.

Murdered, in all likelihood, by his Russian associates in the trafficking and prostitution racket.

His DNA results aren't yet available.

Unless perhaps one of the three men killed him, to stop the trail from leading to them? His wife Zara? No, not her.

She can see the men's faces before her, feels the mobile against her ear, hears Waldemar's weary voice.

Fredrik Kantsten.

Emanuel Ärendsson.

Peder Stålskiöld.

Dirty old men, obscene abusers of power, but killers? Are these the murderous heads of the hydra? Or its pawns? Is Ärendsson lying about the fact that Jenny Svartsjö was alive when Paul Lendberg collected her from the cabin?

Would he dare to lie brazenly in the face of a frenzied Waldemar?

No.

Is there a monster on the loose in the forest?

Maria Murvall.

She suffered a seizure after seeing a picture of Fredrik Kantsten. Should I show her a picture of Paul Lendberg? Yes, at some point.

So it must be someone else. A fifth man. Mustn't it?

The man among the boys who want to be men.

The one with no boundaries at all.

The devil behind the apprentices.

'Are you there?'

'Sorry, I was thinking.'

'Easily done. I'll be in touch.'

Waldemar hangs up.

'Let's go and see Fredrik Kantsten again,' Malin says. 'Confront him with his bloody lies. And the fact that he's paid for whores.'

Fredrik Kantsten's powerful silhouette becomes strangely birdlike when reflected in the mahogany desktop, a cawing black shadow, as if burned into the glossy wood.

Malin and Zeke have told him what they know. That they've got a witness who says he paid for sexual services, and that Jenny Svartsjö was in the hunting cabin. And that he was lying. Claiming that they weren't even in the hunting cabin at the time.

Fredrik Kantsten stands up behind his desk, holds up his hands as if in surrender, and says: 'OK, you win. I knew Paul Lendberg, and we had prostitutes on our hunting trips. I admit that. But they were always above the age of consent, and they always enjoyed it. And we certainly never subjected them to any form of violence. And OK, so Svartsjö was there, but Paul picked her up in perfect condition. He was very particular about that sort of thing.'

'And you expect us to believe that?' Zeke says.

'Tell us what happened in that hunting cabin,' Malin snarls.

'Paul collected her. I don't know what happened after that. I'm not the only one who can confirm that. Who knows what Paul was capable of?'

'You're going down for this,' Zeke says. 'And you know it.'

'For the murder of Jenny Svartsjö? Hardly. What evidence have you got?'

'You'll be pilloried in the media,' Malin goes on, aware that they don't have a shred of evidence against the men, but maybe they'll be able to get DNA samples from them now that they know the men were with Jenny just before she disappeared.

She and Zeke ought to leave, and she sees Fredrik Kantsten shrug his shoulders.

'Pilloried a little, maybe,' he says. 'Just a little. I've always kept a fairly low profile. I'll apologise, and everything will be fine.'

Zeke's eyes narrow.

'Do you really think it'll be that simple? We're talking about murder, rape, the torture of women, at least two of whom you've been involved with. Do you really think this will just die down?'

An image of the Social Democratic politician Björn Rosengård comes to Malin's mind.

He might have married a younger woman, become a high-flying businessman, and turned himself into some sort of lord of the manor, but when it comes down to it, he's only remembered for visiting strip clubs and having a weakness for lap-dancing.

'People will believe me. Us. Even in this country there's a modicum of common sense. We've got nothing to do with mindless violence. An apology, a bit of time, and I'll be back on track. And let me repeat: we had nothing to do with the more serious crimes. I might have to resign from being a prosecutor, but I can always become an independent lawyer. There's more money in that anyway.'

You have an inflated sense of self-confidence, Malin thinks. What does that mean? Guilt? Successful men always shrug things off. Would I do that? As Olof Johansson, former leader of the Centre Party, said on television in connection with the Geijer scandal of the 1970s: 'How can you believe that *I*, a former energy minister, would have met a lady of this sort?'

You would, Malin thinks. And plenty more men like you. Didn't the most recent case involve trade union bigwigs?

You're hiding something from us, aren't you?

Who are you protecting?

Whom are you being loyal towards?

'Jessica Karlsson,' Malin says. 'Did you kidnap her as she shut up the hotdog kiosk, then subject her to your sick fantasies? Is that what happened to her? What drove her to her death? You couldn't get hold of any whores, so you sorted it out yourselves? And things got out of hand? Is that it? Did you stuff a rag soaked in hydrochloric acid in her mouth? You sick bastards.'

'As I told the police in Hälsingland, I don't know anything

about a Jessica Karlsson. We were up there hunting, that's all. And we never went hunting in Skåne.'

'Why did you lie about Paul Lendberg? Pretending you didn't know him?' Zeke asks.

'Of course I lied. Otherwise I'd have made myself one of the suspects. A defence mechanism. And that's why I lied about being in the hunting cabin with Svartsjö. Everyone will understand why.'

That feeling again, that he's hiding something.

A fifth man?

Could that be it? God knows who Fredrik Kantsten might know and want to protect, Malin thinks.

'Why did you shut down the investigation in Malmö?'

'Because it was time to shut it down.'

'Not to protect someone?'

'And I didn't put any pressure on Jimmy Kalder either.'

'Have you ever been hunting around Malmö?'

'No.'

'Was it you who raped the woman in Lund?'

'What a ridiculous idea. I was trying to solve that case.'

'And what will your family say when this gets out? Your children?' Zeke says.

'I'm divorced and my children are adults. And what they think, Inspector, is my business.'

'Did anyone else go with you on your hunting trips? A fifth man?' Malin asks.

Fredrik Kantsten thinks before replying.

'No. There were three of us, four when Paul made his deliveries. Like the seasons. We used to joke about it. I was summer, Emanuel autumn, Peder spring, and Paul a very cold winter. And, as you know, there's no fifth season.'

'Funny,' Zeke says.

'Perhaps the girls were the fifth season,' Malin says. 'The one that's going to ruin you.'

'Are you going to arrest me?'

You're saying that too lightly, Malin thinks.

'No,' Zeke says. 'What you've confessed to is punishable by fines. We can't take you in for anything else yet, and you know that. But we're going to get you. Don't doubt that. We never give up. And we're going to want your DNA.'

'You can have that now.'

'We don't have the equipment with us,' Zeke says.

'If it wasn't any of you who harmed these girls, didn't you wonder why they kept turning up murdered and torn to pieces? Close to where you'd been? Didn't it ever occur to you to wonder about that?'

Fredrik Kantsten looks at Malin.

'I know I'm innocent, so why should it bother me?'

Fredrik Kantsten has just spoken to his friends Peder Stålskiöld and Emanuel Ärendsson.

The police don't know everything yet. He's aware of that now.

And there's no need for them to find out everything either.

The phone is still warm when it begins to ring again, angrily, signalling to him that life as he knows it is over.

He managed to maintain his mask for those detectives, that bitch from Linköping.

A prosecutor loses his job if he's convicted of the crimes he's going to be found guilty of.

Paying for sex.

Misconduct in office when he shut down the investigation.

He had good reasons for doing so.

That was how he got his post in Stockholm, when his career was in the doldrums.

But it has to end here.

Doesn't it? It can't go on.

Now it's kill or be killed. Because how else did Paul end up in the water? OK, it might have been his business associates, but there could also be another explanation.

He doesn't want to think that thought through to its conclusion, doesn't want to think about what it means.

Instead he gets ready to leave for the day.

He told the others to be careful, if and when the police visit them again. Not say anything. Emanuel had been shaken, upset. 'Should I report that maniac policeman?'

No.

Not now. Definitely not now.

'Play it softly.'

'But no one can treat me, us, like that.'

'Your time will come, Emanuel, but right now you have to calm down.'

But Emanuel was right. Who does that police cunt think she is?

I need to seize the initiative in this. I'm going to lose my position as a prosecutor, that much is clear, but I can still practise as a solicitor, maybe even a lawyer.

I can have a life.

Even the children will forgive me a bit of sexual weakness. I've got grandchildren on the way. They need a grandfather they can look up to.

This can't go any further than it already has.

I'm going to do something about this.

I'm not just going to sit here and watch my life come to an end.

49

Need to ask Sven Sjöman.

Need to make some sort of sense out of this.

Malin has just spoken to Conny Nygren on her mobile, while they were walking towards Police Headquarters from the central courthouse.

Work was still going on out in Lidingö.

Fredrik Kantsten and Emanuel Ärendsson may have admitted to paying for sex and lying, but Conny Nygren thought it best to hold back and see what else they could find out, if they were actually involved in the murder of Jenny Svartsjö.

They had been in a hunting cabin nearby.

With Jenny.

Karin Johannison and her colleagues were probably busy examining the cabin right now.

In and of itself, it wasn't a crime for the men to have been there. Nor were their lies or withholding of information.

But they had enough on them to take DNA samples. Kantsten had volunteered. That alone probably indicated that he was innocent.

Conny Nygren reasoned that one of them might make a mistake.

Malin wanted to push harder, maybe leak the story to the press, scare them with a night in custody, but as she listened to Conny Nygren she felt that he might be right, felt that this case might open up its dark arms to embrace them.

Because Fredrik Kantsten was definitely hiding something, wasn't he?

He wasn't telling them everything.

And they still hadn't found any connection to the woman in St Lars.

Kantsten knows who the murderer is, Malin's sure of that, but he'll never admit it. So they're going to have to find the answer to the biggest question in the investigation themselves.

'OK, we'll do that,' she had said to Conny Nygren. 'We hold back, keep an eye on them,' then, after they hung up, she changed her mind.

And felt she needed to talk to Sven.

Zeke could tell she wanted to call, and now they're standing outside Stockholm's dour Police Headquarters, feeling pressed into the pavement by the overblown, brutalist 1970s architecture.

The clock on her mobile says 17:15.

The day has passed in a flurry of chases, meetings, interviews and attempts to bring some sort of order to the mess of information and events that make up this case.

'Sven here.'

Malin gives him a brief summary of everything that's happened, what they've found out, and what the gynaecologist and district prosecutor had admitted, and she asks if he's requested a search warrant and sent Karin out to Stålskiöld's hunting cabin.

'I've done nothing of the sort. We've only got the word of the other two to go on, and if Stålskiöld denies any involvement it could hold up the investigation. Anyway, you've already been out there. You said yourself that it was spotlessly clean. We aren't going to find anything there.'

Sven's right.

We've got so much else to do.

The truth isn't out there. Possibly some supporting evidence

The Fifth Season   433

for an eventual trial, but nothing that can move things on now.

'We could send Waldemar out to see Peder Stålskiöld,' Malin says. 'I've just got a feeling we don't know everything. And we need to question him.'

'No more Waldemar,' Sven says. 'We've just had a phone call from the aforementioned gynaecologist, making a formal complaint. About alleged abuse on Waldemar's part that's so brutal that not even I can believe it. He said he was on his way to hospital to have his injuries documented.'

What's Waldemar done?

She doesn't want to know.

But she'll have to find out, because if she shuts her eyes she's no better than everyone else.

'Maybe you could send him anyway?'

'Yes,' Sven says. 'If he can manage to stay calm.'

'Katerina Yelena is going to be OK, they're sure now. But they daren't bring her round just yet, so we still can't talk to her.'

More good news.

'We'll have to talk to her as soon as they let us.'

'And Andrei Darzhevin's family has been in touch from St Petersburg. His body's going to be shipped back there for burial.'

Malin finds it hard to concentrate on Sven's voice.

The late afternoon light is glaring into her eyes and the chaos of Stockholm is crashing through her, buses, cars, vegetables tossed into a wok in the Thai restaurant on the other side of the street, boxers beating each other senseless in a basement around the corner, gays, trannies, gypsies, Chinese, Turks and all the fucking blond Swedes, then Sven's voice cutting into reality again: 'I agree with Nygren. We hold back. I'll dig out whatever funding we need here in Linköping, and Nygren will have to deal with Stockholm.'

They hang up.

Malin and Zeke walk towards the entrance of Police Headquarters.

The moment he discovered the information in a hidden database, Johan Jakobsson wanted to call Malin at once.

He's read the names in the membership file of the Skulls Society. The society's statutes were attached to the file. Evidently tidied up over the years until it turned into something not immediately offensive.

But it made uncomfortable reading when you considered that this was the sort of thing that helped shape young men's views of the world, that of future leaders.

But at the same time Johan can see the attraction.

The feeling of being chosen, the camaraderie, sense of belonging, the feeling of entitlement that comes with a belief in your own elevated status.

Members always protect each other and act in each other's best interests.

Members always help each other, no matter what the circumstances.

Members never betray one another.

Members will always be loyal to the Society and its members. This applies even when the interests of the individual conflict with this.

Members will strive to gain influence over society, and will exercise this influence to the benefit of the Society and its members.

Members of the Society belong to an elite, the best of the best, and will treat outsiders with consideration: not as equals, but as people who need to have their paths mapped out for them.

Members know that the Society's path is the right one,

and that any individual is fundamentally insignificant.
    We are members of the Society.
    We have the right, because we know what is right.

Does Malin need to see this?

No, he thought. She's got enough to deal with, and this would only make her angry for no good reason.

But some of the names could help her.

He picked up the phone on his desk. Dialled Malin's number.

Malin and Zeke don't even have time to get inside Police Headquarters before Malin's mobile rings again.

'Johan here. I've got something seriously bloody interesting for you.'

The orange panels covering the façade of Kronoberg Prison look as if they're on fire in the afternoon sun, melting, as if they wanted to free all the tormented souls that have ever been contained within.

'Out with it, then.'

'I've got hold of a membership list for the Skulls Society, dating back to when our lot and Paul Lendberg were in Uppsala. There are several interesting names. One in particular.'

'Whose?'

'I'm not going to tell you now. I want to give your crazy head the chance to draw its own conclusions. I'll email the list to you instead.'

She wants to protest. Can't be bothered to play games, but sometimes it can be best to put the pieces in place yourself.

Listen to those voices in the investigation that only you can hear. Listen, because they're there, they always are.

'OK, do that,' Malin says.

She ends the call.

Opens the door to Police Headquarters.

Blinded by the light reflecting from its impenetrable re-inforced glass.

And then the noise of the city seems to vanish, and at first there's just an all-encompassing silence, then she hears a voice whispering quietly, the faintest woman's voice she's ever heard, but also the strongest, as if all the voices of one person throughout her life had been forced together into one moment, one distinct message.

This isn't the screaming woman she's heard before.

A different woman.

And the voice is strangely firm, focused, even though it's impossible to hear the words it's trying to say. Drowsy, as if it's trying to push through fog to reach this moment.

It's a voice she's been waiting a long time to hear.

What's it saying?

What is it whispering to her?

Maria Murvall is sitting on her bed, leaning against the wall, her legs tucked under her, hands on her knees.

She's found her way back. She had been crying out to herself, even though her voice had seemed reluctant, telling her: 'Maria, don't bother with that. You're better off where you are. You're only going to end up as the embodiment of pain again.'

But she had shouted, listened, heard the echo of the noises she was making, and had known she was there.

Gurgling at first, to start with.

Hissing.

She'd heard that.

And knew she had to fend off that snake.

Silence. Sound.

'Maria. Maria? Where are you?'

'Where are you?'

'I'm here.'

'I'm here.'

And in the echo of her own voice, that's where she appeared.

Incomprehensible syllables. Language that isn't a language.

As if her head, body, brain and heart needed to wake up, be caressed, fired up with trust and intimacy, as if unconscious words needed to be replaced with conscious ones, if only for a short while, and that has just happened, the world has just locked itself into place inside her, and now words are pouring out of her, babbling, a chanted litany of words.

'I want to see Malin Fors, I want to see Malin Fors, I want to see Malin Fors, I want to see . . .'

A nurse is standing silently in front of this long mute patient who is now talking.

She presses the alarm button.

Waits for a doctor to show up and explain what's happening.

The world, Maria.

What are we going to do with it? I'm drifting close to you now, I don't know what it is you want to tell Malin, but I'm sure she's going to want to listen to you.

We're one and the same, you and I, Maria.

Even if I am, was, Jenny.

Perhaps you do want to come back here, but I don't believe that, why would you want to? There's no need for you to come here to me, and you've got a task, there's something for your words to accomplish, you've got a mission to fulfil.

What names are on Malin's list, Maria?

What are you going to tell her? The truth about what happened to you? I want to believe that, but I can't know for certain. Perhaps it's impossible for you to reach the truth, because then every second of your life will be unbearable.

You are brave, Maria.
You are everyone's courage.
You are the angel for all those in the front line.
Those fighting and never giving way.
Those who never compromise when they stand face to face with evil.

'Malin.'

She's standing in the reception area of Police Headquarters when she gets the next call.

The time is now half past five.

She recognises the voice.

Maria Murvall's doctor.

With her beautiful Polish accent.

'There's been a major development,' she says.

And Malin knows who the voice she just heard belongs to.

'Maria,' the doctor says. 'She started to talk. And she says she wants to meet you. That's the only thing she's saying.'

50

The forest silent beside the road, the trees seem to be moving towards the car, reaching out for Malin, to drag her off to places whose names no voice can speak, places containing the names of all the women the forest has taken deep within its infinite, dark silence.

The sky is uniformly grey, and hail the size of geisha balls is hammering on the roof of the car, trying to force its way through the metal and crush her and Zeke.

Maria has started talking.

Wants to talk to Malin.

Zeke is at the wheel, and she looks down at his foot on the accelerator. Wants him to drive faster, put his foot on the floor.

What can Maria have to say? Does she remember what happened now? Who or what harmed her in the forest?

Her brain has been bubbling ever since Maria's doctor called.

The mute can speak.

What forces are in motion?

Think, think clearly.

And then she remembers Johan Jakobsson's list, the members of the Skulls Society, and she brings it up on her mobile.

Scans through it quickly.

Unknown names.

But posh-sounding.

Not many Svenssons, Anderssons or Johanssons.

Then she sees the name Johan must have meant.

Her stomach clenches.

She flinches and Zeke takes his eyes off the motorway and looks at her.

'What have you found? You look like you've seen a fucking ghost.'

'Sten Dinman,' she says, and can see Zeke searching his memory.

Hammering hail.

He's forced to slow down and they can't see more than a hundred metres ahead now, and the rear lights of the car in front are blurred and pulsing.

'Former minister for equality, then considered for the post of equality ombudsman, currently chief executive of Save the Children.'

Zeke sucks in his cheeks, making him look more skull-like than ever.

'Shit.'

'I know. Shit is only the start.'

'Do you think he could have anything to do with this?'

'I'm not ruling anything out,' Malin says. 'He was in the same student association at exactly the same time as the others, he's the same age, and they seem to have formed a sort of sect, don't they? A boys' gang where people help themselves to whatever they want.'

'But that doesn't necessarily mean anything, any of the other, less well-known names could have been involved. If there is anyone else apart from Kantsten, Stålskiöld and Ärendsson.'

'There's just something about this . . .'

'Can you bring up a picture of him?'

Malin goes online and googles Sten Dinman. Hundreds of pictures. She picks one of him standing next to a younger blond woman outside a cinema, smiling on his way into a film première.

He has a peculiarly large crocodile-skin case in his hand. One hand clutching the case tightly.

Minister Sten Dinman and his assistant Vera Bodlund. His face.

He looks like Peter, but not quite.

Broad cheekbones, almost Sami-like, and blue eyes with a curious, satisfied expression.

Short fair hair, receding badly. Look at me, I'm reliable, handsome enough to run a country.

By all accounts charming, attractive, a real ladies' man.

But there's something wrong with those eyes.

Deep within the black of his pupils.

Malin can see the disconnect, and can tell that Sten Dinman is acting, posing.

Has he been in the cabins?

She holds the picture up for Zeke.

He glances away from the road again.

'A born ladies' man.'

'Maria,' Malin says. 'I'll show Maria his picture. And Paul Lendberg's. But Conny probably hasn't managed to sort one out yet.'

She googles Sten Dinman + Fredrik Kantsten.

Then Sten Dinman + Emanuel Ärendsson.

Sten Dinman + Peder Stålskiöld.

And is astonished by what she finds.

News articles. Wikipedia. Fredrik Kantsten is on the board of the Workers' Education Council with Dinman.

That's the most striking result.

But there are others.

Emanuel Ärendsson and Sten Dinman were on the same county council committee looking into ways of reducing hospital waiting times.

Fredrik Kantsten was the legal expert on Dinman's public inquiry into the taxation of environmentally friendly vehicles.

Peder Stålskiöld was appointed agricultural advisor to the Latvian government on Sten Dinman's recommendation.

He and Emanuel Ärendsson are both on the board of a Danish pharmaceutical company.

They know each other, all right.

They've helped each other out, all right.

From the look of things, they've certainly kept in touch over the years. Sten Dinman always just behind the others, like a shadowy protector, something to lean on.

Could Fredrik Kantsten have got his job as a district prosecutor in Stockholm because of pressure from Sten Dinman? As thanks for services rendered? Is Kantsten protecting Dinman? Was he with them in the hunting cabins?

Malin feels her brain move into top gear.

Like the engine of the car.

Should we have seen this before? But none of us made the connection, the information only appears if you cross-reference those specific names, and up to now there's been no reason to look for Sten Dinman.

Not even Johan has seen his name until now.

But the society's membership list connects the four of them.

The Skulls Society.

The association.

The boys' club.

She cross-checks some of the other names on the list, but doesn't get any results when she matches them with any of their five names.

The Destroy Women Club.

It was the five of you, wasn't it?

What have you done together? Malin wonders, and feels

tiredness spread through her body, as if years of tension and work are finally approaching their conclusion.

Google Images again.

Another film première.

Sten Dinman next to a smiling Count Stålskiöld.

The case again. The glossy skin of a predator.

What's in that case?

Nauseous now.

How many of you are there? What have you done? It must have been one of you who harmed the women so badly.

Are the rest of you hiding Dinman?

Is Dinman the fifth man? The leader? The man with no boundaries? The shadow? The one the rest of you are protecting, the one you'd all like to be, or at least be admired by?

Malin's mobile rings.

Conny Nygren.

He says: 'I just wanted to let you know that we can't locate Fredrik Kantsten. I was trying to find him so we could keep an eye on him, but he's not at home. Nor at his office, and he's not answering his mobile.'

'He could be anywhere,' Malin says. 'The gym, even.'

'It still seems a bit odd.'

Then Malin tells him what she's found out about no less a figure than Sten Dinman, and his connections to the others.

Conny Nygren falls silent.

'This is growing,' he says eventually. 'This is like some bloody snake with more than one head. But it doesn't necessarily mean anything. He probably hasn't got anything to do with this whole damn business. Former minister for equality. Surely he should be above suspicion? A man who's promoted women's rights in every newspaper, surely he couldn't be involved in this?'

Then Malin tells him about Maria.

That she's started to talk.

Has emerged from her mute state.

And wants to talk to Malin.

She apologises for not calling earlier to say that they're on their way down to Vadstena.

'Bloody hell,' Conny Nygren says.

'I've been waiting for this,' Malin says.

'I think you should show her a picture of Sten Dinman.'

'Exactly what I was thinking,' Malin says. 'Sven has people checking what Stålskiöld and Ärendsson are up to, and I daresay Fredrik Kantsten will show up again before too long.'

'I'll speed up the photograph of Lendberg. And I'll pay a visit to Sten Dinman. Ask a few questions about his friendship with our gang. It can't do any harm. He ought to be home at this time of the evening.'

Fredrik Kantsten looks down at the seat beside him in his Mercedes, at the shotgun and rifle sitting on the black leather in their green case with its lovely worn, brown leather trim.

He's just picked up the guns from storage in Grev Turegatan, arriving just before they closed at six o'clock.

For ten thousand kronor a year his guns are stored legally and securely, and they clean them after he's been hunting, and make sure he always has ammunition.

The inside of the large car smells new, with a hint of gun grease, but right now everything feels old, as if his entire life is catching up with him, to a present where anything at all can happen.

The garage by Östermalmstorg, not far from the newly built glass monstrosity just across from the old market hall, is dark, no one can see him inside the car.

We've all gained from knowing Sten Dinman, Fredrik Kantsten thinks.

And he from us.

But mostly us from him.

Fredrik Kantsten knows what happened, has always known, but hasn't wanted to see, and now that everything is about to explode there's only one way for him to save himself.

But where is Dinman? At home?

I can check there.

At his country house out in Värmdö?

I can look there as well.

But can I use these guns? They can be traced back to me.

Use your prosecutor's brain now.

Think clearly.

But my mind won't settle.

If I dump the guns afterwards they'll never be able to prove anything. They've been stolen! Anything, really.

I'll be able to have a life. And if that youngster, Jimmy Kalder talks, I'll deny everything point blank. Evidence. So easy to dismiss. Confessions so easy to retract. I know all about that.

But I need to deal with this.

What I might have known can never become public knowledge.

That I have come anywhere close to absolute darkness.

I'll go out there. To see him.

Fredrik Kantsten puts a hand on his guns.

Plenty of animals have fallen to their bullets.

Now it's time to bring down a human being.

Things are heating up now, Malin.

People on their way in different directions, the same direction.

Pictures to be shown to the no-longer mute.

Houses to be visited.

Paths to be crossed.

I shall drift and watch the truth be revealed.
I shall stop being scared and alone.
Malin.
I'm relying on you.
I'm relying on the fact that I can become that little girl again, the one running over a meadow, towards a freedom that she still believes can be hers.

51

Börje Svärd and Waldemar Ekenberg sit down in the large sitting room in the manor at Sjölunda, and both lean forward in the low sofa from Svenskt Tenn, upholstered in Josef Frank's colourful snake patterns.

Sven Sjöman told them to head out here.

But to play it seriously cool.

Emanuel Ärendsson's complaint against Waldemar could prove difficult to ignore.

A doctor had called earlier to ask if a police officer could really have done that. Bruising to his scrotum, abrasions on his wrists from cable ties.

But the complaint will disappear.

Because what's the evidence?

And who's the person making the complaint?

An eminent gynaecologist, admittedly, but mainly someone who uses prostitutes. And that's a label that sticks. Desperate to shift the focus away from his actions, he harmed himself. And the doctor had agreed. Theoretically he could have inflicted those injuries on himself. A passive sadist might even take pleasure from doing so.

Count Peder Stålskiöld sits down in a worn Chesterfield armchair by the unlit open fireplace.

'Things are heating up,' Börje Svärd says. 'Don't you think?'

'I don't understand what you mean,' Peder Stålskiöld says. He was fairly amiable when he let them in just now. 'What's heating up, and in what way?'

They've already told him what they know.

About the prostitutes. About Jenny Svartsjö in the hunting cabin. And how Sten Dinman has cropped up in the investigation, that they seemed to have belonged to the same group of friends, that they've seen the picture of him and Dinman at a film première. That he's been telling the police barefaced lies.

Waldemar moves onto more personal matters: 'What does your wife think about all this? Does she know?'

'She doesn't care,' Peder Stålskiöld replies. 'She's known about the prostitutes for ages. She's had gigolos herself, when she's abroad. That's our arrangement. You can leave her out of this.'

Peder Stålskiöld makes a sweeping gesture with his arm towards the rest of the room.

'This is all she's ever wanted. Being the wife of a wealthy landowner.'

Waldemar nods.

'And Dinman?'

'We knew each other in Uppsala. And we've met up a few times over the years.'

'Did he usually take part in your hunting trips?' Börje asks.

'No.'

'Never? We can find out if you're lying. Your friend Emanuel Ärendsson is a proper little songbird,' Waldemar says.

'I know what you did to Emanuel. And by the way, I've fired Victor Johansson, I understand he's been speaking to you. That wasn't his place. And he told me, the idiot.'

'Who usually hires the hunting cabin?'

'Like I said the first time: the cabin has never been rented out.'

Waldemar raises his eyebrows.

'And how do you explain the fact that you were there with Jenny Svartsjö? You lied about that before.'

'I didn't think you needed to know. And, as you are aware, Lendberg picked the girl up. I don't know what happened after that. You're welcome to take a DNA sample from me, if you think that would help. I've never given a sample before. It might be an interesting experience.'

'And we're supposed to believe that?' Börje asks. 'That she was picked up? No, you were the ones who violated and raped her.'

'You're mad,' Peder Stålskiöld says. 'What a ridiculous idea. Please, feel free to do a forensic examination of the cabin.'

They've been talking among themselves, Waldemar thinks as he tries to keep a grip on his growing anger.

But surely the count wouldn't do something so stupid in his own hunting cabin? he thinks, as his anger fades away. It feels almost as if his rage found some sort of ultimate expression with Emanuel Ärendsson.

People out here in the countryside have big ears, and quick tongues.

Ärendsson didn't tell me everything, Waldemar goes on to think. He didn't mention Dinman. And I promised to return if he held anything back. I'm going to keep that promise.

Peder Stålskiöld makes himself more comfortable.

Shuts his eyes.

'Did Sten Dinman ever go hunting with you?' Börje asks again.

Peder Stålskiöld lets out a deep sigh before replying: 'He came along a few times. Here on the estate, and up in Ljusdal.'

'And he helped himself to the entertainment on offer, like the rest of you?'

Peder Stålskiöld's expression becomes sharper, he's trying

to turn us into farmhands, Waldemar thinks, tenant farmers sitting here, cap in hand.

'Did he fuck the whores? No, he didn't, actually. He didn't seem very interested in that.'

'But you were?'

'Of course. I admit that. How would you like me to pay the fine? To you? The bailiffs of the state.'

Then the count laughs, a loud, forced laugh that echoes around the large room, as if this is all a game to him, a wearisome adults' game, a game to a man who has never had to worry about anything, never needed to take responsibility for anyone but himself, and has spent his whole life satisfying his own desires and keeping himself entertained in various ways, seeking suitable company wherever it was on offer.

'You think this is a joke?' Waldemar Ekenberg snarls. 'This is no fucking joke. We're dealing with murder here, and even if you aren't guilty, you're an accessory. Shielding a criminal is a serious crime. What do you know?'

'About what?'

'About what happened to Jenny Svartsjö. What happened to Maria Murvall. Jessica Karlsson. The girl in Lund. What do you know?'

'I don't know anything. Are there actually any connections? As far as I understand it, the victims are entirely unconnected?'

'And why didn't any of you mention the fact that Sten Dinman was with you? We asked all of you if there had been anyone else there.'

'He's a friend. A very prominent man. He shouldn't have to get dragged into something like this without good reason.'

Conny Nygren parks his car outside the house on Charlottenhill on the island of Djurgården.

An enormous *fin de siècle* red-brick villa that has been converted into five separate apartments, each of them at least two hundred square metres in size. Broad flights of grey stone steps lead up to hidden terraces, and the windows are divided by what looks like white-painted steel frames. The overall impression is welcoming but simultaneously extremely exclusive: Who are you? What are you doing here? Take your poverty-stricken arse and get lost.

Birch trees set closely around a gravel courtyard, tall, planted a long time ago, this privileged abode has old roots, class differences nothing new in this city.

A king who seems to have fucked anything that moved.

Building homes for the rich on his land.

The way it's always been.

His daughter flies to the South Pacific on a billionaire's private jet.

Power lining up alongside power.

Conny Nygren feels nauseous at the thought of the shameless corruption among networks of friends in this society.

But at the same time . . .

Those who live here are still only people. With failings and faults and longings for love.

Sten Dinman evidently lives in the ground-floor apartment, and has the use of the cellar below.

Conny Nygren has made some calls.

Sten Dinman wasn't in his office at Save the Children, and wasn't answering his mobile, so it seemed to make sense to drive straight out to Djurgården.

To have a chat with him.

Beyond the greenery of the garden Conny Nygren can make out the inlet to Stockholm harbour, the Viking Line ferries lined up in front of the cliffs of Södermalm, the ochre-coloured houses that seem to cling to the rocks.

He presses the button on the entryphone.

No answer.

He uses the police access code to get in.

The name 'Dinman' is listed on a panel just inside the door. A long strip of carpet runs the length of the hall, blue, with an oriental pattern, and a small alcove leads to Dinman's door, painted to match the grey marble of the stairwell.

He rings on the door. A square chrome doorbell.

No answer.

No one at home.

Shall I go in? Conny Nygren thinks.

I'll go in, and he checks the door for stickers warning of security. Nothing, but surely the flat must be alarmed?

He decides to risk it. He can always make himself scarce if anything does go off, or come up with some excuse.

He gets out his picklock, listens for noises in the stairwell, but there's no sound from the other flats.

The door opens and he goes in.

No alarm.

He moves through the apartment.

White walls.

Hundred-year-old panels of dark oak, designer sofas in thick, shiny fabric, modern art on the walls. Photographs. Naked models and dreamlike landscapes. All black and white, as if the world were more comprehensible, more beautiful like that.

No national romanticism in here.

The dining table has a white marble top and sits on a speckled grey carpet. The chairs look uncomfortable.

He gets a message from Paul Lendberg's pathologist, containing a picture. He forwards it to Malin.

It seems odd that there's no alarm. Dinman probably doesn't want anyone from a security company in here, Conny Nygren thinks. Maybe there is something hidden here after all, because surely a former government minister's home ought to be alarmed?

He can feel it now.

There's something here.

Another dungeon?

Women?

He sees a door that must lead down to the cellar.

He opens the door and is hit by a strong smell of sulphur.

He holds his nose.

Acclimatises himself to the smell.

Heads down the steps.

Sten Dinman wasn't at his house out in Värmdö. It was shut up, and Fredrik Kantsten drove away again, and now he's sitting in a traffic jam on Strandvägen in the centre of the city, alternately glancing up at the ornate façades of the buildings to his left, or out across the water of Nybroviken towards the island of Skeppsholmen, where old, white-painted boats are bobbing up and down.

The apartment on Charlottenhill.

He's never been there, not once, but Sten showed him pictures on his mobile when they were hunting. Showing off the works of art and the new furniture he'd bought with his salary from Save the Children.

Could he be there now?

Fredrik Kantsten doesn't want to think about what Sten Dinman has done, what he must have done after the others had left the hunting cabins where they met up.

Occasionally he suspected that Sten had gone back to the cabins. He had seen Sten talking to Paul once, when he came to collect the girls from the count's hunting cabin a long time ago, and Fredrik hadn't heard what he said, but the soundless words were still there in the forest as a sort of muttering, and he could tell from the look on the men's faces that they were talking about something beyond his and Peder's and Emanuel's inclinations and capacity.

And whatever it was they were discussing, it had something to do with the women.

With Jenny Svartsjö.

Jessica Karlsson.

The nameless woman in Skåne.

And whatever was going on, it mustn't be allowed to get out.

It would ruin his reputation beyond any hope of salvation.

The guns on the car seat beside him.

No one can see them through the tinted windows.

The traffic eases.

He turns off right towards Djurgården, drives past the Natural History Museum and the rabble milling about outside the tourist attractions of Gröna Lund and Skansen.

Following his satnav to Charlottenhill.

An empty wine cellar.

A laundry.

A television room with a big black sofa and a wall-mounted Loewe screen.

Then a white wall with a black-painted door.

This cellar ought to be much bigger, Conny Nygren thinks.

He listens for sounds above.

Silence.

Or did he hear something?

A sound?

No.

It was nothing.

Quickly he opens the door.

He feels suddenly angry at having to be in this cellar, poking about in the very darkest corners of masculinity.

A perfectly ordinary workshop. With a carpentry bench. Tools neatly hung up on one wall.

A lathe.

Oil stains on the floor.

I did hear something, didn't I? What was that?

But it's probably just the natural sounds of an old building.

Carry on.

Don't get paranoid.

An open toolbox on the bench, full to the brim with packs of nails and screws.

In one corner of the room is a shiny case made of brown crocodile skin, roughly the same size as a piece of cabin luggage, but without wheels.

The case doesn't seem to belong in here.

Conny Nygren goes over to it and kneels down beside it.

A gold lock twinkles in the dim light from the tiny windows up by the ceiling.

He picks the lock.

Opens the lid.

Fuck.

What the hell is this?

Little polished knives strapped to the lid, a spiked metal dildo, soldering irons, small plastic bottles containing what might be corrosive acid, electric cables, lengths of tubing, scalpels, and a dentist's drill. A hammer and a small vice.

Torture.

A case belonging to a travelling torturer.

A case for pain and fear.

For violation and rape.

A tiny little portable space containing the very worst in us. The things we can never escape.

He listens for noises from above, thinks he can hear a car stopping on the drive.

He can definitely hear something now. Unless the car is leaving?

Silence again.

How did Dinman get the women here without being seen? How did he get them out of here? Perhaps the stuck-up neighbours preferred not to see anything. Made themselves blind.

Has he even had any women here? Or has he just travelled around with his case?

The feeling that he isn't alone is back.

Did I hear something?

He tries to ignore the chill feeling in his stomach.

I closed the door behind me. I definitely did.

He gets out his mobile.

Keen to call Malin and tell her about his discovery, to call Forensics in so they can start their work. Examine the apartment, the room, the case.

A signal.

The building must have its own transmitter.

Malin answers.

He tells her what he's found, and she listens, says she's about to go in and see Maria, that she can't wait to hear 'her liberated voice'.

They hang up.

Then Conny Nygren turns around.

And finds himself staring down the barrel of a gleaming elk-hunting rifle.

52

Maria.

What are you going to tell me? What corners of your soul am I going to gaze down into? What darkness, what light is yours?

Words like bullets firing out of you. Well-aimed projectiles aimed at what must die.

Malin opens the door to Maria's hospital room.

It looks the same: the bed in the corner, the two chairs. From the chair in front of the window, nothing but sky is visible. It's as if nothing had changed. As if everything were the same as usual.

But nothing's normal. Is it?

Inside her she can see Sten Dinman's shiny crocodile-skin case, the way Conny Nygren has just described it to her.

Soldering irons.

The burn marks on Maria's lower arms.

The acid. Jessica Karlsson's ruined mouth.

Before entering the hospital she emailed the pictures of Sten Dinman and Paul Lendberg to Sara Markelberg down in Lund.

'Show these to your patient, see what reaction you get.'

Zeke is waiting in the dayroom.

She takes a deep breath.

And steps inside.

A weary evening light is falling, almost hesitantly, through the window, and Malin can see Maria in silhouette, sitting in her chair. She is sitting in silence and seems to be looking out at the steely grey air, which has a strange shimmer to it from the reflections off Lake Vättern.

'Maria,' Malin says, hoping she'll turn around, but she doesn't turn around. She goes on staring out of the window.

Malin moves the other chair and sits down next to Maria.

'I'm here now. I heard that you wanted to talk to me.'

Maria turns towards Malin.

And there's something different, something new, something familiar in her eyes, something that belongs to this world.

'Talk to me, Maria.'

But Maria says nothing, as if the words aren't there, as if they aren't enough to describe what she wants to say.

'It's OK,' Malin says, but she wants to hear Maria's voice. Wants to hear how it sounds.

'Talk to me.'

And she puts her hand to Maria's cheek, she's never touched her before, but now she does, and Maria doesn't draw back, just moves her mouth, looks at Malin, but no sound comes out.

'I'm here now. Tell me. I'm going to put everything right.'

She can feel her mobile in her pocket.

The pictures of Sten Dinman are easiest to access.

It was his torture instruments that made you suffer, wasn't it? Malin thinks.

His evil, a distillation of the very worst of human beings.

'Talk to me.'

She's pleading now, and then Maria opens her mouth and says: 'I want to talk to Malin Fors.'

Her voice.

Fragile as an orchid flower. Distant but still close. Full of courage but still hesitant, a stranger to language and the air that will make it comprehensible by carrying its waves.

Your voice, Malin thinks, is the most beautiful I've ever heard. Not even Tove's voice is this beautiful.

Actually, it is.

It's the same pure love I can hear in the tone of both voices. The same goodness.

A muteness that doesn't exist.

An openness, pure and unforced. A dream of what could have been. The people we could all have become.

There are some apples in a bowl on Maria's bedside table.

'I'm here. It's me. It's me you're talking to.'

'Are you there?'

'Yes.'

'Who's there?'

'Me. Malin. Malin Fors.'

And Malin looks out of the window, wonders if Maria can see the stars already, all the beauty that's hidden by the light.

'What can you see, Maria?'

'I can usually see the stars,' she replies. 'But I can't see them any more. It's too light.'

And then Malin gets her mobile out.

Shows Maria the picture of Paul Lendberg.

No reaction.

Then she holds the picture of Sten Dinman in front of Maria's eyes, and the moment she does so she realises her mistake.

Maria sees his face.

And she stops breathing.

As if her entire body is refusing oxygen.

As if her consciousness is capable of defeating the reflexes of her brain. Logic, the triumph of emotion over innate will.

Every muscle in Maria's body tenses, and she knocks the mobile out of Malin's hand before screaming out loud, and now Maria is howling, syllables and sounds expanding like an explosion, driving all light from the world.

Don't want to hear that sound.

Don't want to hear this.

The howl is the opposite to the sound of her voice, Malin thinks.

'Sorry,' Malin whispers.

'Sorry,' she shouts.

I should have thought before, what good is sorry now?

Then an unfamiliar male doctor flies into the room followed by a nurse, and Malin turns around, sees their fear, sees how they want to run from the scream, but there's no escape.

Maria is screaming without breathing.

And gradually the scream dies away, and she relaxes and what Malin saw in her eyes a few moments ago is gone once more.

'It was him,' Malin whispers.

'It was him, wasn't it?'

'He was the one who hurt you, wasn't he?'

'Where did he do it?'

'How did you end up in his clutches?'

'Were the others there?'

'He was the one who hurt you, wasn't he? It was him.'

Malin's words like bullets from a machine gun.

And Maria seems to subside, the energy vanishes from her muscles and her chin drops to her chest, her eyelids droop and perhaps she is sleeping now, Malin thinks, even though her eyes are still open.

'Come back,' Malin says.

She strokes her cheek with her hand.

Her cheeks are hot.

Come back.

She thinks, and realises that her gaze is clouded by the tears welling up and running down her cheeks as if they came from an ancient well.

'Come back to me, Maria.'

Malin slips off her chair and sinks onto her knees beside Maria, takes hold of one of her legs and clasps it. Leans her cheek against it.

'Come back,' she pleads. 'Come to me. I'm going to put everything right. Everything's going to be all right.'

A hand on her shoulder, a gentle but firm hand.

Elena Kaczynski's voice: 'Malin, you have to leave now. That's enough now. That's enough.'

Three hundred and fifty kilometres away, in a similar room in St Lars psychiatric hospital in Lund, another woman, an unknown, younger woman, starts to scream when she sees the picture of Paul Lendberg.

Her scream is wordless.

The scream rises in intensity when she sees the picture of Sten Dinman.

A scream as empty of content as she is herself.

A scream that is the present, without either future or past, a scream that somehow contains an awareness of all the evil that exists in the world, and the pain that evil has caused.

But this woman's scream doesn't stop.

She screams and screams and screams, into an infinite space.

And people in white coats put a syringe in her arm, watch her fall asleep, and believe that they are giving her peace.

I have Jessica with me now.

We can see you all, Malin, at the same time.

She isn't in pain any more, she's whole, the effects of evil belong with you, here they don't exist.

That's good to hear, isn't it?

Maria has vanished again. Further in. Deeper. And it's happening again now, Malin, what happened to us, and you'll have to hurry, because it mustn't end for her the way it ended for us.

The last woman, Malin, it's her.

So get up from the floor now.

And go on hunting.

There's still time, she hasn't followed Maria's path yet. If you save her maybe you can save yourself, but be careful, think about what's inside you now, think about the fact that you're not alone, you're not alone, Malin, feel what's growing in you, feel it, and then prove what that's worth.

Malin hears the voice.

But not what it's saying.

She wants to stay on the floor of the hospital room all night.

Clinging onto Maria's leg.

Pleading and cursing, trying to bring her back, then fall asleep and never wake again.

But the voice, the voices, want something different.

And she can feel it now, what's inside her, but she daren't believe in the miracle, daren't believe that such a future is possible.

Not for her.

Not for such a failed, broken person as her.

Not for someone as worthless as Malin Fors.

'Get up,' the voice says.

And Malin gets up.

And sets off towards her future.

53

Who was that, suddenly standing in front of him down in the cellar?

And what was that case he could see behind the unknown figure?

Fredrik Kantsten had parked outside Charlottenhill.

He had made sure no one could see him. Then he had unpacked the rifle and hurried into the building.

The door was unlocked.

It looked as if the coded lock was broken.

Then he had stopped short outside the door of Sten's apartment, which, remarkably, was ajar.

He had to be at home.

Fredrik Kantsten had felt the weight of the rifle in his hand.

Reflecting on how many times he had fired it, though never at a human being.

But now there was no alternative.

Sten Dinman, he had thought as he stood there in the hall outside his apartment.

They had known each other for thirty-five years. But could Sten be anyone's friend?

No.

An acquaintance, perhaps. A powerful acquaintance who could get you into places and situations that led in only one direction: upwards.

But he somehow never really seemed fully engaged in

the moment at hand, and there was always some ulterior motive behind every favour, he always wanted something in return.

Ideally something that gave him a hold over the other person.

As with me.

In exchange for him using his contacts and procuring me a post in Stockholm, I was obliged to do two things: shut down the investigation into the woman who was found raped and abused in a field outside Malmö. And get hold of a block of hash for him.

He doesn't even smoke. But he wanted that extra hold over me.

Calculating. And he seemed to enjoy it, Fredrik Kantsten had thought as he made his way deeper into the apartment.

Yet at the same time Sten is funnier, more charming, more captivating than most. A bit of spice in the higher echelons of the Social Democrats.

The handsome, charismatic swan among the ugly, lumpen socialists. The chocolate hidden among the bark bread. Always on the side of the good in the media, whenever the opportunity arose.

He had crept through the apartment, moving from room to room with the rifle raised, looking for Sten.

But Sten wasn't there.

And then Fredrik Kantsten had found the cellar door and heard someone talking down there. It could be Sten. It sounded like Sten.

Didn't it?

The same slightly nasal, assured tone of voice.

He crept downstairs.

Past the wine cellar.

Then suddenly the unknown man was standing there, looking surprised and scared, and he had to be either a burglar or a police officer, but it really doesn't make any difference, Fredrik Kantsten thought, it doesn't make any difference, no one can see me here, no one, and I have to do this, and inside him he saw the faces of all the prostitutes.

Jenny Svartsjö, whom he had fucked up the arse on the sofa of the hunting cabin on Peder's estate while the others watched.

And all the others. Who had vanished from his life after numerous acts, and he had convinced himself that they liked his erect cock, that they enjoyed having sex with him, the cool prosecutor, the passably handsome man. And he had enjoyed the others watching. The way they goaded each other on, just like they had done long before as young men in Uppsala, when they used to get high and take young high-school girls back to the Skulls Society premises.

Sten had been there.

In the Society's cellar. In the hunting cabins. Getting hold of the girls from Paul. Assuming the role of leader, obviously, and we all wanted to be like him. Handsome, dynamic, tall and elegant, the sort of man who permits himself to do everything and gets admired for it.

But he was never interested in the women.

Over the years Sten had hardly even watched, and had never done anything with any of the women. As if he were waiting for his very own turn.

His eyes.

And Fredrik Kantsten realises that he has known all along.

But refused to see what was right in front of him.

And that case he always had with him. Crocodile skin. The anger he showed if anyone mentioned the case, wondered what he had in it.

'That's where I keep my soul,' he said. 'And I keep that to myself.'

Blindness acts as a sort of manure for evil.

And Emanuel's disgusting, perverse wish to join in. He was prepared to do anything, even licking the whores' arses if Peder told him to. Without protection.

So who was the man standing in front of him?

He could make out the room behind the man, saw the contents of the case, and finally he realised, understood how everything had happened, and was convinced that he had to pull the trigger of the rifle.

'Don't shoot,' the man said. 'Don't shoot.'

And Fredrik Kantsten shot. Pulled the trigger of the rifle as hard as he could.

Don't shoot, Conny Nygren thought, it was the only thought in his head.

'Don't shoot,' he said. 'Don't shoot.'

He knew who the man was.

He was the man who had been following in his footsteps his whole life. The face, the body, the being he had always known would catch up with him.

The man had a name that he couldn't remember.

But he knew the name of the essence.

And then the noise, the fraction of a second after firing, then the pain and the feeling of being thrown through the air as the bullet hit him, and collapsing onto the concrete floor and the open case, and the feeling as the razor-sharp dildo cut right through his shoulder.

He had time to see different people.

His mother, calling to him in a playground surrounded by low, newly planted bushes, which would grow at the same rate as him. His wife, the woman who left him for a better man.

The boy. Driving him in a car made out of boxes outside the terraced house in Huddinge. Dad in his bed in the care home. The girl. Running across a summer meadow. Grandchildren. Incarnations of himself.

The boy and girl as they are now, as adults, and he saw them standing on a windswept, isolated cliff top facing the sea.

The world around them grey.

They waved, and the grey sky grew darker.

Then everything turned black.

And then Conny Nygren noticed that all sound had gone, that one world had been irrevocably replaced by another.

Fredrik Kantsten walked over to the body, which was lying as though fused to the case, trying to avoid standing in the blood that was seeping out of it.

He could feel his adrenalin pumping.

And then a sense of panic. Who have I killed?

Who have I become?

He searched the dead man's pockets.

Found a wallet.

Carefully picked it up, it can't be a burglar, because surely they don't carry wallets? He pulled an ID card from the leathery darkness. And recognised it all too well.

Fuck.

What have I done?

A policeman.

A Conny Nygren. Should I know who that is?

They'll never stop chasing me.

Think. Think clearly. Force yourself to be calm. This doesn't change anything.

Then Fredrik Kantsten returned the wallet, left the room and went back upstairs.

He sat down at the curved white table in the kitchen.

They'll think Sten found the policeman here and killed him.

That's what they'll think.

I can dump the rifle, and use the shotgun on Sten. Wherever he is.

Where the hell can he be?

Where would I go if I were Sten? Where would I be now?

Somewhere I could be safe to be the person I am deep down. If that's what he's actually doing.

54

Sten Dinman

I can be myself here.

The bag of skin crammed with testosterone-fuelled flesh that is really me.

In this room.

One of my cases is open, the other is still in Djurgården.

I love my cases.

I love them like an old woman loves her handbag.

The possibilities contained within them. That everything is somehow present, nice and simple. I had them made in the Burlington Arcade in London. Filled them with what I needed.

Wonderful things.

I've covered the walls and windows with broad strips of aluminium foil, the floor with lining paper, shiny side up, and I've hung spotlights from the ceiling.

The world is shiny now.

Glowing, as if it's never been more beautiful.

I want these moments to be bathed in light.

I don't know why.

It just feels right with this sort of light. Everything becomes clear, clean.

It was an idea I had, a whim, so I went to a DIY store to get what I needed, and she, the woman hanging from the roof in chains in front of me, was still here when I got back, I've got better at that over the years, stopping them escaping, even if I have a certain appreciation for cat-and-mouse games.

And once they are quiet, then they can go.

The forest takes care of them.

Ripping their innermost walls to pieces.

And then I come along.

I'm surprised that they never give up.

And no matter what I do to them, they never stop hoping or pleading, and sometimes I stuff rags in their mouths when they fuck about with me.

Sometimes I soak the rags in something.

Raspberry syrup. Everyone likes the sweet taste.

They're like children with sugar. Trusting, naïve.

Jessica Karlsson liked raspberry syrup. She didn't like hydrochloric acid.

It was easy with her.

I had rented a second cabin. And picked her up when the others were busy doing their own thing. And then I stayed on after they thought I'd gone home.

They must have realised.

Must have known. But they chose to be blind for their own sakes. A person can understand things in many ways, but they know, and someone who knows is never free from guilt, if you happen to believe in such a concept.

Drink. The women like that as well.

And sometimes I dip the rags in hydrochloric acid and they try to scream and their eyes turn white and then red and swollen and they swell almost to the point of bursting or popping out of their sockets.

That's fun.

Their mouths and flesh burn and hiss and smell as the acid caresses them.

A well-marinated lamb chop under a grill.

That's more or less what it smells like.

Why do I do this?

All this evil.

Towards Maria, Jenny, the one in front of me now. All the others who are dead and buried, the forgotten, the missed, the not-missed.

All the women. Thousands and thousands of women. Mine, and others'.

Why am I moving the knife towards her breasts in this room that is crackling with light?

Why have I poured scalding hot water on the bottom of her left leg, watching as the skin falls off in great lumps as she screams for help in the gibberish of her own language?

Why do I do these things, and much, much worse to her?

Why did I do what I did to the other women?

You're wondering, aren't you? You're screaming, howling.

To be honest, I'm wondering as well.

This would be the place for me to talk about a terrible childhood, with sexual abuse and a father who beat me and a mother who drank, about divorce and drugs and bullying, about addiction and poverty and misery.

But there's nothing of that sort.

I can say that I had a happy childhood. Nice, Swedish, middle-class, in a nice, Swedish, suburban house with an older brother and a younger sister and two parents who only had eyes for each other, and never ever argued.

It was all strawberries from the garden, glasses of milk.

Sandwiches and hot chocolate.

Homemade meatballs.

It's true.

I swear.

My work has sent me to war zones. I've taken inspiration from them. Admired the inventiveness.

Witnessed epidemics. Seen what disease can do to the human body.

Terrible.

Horrific.

Yet here I am, cutting into her left breast, listening to her scream, but I go on cutting something resembling a Chinese character.

'Art is war', that sign. Or was it 'the art of war'?

Well, it's war, anyway.

And in war things aren't that particular. Anything goes, as the Americans say.

I'm evil, aren't I?

Maybe I am evil itself, in which case, why do I exist?

Yes, why do I exist? Or you? Why does evil exist? Why do we never know what it looks like or where it comes from?

My balls itch. And I scratch them.

Erect now.

Look at how erect it is.

Girls, women, of all ages know what it can do.

But evil.

Why do we choose not to see it, even though it's right in front of us?

Behind one of the country's most winning smiles, even?

Evil exists anywhere, at any time, in any guise.

Don't be scared if you don't understand, because there's nothing to understand. It is what it is.

For you.

For me.

The others have their weaknesses. But not me.

You can regard evil as a talent, and that talent exists in every human being. But there isn't much cultivated talent, in any area, and that includes evil.

That's one way of looking at it. But doesn't evil need a goal?

I haven't got one.

So am I still evil?

The woman here with me probably thinks I am. Jessica, Jenny, Maria . . .

So many people. So much insignificant pain.

The aluminium foil rustles. Dazzling light, and I gag her to put a stop to the howling, first soaking it in something from one of the bottles of acid, in front of her so she sees it and has time to think: I'm going to burn now. My tongue and my larynx are going to melt.

But there's only elderflower syrup in this bottle.

My ex-wife made it, from the tiny flowers she picked in a beautiful Swedish meadow.

We've been divorced for a long time. Our children are grown up now, and I've been a good father to our son and daughter.

The sex, you might be thinking.

It's the sex, that's why he does it, but that's not the case. Certainly, naked women's bodies turn me on, but the sexual element is a by-product, nothing I long for, or even regard as a big deal.

It isn't a goal in itself. No compulsion of the soul.

I'm no Jeffrey Dahmer. Or some ridiculous Anders Eklund. Or Marc Dutroux. Those slaves of ridiculous, uncontrolled lust.

My friends.

They're no better.

But, oh, they're such male human beings.

Sometimes I can't actually get it up. But I like the idea of violation. And then there's Viagra. Don't ask me why, no one has ever violated me in any way at all, I'm no hopeless victim of sexual abuse.

The Nobel Prize for medicine should go to whoever invented Viagra.

Jenny.

I violated her through a new hole I made in her body.

My pulse didn't increase while I was doing it. I don't remember any beautiful moment. I just did it because I could. Because someone had to.

I get Viagra from Emanuel. I get the morphine for the girls from him as well.

He's just happy he can be part of our little hunting party. Belonging.

I've never needed to belong to anything. That's why I'm so good at it.

I don't feel the intoxication of power, or the pleasure of ownership, when I do my 'terrible' things.

I feel nothing. Mean nothing.

The one outside Lund. I was there without the others to hunt woodcock. The finest and tastiest of our game-birds. I had Paul drive her down to me from Stockholm. Fredrik shut down the investigation, and in return I sorted out a job for him in Stockholm. He was so grateful, like a little puppy being given a bone to chew.

'Why?' Paul Lendberg would ask me occasionally when he delivered the girls to me, to us. When he came back with them after the others had left.

Why?

I never answered, because there was no answer.

There is no answer to that question.

Perhaps I could answer by rephrasing the question: Why not?

But I never played the why, why not game with Paul.

Instead I paid him well, and money was the only answer he was ever really interested in.

He got three hundred and fifty thousand kronor for each girl I ruined. That way he could justify it in business terms.

And it's this lack of an explanation that makes them so

scared. So scared that they escape or want to die in the end, or just become mute, fleeing from life even though their bodies are demonstrably alive. The fact that there's no logic in my behaviour, no reason for me to do what I do.

That I'm just doing it.

That terrifies them.

More than anything else.

Even more than the pain.

It terrifies them because in the end they understand the emptiness of evil, and because they see themselves in me and recognise it as truth.

Perhaps the silence of the living is my only victory.

Suppressed memories, denials that become a living un-life, a sort of anti-feeling of evil. A perfect nothingness, that still pumps oxygenated blood.

A bag of skin, full of flesh.

Evil just is.

Just like this white-hot knife just is. The glistening white, hissing metal that I raise slowly, with a tantric gesture, up towards her, shall we say, G-spot?

55

What happened to you in the forest, Maria? What were you doing there?

Who, what did you meet?

All questions Malin should have asked her in the brief period when she seemed to have returned to them.

The questions are tumbling around inside Malin as she sits beside Peter on the sofa in her living room late on Tuesday evening, feeling the saggy padding chafe against her back, but then the fact that she is so close to Peter overrides everything else.

The late night news has just started.

It's leading with their case. Somehow they've found out that prominent figures might be involved, but mention no names, merely stating that the case has connections to the very highest levels of society.

Nothing about Sten Dinman, and that the Stockholm Police have found a case full of torture instruments in his cellar on the royal island of Djurgården.

Conny Nygren must have called in his colleagues hours ago, even if that didn't make it onto the news. She hasn't heard from him yet, but it's only been a few hours. Presumably he's put out a national alert, and Forensics will already be hard at work.

She told Peter about Maria.

The way she screamed when she saw the picture of Sten Dinman. And about his torture case.

And what Sara Markelberg in Lund had said about the reaction of her patient, the nameless young woman, when she saw the pictures of Sten Dinman and Paul Lendberg.

That she had screamed a scream that sounded like nothing else on earth. Sara had called it 'the mother of all terrified screams, as if she'd seen the face of pure, unadulterated evil'.

The things Sten Dinman might have done.

Conny Nygren ought to have phoned by now.

The only call all evening had been from Tove.

A short conversation.

Fresh promises.

Once again she had promised to go to the end-of-year concert and hear Tove sing, watch her onstage beaming with pride and confidence, then go to dinner with Tom's family.

Only ten days away now.

By then this case, this descent into the very hottest chambers of hell, must have come to a conclusion. By then I must have managed to cut off all the spitting heads of the hydra.

She curls up next to Peter on the sofa.

Feels his warm, hard body. Should she mention what she can feel happening inside her? Should she? Deep inside her, in her warm core?

No.

Because he'd probably want her to take a test, and she sees herself in the pharmacy at Fridhemsplan again, putting the pregnancy test back on the shelf.

Peter puts his arm around her, concentrating on a report about three French doctors who've been murdered in Sudan. They had been working for Médecins Sans Frontières.

'I've thought about doing that,' he says.

And Malin feels like pinning him down on the sofa.

Remembers the way Janne would head off to Bosnia and Rwanda with the Rescue Services Agency the moment things got tough at home, the way he would use humanity's catastrophes as an emergency exit.

'You're staying here,' Malin says. 'Otherwise I'm going to glue you to the sofa.'

'I said I thought about going. Before, I mean. Not now.'

'Why not now?'

'You're fishing for compliments.'

'Indulge me.'

'I'm staying here for your sake. For our sake. And what we're trying to do.'

'Do you want to try now?'

Malin defies her body and the feelings inside it, if she's wrong they can try again, and she wants to try, and gets up from the sofa, pulling him with her into the bedroom.

She undresses him.

Unbuttons his shirt.

His trousers.

His underwear, and she feels him, his hardness and heat, and he undresses her, pulling her top over her head, and outside the bedroom windows it's dusk now, a couple of swallows are swooping over the rooftops, and above them are stars, the stars that were reluctant to show themselves in Maria's hospital room a short while ago.

He undoes her bra.

Pulls down her pants and she doesn't want to wait, wants him immediately, and she sinks onto the bed and holds out her arms, opening herself to him, to what she wants to happen.

He's lowering himself towards her when her mobile rings, shouting from where she left it on the worktop in the kitchen.

And she wants to ignore it.

But she can't.

Because in the sound of the ring she can see Conny Nygren's face.

She sees his eyes closed.

The bloodless sheen of his skin.

'I've got to get that,' she says.

'Malin.'

'I've got to.'

'For fuck's sake, just this once can't you . . .?'

But she's already up from the bed, pushing him aside.

Standing naked in the kitchen.

Sven Sjöman at the other end of the line. There's sorrow in his voice, and she realises what's happened immediately.

'It's Conny Nygren. He's been found shot in Sten Dinman's cellar out on Djurgården. He's dead. A neighbour saw that the door was open and found him in the cellar.'

Fuck, Malin thinks.

She forces her grief aside, her anger, the desire to go out and kill the first person she finds in revenge at what happened to Conny.

She forces all her irrational reactions aside.

'Malin, are you there?'

'I'm here. Thinking.'

It must have happened just after she spoke to him, Sten Dinman must have taken him by surprise before he had time to report what he'd found in the basement of the apartment and call for reinforcements. Then no one had missed him for a couple of hours. That's why she hadn't heard from him. That's why there hadn't been anything about it on the news.

Fuck.

She should have called Police Headquarters when he didn't answer earlier.

'Have we sent out a national alert for Sten Dinman?'

'Yes, fifteen minutes ago.'

Malin had given Sven a quick update on the situation after her visit to see Maria, and he had told her that Stockholm were taking care of the necessary procedural matters. Evidently he hadn't checked with them either before he got the call about Conny.

Mistakes.

But they couldn't have saved Conny.

'Where could Sten Dinman be?'

'No idea,' Sven says. 'Could be anywhere.'

'He could be somewhere around here,' Malin says. 'He's been in these parts before.'

'Or he could be somewhere else entirely.'

'What about Fredrik Kantsten?' Malin asks. 'Did Stockholm say anything about him, I know Conny wasn't having any luck finding him?'

'Nothing.'

'What sort of gun was he shot with?'

'Something high-calibre. Probably a hunting rifle.'

'OK.'

Thoughts are whirling through Malin's head, refusing to settle. She tries to make sense of them as she stares at the faulty Ikea clock on the wall, but all she can see are faces.

Women's faces.

Jenny, Jessica, Maria, the woman in Lund.

The men's faces.

And then Conny's death mask.

Paul Lendberg dumped in the water. It must have been his associates from the East who were responsible.

Mustn't it?

Death, drifting in the air like smoke.

Who's its next victim?

And she tries to bring all her suspicions together to form a whole, to understand how it all fits together, understand what Maria was doing in the forest, but she can't make sense of it, just knows that this hasn't reached its conclusion yet, its very deepest darkness.

'Johan's digging up anything he can find about Dinman.'

'Good. I'm on my way,' Malin says. 'I need to do some work on this now. There's something we're not seeing.'

'Do you think he's got any more women somewhere?'

'I don't know,' Malin says. 'But he did have access to them, via Paul Lendberg.'

The women in the basement.

Ten rings, nine women.

The tenth, last woman.

'There were ten rings and chains in that basement, but only nine women,' Malin says. 'He could have one more woman. We have to accept that as a possibility.'

The sound of Sven's breathing.

The weariness of insomnia in its rhythm.

'Is there any way we can get hold of Dinman's DNA quickly? We've got the DNA of the man who killed Jenny Svartsjö, and the results of Lendberg's DNA test. It wasn't him who violated Jenny Svartsjö out in the forest.'

'I'm sure we could get it,' Malin says. 'But there isn't time for that. Not now. He's holding another woman captive. I'm sure he is. He uses the women to escape himself. Uses what he does to them. He's never going to stop.'

56

It's been an endless day, Malin thinks. And it's not over yet.

She, Johan Jakobsson, and Sven Sjöman are sitting around the table in the meeting room. The others in the investigating team have gone home for some much-needed rest.

The hospital and blocks of flats down towards the river are sea anemones under a black sky, where all the stars have now ventured out.

The preschool is dark and deserted.

The whiteboard in the meeting room wiped clean.

No names needed there any more.

They know who they're after.

But now it's no longer just the murder of a prostitute and violence towards women, it's also about the murder of a colleague. The case may fall under Stockholm's jurisdiction, but that won't make any difference to their response.

They're tired.

Almost night now.

Malin has spread all the papers from her file about Maria across the table, and the three detectives are looking at them, as Malin says: 'I know the answer's here. Somewhere.'

Sven shakes his head.

'You really are obsessed, Malin, you know that?'

She nods.

'The answer's here, though.'

And Johan looks down at the documents. Profiles of

people in Maria's life, printouts of dozens of interviews with her clients, the story of her whole existence.

'It's struck me sometimes,' Malin says, 'that I might have missed one of her contacts. That not everything was documented in her case files.'

'I can check,' Johan says, pointing at his computer. 'See what I can find.'

'I'll do some digging on Dinman,' Malin says.

'And I'm going home to get some sleep,' Sven says. 'I haven't heard anything more from Stockholm, but I guess the force has gone into the sort of paralysis that happens when an officer gets murdered. And Conny was in charge of the preliminary investigation, so I daresay they're seriously confused right now, trying to sort their own case out.'

'It's up to us now,' Malin says. 'To solve this before it gets worse.'

Sven nods.

'I'm sure there's another woman,' Malin hears herself repeat. 'No one else has been reported missing, but he's taken women that no one's missed before. It's really urgent now.'

Listen to the voices of the investigation.

Sven's mantra.

And both he and Malin have listened.

Another woman, the voice is saying. *The last woman.*

'Isn't he just on the run?' Johan asks. 'Wouldn't that be the logical thing to do?'

'His evil has no logic,' Sven says. 'It's pointless trying to find any logic in his behaviour.'

Then the three of them sit in silence around the table.

The men.

The weapons.

The murder of Paul Lendberg.

The hunting cabins.

And however much Peder Stålskiöld, Emanuel Ärendsson

and Fredrik Kantsten stand to lose from this, being revealed to have paid for prostitutes, they can still get away with it, even if it did happen systematically, by making a full apology, and showing how much they regret it and want to make amends. Even the connection to Paul Lendberg can be explained by the fact that they were kept in the dark and didn't know anything.

And they had nothing to do with Jenny's murder, nor the brutal violence against the other women.

Malin's sure of that now.

With their little male terrorist cells, they protect each other. Choosing not even to see the worst crimes and abuses.

Prominent men can get away with a lot.

But proximity to a sexual sadist like Sten Dinman, possibly even protecting him? That connection will never fade. But if Dinman dies before he gets caught, before he manages to tell his side of the story, if he wants to, then Kantsten, Ärendsson and Stålskiöld's relationships with him would remain unclear. Bringing them in for questioning would be pointless.

'We didn't know anything.'

'Like everyone else, we thought he was above suspicion. We thought he was a good person.'

This can end in several different ways, Malin thinks in the silence of the meeting room.

Conny Nygren.

In all likelihood, Sten Dinman found him in the cellar, he had a licence for several hunting rifles, he could have shot Conny with any one of them.

So far they hadn't been able to find out where the guns were.

But there were also other possible scenarios.

Perhaps one of the others, or more than one of them, had realised that they had to get rid of Sten Dinman in order to safeguard their own futures, and were then discovered by Conny Nygren out on Djurgården? And shot him in panic?

Bang, you're dead.

Conny.

I could have imagined working with him in Stockholm.

And Malin realises that she didn't actually know anything about him. His life, his dreams.

Ärendsson.

Sven had called him an hour or so ago. He had been at home. Same with Stålskiöld. As of now they are under surveillance.

But Kantsten was still unaccounted for. Maybe he was the one who went out to Charlottenhill to kill Sten Dinman and was taken by surprise by Conny Nygren?

If that's the case, we're now hunting both Kantsten and Dinman.

And both of them are presumably pretty desperate now.

Fucking self-justifying bastards.

'I'll look into Sten Dinman's background,' Malin repeats. 'Maybe I can find something there that can lead us to him.'

'I didn't manage to find anything interesting before. But go ahead. It's going to be a long night,' Johan says, and gets up, takes his laptop, and leaves the room.

Malin and Sven are left sitting at the table alone. Sven seems to have forgotten that he was going home.

He pulls in his stomach and lets out a deep sigh.

'I've never looked forward to retirement more than I am right now,' he says. 'It feels like I've done my bit. I just haven't got the energy to go on.'

The preschool lights up as a lamp is switched on.

A black cleaner in the child-aquarium.

'Don't say that.'

'Don't you think I've earned the right to say what I like?'

Malin smiles.

'Oh, yes.'

'So when this case is finished I'll be putting in my retirement request. I wanted to tell you first.'

We won't be able to manage without you, Malin thinks.

The entire investigating team will collapse without you, Sven.

'I got the results of the tests back from the hospital today,' Sven goes on. 'They didn't find anything definite, but my cholesterol's too high and my PSA is through the roof.'

'What does that mean?'

'I might have prostate cancer.'

No, Malin thinks.

'It's not certain, not yet,' Sven says. 'But it's time for me to do something else now.'

Malin looks at her mentor.

The furrows in his face.

Cancer.

Does it never end?

'I don't know what to say,' she says.

'You know you'll be the one who takes over when I go,' Sven says.

It's not a question.

More a statement of the obvious.

'You're the one who sets the tone, Malin. Your obsession. All police officers who deal with murders need obsession. Their own, or someone else's.'

57

What do we know about Sten Dinman? Malin wonders as the screen flickers before her eyes and the open-plan office around her seems to dissolve at the edges, becoming a grainy mirage.

It's a quarter past midnight.

Dinman was a Social Democrat.

Raised in Växjö.

His father worked for the railways, his mother for the social welfare board, and she was also a deputy member of the local council for the Social Democrats.

Two children, both grown up now, living abroad.

Divorced ten years ago.

Single since then.

A meteoric career, the golden boy of the Swedish Social Democratic Youth Movement, although never its chair; speech-writer to one prime minister, then a key member of a think tank, followed by appointment to the post of parliamentary undersecretary of state to the employment minister, a former colleague of his mother's. He made a name for himself as an advocate of women's rights and equality.

He's on the boards of the Folksam insurance group, the Vattenfall energy company, and the Workers' Education Council.

Minister for Equality, then, after the change of government, hand-picked to be chief executive of Save the Children.

Always handsome.

Always smiling.

Always fake.

So where the hell can he be? If he's actually gone into hiding somewhere?

Malin rubs her eyes. The letters on the screen are starting to blur.

All this surfing and searching into Sten Dinman's background hasn't thrown up anything useful.

The online edition of one of the evening tabloids is leading with Conny Nygren: 'Policeman shot in ex-minister's home'.

Nothing about the instruments of torture. No link to their case, to everything else that's happened.

Her brain feels foggy.

Best get some sleep now.

Best to sleep on everything they already know, and hope it settles into a new, clearer pattern.

Sven's suggestion. She can't even think about it at the moment. And the timing would be terrible, if she's right about what might be happening in her life.

Sven.

She can't imagine working without him, without knowing that he's always there somewhere to provide support.

Unless it really is time. For him. For me. Time to take the next step.

And she steps back from her own thoughts.

How ridiculous it sounds: the next step. Like some lousy, second-rate psychologist, and she tells herself that she has to get some sleep now.

What he said about his prostate.

Can't take it in right now. For the time being, it doesn't exist.

She can't make sense of her thoughts.

Sleep.

That's the next step.

Johan Jakobsson seems inexhaustible.

He's sitting at his computer, and seems to have something like twenty documents open at the same time.

Malin's standing behind him.

He hasn't noticed her, and starts when he hears her voice.

'I'm going to lie down,' she says. 'I'll try to get a couple of hours' sleep in the bunk room.'

'I'll wake you if anything crops up,' Johan says, and Malin says goodnight and heads off towards the bunk room via the kitchen, where a pot of coffee is sitting on the hotplate of the machine, spreading a bitter, burned smell.

The bunk room has no windows.

A cell.

Not much more hospitable than the room in which they found the women.

She shuts the door behind her, turns off the light, and lies down on the hard bunk without even taking her shoes off.

She shuts her eyes.

Tries to feel whatever it is that's moving out there in the darkness.

Tries to see Sten Dinman before her.

His blond fringe. Those innocent blue eyes. The wry smile, the roguish look. And then he changes, and his face becomes a hard mask, his eyes reptilian, and she sees him standing naked in a room whose walls are covered in aluminium foil, and spotlights spew out a harsh, burning light onto the bleeding woman lying on the floor.

Then the image is gone.

And Malin knows that it's happening again.

She sees a forest full of snakes.

Faces like glowing spheres against the sky of that world.

The men's faces.

It's happening again, and she feels like rushing out, but knows she has to get some sleep, and will have to trust that even evil needs to rest sometimes.

Eyes closed. Open, closed, open.

The Workers' Education Council.

The Social Democrats.

Eyes closed.

Stjärnorp.

Open.

Closed.

Then she falls asleep.

The woman on the floor comes round slowly, torn from sleep by a bright light that wants to burn the rest of the skin from her body.

Her mouth stings, she can't breathe through it, or talk, but at least it wasn't acid on the rag he gagged her with.

Have I got a body?

It feels like I've abandoned it. Because I can't feel pain any more, pain no longer exists.

Yes it does.

Here it comes again, and I want to stay asleep because now I can feel how my whole being is an intense, burning flame of pain, getting worse and worse by the second.

What's been inside me?

I move my legs.

I can move my legs.

I am lying down, and I can see him, he's lying down as well, and I can hear him snore, and the whole room is shining silver, and he's asleep, he's asleep.

I'll get up.

I'll escape.

I can do it.

And she crawls forward, with her hands tied behind her back, snaking forward like a lizard towards the door, without having any idea what might be behind it, but the door is the only way forward she can see.

Past the closed case.

She reaches the door.

And she gets up, there are open wounds on her legs and she tries to push the door handle down.

And it works.

The door is open now.

It is dark and cold, the cold like heat against her hot, burning body.

The forest.

That's all there is here. She can see that. And a few ramshackle, derelict buildings.

Who am I? she asks herself. What am I? And she realises that she no longer knows her own name, who she is, and that it really doesn't matter right now.

Forward is the only thing that has any meaning.

Forward.

We can deal with the rest later.

Then she hears something behind her.

Is it him?

Waking up?

Is he coming now, coming to wipe out the last vestiges of the self that I can no longer feel?

A body moving forward. Her body.

Into the forest now, into the very darkest hour of night, into an unfamiliar season.

58

His eyes seem to be crackling.

The clock on the screen says 5:15.

Johan Jakobsson looks around the open-plan office.

The words of the document are blurring together. He's found his way into the social service register, has managed to bypass the security protocols and knows that he's crossed the line now.

Maria Murvall's clients.

The ones in Malin's file.

The ones registered on the computer.

Johan tries to cross-reference the names on the screen with the names in the file. Has Malin missed anyone? Maybe there's a discrepancy between Maria's own notes and what she logged in the computer? Could any documents have got lost?

There's no way Malin could have gained access to the register he's found his way into.

Maybe someone will notice the breach?

Maybe, maybe not.

He'll have to deal with that later.

Waldemar Ekenberg uses his fists, whereas he sneaks his way in. Needs must.

But everything seems to match.

He turns the document over. Blank paper, just Malin's greasy fingerprints.

No more names there.

But on the last line of the computerised record of Maria Murvall's clients there's one more name.

One final name.

One last woman, a Krista Överlund, born 1975. Drug addict, prostitute.

Malin.

Have you checked her out, spoken to her? Not much to go on, but it might be worth trying.

He looks up Krista Överlund in the police database.

She served one year in Österåker five years ago, for burglary.

And her address?

He checks the population register. There's a serious risk that this Krista Överlund isn't alive at all. How many drug addicts make it beyond thirty-five?

But she's alive.

And lives in Linköping.

In a flat in Johannelund.

Johan gets up, this new discovery has given him fresh energy, and he goes over to the bunk room and knocks, but Malin doesn't answer, so he opens the door and steps inside and in the weak light from the doorway he sees her lying on her back with her shoes on. She's snoring loudly and looks as if she could do with sleeping for a hundred years, a dreamless Sleeping Beauty sleep, then wake up in a new, better world.

But she needs to wake up now.

So he turns the light on, goes over to her and says: 'Malin, you need to wake up. I've found something.'

And her sleep couldn't have been as deep as he thought. It couldn't have been, because she sits up, squinting against the light, and asks: 'What have you found, Johan?'

The Statoil petrol station with its adjoining Route 66 restaurant is ten kilometres south of Norrköping, at the foot of a forested hill that's been split in two by the E4.

Tables with green laminate tops. Red plastic chairs on a bare brown floor. An open kitchen where an immigrant in a hairnet is frying sausages. Only a few customers: a fat lorry driver, a dad with a young son.

The coffee has been stewing all night and is hot and tastes scorched and stale.

But it clears his head.

Fredrik Kantsten has worked out where Sten Dinman might be.

It was perfectly logical, really.

If he is actually there.

But it would be characteristically arrogant of him to pick somewhere so close to the place where they recently found one of his victims.

Dinman had showed him the place when they were hunting on Peder's estate. Chuckling and saying it was the perfect symbol for why the country was so fucked. Then he had said that he would use his influence to get the place sorted out.

Then he had changed his mind and dropped the idea.

There were already too many places like that.

But there had been a spark in his eyes. As if Sten already had plans for the place.

As if he'd been there before.

And wanted to go again.

Fredrik Kantsten takes a gulp of the coffee, registers the smell of frying, but he isn't hungry.

And something makes him feel sure. He's going to find Sten there, at the place he's heading towards, and he doesn't even want to imagine what Sten might be doing there.

The bastard.

I should have done something.

I pretended not to know, not to have any idea at all. But

I knew what he had in his case, what was hidden behind that crocodile skin.

But it must all end now.

And I will have a fresh start.

He got some sleep in the car. He dumped the elk-hunting rifle in a small lake deep in the forest outside Järna. No one will ever find it there, and he knows that the murder of the policeman will be blamed on Sten, as long as he can be done away with.

No one will lift a finger to uncover any other truth.

And he wishes he could feel guilt, regret about what he ended up doing, what he's thinking of doing.

But he feels nothing of the sort.

He's reached the point where everything is at stake, the point at which compromise is no longer an option, and he feels no shame at attempting to save himself.

He stands up.

Has to keep going.

The smell of the previous evening's cooking is lingering in the stairwell in Johannelund. Malin leans against the wall, feeling its chill under her palm. Her body is aching with tiredness, her muscles straining with every movement, as if someone had injected a slow, paralysing poison into her veins.

She rings the doorbell of the flat. The clock on her mobile says it's a quarter past six.

The stairwell is freshly painted, in a shade of vomit green, with a pink floral border around the ceiling.

The third floor.

The lift is broken, and Malin is panting.

Then the door opens, and in front of her stands a skinny woman in a white nightdress, holding a hand-rolled cigarette in one hand and a chipped coffee cup in the other.

Her skin is tight across her cheekbones, and her eyes are grey and tired, set deep in her thin face with a look of resignation. She looks older than she is, Malin thinks.

Then the woman raises her sparse brown eyebrows and a thousand wrinkles appear on her forehead, every one of them gained the hard way.

A moment of surprise switches to realisation, and she gestures with the cigarette for Malin to go in.

Krista Överlund.

'You are Krista, aren't you?' Malin asks, and suddenly feels that those few hours' sleep have done her good, she can carry on now.

Krista Överlund nods.

The flat is small, just one room.

Tidy, but the furniture looks as if it came from markets and charity shops.

A speckled green sofa. A little Swedish flag on a shelf on the wall, next to the EU flag.

Krista Överlund sits down and looks at Malin, who remains standing, and says: 'It's a fucking nightmare.'

'What is?'

'Staying clean. Or in your case sober. I'm right, aren't I?'

And Malin sinks onto the unmade bed opposite Krista Överlund, and looks at the yellowing aerial photograph of a farm on the end wall of the room.

Nods.

'It's fucking shit.'

'I haven't touched anything in two years,' Krista Överlund says. 'I'm a cleaner at Åleryd Care Home. This is my flat, all mine. First one I've ever had.'

Malin nods again.

'But it's fucking awful.'

'Aren't you wondering why I'm here?'

'It's because of Maria, isn't it? Maria Murvall?'

'She was your social worker.'

'She was more than that. She helped me outside of work as well, wanted me to get back on my feet, stop all the crap. But I was out of reach back then.'

'You know what happened to her?'

And Krista Överlund stubs the cigarette out in an ashtray on the floor next to the sofa and takes a sip of her coffee.

'I know.'

'And?'

'For a long while I couldn't remember anything. I suppressed it, couldn't bear to think about it, and it was like I managed to stop myself remembering with all the drink and drugs.'

'Remembering what? You have to tell me,' Malin says. 'Maria can't say anything, you know that, don't you?'

'I was there a month ago, outside the hospital. In the car park. But I couldn't go in. I left her there, with him. In the forest.'

'Tell me,' Malin says again.

'Sometimes, when I was at my worst, I know Maria used to follow me in her car, sort of watching over me. And once, I was working on the street in Norrköping, out by the harbour, I got picked up by a bloke, a nice one, and he drove me to some cottage, I was so off my head I had no idea where, and he put on a pair of overalls and I thought he was going to start hitting me. But instead he opened this shiny case he had with him, but I never saw what was in it, because that's when Maria showed up.'

Krista Överlund falls silent.

Crying gently.

You have to bear it, Malin thinks.

She strokes Krista's back and says: 'You have to go on.'

And Krista Överlund straightens up.

'I remembered in the end, when I was on my own,

cleaning the corridors in Åleryd, I could feel all the poisons slowly draining out of me, and I remembered.'

Malin is on her knees now, as if she's praying beside Krista Överlund.

'Tell me.'

'Maria gave him money to let me go, she was shouting, I remember that, saying I was so high I wouldn't remember anything, telling him to let me go and take her instead. She knew he wasn't going to let us both go.'

'Who?'

'Him.'

And Malin knows who 'he' is.

But she lets Krista Överlund go on.

'And he let me go. He couldn't have needed the money, but that was what he wanted. Money. And I did it. I took her car and drove away. Even though he was a monster. Even though I had an idea of what he was going to do.

'I wanted a fix, so I drove off, and after that everything was foggy for years. I didn't realise until a long time afterwards what must have happened up there in the forest.'

'Where?' Malin asks. Too eager now, but she can't hold back.

'Somewhere north of Stjärnorp. I can't tell you where exactly. But he seemed to feel at home there.'

'So Maria sacrificed herself for you?'

Krista Överlund nods.

'You know what he did to her?'

She nods again.

'The bastard,' she says. 'He didn't have time to do much to me.'

Krista Överlund shows the scar of a burn on her lower arm.

But to Maria? Malin thinks. On her own path to Calvary in that cold, fucking forest. Why? Why?

'You know who he is?'

Krista Överlund nods.

'I've worked it out,' she says. 'I've seen him on television. In the spotlight. Trying to look like goodness personified.'

59

A beaming, crackling light.

Sten Dinman has changed into a set of black overalls, and brushes a lock of hair from his forehead.

He's hung her up in the chains again, and he looks at her skinless legs, the wounds leading up to her crotch.

He had dozed off.

Woke up when the wind slammed the door behind him, and then it was time for a bit of cat-and-mouse again.

She didn't get far.

Didn't manage to escape like Maria or Jessica or whatever her name was in Skåne. Didn't get as far as Jenny or that other Ukrainian girl he dumped in the lake.

He caught her just fifty metres into the forest, he was the branches twining around her legs, his hands were the millipedes' fangs, his fingers ancient roots reaching out of the ground to trip her up, catch her, overpower her with his strength, and the ferns beneath them were wet and the ground full of crawling insects, and he pushed her down into the teeming earth and laughed at the vanity of her attempt to escape.

He held her down on the ground.

Was the very hungriest of the hydra's heads.

Digging his fingers deep into the wounds on her legs.

Then he hit her, knocking the last teeth from her mouth, and he saw millipedes crawling, hungry flies with green eyes buzzing around them, eager to lay their eggs in her open flesh.

'Don't be scared,' he whispered in her ear. 'It won't do any good. I've got more heads than you can count.'

And she didn't resist when he dragged her through the forest like a freshly shot elk-calf.

She had given up.

And he dragged her across the gravel in front of the cabin, and back into the warmth and light.

He felt at home in this forest, proud of having the courage to be back, so close to where they found the last one.

He strung her up in the chains again.

Sorted out the contents of his case.

Dozed off once more, and when he woke up this time she was still hanging there, and he was starting to get tired of her, bored, and she was no longer a pretty sight with all those wounds, all that hopelessness, and skin that was more lilac-blue and yellow than anything else.

But she was still breathing.

Moaning.

She hadn't given up breathing yet.

And he wonders what to do with her now.

He plugs the soldering iron back into the wall. Then he makes himself a cup of coffee in the cabin's little kitchen.

North of Stjärnorp, Malin thinks.

She knows this all fits together somehow.

And it's urgent now.

The woman's scream has fallen silent.

But Malin can feel that she's alive, somewhere.

What else is north of Stjärnorp?

She gets in the car and drives aimlessly around the waking city, driving past Janne's workplace, the fire station down by the river, carries on past the railway station up towards the construction site near the Berg roundabout.

How does it all fit together?

And she wonders if she should call Zeke.

Johan Jakobsson.

And her tiredness is back.

Look inside the tiredness.

So she drives past the abandoned old Dagab food distribution warehouse and sees the little red signs in the ground-floor windows of the beige brick building, and then she remembers.

Knows.

The Workers' Education Council.

Sten Dinman is chair of the committee.

Fredrik Kantsten a committee member.

And ten kilometres or so north of Stjärnorp, towards Finspång, is the Council's old, long-since abandoned residential training centre.

Deserted for the past two decades.

In the middle of nowhere.

She went out there once, when she was trying to work out what had happened to Maria.

Five small cabins in a clearing in the forest, a larger building at their centre, with a classroom and a half-dismantled kitchen.

Abandoned. Derelict. It had looked like no one had set foot there for years.

But what if Sten Dinman knew about the place as a result of his involvement in the Workers' Education Council? That it was there he had driven Krista Överlund, there that Maria followed them, and then staggered twenty kilometres before emerging onto the forest road where she was found?

That it was from there Jenny Svartsjö set off, running almost fifteen kilometres before meeting her nemesis? Before Sten Dinman caught up with her, like some crazed hunting dog? What about the other locations? Were there abandoned education centres there as well?

That doesn't matter at the moment, Malin thinks. He could be there now, he could be holding someone there now. The last woman. That would be typical of him, showing his power by choosing the same place, even though our investigation is centred upon the area.

You're there, you bastard.

And she knows she ought to call for backup, but doesn't. She switches her mobile off instead.

She needs to do this on her own.

I have to confront this alone.

It's urgent, so urgent. It mustn't be too late.

She turns off at the Berg roundabout, heading past the retail warehouses in Tornby, over the E4, and the sky seems to be dancing in the water of Lake Roxen, and off on the horizon the grey spires of Vreta Kloster rise high above the plain.

Her pistol is in its holster, nestled against her chest.

Cold.

She's not scared.

Whatever is, is.

Whatever is going to happen will happen.

She takes one hand off the wheel, puts it to the lower part of her stomach, on the white fabric of her skirt.

Lets her hand rest there.

Knows what's alive in there.

Close now.

Fredrik Kantsten had dozed off again in his car, outside the Route 66 restaurant. He allowed himself a bit more sleep.

He woke up an hour or so later, and now he's pushing the car on. He turns off the E4 by the Ikea store, at the sign for Vreta Kloster, and the car is sweeping across the Östgöta plain without him noticing the farms, fields, and orchards, where the apple trees are still hesitating before bursting into blossom.

Is Sten Dinman there?

The shotgun is lying beside Fredrik Kantsten, diagonally across the passenger seat.

His own name engraved on the butt.

The clock on the dashboard says seven o'clock.

He thought about calling Peder or Emanuel, but decided against it.

From now on, it's every man for himself.

No more, no less.

This needs to be done, that's all there is to it.

He reaches Vreta Kloster. The old church is shining white in the tired morning sun, and on the other side of the road is a peaceful school, also white.

He turns off towards the forests around Stjärnorp, to where he knows the education centre is.

I want to hold her now.

We want to hold her.

You, Malin, are on your way to rescue her, although you aren't sure she's actually there, or even if she exists at all.

But you have to go, don't you? You have to destroy him, the man who has harmed so many of us women so badly.

Shoot him, Malin.

Shut that crocodile jaw of his.

Kill him.

Amputate him from the body of humanity.

Cut off his heads.

Burn him and bury his remains in nature, and let the snakes and millipedes and flies eat him.

Give us justice.

Give us revenge.

Give us peace.

There's a car driving behind you, Malin.

Be careful, look over your shoulder, because everything has a cost, you know that, don't you?

Life, death.

Caresses, pain.

Hurry up, Malin, he's doing terrible things to her now, and she's on her way, but she can still be saved.

Hurry up.

Let this story end here and now, in this early hour of the morning.

60

'Where is she?'

The voice comes out of the night, but it's morning now, isn't it?

Johan Jakobsson fell asleep in the bunk room after giving Malin the new information about Krista Överlund.

And now Sven Sjöman is standing over him.

'What have you done with Malin?'

Johan quickly crosses the boundary between sleep and wakefulness, and then he knows where he is, what's going on.

He sits up.

Looks at Sven.

Sees how worried Sven is, that his instincts are telling him that something's in the process of going wrong.

'Where is she?'

Johan tells Sven about Krista Överlund, and Malin heading off to talk to her while Johan got some sleep, and how they agreed to let Sven sleep, not to call him in the middle of the night with information that probably didn't mean anything.

'OK,' Sven says. 'But now I can't get hold of her.'

'She's probably at home. Sleeping. She might have switched her mobile off.'

'You know as well as I do that she'd never do that. She must have found out something from Krista Överlund.'

'We can ask her.'

'There might not be time for that. Malin's not answering. She could have worked out where Sten Dinman might be, and is on her way there now. Have you any idea where?'

'No.'

Johan looks up Krista Överlund's mobile number in the online directory.

Calls.

Krista Överlund answers.

Tells him what she told Malin.

They hang up, and with Krista Överlund's words come clarity, connections, and Johan knows where Malin is heading.

'She's on her way to the abandoned Workers' Education Centre north of Stjärnorp.'

Sven doesn't question him, doesn't hesitate. Instead he says: 'Let's get going. You, me and Zeke, he's just arrived.'

Don't kill me.

Don't hurt me any more.

I'm swaying in these chains now. And you're getting closer with whatever heat or sharpness you've pulled from that case on the floor and I can't scream any more, because I don't care any longer, I don't care, I no longer exist.

A clanking sound.

Is that what the door to emptiness sounds like?

I'm not scared.

Not angry.

Not alone.

Do what you like with me.

Because I am nothing.

Not even forgetfulness.

Sten Dinman feels a smile take shape on his face.

She's hanging in front of him. Her body is glowing in

the reflections of the foil, almost seems to be burning in light. A cold fire, a warm chill.

Time to put an end to this.

Time to move on.

Beyond this, because there is such a thing, I'll take one of the false passports from my case and escape to the Philippines or some remote Indonesian island, and carry on doing what I do there.

The policeman they found at home in my apartment. I saw it just now on my mobile.

It was bound to happen in the end. They're trying to kill me.

The one who shot the policeman. I have an idea who it might be.

How sharp is my knife now that I've just honed it?

Her neck.

I've left it untouched.

The snap when the throat gives in to the knife and the head lolls forward from the weight of the hanging body is like nothing else, either as sound or movement.

He walks over to the portable stereo.

Turns on the CD player.

Grieg's symphony fills the room. Notes and light.

And the knife that will soon slice through her white neck.

Malin turns off towards the training centre and cabins.

The car bounces and lurches over the uneven gravel track.

The forest denser here.

Almost ancient. The firs and pines reach up towards the sky. Their branches reach lower than usual, and the forest seems airless and hungry, as if it devours all living creatures that dare to step inside it.

She takes her pistol from its holster, holds it in one hand and steers the car with the other.

Drive faster, have to get there, and then the forest opens into a large clearing.

Buildings with peeling yellow paint, small, basic cabins, and a larger building in the centre, just as she remembers. That one's painted red, with some sort of plastic-based paint that seems to want to stifle all life that enters the building, or this forest.

A car, a black Mercedes, is parked on the gravel in front of the buildings.

She stops on the edge of the clearing, maybe three hundred metres away, so that he won't hear her coming.

Gets out of the car.

A faint, sulphurous mist is clinging close to the ground.

Unquiet smoky shadows.

She moves quickly, creeping across the gravel, carefully, trying to muffle the sound of her shoes on the ground.

The first building.

Door locked, and she looks through the window.

Empty.

The same with the second, third, fourth building.

Then the large building.

Empty.

Is there a cellar? No.

He, they, must be in the last of the small cabins, the one closest to the forest.

The car.

She looks inside it, sees the shiny black leather seats.

It's obsessively clean. She wonders about calling in and checking the number, but she's sure the car belongs to Sten Dinman.

Is he asleep in the last cabin?

No light from the covered windows.

Aluminium foil? It looks as if the windows are covered in aluminium foil.

She approaches the cabin.

Hears the music now.

The way the entire force of a symphony orchestra seems to be trying to explode the little building from within.

Fredrik Kantsten turns off towards the training centre, into the confining, compressed vegetation of the forest.

This must be the place, he thinks, dodging a pothole with the wheel.

Close now.

I have to put an end to this.

I'm going to ensure that I have a future, and don't end up in prison.

He drives carefully. Doesn't want to have an accident now that he's so close.

Forest.

Denser.

Like barbed wire where escaping bodies have got caught and died, strung up as food for hungry flies.

The knife against her throat now.

Her body is hanging.

The foil is glowing.

I am glowing.

I just need to press a little harder and she'll die like a pig.

But quietly.

Without a sound.

Powerless.

Resigned.

I press now.

Pull.

Pretend.

Measure.

And now I'm doing it.
Unless?

Something cold and hard against my neck.
I can feel it.
So I'm still here.
Yes, I'm still here.
Can't someone save me? Save me.
Please, save me.

Malin kicks open the locked door.

Throws herself into the cabin's only room, into shrieking light and thundering music.

She sees him standing by the woman hanging from chains, with the knife in his hand, pressing it to her throat.

He's dressed in black overalls, his face turned towards the woman.

What do I do? Malin thinks, and feels adrenalin taking over her circulation.

The pistol in her hands pointing straight ahead, and he hears her, notices her, and turns around, then he sticks the knife in and Malin pulls the trigger again and again and the ear-shattering blasts drown out the music and his body collapses to the floor with blood squirting from a hole in the left side of his chest.

The woman.

Her neck.

Her body more wound than body.

Malin rushes over to her.

Blood is running from her neck, but not pumping, he didn't manage to cut her aorta.

Malin gently places her hand to the woman's chest, her heart is beating.

She presses her top against the wound.

The woman is breathing.

She's alive.

I got here in time.

An open crocodile-skin case by the door, shiny instruments inside it and strapped inside its lid. Containers full of fluid.

'I'm going to get you down,' she whispers. 'You're safe now. I'll get you down,' and she can no longer hear the pounding music, hears nothing, not even the sound of the car pulling up outside.

Sven Sjöman, Johan Jakobsson and Zeke are all sitting in silence in the car, a rattling cocoon where no words are needed.

Thinking about Malin and what's happening to her in the forest.

One hundred and eighty kilometres an hour, past Stjärnorp Castle, past Sjölunda, always with the dancing water of Lake Roxen to their right, the expanse of water like an escape route if the whole world should suddenly catch fire.

Deeper and deeper into the forest.

Zeke at the wheel.

Faster.

Sven makes no comment about their speed.

Just wants them to get there.

Faster.

Wants them to find Malin before it's too late.

Who knows what might be happening in the forest? Who knows what depths of depravity this infernal investigation will have to plumb before it's over?

A car at the edge of the forest. A white Golf.

Then Sten Dinman's Mercedes on the gravel in front of the big red building.

Fredrik Kantsten drove past the first car, up to the buildings, and pulled up beside the Mercedes.

No one seemed to have noticed his arrival, there didn't seem to be anyone there. But Sten was somewhere in the vicinity, he was sure of that.

The Golf?

Never mind. This has to happen.

Fredrik Kantsten got out, walked around the car and took out his shotgun, then saw that the door of the furthest cabin was open.

And now he's walking towards that cabin.

With the gun pointing in front of him, and a wind blowing through the tree tops, and the sky is gradually filling with low grey cloud sweeping in from the east.

Music from the cabin.

A strange light streaming out of the door.

Then he runs forward, wants to surprise Sten and whoever else might be in there.

In through the door.

A woman is crouching beside a lifeless body.

Sten's body next to her on the floor, his face white, the sheen gone from his blond hair. So it's been done already.

Beyond the crouching woman a naked, wounded woman is hanging from chains in the ceiling.

Dead?

Maybe.

Is the woman beside Sten's body looking for the keys to the handcuffs around the hanging woman's wrists?

But who is the crouching woman?

Ah, Fredrik Kantsten recognises her, it took a while but now he knows, it's that stubborn fucking police cunt.

And he knows that she has to be done away with as well.

Both women have to be done away with.

He aims the shotgun towards them.

Feels the coolness of the trigger against his right fore-finger. Dinman is dead. Perhaps I can take his place now?

Malin doesn't hear him.

But she feels him.

She turns around and finds herself staring into the twin barrels of a shotgun, then she looks up, sees Fredrik Kantsten's face, the contorted, confused and determined look on it.

The acne scars. The sharp nose. The weak cheekbones.

Everything falls into place for her in an instant.

She knows what he's doing there.

Knows she has to fight for her life now.

Her pistol.

She'd put it down a metre away from her, it's glinting in the light from the spotlights and the reflections from the aluminium foil on the walls.

No words now.

Too late for that.

I should have called the others, and as the blast goes off from the shotgun she throws herself aside but still feels the sting in her stomach, and from the corner of her eye she sees the hanging woman almost torn in two by the storm of shot.

So it was too late.

I didn't make it in time.

I let you down.

But I'm not going to let the others down. Not let any other woman down. Not give up.

The pistol.

There it is, and she grabs it, feels the sting of a thousand blowtorches in her stomach, and she sees the gun pointing down, straight at her now, sees the empty look in Fredrik Kantsten's eyes, and she pulls the trigger.

Twice.

One shot.

She sees a red flower blossom on Fredrik Kantsten's forehead, then she clutches her stomach.

The world starts to go fuzzy around the edges.

As bad as that?

And she sees herself from above, the bodies around her in the room, and she sees Zeke and Sven Sjöman come storming in, rushing over to her, and she sees herself tell them that she's OK, that she just got hit by a bit of shot, that she's OK, but that it hurts like hell.

The case by the door is on fire. Burning brightly. Sparks from the shotgun must have set light to the liquids in the containers.

But why am I drifting?

Why am I seeing myself like this if I'm fine?

Then she realises.

And she feels something leaving her, heading out into an endless, lonely space inhabited by particularly beautiful stars. She feels herself fall back into her body and then she screams, screaming out her grief at the life that never was.

The forest hears her scream.

And shakes it off, like a wind.

Epilogue

Lundsberg chapel, Friday, 3 June, 2011

Malin.
   We're whispering to you.
   Can you hear us?
   We're here now, me and Jessica and Silvana, who ended up being the last woman.
   You weren't able to save her. But she's OK now, here with us.
   There are so many of us.
   Some of us for ever unknown, others forgotten.
   Thank you for your sacrifice, Malin.
   He is here with us, like a tiny drifting light, a beautiful, glowing atom.
   Thank you for fighting, for not giving up.
   Give birth to all the children we never had.
   Tove, look at her, Malin, see how radiant she is, see the beauty of your life.

Tove.
   Summertime.
   Wearing an ankle-length white dress and with her brown-blond hair in plaits.
   She's standing at the front of the stage in the chapel at Lundsberg, the student choir dressed in white sarongs behind her.

And she's singing.

And the living is easy.

Gazing out at all the stuck-up, arrogant people here, and they're looking at her, and Malin can see that the looks they're giving Tove are appreciative and impressed.

And Malin feels herself grow as she sits there in the pew beneath the whitewashed arched ceiling in the flood of summer light pouring through the windows.

The season is no longer hesitant.

The mad season is over.

A burning sensation in her stomach.

The single fragment of shot that must have killed what was inside her.

She started to bleed in the ambulance on the way to hospital from the training centre.

The child must have left her then, the cells it had managed to become. She hasn't said anything to Peter about what she thinks was lost out there in the forest.

She's carrying that grief alone.

The doctor who performed keyhole surgery on her after she was shot in the cabin had seen her medical record, and seen that she'd recently had her coil removed. He told her there shouldn't be any problems having children, as long as the tiny hole in her womb heals.

Malin looks at Tove.

Hasn't said anything to her about the child either.

Or that she and Peter are trying.

Do you always have to be honest with your daughter?

Malin focuses on Tove instead of letting her thoughts and feelings drift off.

She really can sing, she never showed any interest in it until she moved up here.

Malin met Tove's housemother, Klara Groberg, outside the chapel. She seems to be a sensible woman with her feet on the ground, not in Chanel sandals like most of the others in here.

Tove.

The light in your hair.

What price, Malin wonders, do we have to pay in return for life? What price do we have to pay for love?

She lets the question pass her lips, and silently it moves through the full chapel, but no answer echoes back.

Maria.

The still nameless woman in Lund.

I haven't given you back your name, like I promised.

Do you even want it back? Maybe you're better off the way things are?

But I promised.

And perhaps some promises have to remain unfulfilled. We all die with promises that weren't kept.

You're both still out of reach, but the evil that hurt you can never harm you again. You know that.

Katerina Yelena is at a rehabilitation centre in Motala. She came round of her own accord in the end.

Sven Sjöman has put in a retirement request. He hasn't mentioned whether or not he's got cancer. And, as the prosecutor in charge of the investigation, Vivianne Södergran dropped the assault charge against Waldemar Ekenberg, decided there was no evidence to suggest it had ever happened. An independent doctor had confirmed that Emanuel Ärendsson's injuries could well have been self-inflicted, or by someone else during a sexual game.

She has also dropped the investigation into Andrei Darzhevin's suicide, and how the multiple injuries on his body occurred. There was no evidence of negligence, and he must have received the injuries when he resisted arrest.

As soon as Malin was discharged from hospital she had gone to see Maria.

She told her she knew what had happened in the forest.

Praised her courage, thanked her for it, for daring to show the way with her goodness.

Maria didn't show any reaction. She was back where she was before.

Malin's been down to Lund with Peter.

She spoke to the other mute woman, said the same thing to her, but it was impossible to tell if she understood or could even hear her.

Everyone's like that, one way or another, Malin thinks as Tove sings the last note.

Mute when confronted with their own lives.

Blind.

More or less.

She and Peter went to see Stefan on the way up to Lundsberg.

Janne drove with them from Linköping, but waited outside the care home in Sjöplogen.

Stefan was sitting in his wheelchair by the window, and he smiled when she arrived, but said nothing during the half-hour they were there.

Malin held his hand, the way she takes Tove's hand now as she comes down from the stage and sits beside her in the pew.

'You were wonderful.'

A newly appointed headmaster gives a speech. An authoritative man in his fifties, dressed in a beige suit.

He talks of hope and encouragement for the summer.

Malin said hello to Tom's parents outside the chapel.

Exactly the sort of idiots you'd expect. Lovely people wearing loafers from Tods.

Posh.

Just like Sten Dinman. Quite possibly the worst killer of women this country has ever seen.

The worst torturer of women.

He tortured Jessica Karlsson and Maria Murvall and the woman in Lund. He murdered Jenny Svartsjö, and no one knows how many more. An inquiry has been set up under the auspices of National Crime, with the young Linköping prosecutor Vivianne Södergran drafted in to be in charge of the preliminary investigation.

It turned out that Fredrik Kantsten was the cop-killer. His fingerprints were found on Conny Nygren's wallet.

They haven't found Paul Lendberg's killer, or killers, but they're assuming that his business associates wanted to silence him, unless Dinman was responsible for that as well. The case is still open in Stockholm.

Emanuel Ärendsson has lost his job at the University Hospital. He's been fined for purchasing sexual services on five occasions.

Count Peder Stålskiöld has confessed to the offence as well, also on five occasions. He's paid his fine. Malin's heard rumours that he's going to move to New York to get away from the relentless media attention.

The media had a field day when the truth was revealed.

Tearing into facts and people alike, like a pack of hungry predators.

What a scandal.

What monsters.

What a beast.

And then the questions everyone was asking: How could he? Why him? How did he get like that? Was he the devil incarnate?

Why?

The chapel.

The whole room bursting with love on a day like today.

Malin squeezes her daughter's hand.

Tove squeezes back.

Then another song rises to the roof of God's house, and Malin looks up, and sees a glowing point of light drifting back and forth above the altarpiece.

A tiny, lost light, all alone, anxiously looking for its mother.

Don't miss the other titles in the Malin Fors series

MIDWINTER SACRIFICE, SUMMERTIME DEATH, AUTUMN KILLING and SAVAGE SPRING

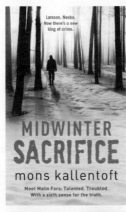

Out now in paperback

**Also available as eBooks
and as Digital Audio Downloads**

www.hodder.co.uk

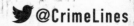